THE CRIME TSAR

THE CRIMETSAR

THE CRIME TSAR

NICHOLA McAULIFFE

BLOOMSBURY

First published 2003
This paperback edition published 2004

Copyright © 2003 by Nichola McAuliffe

The moral right of the author has been asserted

Bloomsbury Publishing Plc, 38 Soho Square, London WID 3HB

A CIP catalogue record for this book
is available from the British Library

ISBN 0 7475 6826 X

10 9 8 7 6 5 4 3 2 1

All papers used by Bloomsbury Publishing are natural,
recyclable products made from wood grown in
well-managed forests. The manufacturing processes
conform to the environmental regulations of the
country of origin.

Typeset by Hewer Text Ltd, Edinburgh
Printed in Great Britain by Clays Ltd, St Ives plc

www.bloomsbury.com/nicholamcauliffe

For
Don Mackay who had Faith,
Misty Spring who had Hope,
Mary McAuliffe who all her life has had Charity,

and for
Liz Calder who had the manuscript

PART ONE

There was no difference between the blood. Moslem and Christian. It still ran through the gutters of the estate. The rain whipping down heavy and hard swilled it over the rubbish of the day into drains full of cigarette ends, sump oil and polystyrene cups.

The bloody mud continued its journey searching for a place to hide.

But they didn't stop trying to kill each other. The baseball bat smashed an eye socket, the machete hacked through an arm. Two lads, the dark of the storm making them identical. The crowd roared them on. Lightning lit up the faces, thunder effortlessly covered the shouting. More lightning, strobing the blows of machete and bat into Keystone harmlessness. The rain sluicing the blood off their faces, painting their hair to their heads.

A car now turned on its back, a tin turtle turned by hatred. The petrol tank smashed open with a paving block. A fire so fierce it defied the sheeting rain for twenty minutes before flickering out in a lake of black sludge.

And still the boys fought on. African against Asian. Black against brown. Nike versus Reebok.

'To Me! To Me! To Me!'

She was no more than young, no taller than small. Her roundel shield beaten with all her strength with her baton. Her visor down, the rain making vision impossible, she flipped it up between beats. Inspector. Female in riot situation. Her men, her squad, came at her barely audible call. Men who'd been Special Patrol Group until rebranding became necessary due to excessive force being used on more than one unarmed individual. Long Roman Shields, greaves, helmets, sheer muscle pushing the crowd back. The thickness of a blue serge uniform separating them from the thugs they faced.

From the side she could see the opportunity to go in and snatch the fighting cocks. As another streak of lightning lit the estate her lads went in to grab their lads. The two crowds of youths were now one mob united against the police. Paving slabs were ripped up and thrown. In the supernatural thunder and lightning bodies smashed by the stones fell and were dragged away with no sense of reality. The only reality was the rain. Best policemen in the world. But not tonight. The energy of the raging elements seemed to have entered the bodies below making them oblivious to the worst storm for four hundred years.

More police fell and still their Boadicea urged them on, but now they needed no urging. They wanted to feel bones crack; they were hungry to feel bodies under their boots.

The mob fought back with bricks, knives and finally the petrol bombs they'd been saving to use on each other.

Then the rain fell harder, the wind whipping it across faces, into eyes. The falling torrent put out the childish flames as the bottles broke around the police.

Now there was confusion. People falling, unable to stand under the force of the storm. And suddenly there was fear, not of their fellow men but of the blind biblical force of the elements tossing them about like so much rubbish in the flood.

But God sent no Moses to ford the rivers of blood.

A Pakistani boy aged about fifteen blown on to a scaffolding pole. It went through his face like a straw into milkshake.

Roof tiles falling, smashing heads and shoulders.

The earth whipping up as if the dead awoke.

Now everyone was running as the storm, like an angry parent, lost its patience.

They tried to find shelter but found the ugly buildings of the estate funnelled the energy of the wind, flattening bodies against walls and sucking the breath out of them.

Many collapsed where they were, curled over in an attitude of prayer, crying out to whichever god they knew. But the storm took their voices away. God was somewhere else.

Only the devil was listening.

A stroke of lightning struck the ground-floor flat opposite the pub and blue flames snaked into the sky. Flames the rain couldn't quench.

And below the flames, coils of oily smoke covered the stunted grass that had once been a garden.

And there, as the opportunistic desert blooms after years of drought, strange life stirred once more.

In thunder, lightning, and in rain.

'What were you saying?' Jenni said. 'About adoption?'

'Oh . . . nothing. Just waffle,' Lucy replied, regretting she'd mentioned a subject so close to her and so far from Jenni.

'They'd never let you, of course – you're probably too old and Gary . . . well, Gary's –' Even Jenni's sublime insensitivity paused at saying 'a cripple'; she settled for a rather lame, 'Disabled.'

Lucy wanted to slap her pretty face. Lucy resented her prettiness. Jenni with an I. Perfect hair, perfect nails, matching husband and children. Pretty. A little crêpey round the neck in a harsh light, but Jenni never allowed harsh light to shine on her.

'We weren't thinking of adopting – I was just saying . . . it must be nice to have children.'

Jenni wasn't listening. Why should she? The conversation wasn't about her.

Lucy sighed. 'How's Tom?'

Those two words put them back on to Jenni's ground. Her Husband. The Chief Constable. Her Children. The Chief's Children. The Chief's Wife. She loved the power the title conferred, though it was frustratingly local.

'Well, you know he gives a hundred and two per cent. Of course it's easier now, but when he took over the force was a shambles, but you know Tom Shackleton.'

She always referred to him by his full name. A strange mixture of display and insecurity. He was a Success. They were a Success. But there was some part of her that had no idea who her husband was. No insight into his empty policeman's soul. By repeating the full resonance of his name she could make him exist.

Lucy always thought of him as a large cold hall with a small pale boy curled up in the corner, afraid.

When Lucy refocused Jenni was still twittering on about the Chief. About his devotion to her and her ability to tug his chain occasionally to bring him back into line.

'Honestly, Lucy, I watch that man and, of course, I'm proud of him.' She looked at Lucy through the mirror and said, 'But I'd never tell him that.'

Lucy wondered why not. Why withhold affection? Maybe it gave Jenni a feeling of power. Lucy imagined her dispensing small amounts of approval weekly, like pocket money. Earned but grudgingly given.

Sitting at the breakfast table in the television-perfect kitchen, Amtico floor, Maple cabinets, granite work surfaces, Jenni was repairing her already immaculate make-up. To go shopping. Lucy had seen the remains of it on the pillowcases, small veronicas of mascara. It was fascinating to watch how Jenni always laid out the pencils and brushes in the same order, always applied the colours in the same order with precisely identical strokes. The fastidious wiping of the brushes after and replacing them in the make-up bag. Lucy saw ritual and order where her life was chaos and make do and mend.

'Have you ever thought of having an affair?' Jenni asked, staring at Lucy through the mirror with those strange, unblinking eyes.

'No . . . I don't think I could be bothered shaving my legs on a regular basis.' She left the right length of pause. The one that says, I'm not really interested but it's only polite to ask. 'You?'

'Oh . . . don't be silly.' Had she been twenty years younger Jenni would have dimpled, and giggled with a sound like silvery bells. But she was around forty. Older than Lucy though better tended. She turned scarlet, prettily.

'The Chief would kill me. I'd soon have my marching orders. Anyway, he's very demanding, I don't think I'd have the energy.'

Jenni looked at Lucy, coyly willing her to see them in scenes of sweat and carnality. She looked suitably impressed, even though she knew they hadn't had sex for six years. He'd never called it making love.

'But . . . ?' Lucy left the question hanging. Genuinely interested in the way one is when a beetle falls in a glass of lemonade. Will it find the straw and climb out?

'Well . . .'

The legs were clutching at the pink-and-white pole.

Jenni turned to face her, her lipsticked mouth vivid against her smiling teeth.

'Well . . .' She said it again.

Lucy wanted to slap her but she said softly, with a gratifying urgency, 'Come on, Jenni, you can tell me.'

'Oh, I know.' Her loyalty was dismissed, swatted away. Lucy was, after all, less equal now she cleaned the house. Not in the same way a friend.

'It's just that . . .' Again the adolescent pause and giggle.

Lucy's hand itched to slap her.

'He's in politics. A politician.'

Lucy looked at her.

Jenni misinterpreted her stare as interest. It was actually horror. 'Very, very big.'

'Which side?'

'Oh ours, darling. New Labour – New Lover.' She was delighted with her wit. 'You mustn't breathe a word, Lucy. I really shouldn't have told you.'

'And have you . . . er . . . ?'

'Not yet. But . . . I'm in training. No wheat, alcohol or dairy products. And it said in my horoscope this was going to be a period of intense activity.'

She was positively bubbling. Breathless with anticipation. She returned to applying her immaculate mask.

Lucy watched her with the blank, pale-eyed stare of an uncertain sheep and thought of the afternoon months before when Tom seduced her. She was taking him a cup of coffee in his study. Jenni was too busy on the phone to her daughter, Tamsin. Tamsin, Jacinta, Chloe and Jason. Aspirational for Tracy, Michelle, Kylie and Wayne.

She remembered he'd spilled the coffee into the saucer as he took it from her and been sweetly embarrassed. Lucy had said she did that all the time and smiled at him. He smiled back. Not the confident square-jawed smile so popular with newspaper picture editors but a shy movement of the lips and dip of the head. A humble little smile.

When Lucy turned to go he gently put his hands on her shoulders and started to kiss her ear and cheek. Lucy stood absolutely still. Guilt had pushed her half-formed fantasies of Tom Shackleton away so many times since they'd first met but now . . . now . . . He said he wanted to release her breasts and play with them. Curiously formal. Stilted. She felt a moment's panic that he'd see her bra, old and grey from being washed with her husband's socks. But his eyes were closed. She wondered, if she went and left her body behind, whether he'd notice.

He told her, without looking at her face, about the sexless years after his children's births. They shared Jenni's bed and soaked up what affection she was capable of. Sex for her was a means to an end.

She was looking at a photograph of his year at Hendon Police Training College when his hand moved to her neck. Holding her, not painfully but firmly, he stood back from her slightly. She thought he was pushing her away but then she felt his other hand on the back of her thigh. She didn't move. She stood absolutely still, concentrating on the picture, not wanting him to stop. She couldn't pick him out among the low-slung helmets and shiny young faces. He pushed her skirt up very slowly.

She remembered her knickers being lowered like this when she was small, when underwear was still too complicated for little fingers. It was oddly comforting. He moved close to her again, enclosing her, leaning over her, his right arm across her chest, his hand holding her left shoulder, his face bent into her cheek and neck. He curved her over slightly, taking her weight on his arm. She felt safe, secure, surrounded by him. Again, curiously formal, he whispered, 'May I?' Lucy thought it was a silly question as she had her naked bottom pressed against him but by the time she'd decided to say, 'Of course,' or, 'Feel free,' something that would impress him as sophisticated, he had gently, and with no resistance from her welcoming body, slipped inside her. Neither of them moved for a long moment.

Lucy had a vision of unused condoms and apocalyptic results and was surprised to find she didn't care.

He moved very quickly – not the long slow strokes of popular fiction but with almost rabbit-like rapidity. A wide vibrato. Lucy just stayed in the position he'd placed her in.

When he came his breathing quickened but he made no sound. Lucy didn't see his face. But she felt the soft quiet kiss just below her ear as he withdrew. Not wanting him to let her go she raised her hand and stroked his cheek.

Her legs were shaking when she pulled her pants up and adjusted her skirt.

It seemed inappropriate to say anything.

8

Jenni was still on the phone when she got back to the kitchen with Tom's empty cup.

Hours after the conversation with Jenni, when the nurses had put her husband to bed, Lucy realised why she had felt so angry. It was because Jenni wanted her to know about the politician. It wasn't the affair, it was the chance to publicise it. Where was the moral rectitude in thinking it more virtuous to be unfaithful but silent? And she was the only person Jenni could tell because she was bound to Jenni by gratitude.

When her husband, Gary, became ill and Lucy became a carer she slipped out of the world they'd known. They'd joined the socially excluded, gently impoverished but not poor, not struggling on a sink estate so not even really included in the excluded.

Gary didn't give in; he had tutored kids at home and when that became too much he held a 'virtual' maths class on the Internet. He discussed Mozart the pre-revolutionary humanist in a chat room dominated by ideas of Mozart the political subversive. Gary had never defined himself as the sum of public opinion but Lucy, never certain of her own value, dwindled in her own eyes as she saw herself shrink in the eyes of others.

Lucy, wife of one of the most successful and sought-after heads in the country, who made stained glass to commission, would never have allowed Jenni to patronise and dismiss her. But her label had changed and she saw herself as a distressed gentlewoman who deserved no more than well-intentioned condescension. And now 'poor Lucy' did a bit of cleaning for Jenni and Tom, ran errands: not a servant, no, but no longer in the same way an equal.

The only thing that made her husband really angry was her assumption of this veil of martyrdom and her neglect of her art. He had encouraged her to be ambitious, to believe in herself, and couldn't understand her willing transformation into a doormat. He wanted to move away, for her to return to work; it was bad enough that change in him was inevitable – he needed her to stay the same. But he didn't see the silt of depression dam up her spirit, didn't understand that it was easier for her to let go than cling on to a life for which she had no confidence without him. The idea of being superwoman frightened her so she had gradually allowed herself to drift downwards and, like a bottom-dwelling fish, she found sustenance sifting through the detritus of others' lives. She had never flown as high as Gary or the Shackletons and had often felt panic at the thought of trying to keep up with them, feeling safer in the company of her tiny miniatures of coloured glass. Though she'd never admit it, Gary's illness had provided a sort of relief but had taken away her desire to create beauty.

They had been the Policeman, the Social Services Manager, the Artist and the Headmaster. Equals. Close but not close enough to threaten intimacy. Jenni was always suspicious Gary and Lucy were trying to 'keep in' with the Shackletons, as if they might use Tom's rapid elevations to advance their social standing. It was beyond Jenni's comprehension that Gary, and so Lucy, wanted nothing more than easy-going friendship or that Gary's standing in education was on a par with Tom's in the police. In Jenni's experience everybody was after something. Lucy had learned how important it was to Jenni to keep her in her place when Jenni had once heard her sing. 'I heard you screeching,' she laughed. Lucy had been hurt, but that wasn't the intention – Jenni simply needed to maintain her position and Lucy's . . . But now there were the £10 notes popped into her jacket pocket. Slipped into her pinny. Jenni could give and generously – she just couldn't share. And now Lucy was no competition, it was safe to like her.

'Oh Lucy darling . . . would you mind? Could you just wipe out the cutlery drawer? Run a duster along the dado rail? I got you a little something in Harrods. I thought you might like this La Prairie moisturiser.'

Always in that tone, the one reserved for 'poor Lucy'.

Lucy sat in her living room on a once fine sofa, now, like everything else, in need of care and attention, thinking about her father and Tom Shackleton. She would have walked on water for her father, but if she had he'd only have accused her of showing off. She'd always wanted him to hold her safe, fold her up and put her in his pocket but he'd never really liked her. Her arrival had been an unwelcome intrusion in an ordered life. Perhaps if she'd been a boy. Maybe if she'd been as pretty as Jenni he'd have liked her more. But Shackleton had found comfort in Lucy, or had he just taken advantage of her neediness, her craving for affection? She knew she was still chasing the smile of a man who'd been dead ten years.

It got dark. She didn't turn the lights on. She looked across at Jenni and Tom's house with its gravel drive and wrought-iron gates: 'We had to have them, Lucy – for security. The Chief is vulnerable to attack, you know.'

Not least from sexually frustrated neighbours in fluffy panda slippers.

She sat eating rice pudding out of the tin.

Putting Gary to bed always exhausted her, even though she was little more than a spectator to the changing of the catheter, the washing, the hoist. The invasive smell of talcum powder. When she allowed herself to think about Gary's dying, one of the things she looked forward to was throwing away the medicated talc. And the incontinence pads, the plastic apron, the latex gloves.

She remembered Gary at Labour Party conferences, passionate about the care of the less fortunate, those who had no place in a Britain led by a mad woman.

The four of them so sure the revolution would come, not seeing how far they had moved from their old ideals. How contaminated they had been. They had become defined by their jobs, their cars, their ambitions.

Now Lucy and Gary were the less fortunate and the books they'd read, the music he'd played on the boudoir grand, now silent and covered in the contents of a chemist's pharmacy, the things they still had inside them counted for nothing. They had crossed into the vacuum.

The Chief's dark-blue Jaguar stopped in front of the gates. Gordon, his driver, a dull man who didn't read for pleasure and only rarely for information, pressed the buttons and eased the car close to the front door. Lucy watched Jenni's husband get out and felt that internal pancake throw of excitement.

His suit was expensive, his shoes very nearly Gucci. She could feel his breath on her neck again, the softness of his lips. His eyelashes on her cheek.

The security light went out. He was inside with Jenni. She wondered if he'd have a whisky and soda. If Jenni would scream at him for putting the glass in the dishwasher. Lucy wondered if tonight she was 'doing a Diana', as her eldest daughter, Tamsin, had

11

once described it. If the mood swings made famous in the legend of
the Princess of Wales were condemning Shackleton to an evening of
appeasement.

Gary's bell was ringing. She went in to see him. The remains of
their dining room framed the ripple bed, the wheelchair, the debris of
slow dying. Gary's spine was hurting.

'Lucy, will you give me a pull? Sorry.'

'Will you stop apologising? Ready?'

She got him under the armpits. The idea was to pull him so his
back would realign itself more comfortably. When the pain was
really bad she'd get him into the wheelchair, put him in the van and
drive over speed bumps. Gary would yell out the Dam Busters march
with tears of pain running down his face, till the thumping up and
down shifted something in his vertebrae. But this was a different
principle – she had to stretch him slowly. Sudden movement could
put him into spasm.

'What is it he's got?' asked Jenni after he'd fallen over at school
again.

'Multiple sclerosis.'

'Oh, my uncle had that.' She always pulled the focus back to
herself. 'I found him a diet, you know, no refined sugar, no caffeine
or oranges – don't know why oranges – and he was fine for years.
You'll have to put Gary on one, oh and I'll get you a healing crystal,
they are fantastic. In fact, I've heard there's a new tantric meditation
which does wonders for MS patients. I'll have a word with my para-
diviner, she knows all about these things. And of course cannabis,
but don't say I said so.'

'Yes . . . yes,' Lucy remembered saying blankly, too numb to be
hurt by Jenni's casual packaging up of Gary's death sentence into a
New Age bundle of hope.

Lucy thought vaguely about no good marriage having a happy
ending. But that was before she knew release could promise a kind of
happiness. Before she gave up work, before she had to be grateful to
Jenni. Before Tom had touched her, kissed her, quivered inside her.

'Here goes, then.' She pulled, leaning her whole body back. Gary
was gasping for her effort and his pain.

'That's it. Yes, I think that's it.'

She released him and waited a moment in silence to see what his
back would do. The crumbling of the bones in his spine was found

after the MS. A little bonus, a little addition of pain to sharpen his appreciation of loss of feeling elsewhere.

She filled the time by pulling his anti-clot socks further over his feet, swollen and smelly, the skin stretched so much sometimes she imagined popping them with a pin. Those feet that had searched for hers in bed. So they wouldn't be lonely.

'Better?'

'Perfect.'

He smiled. No shadow of self-pity, no whiff of the pathetic. The (then) shadow Education Secretary had called him a remarkable man but he had no idea how remarkable. There was no one who met Gary who didn't feel happier for the encounter. She looked down at him and wondered how she could still think him handsome. Ridiculous in red pyjamas with blue piping. The man who never wore anything in bed. Who was so proud of his long, lithe body. His chest now a sort of medieval soup bowl, an old man's turkey neck growing out of it. The flesh of his face unable to cling to the bones, falling away to gather round his ears. The once blond hair brittle, colourless, thin as a chemo patient's, even though that was one treatment he had not yet been subjected to.

His eyes were fixed on the ceiling rose, listening to the pain. Still smiling. Staring out a cruel God. He let his breath go, sure it was quiet. Relaxed. She leaned over and kissed him. Lucy had married him before she'd learned gratitude for affection wasn't love. It had taken time to put aside fear of rejection, and learn she wasn't a supplicant to be granted the occasional emotional concession. She had grown to love him, encouraging healthy feelings like blind crocuses. Now she was closing down those small emotions. Putting them into hibernation. Protecting herself against the day her black suit would be once more worn in anger.

'I don't half fancy you, you know.' The old words.

He smiled, knowing it a lie.

'Go and watch the television, woman. Go on, give us peace.'

'Sure? Want anything else?'

'No . . . go on.' She left him reluctantly but knew he needed privacy to give in to the exhaustion.

She sat in front of the television. A political talk programme was just starting. The ringmaster one of those plump media graduates still relishing popularity with the Labour government. The debate was about inner-city policing and racial tensions on the streets.

'We're joined by the Association of Chief Police Officers' spokesman, Tom Shackleton, on the borders of whose area last night's disturbances occurred. Good evening, Mr Shackleton . . .'

Again the pancake flip. The sweat, the shaking hands. She smiled at the thought of the Pope's blessing only working if it was a live broadcast. Tom Shackleton was just as potent recorded. He was in uniform, the darling of the tabloids, the people's copper, the liberal chief constable who could be relied on to speak out on behalf of debate and openness. Tipped to take over the Met if Labour got in at the next election. If? Where was the competition?

She wondered if Jenni's ambition for her husband was the lubrication for her potential affair. Jenni's obsession was the furtherance of her family. Her husband was her creation no less than her children. Her hysterical outbursts were not the result of an excess of emotion but a fear of loss of control.

Tom took refuge from the volatility of his wife in the masculine predictability of the Job. Lucy, unwilling to betray Gary or Jenni, had tried briefly to play therapist, that day in the study, while he was talking about his wife's treatment of him.

'You must love her very much,' Lucy had said, unwilling to believe the fairy-tale marriage was just that, a fairy-tale.

'I think I despise her,' he had replied without anger. Indeed he spoke about Jenni with a curious hurt.

Lucy watched him on the television and couldn't believe this powerful, confident police chief was the same man who'd made such gentle, apologetic love to her.

Jenni was watching him too. Her head at an angle. He sat in the armchair opposite her, intent on the television screen. The interview was opened out to include some other talking heads.

'He thinks you're a fool,' said Jenni dispassionately. 'The BBC want Geoffrey Carter to get the Met. He was at university with most of them.'

Tom didn't say anything. He could see the interviewer becoming irritated with his replies. With his pedantic police speak, his uniform. The others on the programme were intellectuals. There was still that prejudice among the chattering classes towards plod, no matter how high plod rose.

He knew Jenni was right, the intelligentsia would prefer Carter. He was as reasonable and charming as Tom Shackleton but he was an Oxford graduate. Double first in theology, organ scholar and now Chief Constable of Tom Shackleton's neighbouring county.

Shackleton had a degree too, first-class law degree. From night school and day release, done while fast-tracking through the force. Where Jenni and Tom had come from, Oxford and Cambridge were just words on the front of coaches leaving the bus station by the chip shop.

Geoffrey Carter spoke French, relaxed in Provence and Tuscany and came from a family with immaculate old Liberal credentials. An unusual policeman and outspokenly critical of knee-jerk home secretaries who used the police as a blunt instrument. Urbane, intelligent and popular with the politicians. He and Shackleton had known each other over the years, meeting at various command courses and colleges around the country. Their wives had shopped and taken coffee together. They got on. Everybody got on with Carter. Everybody, even Jenni, was drawn to Eleri, his wife.

When Tom arrived at the studio the researcher let it slip they'd asked for Carter first but he had a meeting in London. Tom knew he'd be schmoozing the Home Office. No, not schmoozing – Geoffrey Carter would never do anything so vulgar. He'd never need to. He had charisma, natural unforced charm, exquisite manners and a formidable ability driven by a good brain. Shackleton had often felt inadequate beside him but knew, like a shark faced with a tiger, each had strengths the other lacked. And like the tiger and the shark each must avoid conflict in the other's element.

The programme finished and Jenni left Tom to catch up on the news while she went to fetch his supper, lightly grilled chicken, salad and a small pile of wild rice. She put their drinks on the tray and carried it through to the living room.

'Thank you,' he said, watching the screen but thinking about the interview.

'I'd put it on your lap but your stomach's in the way.'

All day he'd been Chief Constable, sir, the power in his fiefdom. She had just reduced him to a fat man being served a television dinner. Subconsciously he tightened his stomach muscles. It didn't make much difference.

'Looks very nice.' Shackleton was careful to appreciate the food; Jenni was usually too busy to cook for him.

'Oh, it's only a bit of chicken,' she muttered, but he'd said the right thing.

She took her drink and sat down, watching him eat. Almost immediately she got up and straightened the cushions on the sofa. She sat down again. Took a sip of her drink.

Tom didn't look at her as she got up again and straightened the already regimented cushions.

'Did you have a good day? Has Jason done his homework?'

He hoped he could distract her. Long years of experience taught him the distance between Jenni the attentive wife and Jenni the critical harpy was the length of an obsessive thought.

'That interviewer made you look a prat.' Jenni's tone warned Tom not to reply. She turned off the television. The following silence was leaden with her anger.

He knew that anger came out of fear but it didn't make it easier to live with. What was she afraid of this time?

'I said they'd try and make a fool of you. But you wouldn't listen. They're out to get you, T.'

He carried on chewing, longing to say his name was Tom. But she'd always thought it a rather common name. Like her own, Monica. She'd changed to her middle name as soon as she could, to the incomprehension of her parents who never understood the beautiful but alien daughter they'd bred. Jenni saw nothing to be proud of in being lower middle class.

'I don't understand you, I really don't.' She was turning her glass slowly on the arm of her chair.

'Oh there's nothing to understand, Jenni. You know that. This is delicious, by the way. Thank you.'

But she wasn't to be deflected by his humility.

She spoke quietly. To his surprise she was smiling slightly, her head tilted to one side, looking at him affectionately.

'You want to go further, don't you? You don't want to end your days as just another seven-year-spin chief constable. You've always said you want to make a difference. And,' she leant forward, 'the only place to do that is the Met? Isn't it?'

He dipped his head. Neither yes nor no.

'I know you want it but I don't know if you've got it in you to get it.' She said this very softly, with no malice. 'Carter's the favourite but we can change their minds. You're a better man than he'll ever be.'

That was too close to a compliment to be comfortable for either of them. He took refuge in his whisky.

'But what if we don't persuade them, Jenni?'

It was the wrong thing to say.

'You find your balls and we'll persuade them.'

His timidity infuriated her – she was seething with resentment. Going back to the interview, the imagined slights were now insults. Jason, his son, hearing her voice raised, quietly closed the door of his room, knowing his mother was heading for one of her moods. When he'd come home from school Jenni had been hoovering the curtains in the downstairs cloakroom. Something she more often did in the middle of the night, unable to sleep more than four hours at a time.

'What were you thinking of, letting him run rings round you like that?'

'He didn't run rings, don't exaggerate.' Tom's tone was soft, conciliatory.

It infuriated her.

'Oh . . . you're so bloody wet. Carter's going to walk off with the Met and you'll just get some inspectorate of prison lavatories. Why don't you go and see someone? Get down to London and pull some strings.'

'It's not as simple as that, Jenni '

He didn't get any further – the heavy-bottomed tumbler from which she had been sipping a vodka tonic narrowly missed his face.

'God, you're such a prat. Look at you! Christ knows why I ever married you.'

He tried to defuse the situation with a little quiet humour. 'Because you loved me?'

'Don't be so fucking stupid.'

She rarely swore but when she did she had a way of articulating the word, of articulating each syllable, slowly, with a slight raising of her upper lip. Like a dog scenting fear.

'How can one love an invertebrate?'

Tom stood up, unwilling to engage with her. He knew the pattern, that she would not stop until she had listed his failings, his moral cowardice, his domestic laziness, his meanness, lack of ambition, his neglect of the family.

He looked at her as she became more and more agitated, moving round the room touching and tidying the already neatly placed ornaments and statuettes that decorated her dust-free surfaces. Would she throw something else at him? Although he was a tall man he seemed to shrink under her vicious onslaught, though his face remained completely unreadable. He often wondered why she occasionally resorted to throwing things when her tongue could inflict far more damage.

Her favourite trick had been to humiliate him, then, as if nothing had happened, want to have sex. His increasing inability to perform under these circumstances simply added to her ammunition. For a moment he felt miserable, lonely, and desperate for her to be quiet. He wanted her to be affectionate, soft. He wanted to lie on her breasts.

'Are you listening, you shit?' she screamed.

'Yes,' he said automatically.

No, it wasn't her breasts he wanted to rest his cheek on, not her nipple he wanted at the corner of his mouth. With a sense of detached surprise he realised it was Lucy's breast he could taste. The slight smell of soap and deodorant. He hadn't thought about her since their strange encounter in his study.

It was a deliberate blocking out: Lucy had made him unexpectedly happy. He remembered leaning over her whispering, 'You'll never hurt me, will you?' He was embarrassed at the recollection. Asking a woman not to hurt him was like asking a scorpion not to sting.

He had a mistrust of sex, of his libido distracting him. He had satisfied a physical urge and had felt faintly disgusted with himself afterwards. During the act he had no thought of the woman, whether it was Jenni or one of his rare, furtive experiments elsewhere. Sex had been something inflicted on him and now he inflicted it, rarely, on others. He knew Jenni had no more emotional involvement in the act than he had but knew she relished seeing him helpless afterwards, exhausted even if only for a moment. As always giving but not sharing.

He became aware it was silent. Jenni had finished her ravings and had stormed upstairs. She switched off the light as she went and he stood unmoving in the darkness.

It was different with Lucy. She had received him with gentleness and affection. He touched his face where she had stroked him. Had she cried? Or did he imagine that. He looked across at her darkened window. Unseeing she looked back.

'Darling Lucy . . . what would I do without you.'

Jenni was glittering the next morning as Lucy cleared away the remains of a heavy-bottomed tumbler from the living-room carpet.

'Now . . . I've decided to have a little dinner party. Just the Chief and me and our politician friend.'

Lucy glanced up to see if the conspiratorial intimacy of yesterday was still in Jenni's face. There was nothing. The mask of make-up was inscrutable.

'And Lucy . . . I've a huge favour to ask you.'

Lucy composed her face into her 'of course I will' smile.

'Would you be the fourth?'

It was so unexpected Lucy's smile almost slipped. Misinterpreting the hair's-breadth pause for reluctance Jenni applied a little more charm, a little more dazzle.

'Gary could ring across for you if he needed anything. Do say yes, Lucy. It would be awkward if we weren't a four, and his wife lives somewhere miles away, and anyway he only sees her at weekends. From what I've heard about her that's probably quite enough.'

'Well . . . thank you. Yes. I'd love to.' Lucy spoke quietly. 'I haven't been out for ages.'

'Oh it's hardly out . . . but at least you can get your best frock on, and put a bit of make-up on too? Ah Jason . . . at last. Come on, let's go, I don't want to be late.'

Jason thumped down the stairs in boots heavy enough to tackle the Matterhorn. Jenni's seventeen-year-old son, her favoured child, was a negative picture of his father. Where Tom Shackleton was dark-haired and dark-eyed, Jason was blond with pale blue-green eyes. The sensuality of the father's face was a pretty softness in the son's, but the power in the body was the same.

Jason watched his mother, weighing up her mood. He decided it was good and the wariness dropped from his face. He smiled. It was the same shy smile accompanied by a little dip of the head his father had. He saw Lucy watching him and he gave her a stroke with a piece of that smile.

Jenni picked up keys, bag and sunglasses, although it was overcast with rain forecast.

'Lucy, I've got to dash, I'm taking Jason to school. It'll be Thursday – does that suit? Good. About seven-thirty, all right?'

They were gone. A faint odour of Allure by Chanel settled around Lucy. Thursday. Six days. Six days to lose half a stone, get the tone back in her inner thighs, have laser treatment on her frown lines and find something to wear.

She knelt on the carpet picking up tiny slivers of glass with marigold fingers and couldn't conjure up the indignation she had felt about Jenni's infidelity. She had forgotten she could feel this excited.

Jenni stopped the car outside Jason's exclusive academy. He kissed his mother briefly on the cheek. She never returned these kisses, but he knew what trouble there would be if he stopped.

He was always aware of his size around her, or rather he was aware of how fragile she seemed. Exquisite was a word that seemed to suit her and, even though she was technically middle-aged, her skin was almost perfect, rarely exposed to the sun. His hand on her shoulder was clumsy on her tiny bones.

'Mind my hair, Jason.' The rebuke was mild, habitual.

'Sorry, Mem.' As the children grew up 'Mum' was too ageing, 'Mummy' too precious, so when one of Tom's admiring colleagues called her the Memsahib, 'Mem' was accepted as a sweet alternative. 'See you later.' He unfolded himself from the car and lolloped off.

The image of predator as attentive mother was uncannily apt for Jenni. Her treatment of her brood was practical, unsentimental. She never lavished them with overt signs of affection and had always shunned their sticky, childish embraces.

Her physical treatment of them had always been brusque but never rough. There was no room for softness in love – the world was too harsh a place for that. Love, to Jenni, was possession. 'My family', 'my husband'. 'Mine' was the first word she ever spoke. And she would brook no criticism of her children; even Tom's mild observation that one of them might be less than perfect earned a bitter rebuke and several days of icy silence. Especially Jason, who, during Shackleton's long periods away from home, had become her little man. The repository of her bitterness against her husband's neglect. Jason had grown up believing his father treated her cruelly. It was only now he was beginning to see cracks in the flawless portait of his mother.

Jenni watched her son go, proud of his good looks. He was as handsome as his father but the strength of Shackleton's face and body were filtered through the delicacy of Jenni's features. The resulting pure beauty delighted her.

She stretched slightly and eased the Volvo into the traffic. At the traffic lights she absently reached down for her sunglasses, not noticing the appreciative glances from her neighbouring driver.

Her delicacy and femininity were palpable even through side impact bars.

Jenni enjoyed, relished, being the Chief Constable's wife; the position, the perks, the recognition and subtle respect almost as much as being beautiful.

While Tom had been inching his way up the pole she had worked her way up the Social Services system, developing a quiet, sly inflexibility indispensable when parting children from unfit parents. It was a career for which she was singularly unsuited, having no interest in or sympathy for those whose lives were lived in a confusion of ignorance, poverty and cruelty. But with limited qualifications, becoming a social worker had seemed preferable to sitting behind a till. Determined to escape the daily contact with the squalor she found, she worked to get an office-based job, supervising others. She was so successful so quickly she was offered an award, but she declined it. Her determination to stay out of the spotlight was interpreted as modesty; Shackleton knew it was mistrust. In Jenni's experience nothing was given without obligation.

She encouraged Tom to take centre stage, to excel, while she smiled and nodded and watched everything with her disconcerting green eyes. To become Chief Constable or Commissioner of one of the forty-three forces of England and Wales a candidate must leave their region in order to return. So when Tom was offered Assistant Chief Constable on the other side of the country she knew he would be in the ideal position to return, triumphant, as Chief when the present incumbent, a nice old boy who had only thirty-five years' policing experience but no degree, retired.

She had no hesitation in giving up her job to follow him, to make sure he met the right people and was seen in the right places. One of the right people she met and charmed was a local-paper editor, keen to ease her loneliness while Tom worked long hours and neglected his exquisite wife. His infatuation with her led him to invite her to write a personal-view piece about a news story concerning runaway foster children. He re-wrote her words, and her career as freelance conscience and broadsheet agony aunt took off.

Her name was now known around the dinner tables that counted and, though she rarely wrote her own copy for tabloid or broadsheet, she became known as 'the Glory of the Guardian'. Jenni was not stupid, she knew she couldn't write without help, and, having outgrown the provincial editor, made sure the best features writers (male) were always available to her for lunch.

Jenni had that invaluable ability to make them feel unique, important, attractive, indispensable. She would look up, invariably up, with that slight, sly, intimate smile and say, 'I know I'm hopeless . . . would you mind?' And they would re-write her columns, features, occasionally pages, and feel grateful for her attention.

She sat in her car. Now aware of the stare from the man next to her, automatically she raised her chin, not that there was any hint of sag there. Even as she did it he was forgotten.

Her mind was scurrying around the problem of her husband and his rival for the job of Commissioner of the Metropolitan Police. She thought of their conversation after the TV interview. If Tom didn't get it what would be left? The ashes of ambition and a job advising on security for some merchant bank. God forbid he should be reduced to advertising anti-theft devices on television.

But Jenni was, above all, a woman capable of anticipating defeat. Always envying the possibility of another's achievement. If Geoffrey Carter was a hurdle to her husband's advancement then he would have to be overcome.

Jenni's smile was a lovely display of the dental hygienist's skill as she greeted her hairdresser. The parking of the car, the bore of driving into London, the paralysing tedium of conversation with the awkward adolescent washing her hair, were all to be endured for the honeyed cloud of softness cutter Clyde and colourist Tiny created. Jenni watched herself in the mirror as Clyde worked on her. She added just a touch more amusement to her expression as he chattered.

She automatically absorbed the condition of the other women in the salon. Nice face, bad ankles. Cheap facelift. With satisfaction she noted the shortcomings of the other clients. But then arrived a girl. Eighteen, maybe twenty. Obviously a model. Five foot eleven, race-horse limbs and flawless facial beauty.

The girl looked at, and dismissed, the other clients. They were all over thirty-five, some over forty. She opened a magazine for the irritatingly vacuous and looked at the pictures. Jenni was not an exception to this dismissal and felt a surge of anger. She was not like these other women – she was in direct competition with this leggy girl.

She knew she had been put in the middle-aged compartment by this vapid child. Jenni saw her careful perfection was nothing against this girl's real youth and untrammelled firmness of flesh.

Clyde watched Jenni's tightly controlled smile set. Under the noise of the dryers he murmured, 'Anorexic. And coked up to her eyes. Get closer, she never washes.'

He made a little face of disgust.

Jenni's smile unfroze.

Clyde added a little oil to the massage.

'Only does catalogue work now. On the skids at her age. Sad . . .' He left the rest unsaid.

Jenni relaxed.

The manicurist, a suitably plain and subservient girl, started work on her right hand and another prepared for her pedicure. Her mind was now on her prospective lover. Although she had no intention of sleeping with him for quite a while, if ever, all this preparation was for him.

In the next government he was certain to be very highly placed, in recognition of his loyal work certainly, but more for his quiet unreported power-broking. There were few people who mattered internationally who were out when he called. His wealth and influence were immense and his persona acceptable to a sceptical public. High office beckoned.

Jenni thought dispassionately about him, the smallness of the man, the ugliness of him. The extraordinarily sweet smile. His reputation for generosity and tireless work for the disabled, the underprivileged and the impoverished elderly. He was a Victorian giant in a world of shallow, media-obsessed midgets.

But none of this made him an attractive prospect sexually. And he knew it.

She had, while he kissed her with all the subtle sensuality of a drain clearer, unbuttoned his shirt and slipped her long, slim fingers under the double yoke. Her revulsion at what they encountered was covered by her giggling.

'Oh . . . bouclé shoulders . . . how extraordinary.'

He was immediately powerless, embarrassed.

'Don't you like hairy backs? Some women don't.'

She saw her husband's future as clearly marked as an airport runway.

'I love them. Confucius says the bird will not nest in tree with no leaves.'

She snuggled down to kiss his neck. The loose skin moved under her lips. Satisfied with her answer he let his hands move over her. His attempts at caresses set her teeth on edge and she squirmed under his touch. He mistook her movements for enjoyment.

Jenni didn't think of Tom or the way he touched her. Briefly, efficiently. She was one of those rare creatures who thinks only of what is happening in that moment. Jenni never examined her life. If things were bad it was the fault of circumstances or people who were against her and her family. If good, the fulfilment of her plans.

Like a great beautiful fish she swam through life living by instinct, never intellect. What she learned that didn't concur with what she knew was instantly dismissed. The world related to Jenni but Jenni could relate to no one. When she was young she had tried but found herself frighteningly at sea with the demands people made of her. But now she had created her own world, everyone in it a supporting actor. She had finally found some security in control.

The model girl raised her arm to move her hair in a gesture used by young actresses to signify their seriousness. Jenni saw the ugly unshaven tangle in her armpit. Clyde saw it at the same moment. They both laughed. The girl glanced over, oblivious.

'Ooh . . . Mrs Shackleton . . . I went to the most fantastic medium last week. Incredible. I didn't tell her anything about me, not a word, but . . .' Clyde took a breath and leaned close. 'She knew all about Jerry and gave me a message from him.'

Jenni was wide-eyed, hooked. Jerry's death from AIDS six years before had left Clyde ricocheting from seance to Ouija board.

'No!' breathed Jenni. 'Tell me.'

Clyde, his voice an embroidery of excitement, told her about his wonderful discovery, a Danish medium living in a council house near Tower Bridge. Before Jenni left the salon she had the woman's phone number.

Lucy set the alarms and locked up the house. When she got back to Gary he was sitting by the back door in his wheelchair watching the squirrels eat the remains of his breakfast. As she came in he tried to turn the chair but his arms failed him. She tried not to let him see she'd noticed. He had refused for so long to have an electric wheelchair, arguing the manual would keep him fit. But, fight though he did, they both knew he couldn't manage any more. Each week saw an erosion of his abilities. One less thing he could do for himself.

Radio One gibbered out of the portable on the draining board. The unspeakable sadness of his fading had made it impossible to listen to Radio Three any more.

One afternoon they'd been ambushed by a piece of Elgar and the dignity of its English melancholy had defeated them. It was the only time they had cried together. Cried at the inevitability of their future. So they had re-tuned to Radio Four and shortly after sat through a documentary on the last days of an MS sufferer. Now they just listened to Radio One, certain that they would hear nothing but aural Anaglypta.

'Guess what?'

Gary looked at Lucy, pleased at her happy mood, her positive air.

'What? Jenni's taken up DIY.'

Lucy laughed. 'No . . . nearly as unlikely.'

'Tom's turned down a chance to be on television.'

Lucy winced. Gary's name for Tom was John Lewis. Never Knowingly Under-exposed.

'No,' said Lucy, putting the kettle on. 'An invitation to dinner at the Shackletons'. On Thursday. How about that?'

Gary looked gratifyingly impressed.

'We'll have to get the nurses to come late. I'm sure Denise won't mind. And we'd better give this wheelchair a polish – don't want to spoil the look of Jenni's dining room.'

Despite himself, Gary was excited. 'Going out' had been reduced to feeding the ducks in the park. A dinner party would be a wonderful opportunity to pretend he was still normal. He was already calculating how long it would take to get ready and how long he would be able to stay before tiredness, pain and the arrival of the nurses to put him to bed would bring him back to the prison of his downstairs room.

The thought of Gary being invited hadn't occurred to Lucy. She didn't know what to say. But the look on her face told Gary more than a polite 'Oh, I don't think you're invited.' They were both mortified.

'Sorry. My mistake,' said Gary. 'You must go, of course. Do you good to get out for an evening.'

Lucy knew it was too late to backtrack or say anything that would help. She also knew she was so desperate to go martyrdom wasn't an option.

'Only if you don't mind being abandoned for the evening.'

Lucy said it lightly, not allowing herself to think about his hopes lying on the carpet between them. She knew he hated the long evenings after he had been put to bed. Incapable of moving until he was heaved out in the morning. She turned away to make the tea, afraid he'd see in her face her need to be close to Tom Shackleton. Her guilt at her crush on him was worsened by Gary's contempt for the man.

'Thursday?' said Gary. 'Actually, that's great because Jeremy's coming over to talk electric wheelchairs . . . yes . . . all right . . . you're right, it's time to get one. I'd forgotten all about it. You see, I couldn't have come anyway. And no . . . you don't have to be here. I promise no furry dice or go-faster stripes.'

'OK then. If you're sure.'

She knew she'd said it too quickly. Ashamed, she kept her face turned away from him. Her love, like the widow's mite, was all his. There wasn't much of it but it was all for Gary. What she felt for Tom was simply a burning, an excitement, a physical sickness with alternating depression and elation.

'Shall we have a biscuit?' Gary was already struggling to open the tin.

'No.' Lucy took it from him and lifted the lid: 'Think of my bottom. I'll never get into my black dress.'

Gary smiled and took a biscuit. Lucy would never know how

26

much he wanted to hate her for taking the biscuit-tin lid off for him. Or that he was close to tears at not being included in the dinner invitation, at not being a part of life any more. As quickly as the cloud of depression formed he pushed it away, his anger now for allowing it to take shape. Self-pity and resentment had been anathema to Gary the well man and were enemies to be avoided daily by him now.

He shared himself with a God Lucy could only imagine. To her a cruel dictator, to Gary a giver of lessons, joy and sorrow, as opportunities for improvement. His rapid deterioration was his cross, borne with strength and almost gratitude – his suffering meant someone else would be free of it. As if there was a world rationing of pain.

Lucy went upstairs to the bedroom, still burning with her insensitivity to Gary. The room, in quiet need of fresh wallpaper, no longer theirs, now hers, still housed the wardrobe where Gary's work suits hung limply. Unworn for three years and now too big.

She knew she would one day be folding them into black plastic sacks, ready for charity or bin. But not yet, not yet.

She laid out on the bed her evening outfits: a little black number, a dowdy trouser suit, and a silk dress she'd bought on impulse years ago in a designer sale.

Quickly she undressed and looked at herself. Her body was one you'd see in any shop changing room. Politely called pear-shaped. The Great British Figure. It was, in fact, badly proportioned, with a long body and short legs. The bottom heavier than the top. Lucy was resigned to what she saw: mumsy, well upholstered, nothing special. A practical model, built for comfort rather than speed or luxury.

She thought of Jenni with her corvette lines and felt ugly, ungainly. Her excitement at going out, being close to Tom, dressing up, withered in the fierceness of reality.

She picked up the little black number and stepped into it. She couldn't pull it up past her thighs. She didn't bother to re-hang it in the wardrobe, just put it in the waste bin by the bed. The trouser suit had that sad look of clothes bought in charity shops. She sat holding the silk dress for several minutes before she tried it on, unwilling to see herself again so plain and unattractive.

As she sat she saw veins on her thighs that had not been there ten years before, lines on the backs of her wrists, a thickened toenail.

Feeling herself on the cusp of self-pity she got up quickly and tried on the dress. It wasn't a miraculous transformation but she knew she looked good in it. A pale turquoise, bias cut, almost thirties design, falling elegantly to below the knee. Shoes. Which shoes?

As Lucy stood there, vulnerable, she heard her father, tutting: 'Kipper feet. Pick them up, girl. Can't you walk quieter than that?'

Again the tutting. A sound that even years after his death could turn her back into a lumpen fifteen-year-old. The criticism, the sniping at her when no one else could hear. Suddenly she remembered an accident she'd had – 'You should take more care. There's no such thing as an accident.'

He had taken her to hospital where they'd shaved her leg before dressing it. For the first time she had not allowed herself to be self-conscious, convincing herself that doctors handled people all the time, and that her body was all right, in no way out of the ordinary.

She made the nurses laugh and came out of the cubicle a little triumphant. She had got through it and got through it well, without worrying her feet were dirty or her knees unwashed. He said nothing until they were in the car, then, 'Sounded like they were shaving a pig.' He didn't say it with malice, he was smiling, unaware he was the mirror in which she saw herself.

Lucy was pleased with the silk. She would buy hold-up stockings and wear the lace bra and pants she'd bought in the sales two years ago. She put the past away with the dress and went downstairs to make Gary's lunch.

Tom sat in his office. The morning had been taken up with a disciplinary hearing which resulted in an officer of twenty-five years' standing leaving the service in disgrace. The Chief Constable gave the man no more thought after returning to his spartan office. He never ate lunch and so was working on budget sheets and crime figures.

The office was large and his desk dominated the room from opposite the oak door. Past chief constables, stiff in their uniforms, looked out in varying stages of awkwardness from the walls. The desk itself was almost bare. A telephone and paperweight. Behind him a display cabinet containing his first helmet and little else. There were no photographs of Jenni or the children. Like Tom Shackleton the room was minimalist or bleak, depending on your opinion.

Janet, his secretary, knocked discreetly and came in. She was a tall woman with an unexpectedly melodic voice. Always quiet, always protective of the Chief, she was also wary of him. When he first arrived one of the other secretaries had leaned over his shoulder to point something out to him. He had felt the weight of her breast resting on him, he had smelt her perfume, cheaper and lighter than Jenni's. She was moved to traffic the next day.

When he was Chief Constable in his fiefdom his asceticism verged on the monastic. Nothing that might distract him was allowed. His force likened his personal discipline to that of an SS officer.

But he captivated most of those with whom he came into contact. He had a way of making people feel they were special, encouraging them to imagine intimacy, but any subsequent advance towards him was met with coldness and immediate rebuff. As his staff officer said, 'Don't get into bed with Tom Shackleton – he won't respect you in the morning.'

His force, a large one, generally disliked him for his lack of the common touch and his eagerness to be high-profile in the media. But the crime figures were good and his area was high in the league tables of excellence so beloved of the government.

Janet came a little way into the room, not too close.

'Mr Vernon's here to see you – he says it's important.'

Vernon was his deputy. Not a very clever man but doggedly loyal. Shackleton liked him for that and his open good nature. Vernon was already in the doorway.

'Jim, come in.'

Shackleton got up and indicated the two wing chairs either side of the window.

'Sit down.'

'Thank you, sir, I'll be brief. I think we've got a problem.'

Jim Vernon spoke modified Hendon Police College, a flat sound littered with inappropriate words.

'Flamborough Estate's looking a bit suspicious.'

'Not again.'

Shackleton's tone was one of weary resignation. The Flamborough Estate had originally been two estates, Elgin and Forres, but sprawling expansion and a gerrymandering moving of borough boundaries had brought them together to be renamed but not rebranded. The Flamborough was just twice as bad as its component parts and was unique in having two police forces unable to control it.

The DCC scanned his face for the signal to continue. Shackleton gave a slightly irritated nod.

'Yes, a bit . . . suspicious. The situation there, well, we thought we'd nipped it in the bud after that bloody storm. But, well, sir, it seems there's history. The Sudanese kids and the Paki. . . .' He hesitated, mentally reading the sub-sections relating to racism, and corrected himself. 'Pakistani kids had a bit of a ruckus about three month ago, running battle through the estate, couple of cars wrecked and the Credit Union office burned out, nothing serious. Well, our lads went in, rounded up the ring leaders, scumbags – sorry, sir – and when the dust had settled, both sides complained of police brutality.'

'Yes, I remember.'

Vernon was irritatingly pedantic.

Shackleton had gone on local television to defend his officers to a panel of irate elders from both communities. What they regarded as youthful high spirits had left two PCs with stab wounds and a WPC off ever since with post-traumatic stress disorder. But the People's Chief Constable had charmed and promised his way through the confrontation. The matter was closed, until last night.

'Right, well,' continued Vernon, 'we were called to the estate again – a Sudanese kid's battering this Pakistani kid with a baseball bat and he's slashing back with a machete – there's about thirty youths standing round roaring them on. It's like a bloody cock fight.'

Tom was used to his deputy telling him what he already knew but then Vernon wasn't used to chief constables who took an interest in police matters.

'Our lads wade in – literally – that little female inspector played a blinder. The lads reckoned her period was due so she was well up for a fight.'

Shackleton didn't smile. He never encouraged sexist remarks.

Vernon went on quickly. 'The weather was bloody awful' (as if Shackleton's weather had been any different). 'Anyway, we sling these two low life in the back of the van. Ambulance arrives and the Pakistani kid's carted off with two PCs to keep an eye on him and we bring the other lad back to the nick. The Pakistani is declared dead on arrival at hospital and our boy, in the van . . .'

Tom's unreadable expression didn't change – he just nodded for Vernon to continue.

'He starts kicking up and was restrained by two of our lads, maybe a bit over-enthusiastically, and . . . he's in a coma. On a life-support machine. We're looking into it.'

Shackleton nodded again. He could see where this was going.

'The word's got out on the street both lads are dead and it was the police that killed them. You can feel it on the estate – it's going to go off tonight. They've been pouring in from London, Birmingham, all over. Problem is, sir, the Sudanese were dumped on the Flamborough in the middle of the Pakistanis but nobody had worked out the reason they were here in the first place was this bunch of Sudanese are not too keen on Muslims. Seems Christians are a bit of a persecuted minority over there. Rape and torture toughened them up. So there's been trouble ever since they got here and we've been keeping the lid on it. Till now. They're drawing up battle lines. A couple of bricks have gone through shop windows, usual stuff. They've had time now to get themselves sorted. We're pretty sure there are firearms on the estate. Definitely petrol bombs and the usual stuff. If the weather stays fine I reckon we're in for the big one.'

He stopped, looking for Shackleton's reaction. But Tom's mind was on the inevitable battle.

'I think,' Tom said quietly, leaning on the length of his left hand and stroking his eyebrow with the tip of his little finger, as he always did when absorbed, 'they'll set up a fight between themselves again and we'll be called in. Once we're on the estate the lot of them will turn on us like they did last night, but this time we'll have no way out.' He paused. 'Remember the '85 riot?' He went on quietly, not for Vernon or himself but because words gave the horror a dull reality. 'Did you ever see the officer's jacket? In the Black Museum. More than twenty machete cuts. He –' Shackleton automatically corrected himself – both men knew who he was talking about. 'They got away with it and the officer in charge was hung out to dry. For politics –'

Vernon couldn't resist adding his knowledge.

'Yes, sir, but he was cleared. Court One of the Old Bailey. Same dock as the alleged killer.' The emphasis he put on 'alleged' was anything but subtle.

Shackleton continued; his voice remained quiet, unemotional. 'I don't want us caught like that again.'

There was a short silence. The phone rang. Shackleton answered it.

'Tom Shackleton . . . Hello, Geoffrey . . .'

He glanced across at his deputy who immediately made for the door making signs he'd be in his own office if the Chief wanted him.

'Tom, we've got a nasty one here, I think. A Sudan versus Pakistan war on our border. Not what we need, is it?'

Geoffrey Carter's tone was, as always, light, almost amused.

'I think it's more likely to be them versus us,' Shackleton replied.

'Any ideas, Tom?'

Tom wondered if he'd picked up the habit of endlessly repeating the name of the person he was talking to from his sabbaticals in California.

Carter continued without waiting for Shackleton's reply.

'Look, I've got meetings all afternoon but my deputy's going to keep me informed. Why don't we talk around six? And we'll see where we can go from there.'

'Fine,' Tom said and put down the phone.

He sat behind the desk absolutely still, completely focused on the problem. His face took on the blank intensity of a hunting animal when it first sees its prey. Geoffrey Carter was the politicians' favourite, the great administrator, but Tom Shackleton was the strategist, the fighter, the shark. He pressed the intercom, Janet replied.

'Janet, make sure I get hourly reports on the Flamborough situation, more if necessary.'

Then, like a chess player, he sat and worked out every set of moves they might make and every option open to him, both offensive and defensive. This was as close to pleasure as Tom Shackleton allowed himself.

Jenni had arrived at Shepherd's, the politicians' lunchtime refuge, late. She wasn't flustered, she had intended to be late. To make him wait and also to be sure most other tables would be occupied so her entrance would be seen by the maximum number of eyes. She was gratified to see their table was on the far side of the restaurant so she had to pass through a sea of admiring glances and waved greetings. She acknowledged them with a fey, other-worldly smile. But she had to maintain her ethereal expression when she saw he wasn't there. She sat down alone and ordered a vodka tonic. She had calculated everything so she would be in control of this situation and this small defeat, the fear of looking silly, the fear of being stood up, left to read the menu so as not to see mocking glances, started the coils of anger in her stomach writhing.

Before she could decide to leave with what dignity she could command, he arrived. She was pleased to see he looked apologetic and was rushing across the room to her, ignoring the smiles and greetings of everyone. Behind him was a tall man, made taller by the Gnome's smallness. Her irritation evaporated when she saw it was the Prime Minister's personal adviser.

'Jenni, I'm so sorry. Can you forgive me? You know Jeremy, of course.'

She was gracious.

'Only by reputation. How lovely to meet you.'

She held out her hand and the alleged power behind the throne took it with visible appreciation.

'Mrs Shackleton. How do you do. I must say, Robbie here didn't exaggerate when he said he had to get away to have lunch with an angel.'

It was outrageous but she loved it.

'I just had to come and see for myself. We got held up by Robbie here helping some old woman who'd passed out under Churchill's statue. By the time he'd loaded her into a taxi and paid her fare home to Bromley he'd qualified for a Nobel prize and a serious telling off from you. I hope you'll be gentle with him. He's always been a terror for lame ducks.'

Jenni was completely charmed. She gestured to the Gnome to sit.

'I quite understand. Really. Will you be joining us?'

Jeremy's attention was already wandering.

'Mmm? No, no. Ah, there's my table over there. Not nearly as interesting as yours but . . . lovely to meet you, Mrs Shackleton. I'm a great admirer of your husband.'

And he was gone, pressing flesh and waving, to the other side of the room.

Jenni turned the full beauty of her smile on the now forgiven Gnome. Almost immediately his leg sought hers and clamped itself along her thigh.

'I've missed you,' he whispered loudly an inch from her face. The sweet, gentle, ugly face had changed, as if it was a mask passed to another wearer.

She could smell his breath. She expelled the air though her nostrils and turned away prettily, as he thought, demurely. Jenni produced from her bag a notebook and gold pen.

'Ah . . .' he said, sitting back in the banquette seat. 'Business lunch, eh?'

'What else? We can leave pleasure until Thursday. Dinner.'

He smiled and there was the most extraordinary transformation. The ugliness disappeared and was replaced by the face of of the saint again. The black-bearded face with its big, fish-shaped eyes, brown eyes that, looking up, seemed to be praying. It was his smile that made the observer feel they had created beauty. It was his smile that had won him the hearts and votes of a massive majority of his constituents, despite his wealth and unprepossessing physique.

'Oh yes, I'm looking forward to that. Pairing me up with the cleaning lady, didn't you say?' He looked at her, detached for a moment. 'I mustn't tease you, must I, Jenni? I always forget, you have absolutely no sense of humour.'

Under the tablecloth his small, long-fingered hand grasped her knee.

'But you have so much else to offer . . .'

Jenni, despite her revulsion, was fascinated by him. He had never been short of women, though physically he was barely on the acceptable side of repulsive. His beautifully cut suits and obsessive care of his appearance couldn't disguise his misshapen body or odd features.

It was often conjectured in the Red Lion's bar and those of the Commons itself that he was achondroplasic. But to the tabloid hacks, calling a spade a shovel, he was a dwarf. Not a short man with a chip on his shoulder. A dwarf. A Nibelung. He knew only too well the litany of names for his condition. They were like a quiver of darts always ready to be thrown at him. But whatever people's opinion of his looks, he was fearsomely intelligent, and the more power he accrued the more women found him attractive.

For him each conquest was a small act of revenge, for the years when the only female comfort he could find had to be paid for, in cash, and usually beforehand. Now he had Tom Shackleton's fine-boned wife to look forward to.

Jenni was aware of him watching her, his eyes almost closed.

'Penny for them?'

She accompanied her question with an unconscious movement of her mouth that he found very exciting. He took her hand and gently pulled it under the cloth.

'That.'

He smiled at the brief flicker of horror on her face as she touched his penis through the expensive wool of his suit. It made him want to have her more, knowing she found him as revolting as all the others. He always enjoyed the wives of handsome, successful, men – and Tom Shackleton was nothing if not handsome and successful. The devil was wearing the mask again.

'I'm not quite sure why you want me to come on Thursday, Jenni. Can't live without me?'

'Oh . . . I just want you to get to know Tom, that's all. It's important for you to know who your best people are, don't you think? For the future?'

'Your husband's achievements are hardly a secret. But yes, you're right, it would be good to get to know him. Hear his ideas.'

They were interrupted by the waiter. They started to chat, nothings about items in the news, while the menus were handed to them and the specials explained. Jenni put her menu down, having decided.

'Now,' she said. 'I really do have to interview you. I've got a commission to do an in-depth on you – oh, are you all right to have your photograph done? It'll be huge, you know, double page with the photo across the centre.'

'One of those grainy black-and-white jobs that show up the hairs on your nose?'

Stung by his accusation of having no humour she laughed.

'Yes, that's the one.'

'Speak to my secretary.'

Jenni put a small Dictaphone on the table. He looked surprised.

'Do we need that?'

'Oh it's just because I don't have shorthand. I'm a hopeless journalist.' She said this with a disarming smile.

Again he wondered how versatile that mouth would prove.

Jenni saw quite shockingly clearly the desire on his face and not for the first time was surprised at the power of sex.

For Jenni full penetrative sex and all the peripheral fumbling around it were, at best, aerobic exercise, at worst an uncomfortable, unhygienic scrum. But it had proved a useful tool now she had learned how to use it sparingly . . . She hoped she could get what she wanted from this man without having his fingers on her and in her. She shuddered delicately.

'Cold?' he asked solicitously.

'Just someone walking over my grave. Now . . . let's see, what were we talking about? Oh yes . . . you. How nice.'

By seven o'clock bulletins from the Flamborough Estate were arriving at Tom Shackleton's office every fifteen minutes. One of his best superintendents, Don Cork, was coordinating officer in command, codename Gold. Running the show on the front line was Ron Randall, codename Silver. Not a GCSE between them but sixty years' experience of everything from male organs trapped in reluctant retrievers to civil unrest on a grand scale. The reports indicated that petrol bombs and weapons of all sorts, possibly firearms, were being brought into the area. Several cars had been set alight and shops looted.

The big white vans full of edgy young police officers spoiling for a fight were parked around the estate and on the front line, the main access to the estate. It was marked with police tape. Blue-and-white, fluttering in the light breeze. On one side of this fragile barrier the eerily silent blocks of flats, at every window a pair of eyes watching the two lines of uniformed officers who stood, unmoving, on the other side.

The front rank were without weapons or defence, the rear in riot gear, black greaves on dark overalls, helmets with prospect visors, long-handled batons and round Roman shields.

On Shackleton's instructions the police had not responded to any calls since four o'clock. Hysterical residents were dialling 999, screaming they'd been abandoned, threatening to sue, knowing their rights. The telephone operators didn't point out that, in law, neither police nor fire service had any obligation to respond to emergency calls from the public.

The media were gathering, ensuring by their presence a display of testosterone-fuelled aggression from both sides.

On the east of the estate, Carter's territory, there was another line of police, more vans, more tape.

Tom stood looking out of the window – the sky was alight with the red streaks of a shepherd's delight. He knew the real trouble wouldn't start until dark – and until all the television crews had arrived. The audience in place and the theatre ready.

Janet knocked discreetly and came in.

'BBC and ITV, Sky and local and national newspapers have arrived on the estate, sir. Mr Vernon thinks they were called by the youths themselves.'

No doubt about it.

'Thank you, Janet. Oh, and I want to go down there. At nine o'clock. Not in my car.'

The sleek black Jaguar sweeping on to the estate would be bound to cause trouble. And be bad for the image of the Caring Chief Constable.

'Send round a patrol car. But I want Gordon to drive.'

Janet nodded and left. Of course he wanted Gordon. Weasly, unimaginative Gordon. He had only one quality to recommend him to Shackleton. He was armed.

Shackleton went to the phone and dialled Geoffrey Carter's direct line.

He answered quickly.

'Carter.'

'Geoffrey, I'm on my way to the Flamborough – want to join me?'

'What's your plan?'

'Oh . . . I think you and I can talk our way out of this one . . . don't you?'

Carter laughed. 'I think we could talk our way into and out of a Trappist nunnery.'

Shackleton smiled. 'I'll meet you at nine-thirty outside the Crown pub by the station. It'll be just dark by then.'

'Uniforms?'

Shackleton paused for a moment. He was wearing a suit, well cut, grey silk tie, white shirt, good shoes. He weighed up the forthcoming situation. The youths, inflamed against the police, would be taken off-guard by civilian clothes and give them a more sympathetic hearing.

But his own men would expect him to wear the uniform, not to make concessions to these yobs. And the uniform represented authority, an authority not to be intimidated by any section of society. Finally, the impact in the media would be greater if they wore the crowns and insignia of their rank.

'Uniforms,' he said. 'Swagger sticks and gloves.'

'And hats off asap. Yes. Good. Forty minutes then.' Carter rang off.

What on earth was he doing? He felt like a lad who'd just agreed to go joy-riding with the local tearaway. Why had he said yes? Was he trying to prove he was as macho as Tom Shackleton? It wasn't what chief constables did. It was stupid, it was risky and it wasn't by the book. But it was typical Shackleton. And it made the adrenalin run.

If Carter had a weakness it was being human. When he was a DC he had discovered the pleasure of masculine closeness after his team had got 'a result'. The drinking, the physicality, the emotional memory of shared danger and, most importantly, the equality.

As he'd hurtled through the ranks he'd never stopped searching out that camaraderie. Geoffrey Carter was famous for always remembering the secretaries' birthdays, for making sure his driver got proper breaks and was fed on jobs. For caring even when there was no camera or microphone to record his good deeds. It was part of the legend that, when the son of an old sergeant based in the middle of nowhere died in a car crash, Carter visited him and supported the family through their bereavement.

Although not naturally 'one of the lads', wherever he'd served he'd been popular and he'd gained a reputation for having a soft spot for the unconventional, if it got results.

Shackleton, whose natural constituency was the canteen rather than the restaurant, whose background had featured contact sports rather than ballet or opera, disliked the loud bonhomie of the changing room, the physical closeness of the triumphal piss-up. He was a loner whose occasional spectacular acts of daring or bravery were motivated solely by an instinct for self-challenge and self-promotion. He avoided at all costs getting involved. If gifts were given it was Jenni who bought and gave them, out of expediency.

Once, after a meeting, during which Gordon had been kept waiting in the car, the female councillor Shackleton had been lunching with asked if Gordon had been fed and watered. Shackleton looked blank and shook his head, not knowing why Gordon should have been. The woman had stood in the street and said, loud enough for any passer-by to hear, 'You mean bastard!' Gordon was shocked and secretly pleased. Shackleton thought her a fool and did not learn the lesson. He took no responsibility for anyone other than himself.

Shackleton opened the door beside his desk and went into his changing room. Immaculately ironed shirts and uniforms hung on wooden hangers. He didn't know it was Lucy who had pressed each piece, breathing in the steam as if he was in it. If he'd known it would have caused him embarrassment.

He put on his uniform with the care of a priest robing for Mass. He caught sight of himself in the mirror. Not a trace of the excitement he felt showed on his face. He felt aroused as other men did when anticipating an evening with a desirable woman. Alive at the possibilities.

Carter hadn't arrived when Gordon stopped the patrol car outside the dingy pub on the edge of the Flamborough Estate. Shackleton got out. It was dark now and the bleakness of the road was softened by the orange street lights.

Shackleton had chosen the Crown because it was a Caribbean and Irish pub. Its regulars were no fans of the police, but even less keen on the Africans and Asians who were comparative newcomers, accusing them of throwing their rubbish into the front gardens and of being responsible for most of the crime on the estate.

Most of the men and all of the few women customers were older people, the men working on building sites or in the alternative economy, paving and tiling the front gardens of suburbia. Church on Sunday and a good punch-up after closing on Friday. As usual the oldest men were playing dominoes in the saloon bar.

Shackleton stood outside, looking into the estate. It was uncannily quiet, no Bangra or drumming blaring out of flats and cars. No loud, uncontrolled adolescent voices. Nothing. In the distance he saw a flash of light followed immediately by a loud bang.

'Car going up,' observed Gordon. He wasn't frightened but he quivered like a whippet. Fight or flight. With Gordon it was always fight.

Shackleton became aware of three black women sitting outside a flat opposite the pub. It was an extraordinary sight. The occupants had marked out an area on the scrubby grass as theirs. It was bordered with pots containing a riot of flowers, ivies and shrubs. All plastic.

Against the wall of the flat were oil cans, sinks, and even an old

lavatory pan filled with more plastic blooms in vivid colours un-
dreamt of in nature. One of the women was carefully dusting them
and spraying room freshener on those she felt had lost their scent.
The two other women sat in fold-down picnic chairs, a five-litre
bottle of sarsaparilla between them.

'Hello there, Mr Shackleton. You keepin' well?'

He was surprised to be greeted by name; he was sure he didn't
know these women but stepped closer to be sure. The woman who
spoke was the heaviest of the three. She sat, her knees parted by the
flesh of her thighs, watching the evening with a great smile on her
round, shining face.

On her head, she wasn't so much wearing as had precariously
perched a pink hat made of synthetic straw and in the style of old-
fashioned girls'-school felt hats. A wide ribbon of deeper pink went
round the brim to a tight, flat bow at the back.

Shackleton wondered which would give first, the chair or the thin
material of her dress, which struggled to encompass the vastness of
her bosoms and belly. There was something so elementally sexual in
the expanse of her; her cavernous cleavage was so unashamedly
inviting he looked away, feeling inadequate and ridiculous and,
above all, white.

The woman sitting next to her was as thin and dry as she was
voluptuous and moist. Her legs, also apart at the knee, had high calf
muscles and long ankles finishing in large flat feet which pushed out
the sides of larger flatter shoes.

The feet were crossed, resting on their outers, her legs so thin they
looked like crossbones and her fleshless face the skull. She said
nothing but nodded amiably. Her long bony hands, the skin cracked
through lack of care and sun, worked quickly at her crochet. A pile of
doilies and anti-macassars lay on a newspaper by her feet.

Shackleton looked at her and recognised in the sharpness of her
eye sockets and the dullness of her skin the proximity of death. He
glanced away, towards the fire they had made in a small tin bath. The
third woman stopped her dusting to turn and look at him.

The feelings the fat woman and death's companion had stirred in
him were replaced by something like fear when he saw her face. It
was deep black, an African colour without the friendly warmth of the
West Indies. A slate-blue-black with the cheeks deeply scarred by
three slashes on either side.

Her features were without a shadow of the Caucasian in size or position. She was shockingly alien, unexpected. But it was her eyes that repelled Shackleton though he was unable to look away. They were exactly like the cowrie shells used for eyes in African sculpture. As if the eyeball had been folded over and the edges crudely sewn together.

For a second he wanted to get nearer to pull them out, to find the real eyes underneath. After a moment she turned her unsmiling ebony face and unsettling eyes away from him and continued dusting. She bent from the waist, legs straight, and as she did he realised she must be over two metres tall and as slender and supple as a young tree. He had never seen a human being so different, so disturbing.

'You come for the riot, Mr Shackleton?'

The fat woman was still smiling, her teeth perfect white tomb-stones.

'I hope there won't be one,' he replied with his most self-deprecating dip of the head.

'No, Thomas, No . . .'

She was laughing now, laughing at him, joined soundlessly by the death's head next to her.

'You're counting on one . . . counting on it, child.'

And in that moment he felt like a child. Caught in a lie.

Geoffrey Carter's Rover arrived while the women were still chuckling affectionately. Back on safe ground Shackleton turned abruptly, glad to be rid of the women, and walked over to him.

'I don't think the Rover's a good idea,' he said as Carter got out.

'No . . . you're probably right. I'll tell the driver to wait here. We'll take your car, shall we?'

As they walked to the patrol car Shackleton could feel the women watching him. The hairs on the back of his neck rose. With an irritated gesture he rubbed his hand over them and got into the front passenger seat next to Gordon. Carter sat in the back.

They drove slowly towards the estate. As they got closer they saw police vans waiting around every corner, lads in uniforms, tense, ready, not so different from the lads in the flats. Dog handlers standing with their patient animals close by their legs.

And then the black backs of the riot police, legs planted apart, unmoving.

Shackleton signalled Gordon to stop. The three men got out. Inspector Ron Randall hurried towards them. His position Silver, number two in command when trouble kicked off. Both chiefs smiled as if this were a meeting in the social club. Carter shook his hand, bending slightly to speak to him. The same height as Shackleton, he had the wiry build of a marathon runner and looked almost delicate next to the other chief. Thin-faced and fine-boned, he had earned the name of Bambi from his force because of his leggy grace and long-lashed eyes.

They told Randall it was their intention to go in, to try to defuse the situation. Randall was appalled – in his opinion these two clothes horses would only make things worse. He tried to dissuade them, then tried to persuade them to take armed officers with them.

Their faces were grave, concentrating as though listening to him, but he knew the chance of a media coup was more to them than caution. That retiring with no mortgage and a good pension was not an ambition for either of them.

As they turned away from Randall he radioed Gold, Superintendent Don Cork.

'Mr Shackleton and Mr Carter are going in alone. They want to negotiate face to face. We are to keep back. I repeat, the Chief Constables wish us to keep back.'

Unspoken but heard by Cork was the certainty that if it went wrong the resulting chaos would result in nationwide race riots. Randall remembered there'd been a chief constable of Essex who'd exchanged himself for a hostage during a pub siege once but this wasn't about bravery. This was about self-promotion. Gold saw the repercussions for his own career clearly. If it all went pear-shaped and there was an inquiry he would be responsible.

'Gold to Silver. Instruct Mr Shackleton and Mr Carter they are not, repeat not, to proceed.'

'It's too late,' Randall replied.

There was a pause. The radio crackled, then Gold's voice, clear in the heavy silence.

'What a pair of wankers.'

The two chiefs with Gordon a pace behind walked in silence up to the tape. As they touched it a strange wailing sound echoed round the empty streets and the sound of metal pipes being beaten against concrete started up. Rhythmic, frightening.

Out of the corner of his eye Shackleton saw a movement. Too late to be avoided, a flaming milk bottle filled with petrol landed close to their feet. The flames spread out across the road. A roar of approval from the unseen foe; and then they began to show themselves. On the roofs, the walkways and in the doorways young men appeared, all with their faces shrouded in handkerchiefs and scarves. A group of them started to bounce a car parked in their route. Like army ants they swarmed over it and in minutes it was on its back. Alight.

Carter and Shackleton stood, watching, still. Behind them a camera crew, carrying a ludicrous microphone clad in a shaggy fur coat on a long pole.

'BBC, sir,' murmured Gordon.

Shackleton nodded briefly. Unhurriedly he bent down and ducked under the tape. Carter followed, then Gordon. Two officers barred the way of the camera crew but Tom turned and beckoned them on.

'Just them,' he said.

When the small group was under the tape Shackleton and Carter began to walk steadily towards the youths and the flaming car. Randall watched, torn between admiration and contempt. His mind had already dealt with the deaths of the chiefs and the appalling aftermath. He would be the one to start the Armageddon. The air in his radio hissed, waiting for a command. The command to start a race war throughout Britain.

A half-brick was thrown and skidded along in front of the chiefs. Another. Someone behind Shackleton yelped sharply. He glanced round; the sound man had been struck on the shin. Shackleton turned back, his careful pace uninterrupted. This was his element, the only time he could simply be. No fear and no thought, just a wave of adrenalin and total relaxation.

Carter, beside him, was vibrating with the danger they were in, aware of every eye, every twitching hand. Where Shackleton was experiencing an athlete's calm before the big race, Carter was shaking with stage fright.

Three masked youths, carrying knives and baseball bats, started to walk towards them. Carter almost laughed. It was too *High Noon*. Too melodramatic.

Behind the three masked youths came another six, then seven, ten.

Twenty. All armed. Shackleton saw they were both Sudanese and Pakistani. The police had already united the warring factions. A thought went through his head so fast he almost didn't hear it: he wondered how it felt to be liked.

The crowd was jittery, unsure, dangerous. The police stopped with about five feet between them and the ring leaders. Immediately they were surrounded. The cameraman swivelled round, videoing every hidden face, then moved sideways to get the chief constables facing the rioters.

Slowly Shackleton reached up and removed his gold-laden hat and tucked it, with his swagger stick, under his arm. A fraction later Carter followed suit. Then, just as deliberately, Shackleton removed his soft brown gloves. Carter did the same.

With the ritual tension of samurai they handed their hats, sticks and gloves to Gordon without taking their eyes off the boys in front of them. It was as if they were handing in their weapons. Shackleton knew the psychological effect this disarming would have.

The ring leader couldn't stand Shackleton's steady, unblinking look any more.

'What the fuck do you want? Fucking pig.'

'My name's Tom Shackleton, I'm your Chief Constable and this is my colleague Geoffrey Carter. He is Chief Constable of our neighbouring area.'

His expression softened almost imperceptibly.

'We want to know what your grievances are. What's made you feel this strongly? We want to know what we can do to help.'

A pause. Then a voice at the back, made brave by anonymity, screamed, 'Kill them! Kill the bastards!'

The camera swung around towards the voice.

'Take them hostage!'

This suggestion found more favour with the majority. Their voices swelled in agreement. 'Yeah . . . keep 'em here. Then they'll have to listen, right?'

The excitement caused by this idea swept through the youths, melding them into a mob. The small group in the middle sensed the mood change.

Carter felt the sweat of fear run down his arms and legs. Cold. Hands reached towards them. The camera was knocked to the ground. Shackleton was grabbed by the arms and smashed viciously

44

on the backs of the knees by a baseball bat. Carter was felled by a blow to his temple.

Gordon, anxious to hide his gun, cowered and assured them he'd come quietly. The mob thought this hilarious and several of them kicked him contemptuously. He curled over, apparently in pain, in reality covering the hand gun. They grabbed the hats, gloves and sticks from him and distributed them among the crowd. The camera crew recovered their camera and were simply shoved and pushed along behind.

Randall, unable to deploy his troops without further risk to the chiefs and the situation, stared helplessly. It would soon be canteen legend that he'd stood repeating over and over again, 'Idiots. Fucking stupid fucking arrogant fucking idiots.'

When the mob stopped, Shackleton, Carter and the camera crew found themselves in the community centre. Moulded plastic chairs were hastily unstacked for them and they were pushed down on to them. The young man who seemed to be emerging as the leader ordered the camera crew to keep filming.

'Right . . .' said the leader, a shade too loudly. 'What we want is this . . . we want justice, right? The police murdered two boys from this estate and we want justice.'

There was a roar of approval.

'So you're going to stay here till we get it.'

'Fine,' replied Tom reasonably. 'First of all . . . what shall I call you?'

There was a suspicious pause, then, 'Ali. Call me Ali.'

'Well, Ali,' he continued seamlessly. 'I think you ought to know one of the boys, Sammi, is in a serious but stable condition in hospital. He is not dead.'

This caused a furore. Some believed him, others shouted 'Liar!'. Ali joined in the shouting, saying even if it was true, the other boy was still dead, at the hands of the police. Someone punched Tom on the side of the head, spitting at him. He reached into his pocket and took out an immaculate cotton handkerchief. Lucy had put a drop of her perfume on it. He didn't notice it as he wiped the spittle off his face.

'I want to speak to Mr Qureishi.'

'You talk to us – no one else.'

He smiled. 'You're not afraid, are you? Let me speak to him. You know he doesn't take sides. He is the father of your community, isn't he?'

This caused uproar: this white symbol of the establishment was calling the Pakistanis to order as Muslims. The Sudanese were equally loud in their Christian outrage.

Shackleton's voice rose to be heard.

'You won't believe whatever I say. I have the results of the post-mortem on the other boy but you want to believe it was murder. I can't change your minds if you won't listen. If you don't want to hear the truth. Why not let Imam Qureishi and Grandfather Joseph decide if I'm lying?'

The roar of 'No's was deafening. One lad had a can of petrol and showered it over the two chiefs. He was immediately knocked to the ground by others screaming they had cigarettes. It was degenerating into anarchy. Ali was losing control. At the back of the prefabricated room two groups of elderly women watched, expressionless.

As Carter was dragged off his chair by the shoulder of his uniform, sending silver buttons rolling across the floor, an old, bearded man in calf-length shirt over baggy cotton trousers and wearing a brown knitted hat over the crown of his white hair pushed his way into the room. Behind him a second old man in white robes. His Modigliani face the dark, delicately featured oval of the Sudan. Their arrival seemed to inflame the crowd further.

'This isn't your fight.'

'There's no place for old men here.'

'Go home and watch the telly, Grandad.'

But the voices were less sure, less strident.

The old men approached Carter and Shackleton.

'Chief Constable . . .'

Shackleton stood up. Carter followed.

'Ah and Mr Carter. How do you do.'

The four men shook hands.

Shackleton was solicitous.

'Mr Qureishi, how are you? And your family?'

'As you see,' said the old man wryly. 'My grandsons are here.'

He lowered his thin body on to one of the chairs.

Grandfather Joseph nodded but said nothing. He sat gracefully and exchanged a look with Mr Qureishi, who began to speak quietly but with some strength.

'You have heard the grievances of the young people. They believe the police are murderers. That the life of an Asian or an African is not

46

so important as the life of a white or even a Caribbean child. You always know those blacks will kick up a stink, but we, no, we prefer a quiet life. We are peaceable, running our corner shops and sending our children to university. Well . . . these young people are different. You know that from Bradford. They don't have our patience. You are their enemy.'

Tom waited for the old man to finish, then said, just as quietly, just as reasonably, 'I want to assure you, assure you all, that is not the case. As Mr Qureishi and Grandfather Joseph know, Mr Carter and I have worked hard since we came here to improve relations between the police and your two communities.'

'Didn't fuckin' work, did it?' came a voice from the back.

'Obviously not,' said Tom without a trace of irony. 'And for that I apologise. I want you to know that I deeply regret the death of young Mohammed and if any of my officers were culpable I will not rest until they have been brought to justice.'

He paused, taking in the effect of his words. The majority seemed to be listening but he had spotted a group on the edge of the room, spilling into the street, who would not be mollified. As he was speaking another part of his brain logged where they were and what they were wearing. He was sure they were outsiders.

'I have here the preliminary autopsy report on Mohammed. If you would like me to I will read it out.'

There was a shuffling. An old middle-aged woman in a dull dun-coloured shalwar kameez came forward; over it she wore a polyester cardigan that had lost all shape, like the woman herself. Holding her arm was a Sudanese woman equally discoloured by life in Britain. The young men parted for them.

Mr Qureishi said, 'Mohammed's mother. Sammi's auntie.'

The Pakistani woman was awkward and let go of the other woman reluctantly. Shackleton and Carter stood, gravely polite. The chief constables in their uniforms dwarfed the two sepia women. Carter, without touching Mohammed's mother, guided her to his chair. She sat down reluctantly. Sammi's aunt stood by Grandfather Joseph, her face an unlined version of his own. Shackleton took out the report and unfolded it. The incomers, seeing aggression slipping away, began to jeer.

'It's a load of crap.'

'Don't listen to him.'

'He'll say anything.'

But they were shushed down. Shackleton started to read:

Some bruising to side of head and face consistent with the face and head coming into violent contact with a hard surface. Skull fractured above right ear with rounded indentation. Right cheek-bone fractured. Cause of death: massive brain haemorrhage caused by blows or blow to the head with a blunt instrument, possibly a rounders or baseball bat.

There was a heavy silence.

Shackleton continued in his quietest, most compelling voice.

'I believe Mohammed died needlessly and will do everything in my power to find if any of my officers were responsible for his or Sammi's injuries. I believe Mohammed was hurt during the fight and not by my men. That the bruising mentioned was not serious enough to indicate the gravity of the underlying fractures and so was missed by them. I do not believe – as I know some of you do –'

He paused and looked round the room: every dark eye was on him, unblinking. He turned his head and spoke directly and gently to Mohammed's mother.

'I really do not believe he died after being thrown against a wall or struck by my officers.'

The leader of the youths interrupted.

'Just a minute – rounders bat or baseball bat – why not a baton? Eh? A side-handled baton?'

Shackleton looked at him steadily.

'Because there was a sliver of wood left in the skin. It was painted. Police batons were made of mahogany, which does not splinter, and they were also coated in a rubberised varnish. The side-handled batons which we now use are made of polycarbonate. Not wood. It is impossible for a polycarbonate baton to leave a wood splinter in a wound. However, I will not rest until the exact circumstances of both boys' injuries are established.'

He paused. His reasonable tone almost too quiet so his audience had to lean forward to hear him. Now most were listening.

Carter stood up and began to speak, very gently, with appealing humility. He spoke fluently and persuasively about the dangers of allowing internecine fighting to distract from the real problem of racism. He pleaded with the youths to put aside their enmity and not allow the canker of hatred to contaminate their community.

'There is enough hatred from blacks to whites and whites to blacks, blacks to Asians and whites to Asians for there ever to be any good to be gained from perpetuating prejudice on this one small estate, and worse, to allow religious prejudice to ruin young lives is madness. Many of you have come here because of religious persecution and had to leave many things behind to do so. Surely intolerance should be one of those things.'

The older people nodded, the young made no response.

'This evening you found a common cause against the police. Your hatred has brought you together – is it not possible to use this as a basis for future understanding that might, with patience and dialogue, include the police?'

Carter spoke because he fervently believed in what he said. This was why he had joined the police service. There was none of Shackleton's detatched calculation behind his words. Carter really cared and that made him vulnerable.

Shackleton watched the crowd as Carter spoke. He wasn't listening or thinking: his state of mind was still that animal readiness which admits no abstract thought or distraction. Instinctively he knew the immediate danger of the crowd becoming a murderous mob was over. He was aware that Carter had sat down and the old man was speaking. This was the voice that would swing them one way or the other.

He praised Shackleton and Carter and their efforts to build bridges in the past. Shackleton looked down at his shoes – the old man was admonishing the police and humility seemed the correct attitude. He nodded to each point Mr Qureishi made. He knew they'd won when he saw a few of the young men take off their masks and slip away. There was a feeling of relief in the room.

He stood up, ready to leave after a few words of reconciliation and humble apology; the television camera was pointed directly at him, there was no glimmer of triumphalism in his face. The outsiders by the door seemed irritated by the threat of peace breaking out. One of them, a ringleted individual with sunglasses wrapped over the bandanna obscuring his face, casually took out a cigarette and lit it. Shackleton watched him.

Then, after taking a deep drag, as if in slow motion, he took the lighted cigarette between his thumb and forefinger and flicked it towards Geoffrey Carter, who was leaning over to shake hands with Grandfather Joseph. It described an arc and connected with Carter's petrol-sodden trousers.

Immediately, with an audible sound, like a dog's half-bark, Carter was in flames. As quickly as this happened, in uncanny silence, Shackleton grabbed him in a weird caricature of a hug, trying to cover his burning clothes with pressure from his own body. Both men fell to the ground attempting to put out the flames. After the stunned stillness of the first seconds of the drama people started to shout and throw jackets, shawls and even a rug from the floor on to the two burning men. The television crew filmed it all.

From beneath the comical pile of clothes seeped smoke and a muffled moaning. Gordon pulled the coverings off the two men. Shackleton was wrapped closely, tightly, round Carter in a parody of a sexual embrace. The stink of burned skin and hair rose from them. Gordon thought of roast pork.

'We'll have to call an ambulance in,' he said in his flat Yorkshire voice.

'No.' Shackleton's tone was still quiet. 'I don't think that will be necessary, do you, Geoffrey?'

Carter, in obvious pain, tried to sit up.

'No . . . No.'

Shackleton grasped Carter under one arm, Gordon took the other. They pulled him to his feet.

'I think,' said Shackleton looking round the room, defying them to stop him, 'it's time we left. And it's time you all went home. Quietly. Peacefully.'

There was a silence, so solid with renewed hatred they couldn't move. For the first time Shackleton was unsure, close to fear. He had calculated that their injuries and vulnerability would be their passport out, the natural defusing of the situation. He knew that two burned but brave policemen walking out of a now peaceful estate would be a coup. He knew these things not with calculation and objectivity but in the way an animal knows there's rain coming after heavy heat. But the weather wasn't breaking. The atmosphere seemed heavier.

Sammi's mother, silent and immobile until now, broke the tension.

'Go. Please go.'

Carter murmured, 'Thank you.'

But her biblical face offered no comfort.

'Go and don't come back. We will deal with our young men. You go and deal with yours.'

Dismissed.

The two men, their fine uniforms torn and burned, led the way out of the community centre. Gordon and the television crew followed. They walked back towards the blue-and-white tape.

Bright spotlights were blindingly trained on them. Shackleton knew his snipers would be watching. They saw the lines of riot police, more now than when they arrived. The news teams and fearful senior officers.

Randall, unable to act while the chiefs were inside, was seething with anger at what might have been: two dead police chiefs and an entire estate out of control. Then a nation out of control. Race riots in every town and lynchings of rural newsagents. He couldn't blame these kids for their expressions of unhappiness and frustration but he could and did blame these two arrogant buffoons for the worst few hours of his life. If it was cretins like these who were in charge of policing in the twenty-first century then he'd be gone by the year's end. Better to be a security guard than answerable to such self-obsessed egomaniacs.

Shackleton and Carter walked steadily, calmly, not looking back. Behind them what had so recently been a murderous mob broke up into dribs and drabs of shamefaced young men skulking into the shadows. Feeling foolish, most had taken off their scarves. Their mothers and sisters stood in groups, only their dark eyes showing.

As the chiefs and their group reached the fluttering tape one of the Sudanese women started a strange, high yodelling sound. Like a scream caught in the wind it was taken up by other mothers. The breeze caught their clothes as they stood on the balconies and in the doorways of a sixties urban estate, and the sound they made was the hopelessness of their futures in this cold unwelcoming country.

As Shackleton helped Carter to the tape the sound of eager journalists' voices took over. The warming reassurance of media attention drowned out the lonely ululations of the women. Microphones, cameras, tape recorders, lights, smiles, relief. The curtain call of a great performance.

Shackleton and Carter gave an impromptu press conference. The media hacks were in a frenzy of excitement at the sight and sound of these brave officers who had talked down a riot. The tired smiles of these handsome men would be on every front page in the morning. Their civilised understanding of ethnic minorities' grievances a sign of the police's progress. Of society's progress.

Then Randall and Gordon were trying to force a way through the scrum for a couple of paramedics. Shackleton saw them coming and guided Carter away from them. It wouldn't do for the frontiersmen image to be seen being wrapped in a blanket and loaded into the back of an ambulance.

'Ladies and Gentlemen . . . as far as Mr Carter and I are concerned this episode is closed. We have taken note of the grievances of the people on the Flamborough Estate and will do all we can to put things to rights. Starting tomorrow. But tonight, I think it's time we all went home. Thank you.'

The smile he gave them was his most heart-melting, his most vulnerable and appealing. They were blinded by the flashes of cameras. Beside him the delicate Carter, burned but forgiving. Every reptile and every monkey from every newspaper knew they had the picture story of the year.

Shackleton and Carter sat carefully in the back of the panda car. Gordon, stiff and formal, loaded himself into the front and drove them away, leaving others to clear up the mess. The stars sweeping out of the theatre after a triumphant, if bruising, first night.

The three men were silent during the drive back to the pub. As they got out of the car in the quiet darkness beside the closed building their pain began to make itself heard. Their burns were now raw and blistered black. Shackleton was afraid Carter would pass out. The blue-black serge of his uniform trousers was burned into the flesh of his legs. As the adrenalin dropped away the shock and pain flooded in its place.

Carter vomited holding the bonnet of his car. His driver caught him as he slid, groaning, to the ground. Gordon had ensured the ambulance followed them and Carter was quickly guided into the back of it. Now out of the cameras' range he collapsed, shivering with shock.

Shackleton looked up at him from outside the vehicle.

'All right?'

Carter winced.

'Fine. You coming too?'

'No,' said Shackleton. 'I think I'll go home.'

The paramedic tutted. 'I'm sorry, sir, you need treatment for those burns. You should come with us.'

Shackleton wanted to punch him, to feel his nose smash and see the blood. He wanted to hurt someone and this green-jacketed fool would be the perfect candidate. The surge of violence, the need to hurt. He smiled.

'Thank you. Yes. I'll take your advice and call the doctor when I get to my house. Goodnight. I'll talk to you tomorrow, Geoffrey – I think we did a fair job.'

The paramedic closed the doors, commenting what a sweet-natured man Tom Shackleton seemed. Carter didn't hear him; he had already passed out. His car slid away, following the ambulance.

Gordon sat in the panda car. His tight, athletic body still rigid, his brown animal eyes seeing everything. If he was thinking there was no sign of it.

He had not allowed his weapon to be taken by that bunch of niggers. Gordon was not a bigot or a racist – he had the same contempt and nomenclature for anyone on the wrong side of the law. Criminal women were all toms, convicted homosexuals were all shirt-lifters or nonces, depending on their crime, and anyone from Albania to Zimbabwe stopped on suspicion was a nigger.

But not his colleagues – they were ladies, nellies and darkies, terms of respect from the depth of his ignorance. Not possible yet to police the words used in thought.

The pain and tiredness hit Shackleton with a strong need for a drink. He turned to get into the car when the voice stopped him.

'All right, Thomas? Did you get your fight?'

The three women were watching him. All three now sitting, fanning themselves, their tin-bath fire surrounded by flickering candles. Candles on saucers, candles in jam jars, big ones, coloured ones, huge Easter candles and ranks of tiny birthday candles. The sight was weird and compelling. He didn't want to but he walked towards them.

'Come in! come in!'

The fat woman chuckled and beckoned him into the circle of light. 'Francine . . . get my medicine box. Come here, Thomas, sit, sit!'

*   *   *

Since the story had broken on the mid-evening news Lucy had felt sick. She saw the hand-held shots of Tom walking into the petrol bomb. Of being pushed and beaten by the youths. Of disappearing into a low cheap building surrounded by hatred. Gary had taken a handful of Coproximal which hadn't dulled the pain so he'd followed them with a couple of whiskies and was restlessly asleep.

Lucy was glad she didn't have to hide her agitation. Images of Tom injured made her want him so badly she found herself making sounds, groans, as she washed up the plates from dinner. Imagining him bleeding, helpless, hurt, excited her more than the thought of him whole and dominant. Looking down she didn't see the dark water or floating debris of food but his great eyes looking up at her, trusting, needing.

Lucy yanked the plug out, aware of her silliness but unable to quench it. She stood in the kitchen reliving adolescent feelings. Her life seemed as unfulfilled now as it had at sixteen, her dreams as liberating and her aching need for romance as desperate. Lucy, holding a plate in a wiping-up cloth decorated with spring flowers, slid to the floor crying. Crying and repeating Tom's name over and over. 'Tom . . . oh Tom . . . Oh God, Tom . . . Tom.'

But even in her extremity, her dramatic collapse, she kept her voice down and her sobs controlled. She held her hand to her face and whined, 'Oh God, Tom, I want you.'

Had he walked in at that moment and kissed her, touching her lips with his tongue, she would still have smelt the bleach on her fingers from cleaning the sink. She could never be free of herself. She sat on the floor breathing in the scent of swimming pools from her skin, then quietly got up and washed her hands in scented soap.

Although alone, she was embarrassed. Making a fool of herself. Worse, making a show of herself, as her father would say. Lucy tutted at herself for her excess of emotion. Criticised her lack of control. Having been the child, now she was the parent. After all, she didn't really feel these things for Tom. It was all simply boredom. If she had a hobby, she'd have something to take her mind off him. Golf maybe or line dancing with Weight Watchers. She took a pen out of the ceramic bowl on the kitchen table and wrote his name: 'Tom Shackleton'. Then over it, fitting the letters together, she wrote 'Lucy Campion', her maiden name. Her voices, the voices of her childhood, were in a chorus, telling her not to be so silly, to pull herself together.

She shook her head to dislodge them and opened a drawer to find a box of matches. She put the piece of paper with their names entwined on a saucer, struck a match and held it to the paper.

Making up the spell as she performed it she made a bargain with God: if the paper burned without leaving a trace of their names they would be together. In the same way, she bargained with the Fates when she let her fingers bring her to a climax. She knew if she didn't come with his face in her mind she would never feel him with her again in reality.

Every day she had a series of rituals like not treading on the cracks in the pavement. Little superstitions to try to assure herself Tom Shackleton's coupling with her wasn't just a mistake, and herself not to be more pitied than scorned. She had to believe it would happen again but with, if not love, then affection.

The small black feather of burned paper showed no white, no words. As long as she didn't see a single magpie he'd be all right. As long as the name Tom appeared in the credits of a television programme that night he'd be safe and they'd be together.

She shook her head, put away the childishness of frustration and desire. She was slightly embarrassed, as if she'd been observed sitting on her kitchen floor howling for a man she hardly knew and, like a medieval peasant, making deals with a cold and distant God.

She went into the living room and trawled the television channels for more reports of Tom Shackleton, putting in a blank video despite her good sense telling her not to be so stupid. Why not? Lucy had three videos already of him talking on everything from porn to potato theft in inner-city allotments.

Janet had telephoned Jenni at home when the Chief arrived at the Flamborough Estate. She knew he wouldn't have thought of phoning his wife.

When the phone rang Jenni was in the bath soaking away the physical memory of her lunch with the Gnome of Chipping Campden. She had added lavender oil and a drop of rosemary, the first for relaxation, the latter as disinfectant. Aromatherapy and spiritual douche.

Not that he had had the opportunity to do much more than talk himself into an erection. He had managed to get his fingers as far as the tightly resistant lace of her knickers between main course and coffee but nothing else. Had Jenni not been so used to the change that came over some men when faced with the prospect of sex with a stranger, the schizophrenic Gnome might have intrigued her. But she knew, before her age was in double figures, a standing cock knows no conscience.

She lay in her gently rounded bath in her sunken bathroom conjuring the future. Her husband would be in the Lords. A working peer. They would receive invitations to Chequers and Sandringham as valued friends and advisers, not as part of a duty rota.

The time would come when she and Tom could be kind. The more successful they were, the more they could afford to give. But Jenni never spent capital.

Her mind, wary of complacency, moved on to a newspaper's recent compilation of a list of the country's most powerful people. Her husband had not appeared in the top three hundred. Geoffrey Carter had. He was close to the government. And his wife, Eleri, somehow related to Lloyd George, provided an echo of elevation.

Her thoughts chased round the rat run of frustration and fulfilment, reaching no conclusion.

The phone rang. She let it ring three times. She always did. It might bring luck and she never wished to appear eager. She picked it up and gave her reserved, cautious 'Hello', the one that begged the listener to be gentle with her.

'Oh . . . hello, Mrs Shackleton, I'm sorry to bother you.'

Jenni knew Janet was a good secretary, personal assistant, to her husband. A good, plain soul, no threat, who lived only for her elderly mother and mobile home in Rhyl, but she irritated Jenni. Most women irritated her but for some reason Janet's sing-song apologetic voice set her polished white fillings rattling.

'Janet, yes, what is it? Tom been misbehaving again?'

She always had a little joke with the staff – she knew they appreciated it.

'Mr Shackleton's gone to a possible . . . um . . . well . . .'

Oh for God's sake, you silly bitch, spit it out.

'Well, I suppose it's a riot situation. I think it'll be on the news.'

'I'm sure if my husband's involved, it will be.' Jenni's voice was all smiles and conspiracy. 'Thank you, Janet. How's your mother?'

'Well, you know, Alzheimer's,' said Janet.

She said it lightly, as always alive to the needs of others not wanting to hear the miserable truth. But to Jenni's ear she had the remarkable ability of a bad amateur actor to place the emphasis just in the wrong place so any lightness or wit was flattened under the weight of misplaced stress.

Jenni was automatically gracious and laughed anyway.

'Oh, I do Janet, I do. You're so brave.'

'No, Mrs Shackleton. I'm not. But thank you anyway. Goodnight.'

'Goodnight, Janet.'

She put the phone down. It rang again immediately.

Her daughter's voice was high, excited. 'Mem . . . Have you seen Dad on the news? They're throwing Molotov cocktails at him. God . . . I hate the police. Why on earth couldn't he be an accountant or something?'

Jenni rose from the bath like some New Millennium Aphrodite, cordless phone in one hand, television remote in the other.

'Because he wanted to be a policeman, so he could change things – you know that.'

Or be inside pissing out rather that outside pissing in, as Jason had once unwisely put it. She still remembered the sting in her palm after she slapped him and the white then scarlet imprint of her hand on his cheek.

'Oh God. I'm coming over, you can't be on your own.'

And Tamsin rang off. Her hysterical daughter was coming round to look after her. Jenni found her highly charged reactions to everything tiring but, as with all her children, she didn't judge her. No doubt Tamsin would bring her small son with her and round up her sister too to give Mem support. Thank goodness Chloe, her most neurotic offspring, was 'finding herself' in India.

Jenni found the news on the television. The story hadn't made it on to the national bulletins yet, just the local round-up with a chip-pan fire and a couple who'd been married for seventy-five years without a cross word. Then she saw the two chief constables attacked and dragged into a dingy sixties prefab and she knew it was now real news.

She knew this was going to be a chance for her husband to prove himself. The whole country would see this. If it went wrong he would be finished. She picked up a bottle of red nail varnish. She would force herself to apply it, perfectly.

In front of her hysterical daughter, her concerned daughter and her pride-ridden son she would be the cool centre ready to react to anything.

Jenni looked at herself in the full-length mirror. Naked. She turned, running her fingers down her buttocks and thighs. No cellulite there. Stomach barely rounded despite the pregnancies. The ghost of a stretch mark by her hip bone assiduously massaged with starflower oil morning and night.

Whatever the pressure she always had time to appraise her body; it was as calming as meditation to her. She smoothed the slight shadows of muscles under the fine skin. She frowned mildly when she saw her elbows and knees were ageing a little faster than the rest of her. And was that the ghost of a wrinkle at her cleavage? She shook her head sharply, putting on casually expensive trousers and a loose shirt. Hair up in a Grecian tumble. A touch of moisture to the lips and she was ready.

As she reached the living room the phone rang again. It was the Gnome.

'Isn't your husband brave? And so handsome.'

'Is he? I don't notice any more. I rather like Geoffrey Carter . . .' Jenni let his name hang with a little tease in her voice.

'Oh . . . you want him, do you? Does he make you wet?'

She had thrown out her bait to see if Carter found more favour than Tom and had reeled in slime.

'No he doesn't.' Was her tone too harsh?

'It . . . takes more than a Disney cartoon to excite me. You know that.' She had let her voice drop to be as quietly intimate as his.

'I hoped you'd say that.'

She could hear his satisfaction.

'I'll be interested to see how your Tom handles this. I know the Prime Minister's interested too, I made sure of it. After all, the Met will need a new commissioner soon and we're always looking for someone who can play a good race card.'

Jenni breathed out, a shadow of Marilyn Monroe.

'Oh, thank you. I'll be so grateful . . .'

'I know you will, Jenni. I can feel your gratitude already. What have you got on?'

His voice had changed. This wasn't polite flirtation any more.

'Nothing,' she lied. 'I was in the bath. Thank God this isn't a video phone.' She laughed, trying to get back to safe coquetry.

He had no interest now in politesse.

'I want to see you naked. I want to piss down your back . . .'

The front door opened and Tamsin's small son launched himself at her shouting, 'Granny, Granny, carry.'

She was unsure she'd heard him right but there wasn't time to ask and it occurred to her it would be ludicrous to say, 'I'm sorry, did you say you wanted to piss down my back?' So she said, 'Well, that'll be something to look forward to. Cheerio,' and put down the phone.

Her two-year-old grandson, Kit, launched himself at her. Tamsin caught him before he caused any damage. Jenni was always surprised by the amount of destruction a child was capable of and had never encouraged them to regard her as a climbing frame.

Jenni put the television on and they discussed, as nearly as possible given their temperaments and the presence of a hyperactive two-year-old, the situation until the late-night extended news programme started. It led on the siege and kidnapping as they were now calling it. Tamsin began to cry, over-dramatising as was her habit.

Jenni was abrupt with her.

'Be quiet, you'll upset Kit. Come and sit by Granny, darling.'

The small boy, relieved not to have the responsibility of his unpredictable mother, sat quietly next to Granny who he'd learned could be equally volatile. Having created it, Tamsin was unable to bear the drama and went off into the kitchen to make hot drinks.

Jenni could feel the snake of her own emotions coiling as she watched the television. Her thoughts were constructed in blocks of words. At other times daggers of words tore through the blocks. If Tom messed this up he was finished. Dead in the water. The words repeated themselves, like a faulty CD unable to move on.

She unscrewed the top of the nail varnish and slowly drew out the encarmined brush. The laser moved on, releasing another set of thought words. Her husband was basically a kind man, a good man, but undeveloped, a blank canvas. Ambitious but not focused. His general success was due to his single-minded application to the job; his specific success was due to Jenni's vision, her ability to see into the future.

But she wasn't sure he would know how much depended on the outcome of this night. The words constructed and deconstructed themselves as she painted a perfect line of red down the centre of the pale nail of her index finger.

Kit, seeing his grandfather on the television, jumped up and down on the cushions of the settee, screeching and laughing with the humourless overexcitement of a child. The bottle of nail varnish, as if caught in a cross wind, toppled and spilled on to Jenni's cream linen trousers.

A flaming wall of fury engulfed Jenni. She caught hold of the little boy by the shoulder. He was frozen with terror as she leaned over him. Unable to cry or even breathe, he stared up into Jenni's face. She didn't look like his granny any more – he tried to squirm away, to call his mother, but she held him tighter.

Jenni had slipped out of reality. The child on the settee was detached from her, an object held at the end of an arm in a hand that wasn't hers. She moved her hand up to his throat and held him quite lightly, her long nails barely touching his white unfinished skin. The distress the child was feeling was interesting. Would inflicting more pain on him make it more interesting? Could she go against nature? Jenni had never come so close to the thin barrier between her civilisation and the closed-off, stagnant pools of her barbarity.

She felt a power, a detached desire to see suffering, death. Her hand itched to know how it would feel to stop the life held in it. Giving life had taken control away from Jenni. She had felt herself powerless during pregnancy and birth. Used. At the mercy of a greater force as this petrified child was now.

She knew if she could squeeze the life out of him, if she could cause him more pain, there would be nothing in the future that she would stop at. To know she could torture and kill without pleasure or revulsion would release her from the restrictions of moral teaching. The future would be free of guilt or conscience.

She knew she could do it. A wave of liberation washed over her. She didn't have to go any further; it was her choice not to go on. The voice of society, the threat of retribution, didn't stop her – she stopped herself because she knew she could just as easily go on.

The phone rang. She laughed and kissed Kit, then, releasing him with a caress on his cheek, picked up the handset. The child was too frightened to call out or cry, he just cowered in the cushions unable to take his eyes off his grandmother. She smiled at him and ran the painted red nail gently down his nose. He really was a lovely-looking boy. She could see Tom's sweet vulnerability in those great eyes. That look that at once attracted and infuriated her.

'Hello.'

'Jenni? It's Eleri. What on earth have our husbands got themselves into now?'

Jenni could hear the noise of the television and children in the background. She could see in her mind the domestic chaos of the house and Eleri voluptuous and unmade up, dressed in one of her husband's shirts and a pair of multi-pocketed trousers. No shoes.

'Saving the world, no doubt.'

'Look, Jenni, Geoffrey called me before they went – he had a feeling it might not go too smoothly. Anyway, we thought if you were on your own you might like to come over. You're very welcome. It's just me and the boys.'

Oddly, Jenni's hackles didn't rise at this cosy and utterly inappropriate suggestion. There was something so warm about Eleri and her fondness for Jenni and Tom was so transparently genuine that Jenni, despite her initial suspicion, liked her. She liked Eleri as she would have a scatty but aristocratic red setter.

'Oh Eleri, that's such a sweet thought but I've the family here. And I really ought to be home for Tom when it finishes.'

Eleri quite understood and the two women said their goodbyes without articulating their real feelings about what was happening. Jenni put down the phone, Eleri already forgotten. The little boy was still rigid on the sofa, staring at his grandmother. Jenni smiled at him, although he had provoked her . . . She felt a sudden surge of affection for him. He was, after all, the next generation of the Shackletons. A dynasty she had created.

'Tamsin,' she called. 'Bring Kit some biscuits – I'm going to change my trousers.'

On the television an aggressive young woman was debating with an aggressive young man what the youths would do with the two chief constables.

The three women had taken off Tom's jacket and rolled up the sleeves of his shirt. He was put on a fourth chair. This one two pieces of carved wood that slotted into each other to form a low, high-backed chair. He was nervous it wouldn't take his weight but it was surprisingly comfortable. It forced him to sit back. Relax. The sky was clear and the stars brighter than usual in England. The night was hot. Dry. Good rioting weather. His burned skin was painful now, an insistent pain that pulsed with his heartbeat.

The thin woman had gone into the flat and returned with a plastic bucket and a bulging carrier bag emblazoned with *HARRODS – THE SALE*. She put the bucket down in front of the fat woman and sat in her sagging deckchair. They were now a circle with the bucket in the centre.

The African woman, unsmiling and unblinking, reached into the carrier bag. She pulled out a bottle of oil. It had no label and when she unscrewed the top and poured a thin gold stream into the bucket it smelled of smooth Mediterranean geranium leaves. A sharp sweet smell. The desiccated woman took out a bunch of herbs and tore them roughly before dropping them into the bucket.

Tom watched, recognised the leaves as khat, a drug favoured by West Africans. Illegal. He wanted to say something but, as if from a distance, he saw himself unable to speak. With a sort of removed disapproval he watched the big woman stir the leaves into the oil with his swagger stick. Where did she get it? Where was Gordon? He should be going home – Jenni would be in one of her moods.

As the great brown hand stirred, the other two women added more things from the carrier bag. A bottle of spring water, powders and the foul-smelling contents of three small plastic syringes.

Tom knew he should get up and walk away but couldn't. He'd once been hypnotised at a club. He was a young PC and desperate to fit in; he'd volunteered. Unwilling to say it hadn't worked he went along with the mumbo jumbo and cooperated with the tatty hypnotist. Then he'd decided enough was enough and tried to leave the stage. He found he couldn't. Sitting with these three women round a plastic bucket on the edge of a restless inner-city estate, he felt the same helplessness.

The women were singing softly over the brew, which was giving off a strange attractive repellent smell. With an effort he got his brain to identify it. Tom tried to discipline his mind into creating concrete thoughts. It was the sharp clinging odour he'd smelled between women's legs. At once comforting and repulsive, it was so strong he could taste it.

The African woman moved behind him and leaned over his

shoulder to take his wrists in her long elegant fingers. He felt the skin of her cheek against his own. He was surprised at the softness of it. He couldn't stop himself – he reached up, her hand still on his arm, and touched her face. He couldn't see what he touched but it felt like the scales of dead fish. Cold and smooth one way, cutting the other. He pulled back, shocked. The women laughed.

'Here,' said the big one, shifting her great bulk so he could see the ravine between her breasts. The top buttons of her dress had given up the struggle and the thin cotton gaped open. She scooped up a handful of the sludge from the bucket. The black hands on his wrists gripped him and held out his burned hands. He felt fear but the fear was someone else's. He watched the women apply the ointment to his skin. The relief was immediate, cool, like being wrapped in cotton sheets on a hot night.

'Now, Thomas . . .'

The big woman was smiling at him, holding his hands in hers. Hers were bigger.

'Drink this.'

The thin one dipped a royal-wedding mug into the bucket then diluted the contents with British sherry from a bottle by her chair. He didn't resist. He drank.

'I want you to listen to us, Thomas.'

The three women were now sitting, watching him. The big one continued, still smiling, still vast with welcoming flesh.

'You've got a big future, Thomas. You are going to get what you want.'

'What you deserve,' added the thin one. Her voice was dry and brittle, a voice heard in bus queues.

The African woman spoke, her accent so strong he almost didn't understand what she said.

'That is not the same thing. We are telling him about his dreams. Not his nightmares.'

'Don't confuse him.'

The great warm brown face in front of him was kind, affectionate. She didn't want him upset. He could feel her affection for him. Her maternal care. The care he'd always longed for but learned couldn't be trusted. He wanted to ask questions. He wanted a drink of water. He wanted milk and a dash – no, cup of tea. Milk and a dash was what he'd drunk as a child in rare moments of comfort at his mother's hands. Cup of tea was better. He wanted to leave. He couldn't.

'Thomas, what is it you want?'

Shackleton found it difficult to formulate the words. As if in slow motion he said, 'Commissioner. Metropolitan Police . . .'

He couldn't read the women's expressions. Their faces were closed as if they hadn't heard him.

'I want . . . to be . . . the Commissioner.'

They nodded.

'But . . . Carter's favourite. Geoffrey Carter . . .'

He didn't feel drunk, just distant, as if watching himself down the wrong end of a telescope. He knew it must be a dream because he never told anyone his wants, his needs. No one. Jenni told him what he wanted.

The blue-black face and blank eyes of the African woman came close to his.

'Carter's story is not your story. You want what you want, he'll get what he gets.'

The other two faces crowded in on him.

'So you be careful, Thomas, careful you stay in your story – don't you go stray into someone else's or you'll go mash up the future. You mash up the future and that will bring badness. Death in your soul. You hear me, Thomas? You hear me? The Wages Of Sin Is Death.'

Their voices were as distant as a nurse's calling from the other side of an anaesthetic but they were conjuring pictures of his future. They had made him articulate his desire and in escaping into the air his words had made that desire concrete. His ambition now roosted in the dark trees like maggotpies, choughs and rooks.

Gordon rang the doorbell. Lucy watched from the darkness of her living room. She couldn't see Shackleton in the car. She had seen the end of the siege on television. Watched Tom help his badly burned colleague through the blue-and-white tape. Listened to him talk, relieved and quietly courageous, now his car was home. But no Tom.

The front door opened and Jenni stood talking to Gordon for a moment, then the two of them went to the car, followed by Jason, Tamsin and Jacinta. Lucy watched dully as they pulled Shackleton, inert, from the back seat. They looked so close she felt excluded, irrelevant. They carried him into the house. The security light went off. Lucy felt as though she was straining to see through black glass.

Inside the house an argument had started about what to do with Tom. Jenni was convinced he was drunk and was disgusted. Gordon tried to reassure her he was ill and exhausted. Jason seeing his burns insisted on calling a doctor.

'God . . . he stinks. Where has he been?'

Gordon didn't reply. Whatever he said to Mrs Shackleton would be wrong, it always was.

'Gordon, you weasel, why does the Chief smell like that?'

Gordon gave his impression of a deaf mute with learning difficulties.

'All right, take him upstairs, to the guest bedroom. That stink will get into everything. Is it that stuff on his hands? Jacinta, get some water and wash your father's hands. Who put it there? Was it a doctor? Oh God, I don't know why I bother.'

Gordon watched her run up the stairs and followed, almost carrying Tom. With the Chief's head on his shoulder he tried to separate the poison from the saccharine in Mrs Shackleton's words. As usual he couldn't. As usual he kept his mouth shut.

Jenni immediately opened the windows of the slightly musty room. Gordon started to undress Shackleton, thinking he was to be put to bed.

'Leave him alone.' Jenni realised she was too sharp. Too out of character.

'I'm sorry, Gordon. I'll do that. You go home. Off you go. It's obviously been a long day and a hard one, eh?'

Gordon nodded and smiled, glad to be released. All he wanted was to be rid of the gun and on the outside of a modest drink. The only thing that had really frightened him all night was the Chief's wife.

Jason passed Gordon on the stairs and tried to be polite but Gordon was gone before he could make up for his mother's lack of manners.

Jenni was sitting watching Tom from a distance when Jason went into the bedroom. He was lying spread-eagled on the bed, his shirt half undone by Gordon. He was sweating and mumbling.

'Drunk,' said Jenni.

'No, I don't think so, Mem. Really. Look at him, he's ill. Really. Look.'

But Jenni just sat hugging herself, wanting but unwilling to touch him. The smell she could smell on him she'd come across before. It was the smell of the Gnome's breath. The smell of women.

Jason knew better than to go on. He undressed his father and pulled the duvet over him. Gently he laid the burned hands on the top; there were blisters too on the side of his face and ear. The girls fussed in carrying water and an odd selection from Jenni's first-aid box. Jason saw athlete's-foot powder and surgical spirit.

'I've called the doctor. There are hundreds of messages on the machine and the fax is having a nervous breakdown,' said Jacinta, a sensible girl of nineteen, who had an unfortunately large bottom and thick ankles and was studying to be a stage manager at a drama college Jenni could boast about.

She thumped down on the bed next to her father. Capable and unflappable, she started to wash his hands in the bowl of cold water held by Tamsin but she soon saw the only way the ointment would come off was with the flesh beneath. The water was quickly red with blood. She stopped. She felt sick.

Jason saw what was going on.

'Leave it, Jacinta. Wait for the doctor.'

The children felt awkward. Their mother was, not unusually, wrapped in an internal conflict of emotions and unreachable. Tamsin, having put Kit to bed, was free to cry and carry on like a Greek widow. Jacinta and Jason simply sat either side of their father trying to calm him and cool him.

These two had no difficulty loving Tom Shackleton. There was no complication, no qualification. The room was quiet but for the muffled sobs from Tamsin, each person in their own thoughts.

Jenni knew the messages and faxes would be radio, television and newspapers wanting interviews with her husband. She had deliberately not answered the phone since speaking to Eleri. She would sift them through the night. Come the morning he'd be a hero or a joke.

Jenni thought back over her brief conversation with Gordon. Hadn't he said Carter was taken to hospital? In a bad way. Good. He wouldn't be out tomorrow, Tom would do all the interviews, Tom would have the spotlight. Bandaged and frail, he'd be perfect. Jenni knew she would have to phone the Gnome in the morning to make sure the right people were aware of him and to get the Party machine working for her. Them.

The doctor arrived and she was free to check the messages. They were gratifyingly numerous and heavyweight. The last was a television producer saying the crew that had gone into the siege with him had got some incredible footage. Amazing. They were going to stay up all night editing it.

Jenni sat back, pleased but not complacent. It would be good if he was well enough to speak briefly by phone to the early morning radio news. Serious radio only and no breakfast television except news. No sitting on garish sofas looking silly. Then possibly an appearance on the lunchtime bulletins.

She had a thought that bandages would look good; perhaps she ought to go back upstairs and make sure the doctor was applying them. But she was pleased the whole thing was on video; as long as her husband had been his usual charming persuasive self, it would speak volumes for him. He would be, she knew, irresistible. But to tell him she was proud would be weakness. Her approval must stay always out of reach.

More than a day's worth of soundbites and interviews. She stood up, tidied the faxes, checked her appearance automatically in the mirror, and went back upstairs.

The doctor was still examining the inert body in the bed.

'He seems fine. Just in a deep sleep. As if he'd been drugged.'

'Not drunk then?' Jenni said it as if her husband were a teetotaller. 'Oh doctor, I was only joking.'

'Er . . . Mrs Shackleton, did you put this stuff on his hands?'

The doctor was obviously disapproving of whatever it was but too young to say it: just a locum, not his place.

'No, doctor, I didn't. They were like that when he came home.'

The man was relieved, but slightly worried.

'It's just . . . well, I don't know what it is and I can't seem to get it off without causing more damage, so I'm going to bandage up his hands for now and keep an eye on them for infection. I'll give him an injection too. He's not allergic to antibiotics, is he?'

Jenni couldn't see the point of the fuss over a couple of minor burns.

'No, no, of course not. Doctor, look, will my husband be all right in the morning, only . . .' She finished off with her prettiest smile. 'There is rather a lot of media interest.'

'Oh yes, he should be fine once he wakes up. Whatever it is he's taken seems to have knocked him out pretty well. But that's good – he'd be in quite a lot of pain if he were awake.'

The doctor left leaving a selection of painkillers and a prescription. He was seen out by Jacinta. Tamsin had expended too much emotion on the whole event and had retired to bed, exhausted by her devotion to her father. She had cried real tears and worked herself up to a high pitch of emotion. To her, it wasn't a performance.

Jacinta waited until all was quiet then discreetly went home to the small flat in Earls Court she shared with another student. Her sister was asleep and her mother prowling the house planning her assault on the morning. Jason sat beside his father, not really thinking, just being with him and too tired to go to sleep.

Jacinta looked across the bed at him before she left. They smiled at each other, two whole people in a family of parts. She wanted to but didn't kiss her father. He was shy of intimacy when awake; it would seem an intrusion when he was asleep.

Carter's driver had phoned Eleri immediately after the ambulance left. She sounded calm but he knew she wasn't. As always she asked after him, was concerned no one had been hurt and seemed in no hurry to get him off the line. He wanted to pick her up and take her to the hospital but she was adamant his day had been long enough and that he should go home. She'd make her own way.

The elderly widow next door was only too glad to be of use as a babysitter and Eleri drove herself to the hospital.

Carter had been sedated and his burns dressed. Eleri stood over him stroking his hair and crying quietly. She didn't just love him, she worshipped him.

'He's a very brave man, your husband.'

The nurse was taking his blood pressure and vital signs as he would throughout the night.

'Some might say foolish,' Eleri replied. 'I don't know whether to hug him or slap him.'

The nurse, grey with tiredness and reeking of coffee and cigarettes, looked at Eleri from under outrageous eyelashes, suddenly a drag queen.

'Well, daughter, I know which I'd do.'

PART TWO

A fit of dry-mouthed coughing woke Gary early. Too early. The day would be longer than usual. He turned his head on the built-up pillows to see where his drink was. Behind the pills on top of the Scrabble box. Good. He could reach it, he wouldn't have to wake Lucy. He looked at it for a while. It was to his left. If he used his left arm he could reach it easily but would he be able to turn his hand at the right angle to grasp it?

The cup was slightly behind him so it would mean getting hold of it in a back-hand grip. No. He was sure that would be too risky; the water might end up on the floor, giving Lucy two jobs. But if he reached out and found the cup with the back of his hand then tried to raise his hand above and then behind the cup, like those miniature cranes in fairground arcades, he was sure the bedhead would prevent his arm completing the manoeuvre. Also the cup had a lid fitted out of which stuck a red-and-white bendy straw – they had run out of blue-and-white, his team's colours, on Monday. So the height of the straw would make such a move impossible.

Start again.

He looked at the cup. His mouth was tacky, dry, and there was a crust of mucus and probably blood on his front teeth. His gums were always bleeding – brushing and flossing had become too difficult to do properly. He ran his tongue over them. He was now obsessed with the water, the cup, the straw.

'Oh, it's just a symptom of the illness,' said the specialist.

Just a symptom. Obsession. Included in the catalogue with loss of sight and bodily functions.

If he used his right arm he would have to reach much further. The width of his body more but it would mean he could grasp the cup face on, so to speak.

He put his left hand on the edge of the bed. He could feel the rubber sheet, slippery under the cotton one. He gathered his strength for a couple of minutes. This would be a one-chance mission. To grab the side of the mattress with his left hand and pull himself on to his side while throwing his right arm across with precision-aim to get his fingers wrapped round the cup.

Then he'd pause and worry about how to get it back. The whispering in his head started: What if he missed? What if he fell out of bed? What if? What if? He grabbed and pulled. His right hand landed on the bedside table only a couple of inches from the cup.

Good. Gary lay panting for a few seconds then, like a seal coming up the beach, flopped his hand on to the cup. It moved. Just a bit. Like a girl playing hard to get. Gently. Gently. He willed his sluggish fingers to stroke it, tickle it back into his palm. He grunted through a rictus of effort as he made contact with the handle.

Now what? He was stuck. His left arm was caught under his body and he hadn't the strength to get on to his back and control the position of the cup. He lay there for another few minutes. By now he was sweating. He thought of *Lawrence of Arabia* and the scene when they ride out of the Anvil of the Sun. The thirst. And those little goatskin bottles of water. Even Peter O'Toole couldn't get out of this one, he thought.

'Bollocks, I wish I had a camel.'

He said it out loud and found his voice quieter than his thoughts. He started to giggle. Just another symptom. Laughing helplessly at finding oneself unable to perform simple tasks. Come on, man, think.

Right.

If I grab my pyjama arm in my teeth then heave my right arm back while at the same time moving my head, which is, after all, one third of my body weight, firmly and decisively to the right, I should, with a following wind and the intervention of several saints, arrive on my back with the water, unspilt, in my hand. Well, go on then, don't just lie there. Five, four, three, two, one . . .

Gary bit his pyjama arm and heaved. The plan was good. So effective was it the only thing stopping him falling out the other side of the bed was the wall. As his right arm described an arc across his body he found himself unable to control it and watched the lid of the cup with its barber-pole straw lift off and land in his slipper. The water beneath didn't want to go so far and slapped on to his chest in a reverse belly flop.

'Oh . . . fuck . . . fuck, shit, balls, bollocks.' Gary lay in the cold wetness. 'Oh Christ . . . I've got fucking Tourette's syndrome now.'

It was seven o'clock. He had been trying to get the water for forty-seven minutes. Now he had it.

The television at the foot of his bed snapped on. It should have been the radio alarm but Lucy had messed up the setting and they hadn't been bothered to change it. It took him a moment to recognise what was happening. He had not seen the drama unfold the night before and this was shaky, hand-held footage of the inside of a community centre, but he had heard the name Shackleton.

'. . . where two chief constables were last night held hostage. We will be speaking to one of them later in the programme. The other is being held in hospital with severe burns. Now over to Dodie with the weather.'

Gary was surprised at the strength of his hope that it would be Tom Shackleton with the severe burns. But then, no. No, Lucy mooning over an injured Shackleton would be worse. Her maternal instincts always went on the rampage with wounded puppies.

Gary had never plumbed the depths of Shackleton's shallowness and assumed Lucy's passion for him was because of his good looks and air of reserve. Gary thought he'd be bloody reserved if he was married to a piece of work like Jenni. He smiled. Poor Lucy, she went to such lengths to hide her passion for the man.

If only she could have chosen someone else. Someone with a mind relieved by the occasional flash of poetry. Someone with a soul. Gary wasn't sure if Shackleton had sold it or if he'd just never had one in the first place. Was it jealousy? Gary lay in his wet pyjamas, unable to move, tasting the rottenness of his body in the scum that coated his tongue and thought: Yes. Jealous as fuck.

That bastard has everything I wanted. Including my wife. He turned his head sharply, trying to shift the picture of them making love. He couldn't have loved Lucy more, but wondered why Tom Shackleton would want to have her. Because he could. Same reason as a dog licks its balls.

The mind that had so enjoyed grappling with Proust now wrestled with images of sex between his wife and his neighbour. He was disgusted with himself. With living. Lucy didn't know but he'd managed to save up enough painkillers and anti-depressants to kill himself.

Six weeks before, while Lucy was out polishing Jenni's ego, he'd taken the lot. It took the best part of half an hour. Then he'd sat waiting for death. What he got was diarrhoea. Vast crop-spraying quantities of it. Because of the diarrhoea his body didn't absorb the drugs and instead of a romantically dead body, posed like Marat in his bath over the edge of his wheelchair, she came home to a carpet pebble-dashed in shades of brown and an odour it would take months to shift.

Gary had laughed until he was almost sick. Giving up was not an option. He had a vision of his God, like a cigar-chewing boxing coach, shoving him back into the ring unable to stand with eyes bruised shut to go another round with an undefeated world champion. He smiled. Everyone loved a loser.

And there was one good thing about Lucy's infatuation: she was starting to take a pride in her appearance again. If Tom Shackleton restored her then Gary could and would forgive them both. No, he'd forgive them anyway. That would be his new life challenge. Take his mind off the paralysing boredom of disability. Paralysing. Disability. Ha ha. He enjoyed chasing the thought round that it was the dull repetitive boredom of disability that paralysed, not the illness itself. He toyed with a letter to the *Lancet*, the *BMJ*, *New Scientist* . . .

On the television they were trailing the live phone link with hero policeman Tom Shackleton. Gary could hear Lucy moving around upstairs. His mind started running down those paths that led to the debate of whether she was better off with him or without him.

'Good morning.'

The door opened and his thoughts scattered like birdseed.

'Oh Lucy, I've had an accident. I'm sorry. It's only water – the catheter hasn't leaked. It's just water.'

He repeated the words quickly. He had caught sight of the expression on her face when she saw Shackleton on the television.

'It's video taken last night while he was hostage. Good stuff, I think.'

She wasn't listening. He watched her as she tried to hide the softness in her eyes, the softness that had been his after making love when she'd ask, 'You hungry? Cup of tea?'

74

Not for him, not really, but because she was always ravenous after. Now she was ravenous before. He hoped it was still before. Maybe that's why Shackleton wanted her – if he did – because women didn't look at men like that any more, with that mixture of gentleness and encouragement seen in the faces of Madonnas on Christmas cards. What she gave Gary now was that look mixed with pity. The Madonna after the Crucifixion. When it was all over.

She was undoing his pyjama top now, trying not to look at the screen. But she couldn't stop herself when she heard his voice. Live from his home.

'Recuperating from his injuries . . . bravery . . . modesty . . . an example to his colleagues.'

Lucy sat Gary up to peel off the jacket. She wanted to turn a handle and flush out the thoughts of Tom while she dealt with Gary's poor wasted body. But she couldn't. She was afraid her thoughts of Tom would be so loud Gary might hear them through the thin bone of her skull if she leaned too close to him.

'No . . . Lucy. Leave that. Don't you want to see what Tom's got to say? Sit down a minute.'

Lucy couldn't believe Gary had no idea of her feelings for Tom; thank God he didn't. She felt as if she was wearing a neon sign saying: *I AM OBSESSED WITH TOM SHACKLETON.* But Gary hadn't guessed. And with luck, he never would.

She perched on the side of the bed, composing her face to indifference. Perhaps he'd still be in the house when she went over to do her chores. What did she have clean in the wardrobe? No, the skirt was too formal – anyway she didn't have any shiny tights left, only those nasty dull American Tan jobs from the supermarket.

She settled on jeans. They had an elasticated waist but he needn't see that, she'd wear a short shirt outside. Good. Decision made. Her bottom was still pert for a size fourteen and as she spent most of her working time either bending over or on her hands and knees she thought she might as well show off her assets.

'He's good, isn't he? Very plausible.'

'Oh Gary . . .' She was hurt by his coolness. 'He's not plausible, he's really sincere. He does care about race issues. He cares about people, Gary.'

*   *   *

75

'Very plausible. Not glib at all. Really quite believable.'

Jenni's Gnome sat with the Prime Minister and his *éminences grises*. The five men watched the television screen. The Flamborough Estate story had been running all day. It was a slack news season so every programme was full of it, the fact, the comment, the hopes for the future. Tom Shackleton had gone overnight from being one of forty-three chief constables to being the acceptable face of policing. The One Who Understands. Compassion in National Policing. The People's Policeman. The headlines were writing themselves.

'But is he biddable?'

The Prime Minister looked at his advisers. Shackleton's future was to be decided in this room by these three men, the grey men behind the PM. The Gnome thought of the rhyme from Richard III's time: 'The Cat, the Rat and Lovell the dog, Rule all England under the Hog.'

He smiled.

'I think he is. He wants success more than he wants to be champion of the underclass.'

'He's good, he's very good,' said the Rat, a man whose physical characteristics were almost as appealing as the Gnome's. 'Does he mean all this about the issues? How much does he care?'

The Gnome waited a second before he replied.

'Well, David. Let me put it this way, he's on message with all the right principles but put a family of asylum seekers in his loft conversion and he might think twice.'

'I think we all might,' said the Dog grimly. 'But if we let any more of the buggers in, he might have to.'

'Now, Alan,' said the PM mildly. 'Be careful, we haven't been swept for bugs. Anyway' – the change of tone was abrupt – 'you don't mean that, do you?'

The Dog looked at him. The PM's strange doll's eyes were cold, alert. The Prime Minister's appetite for cynicism was very small.

'Of course not. No.'

The Cat looked across at the Dog.

'Alan, when we make jokes it's often a sign of something we really believe.' He paused, he had their attention. 'I've known Tom Shackleton for quite a while now and it's true what David says, he's not a hands-on type. He doesn't want to get grubby unless there's a camera crew there. Emotional involvement is not his style. It's a job, and if that involves kissing babies or kissing backsides, he'll do it. He's not burdened with deep beliefs or a sophisticated moral code. He's a pond skater, elegant, fast on his feet and unlikely to cause ripples. Most important he's a star turn. Look at him . . .'

He rewound the tape and played it again: Shackleton smiling, nodding, shyly proud, quietly modest.

'The public's going crazy for him. He's got the Kennedy touch. Let's face it, he is what London needs.'

'Yes.' The Rat nodded. 'The Caretaker Commissioner's done a good job –'

'Wasn't his nickname George?' interrupted the Dog.

The Rat nodded briefly, anxious to get on.

The PM raised his eyebrows.

The Dog took it as a question.

'After the play, Prime Minister. *The Madness of George III.*'

'And is he?'

'As a box of frogs, Prime Minister. And very hands-on with his female staff, I'm told.'

The Rat made a movement that, had he been the real thing, would have been a ruffling of his fur, and continued.

'Remember the chaos when he took over? He's done well – but now we need someone with charisma. Media-friendly.'

The Gnome had waited his moment.

'Shackleton's your man. He talks all the right fights, Race, Drugs, Crime –'

The Dog bounded in again.

'And let's face it, the British public will forgive anything if they think you need them. Our heroes are all damaged goods. No one's going to erect a statue to Michael Schumacher or Nigel Mansell – no, it'll be George Best and Princess Di. Now, I'm not saying Shackleton's a loser but he's got that vulnerable look the housewives like. And the men can understand him. Good choice.'

The Prime Minister winced. He trusted the Dog's judgement implicitly but he wished his opinions were formed by something more profound than pragmatism.

'Give him the Met then?'

He looked at the Cat.

'Well, the hoops will have to be seen to be gone through but yes, I don't see why not.' The Cat paused. 'He wants a knighthood, you say?'

The Gnome nodded.

'He'd prefer a peerage. Lower-middle background, can't shake it off.'

'Right. Good. That's settled. Let him have the Met –'

'Yes . . . he gets the K automatically and we can chuck him a peerage if he remembers which knife and fork to use.'

The Dog chuckled at his own wit. The Cat and Rat smiled. The PM didn't lose his expression of concerned sincerity. He stood up.

'And the Crime Tsar?'

'Oh Carter, definitely Carter.'

The three wise men all agreed. No discussion. The PM left the room, hurrying off to a cabinet meeting. Smiling a caricature of a boyish smile.

The Gnome, casually, as if an afterthought, asked the Dog, 'Crime Tsar?'

'Don't tell me you didn't get the memo either. That bloody secretary, she's pregnant and her brains seem to have dropped out when she opened her legs to conceive . . . it's shortform for United Kingdom – what's left of the ruddy thing – Anti-Crime Coordinator. The Cabinet's got plans for a sort of FBI – remember we kicked the idea around about a year ago? Scotland's gone for it too and Northern Ireland say they'll cooperate. Fully paid up members of the awkward squad.'

The Gnome nodded.

'Anyway, all serious crimes will come to this super force under the command of this Crime Tsar. Direct line to Europol, BWD, all of them. He'll be able to take charge of any case from any area. So anything more serious than dropping litter will be his province. He'll be a sort of Supercop.'

The Dog laughed. The Gnome smiled. The Dog was struck again by the sheer niceness of the man. How could someone so transparently a force for good and so patently ugly have risen so far? But then good looks had never been the mark of the British politician.

'Pretty powerful position.'

'God's policeman, Robbie. All the chief constables will answer to him, except Northern Ireland and that bugger doesn't answer to anyone. No, the idea is to try to get all the best coppers, all the best intelligence, under one roof. Natural progression from NCIS. Good idea, eh? Coming down to the bar?'

The Gnome shook his head. The cheerios were loud. Confident voices, confident, powerful people. When the advisers had left the room Robbie – the Gnome – MacIntyre stood looking down at the Thames through the leaded window.

He loved the inside of the Houses of Parliament, he loved the stone of the walls and the wood panelling but most of all he liked the quiet power it exuded. Inside looking out. It was the objective of his life, to be an insider.

He loved being rich, he loved being powerful, but most of all he loved being accepted. Being liked even. Inside this building he wasn't an ugly dwarf any more, openly pitied or scorned. Nobody here would shout after him: 'What you doing for panto this year?' 'Oi, Grumpy, where's Snow White?' Both things had been yelled this week, and he'd smiled, and he'd waved.

His thoughts swirled like the water below.

Jenni. When should he tell her? What would get her knickers down? Telling her and hoping for gratitude or not telling her and dangling his influence like a fishing fly. No contest. Dangle. He smiled. So Carter would get the new top job and all Jenni's scheming would be for nothing. He snorted. Serve her right. And her Action Man husband. He'd have her and have him over. What could be nicer?

Lucy had let herself in. There was no sign of anyone. Disappointed, she went into the kitchen. The coffee cups were on the table, the remains of toast and the lid off the honey. The central reservation, a rectangle of work surface the size of a snooker table, was unchar-acteristically cluttered. Jenni's kitchen could have accommodated any top chef – it was more than equal to the challenge of her occasional forays into lasagne and tossed salad.

The mess meant Tamsin and Kit were there. She bent down to get her cleaning-materials trug from under the sink. Her neat little tray of sprays and dusters.

'Hello.'

Lucy jumped so hard she banged her head.

'I . . . er . . . I didn't hear you come in. Sorry.'

Why she was apologising for being frightened out of her wits she didn't know.

Tom stood over her.

'Did you bang your head?'

'No . . . well, yes, a bit.'

She stood up. He was wearing a tracksuit and no shoes. She noticed how neat his feet were, high arches, pale.

'It's all I could put on with these.'

He held up his bandaged hands.

'Oh yes . . . how do you feel? What an experience – it must have been awful for you. I saw the film, well, the video on television this morning.'

Lucy listened to herself rabbiting on. Making a complete fool of herself. Shut up, Lucy, her brain was shouting. He's bored already. Shut up.

He smiled.

'Could you . . . would you mind making me a cup of coffee? Only Jenni's just grabbed a quiet moment to run our daughter and grandson home.'

Lucy burbled, 'Yes, yes, of course. Coffee, black, isn't it? One sugar?'

As if she could forget. Look what happened the last time she gave him a cup of coffee. She realised her hands were shaking when she tried to fill the kettle through the spout as she usually did. A spray of water soaked her shirt. Oh God, he'd think it was a wet T-shirt competition. She tried to rub herself down with a teacloth. Hopeless.

She took a deep breath, removed the lid of the kettle and filled it properly. She managed all the business with the cafetière and poured the coffee into a cup without spilling it. She turned to give it to him. He had disappeared. She called out, 'Tom . . . ? Excuse me, Tom, I have your coffee. Where would you like it?' She felt silly being so correct but then, as her aunt had said, sexual intercourse didn't constitute a formal introduction.

'Here, Lucy.'

His voice came from upstairs. The bedroom. By the time she got there most of the coffee was in the saucer. She upended it and poured it back then knocked politely on the open door.

'Come in, Lucy.' The room smelt of his aftershave, Czech and Speke 88 with something else, something muskier, underneath. 'Could you help me?'

He had taken off his tracksuit and was standing in his uniform trousers and open shirt.

'I managed to do up the zip but . . . the buttons have defeated me.'

He looked so lost Lucy wanted to throw her arms round him.

'And your socks. Where are your socks?'

'Over there, in the drawer.'

She took out a pair of fine black wool socks and knelt down in front of him. He sat on the bed. There was something symbolic, something sensual about unrolling them on to his feet. She kept her eyes down.

'It's a long time since anyone did this for me. Thank you.'

'Oh, I have to do it every day for Gary.'

Shut up about Gary. Talk about *him*.

'Are you all right? How are your hands? It must be very painful.'

Lucy, an interrogation is not a conversation.

'They feel fine. Thank you. Someone put some ointment on them for me.'

Lucy picked up his highly polished black shoes and guided his feet into them.

'Who was that? The doctor?'

'No. I haven't told Jenni . . .'

Lucy looked up at him. He paused, looking down at her. She didn't breathe, didn't blink, willing him to confide in her.

'It was three women. At the estate. I think they drugged me.' He laughed at the absurdity of the idea. 'And they put this stuff on my hands. Anyway I passed out and I'm fine this morning. No pain, nothing. But I dreamt. Dreams.'

He stopped. Lucy waited. She could see he'd closed down. Excluded her.

'What dreams?'

She saw something in him she hadn't seen before. A glimmer of self-doubt. Confusion.

'Tom? What dreams?' Then softly: 'Tell me. Please.'

He stood up but didn't move away. She took this as a sign he wanted his shirt done up. She stood too. Close to him. Her fingers brushing his skin as she slowly did up the buttons. The centre of his chest was covered in fine black hair, the nipples small and pinkish, hard with cold, or with her closeness? A few hairs around them. High on his chest, just below the neck a small red dot like a biro stain, where a blood vessel had burst. His skin was silky, fine. So much better quality than her own. She was desperate to touch it.

'It sounds daft . . . but there were three women. Three black women and they told my fortune in a way. It was just a dream. Strange.'

'What did they say?'

'Nothing much. Just that I'd get what I wanted. Something like that. Daft.'

His shirt was done up. She picked up his tie.

'Could you bend down a bit? Thanks.'

His face was now almost level with hers. She could see the fine hairs on his cheekbones. The coarser ones of his eyebrows. The small scar on his cheek; was it from shaving or something more romantic?

'Sounds like something out of the Scottish Play.'

He looked puzzled. '*Macbeth*?'

'My aunt told me it was bad luck to say the name. She was in the theatre. Well, she was box-office manager at Eastbourne.'

'Could you fetch the jacket? It's in the wardrobe.'

He said the words flatly. Dismissively. The subject of the women seemed closed.

Lucy fetched the jacket and did it up, struggling with the buttons and belt. Finally she reached up with both hands to flick imaginary flecks from the shoulders, below the crowns and insignia of his rank. Her eyes were level with his lips. It was not a wide mouth – the lower lip was slightly fuller, softer than the upper. Unable to stop herself she looked up at his eyes. He was looking at her, and his eyes which she'd always thought were dark brown were, in fact, indigo blue, an extraordinary colour, the depth and texture of a pair of velvet monogrammed slippers she'd once seen in a Jermyn Street shop.

'What is it, Lucy?'

She didn't move, her hands still on his shoulders, her breasts touching uniform buttons.

'Your eyes . . . they . . . they've changed colour.'

For God's sake, she was thirty-seven years old and was talking like an adolescent groupie.

He frowned.

'Oh . . . I must be happy then.'

She was breathless.

'They're like the sea – deep sea.' Sea you'd want to dive into and allow to rush into every orifice, Lucy thought, then remembered the last time that had happened, off the beach at Coleraine in February. She'd been in bed with pleurisy for three weeks afterwards.

'Jenni says they go the colour of a chemically polluted river. She says it's a sign that I'm happy. And she's always right.'

They smiled at each other conspiratorially. Lucy stayed close to him a moment longer, hoping he'd do something. Desperate for him to kiss her.

'What else did the women say?'

'Nothing. It was just a dream. Like you.'

And he kissed her. Suddenly. The way he did it she knew he hadn't planned it. The angles were slightly wrong and the impact a little hard. His lips weren't open at first and hers were, which made her feel awkward. Foolish. But they adjusted to each other and tentatively their tongues touched and withdrew.

His tongue was quite hard. She liked that, it excited her, she curled her lips round it and met it with the centre of her own. She was astonished by the softness of his lips. Not slackness. No, they were like pillows, yielding but firm. Suddenly she was self-conscious. What were her lips like? A little dry? A little thin? She took a tiny step towards him, pressed herself against him, but there seemed to be no reaction, no responding pressure.

They heard the front door open at the same time. He turned away wiping his mouth quickly as she retrieved his coffee cup and was at the top of the stairs.

'Jenni . . . I'm up here. Just helping Tom with his uniform.'

Lucy was at the bottom of the stairs by the time she'd finished speaking. Jenni just nodded vaguely and went up to his bedroom with a pile of newspapers and a sheaf of faxes which she'd retrieved from the hall table.

'Great show in the third editions. You were just too late for much in the first, but look – ' She spread the papers out across the bed. 'The *Mail*'s a bit snipey but the others are all excellent. Hurry up, Tom, you've got to be at the BBC by twelve-fifteen. Janet's faxed through all the people who are bidding for you. It's good. Very good. Don't make a fool of yourself on the lunchtime news.'

Tom could see how high she was, how little he mattered to her excitement. He watched her picking up and putting down the papers, shuffling the faxes. Her face was set, hard. This was Jenni. The real Jenni. But without her what would he be? Happy? Whenever his thoughts veered towards any other life he shut them down. Brutally unwilling to imagine.

If he did that he might feel frustration, a longing for an emotional life, and he was afraid, afraid that giving up the hair shirt of his unhappiness and isolation would make him less efficient, less able to focus on his goal. Their goal. He had only had relationships with two women. His mother and his wife. He couldn't imagine intimacy with either but now, in his forties, late at night and only rarely, he felt a yearning to be close to someone. To talk. To admit vulnerabilities.

But as quickly as these betraying thoughts began he squashed them, controlling his mind as rigidly as his fledgling emotions. He had made this bed, with Jenni, and would lie in it. Easier, more comfortable than the snake pit of emotional involvement. He clumsily picked up his hat and gloves. He couldn't find his swagger stick.

'I'm ready.' He looked out of the window.

'Gordon's downstairs.'

'Oh Gordon.'

Jenni let her façade of good nature drop in front of her husband, in the way one has no pretence in front of the family pet. She hurried out of the bedroom and down the stairs; Tom followed slowly. She hadn't asked anything about the events of last night. He could hear her:

'Tom, if you want to tell me something, you will, there's no point my asking.'

But he'd lost the way to tell. He talked fluently, at length, but rarely said anything. Nothing that might reveal the small boy curled up in the corner of the large hall.

Jenni was sitting in the back of the Jaguar. Tom saw Lucy was standing at the front door. He nodded as he passed her. He did not look at her. She watched the car leave; Tom's head was bent over papers put into his hand by Jenni. She didn't exist again. The kiss hadn't happened.

Gary watched her from across the road and felt sadness. Not because his wife was gazing like a spaniel after a man he detested, but because she was unhappy. But if he were dead and Jenni were in a mental institution, which he had always felt was her natural habitat, would Tom Shackleton take Lucy to be his lawful wedded wife? Gary thought not.

'So' he said out loud. 'Not worth topping myself then.'

He turned back to the computer console and continued to stab the keys with a knuckle. To keep his mind occupied he had started a paper on the possibility of Mozart suffering from Asperger's syndrome. Now he had to finish it before he lost the use of his hands altogether. He hoped it would be published. He hoped it would be taken up. He never seemed to be able to shake off hope.

The following days were taken up with interviews, photo opportunities and phone calls. Shackleton enjoyed it all. There was no time for free-range thinking. By the Wednesday evening he had become one of the best-known and most sought-after celebrities in the country.

It was noted at Party headquarters that his recognition factor with the public was now 78 per cent. Good for a politician, excellent for a police officer who hadn't let someone die in the back of a van or stolen evidence in a drugs trial. Tom Shackleton, it was agreed by those who counted, was a triumph of presentation over content, politically photogenic and the man for London.

The Gnome had stayed away from Jenni since the riot. She had tried to telephone him and even sent an e-mail but he was unavailable. He wanted her desperate for information. He couldn't imagine Jenni Shackleton ever 'gagging for it', a phrase he privately enjoyed when weighing up the possibilities of a woman's sexual potential.

But he knew she'd be gagging for what he could tell her. It was Thursday: her dinner party was that evening. He lay in bed thinking about it. About her. Would there be a chance of anything tonight? With her husband and the cleaner there? He shook his head on the pillow.

Why was he bothering? He knew the minute he'd had her she'd be no more than a trophy fuck. Another notch on the gun barrel. Well, that's all any of them were, wasn't it?

He looked round at the lump in the bed beside him. His wife. She was snoring slightly. He looked at her with great gentleness. Huge arse and varicose veins now but he still saw the girl she'd been. Married for thirty-two years, two kids, well-balanced, attractive, popular kids. Neither afflicted with his condition. People he liked as well as loved. Big house in town, bigger house in the country. Success.

She enjoyed her kids, loved her dogs and she had never, even in their vilest rows, called him ugly or short or deformed.

The one woman he'd ever met who he trusted. Her snoring got louder. She looked like a beached walrus. He felt a surge of sentimental affection towards her: her intelligence and inelegant ordinariness had long since become beauty in his eyes. The jagged, striving women he ritually humiliated during sex had nothing in common with her.

She had attended a debate he'd spoken at when he was sixteen and she a beanpole seventeen. He'd won the motion brilliantly but, as usual, endured his peers' sniggering afterwards. He remembered standing holding a cherryade he didn't want, pretending to read the fire instructions on the hall wall. As always, isolated by the glory of his mind and the deformity of his body. He hadn't been able to read past 'In case of fire . . .' because of the tears in his eyes. As always, it was the pretty girls he saw as the root of his torture. Encouraging their dim beaux to greater heights of ridicule. One day, he thought, one day . . .

'Bloody good closing speech. Want some crisps? Oh, I'm Elizabeth, Lizie. Not Lizzie. Lizie James.'

She'd taken his small hand in her large one and smiled at him. He'd expected to see pity in that smile, a show of generous understanding to be boasted of among liberal friends and approving parents:

'Oh Mummy, I was awfully nice to a dwarf today.'

'Well done, darling! Did you touch his hump? It's frightfully good luck, you know.'

But she was just smiling at him. All he could see in her big blue eyes was admiration. He was armed against any condescension but completely unprepared for this naked, honest look of adolescent adoration.

Watching her now, his fingers lightly touching her greying hair, he remembered how cruel he'd been, how he'd tried to force her into being nasty to him, into conforming to his view of women. But she wouldn't. She waited patiently for eight years until he recognised her. Looking at her now he couldn't imagine punishing her for what he'd suffered but she'd long since forgiven him and in return he'd allowed her to cultivate his charm, his humour, which previously he'd used to wound, and his raw sensitivity to all things beautiful. Lizie had touched every part of him but that so destroyed and perverted by cruelty. That stagnant pond was MacIntyre's alone and hate it though he did, part of him yearned for the debasement it brought.

Lizie had no idea of his sexual practices outside her grandmother's four-poster bed.

He leaned over and kissed her gently; a stray untweezed bristle caught his cheek.

She opened her eyes.

'Morning, Smudge. Was I snoring?'

'You never snore.'

She giggled and sat up.

'No, I never fart either . . . aren't you supposed to be in London today?'

She lumbered out of bed, her sensible tartan nightie riding up over her good British thighs, the candle-thin girl long gone.

'I'm just on my way. Oh . . . and I've got that dinner tonight, the Chief Constable's –'

'Oh yes, Tom Shackleton. Odd face. Rather too much of it. Looks like a serial killer . . .'

MacIntyre could never believe how differently his wife saw the world.

'He's supposed to be handsome.'

She shrugged. 'Handsome is as handsome does. Well . . . have a good time.'

They kissed goodbye on the lips with warmth. MacIntyre thought for a moment about cancelling dinner and coming back here where he wasn't the Gnome or the machiavellian schemer or the consumer of pretty wives. The thought passed as quickly as it had formed.

One day he'd stop. One day his conscience would get the better of him, one day he'd tire of revenge and just come home. Not just to this house and this wife but to himself. Home was Robert MacIntyre, husband, father and immensely generous but modest supporter of charities and individuals. But for now, in the snake-infested corridors of Whitehall and Westminster, he had to be the Gnome, charming, brilliant, enigmatic, fascinating, loved, hated in some quarters but always warily respected. The side of himself he honestly despised was, in that world, what kept him ahead of the game. And it was intoxicating to be utterly without morals or scruples. To have such power over men . . . and those brittle striving women.

'Kiss the llamas for me. See you at the weekend.'

Robert MacIntyre lingered in the warmth of Lizie's crumpled

nightie while his other self closed the door and got into his chauffeur-driven car.

He had a full day of meetings before the delicious prospect of Mrs Chief Constable's knicker elastic. He opened his attaché case and didn't think about her again until he rang her doorbell at seven-thirty that night.

Lucy's week had been a confusion of highs and lows. So high after the kiss, rock bottom when she saw him the next day and he didn't say good morning. High every time she saw him on television or when she cut out pictures of him from the papers, which she put into an old shoe-box.

In the depths of depression when she saw how little her figure had altered in six days. But today was the dinner party. She woke early – she wanted to get everything out of the way so she could spend the afternoon with cleansers and face packs, exfoliators and depilators. She had got some bikini wax strips and wasn't looking forward to trying them.

She'd heard some dancers plucked their pubic hair, you could do it in an evening in front of the telly, but she didn't have very good tweezers. Creams and razors had a legacy of itchy stubble so wax strips it was to be. She knew Tom wouldn't know if she had or had not a perfect heart of soft hair beneath her pants but . . . he might. If a miracle happened. She wanted to be ready for anything.

Gary had a bit of a cold when she went in to see him and, unusually for him, seemed a bit down. He was always saying some people with MS had feelings of euphoria and he was one of the lucky ones. He was always saying how lucky he was: to see a tree, to hear music, to smell perfume. Lucy didn't believe him, of course, but he rarely allowed the mask to slip. She looked at the clock. Seven-thirty. Only another twelve hours. This time tomorrow it would be all over. The phone rang.

'Oh Lucy darling. Thank God you're in!'

Where else would I be? thought Lucy. Jenni had her 'Darling, I'm desperate' voice on:

'Darling, I'm desperate, only you can get me out of this.'

'Yes, Jenni,' said Lucy obediently.

By the phone there was a half-eaten biscuit. She must have left it there. Absently she ate it while Jenni rushed on.

'The caterers are due here at nine but I have to go out and Tom and I have to go to a garden party this afternoon. They are such a bore, bridge rolls and fish-paste sandwiches, ghastly –'

I'll go, thought Lucy. I'd like to go. Listen to Gilbert and Sullivan and wear a big hat. Why not? Beats manually expressing your husband's stools.

'But, Lucy . . . calamity. I've forgotten the flowers. *Could* you? *Would* you? I'm so sorry to be a pest. I'll leave the money in your pinny pocket. Is that OK?'

No, Jenni, I want you to come the ten yards across the road, knock on my door and hand it to me.

'Yes, that'll be fine, Jenni.'

'I'll leave a list of what I want and you know where the vases are, don't you?'

'Yes, but I'm not very good at flower-arranging.'

'Nonsense, Lucy – I've seen what you can do with a couple of catkins and a bit of oasis.'

She laughed. Lucy knew Jenni had borrowed the line from a comedienne's act, she'd hardly bothered to take the quotes off it.

'And could you let the caterer in? Oh and would you send a potted plant or something to Geoffrey Carter, something frightfully impressive – and exotic, something very me, you know – he comes out of hospital today, poor thing. And maybe some flowers for Eleri, his wife? Their address is in the book on the hall table. If it's more than I left I'll settle up with you later. I don't know how I'll find the time today. But you know my husband . . .'

No I don't, Jenni, I wish I did.

'Can't thank you enough. Oh, there's Gordon. We must go – Tom's got a couple of meetings on the way. You know him. Never stops. My husband, eh? What would you do with him?'

Cover him with cream and lick him clean, thought Lucy, but Jenni had put the phone down. That problem was dealt with. There was no need to spend any more time on it, or Lucy.

I'm very well, thanks, but Gary's got a bit of a cold, nothing serious, but it's miserable for him. You know my husband. Never stops. Never gives in. So brave.

The tone purred in her ear, she hung up. A week ago they weren't going to the garden party. There were always invitations but they never went then a letter had come from the Palace: 'His Royal

Highness would like to meet . . .' and suddenly they were going. Jenni couldn't bear not to. This was her week. Carter was out of the way and her husband was in the ascendant. Jenni wanted it all and she was getting it.

Lucy felt suddenly guilty. Jenni was being as kind as she could be. It wasn't fair to blame a cat for being a defective kind of dog.

Lucy knew the amount of flowers Jenni would want would be roughly equivalent to a day's take at the Golders Green Crematorium so her peaceful afternoon would be a quick hour in the bathroom with a steamed-up mirror. She felt her chin. Spot. Well, less of a spot, more a second head.

Maybe she should pull out of the dinner, say she couldn't leave Gary. No, she'd go. If Tom Shackleton loved her he wouldn't mind her spot. If he behaved the way he had all week it wouldn't matter if she had three heads, he wouldn't notice. She stopped her thoughts and rewound the last few feet. Tom Shackleton and love in the same sentence? Oxymoron.

'Gary, I've got to go out and get Jenni's flowers for tonight. And I want some bath salts so I'm going to stop off at the Body Shop. Anything you want?'

'Yes please, a new one, forty-two-inch chest with an elasticated waist.'

Lucy laughed. She'd heard it before but she always laughed. Tom Shackleton didn't make her laugh. He just made her confused and unhappy so why not just walk away? She pulled a baseball cap on over her unwashed hair.

'Because I don't want to,' she said.

'What did you say?' called Gary.

'Nothing. Just beating myself up. See you later.'

Geoffrey Carter's week had been very different from Tom and Jenni's. The burns to his legs were deep and agonising. No arrests had been made. It was felt by the CPS there was insufficient evidence to bring a prosecution. The video didn't show the young man throwing the cigarette; further action wasn't felt to be 'appropriate'.

Appropriate? Carter knew it would not be appropriate for the government to have an untidy end to the story. The heroics of the two chiefs and the dignity of the community elders had made good copy. Britain Talks. Jaw Jaw Prevents War War in Inner City. Any arrests and prosecutions would be messy. Spoil the big picture and leave open the possibility of criticism. Should he and Shackleton have gone in like that?

In the aftermath Carter saw very clearly how stupid they'd been and how lucky to get away with it. Thinking about it, there was something about Shackleton that made him uneasy. Not scared exactly – frightened was too adult a word for what he felt. What did he feel? Admiration? Yes. Envy? A little, of his lack of compassion, his ability never to involve himself. What else?

Carter was sitting waiting in the hospital foyer for his car, reading a magazine. But he wasn't aware of the toothpaste advert he was looking at – all he could see and feel was Shackleton wrapped around him as he put out the fire. He remembered the same feeling for his housemaster, a rugby-playing hardman who'd cuddled him when his father died. All wrapped up in authority, father, big man, protection, warmth, affection . . . stop. The same feelings he'd experienced at those all-male lock-ins where danger and triumph had released normally closed-off emotions. Carter had never had a homosexual encounter, for all the teasing he'd endured as a young man – pretty boy, Jessie, poof . . . at first he'd been too scared then too ambitious. At the time no gay policeman was going to make it past community beat office. But he wasn't gay. No, he'd never slept with a man, never wanted to, but sometimes, when making love to his wife, unbidden images filled his mind. But not Tom Shackleton. No. Never Tom Shackleton.

He was still on painkillers and hadn't had a nightmare for two nights, though his dreams were vivid and disturbing. It must be the drugs, yes, they were cleaning out the unconscious mind and, like a blocked sink, strange scum was being thrown up. His mind seemed more burned than his legs. Raw. Did he say something to provoke the attack? Could he have done more? Every minute, from ducking under the blue-and-white tape to vomiting over the bonnet of his car, he lived and re-lived.

Where Tom Shackleton's conscious mind was a desert, Geoffrey Carter's was a rain forest. Teeming with life on all levels, with great beauty and dangerous darkness jostling for space. He wished his mind would be quiet. That it would leave him alone, just for an hour of tranquillity. A moment of Shackleton's spare inner landscape.

His deputy chief arrived to take him home to his wife, his children, his home. Normality that would chase away the demons.

'Ready, sir?'

'Yes, thanks.'

As he left the hospital a couple of reluctant hacks were standing waiting for him. A photographer whose mobile phone was bleating insistently got a couple of smudges.

'This way, Chief Constable. Can you hold your walking stick up? Great.'

A rattle of shutter clicks and the man was running to his car, talking into his phone about catching a footballer drunk at an awards ceremony.

The journalists asked him what his feelings were towards the people who set him on fire. Had it changed his attitude at all towards ethnic minorities, this last question from a tiny, ferocious girl from *The Voice*. His driver held the car door open for him; his deputy lightly held his elbow as he lowered himself carefully on to the back seat.

A car swerved in ahead of them and a television crew jumped out as if they were about to cover an armed siege in Africa. They wore camouflage trousers and multi-pocketed sleeveless jerkins. The director, a vacuous girl not long out of Sheffield Hallam with a second-class degree in media studies, shoved a microphone at Carter, looping her lank hair behind her ear as she did so.

His legs were hurting and he was suddenly tired, desperate to get back into bed and sleep. But he was polite and charming. She knew he'd make a splendid martyr on the early evening news. As his car drove away she remarked to the cameraman that he seemed quite bright for a policeman.

Carter didn't have the energy to talk on the way home. His deputy sat in the front watching him in the mirror. There was quite an affection for the Chief among his staff and they had all been worried about him.

'I'm all right, Danny.' He caught his deputy's eye in the mirror. 'Thanks.'

Danny, who had been an accelerated-promotion candidate since Hendon, had found himself virtually in orbit when the police started looking round for non-white talent to promote high and fast. He was the first black DCC and was on track to become the first black chief. But he would never know if it was because he was good.

Carter told him not to dwell on it.

'Becoming Chief Constable has nothing to do with being a good copper. It's being a good politician, being a good accountant, and not allowing anything to distract you from what you want. It has very little to do with care in the community or any ideals you came in with.'

Danny knew if that were true Carter would never have made it, but he was a rarity. Danny admired his intellect and his beliefs.

'And, Danny, if it is only because you're black, not because you're good, you'll soon make a mistake and there'll be plenty to pull you down.'

The car stopped at Carter's house. Danny helped him out and up the steps of the Regency-style terrace. Carter had his door keys ready but was looking at the windows of the house. Danny misread the look as apprehension. In fact Carter was disappointed, no, worse than that, he felt as if his birthday had been forgotten or he'd come first in the hundred metres and no one had seen him. He'd thought there would be excited sticky faces at the windows, shouts of excitement, something more than silence.

'Shall I come in with you, sir?'

'No, Danny, thanks.' He opened the front door. 'Bloody hell, what's that?'

In the middle of the hall, impossible to pass, was the largest potted plant Carter had seen outside Kew Gardens.

'Good God, it's a triffid. Where's the card? Is there one? Do you think it's a terrorist bomb?'

Danny handed him the small square envelope.

' "From Jenni and Tom. Get well soon." '

He looked at his deputy. They had both seen the acres of newsprint devoted to Tom Shackleton since the night of the siege, the television chats, the modest acknowledgements of bravery, and since the first hours after they had got out Geoffrey Carter's name had hardly been mentioned. It was, at best, as if Shackleton had saved his life, at its worst it was made to look as if he had been a liability in a delicate situation. The footage shot in the community centre had been edited to feature Shackleton, a lighted cigarette and his subsequent smothering with his own body of the fire that engulfed Carter.

Danny looked at the plant.

'Nice gesture. And so subtle.'

Carter smiled. 'Mrs Shackleton will have sent it.'

'Don't put it in your bedroom then. It might strangle you in your sleep.'

They stared at the monstrosity. Danny tried to move it.

'Oh come on, Danny, she's not that bad.'

Danny grunted. Carter decided it was because of the effort, not a comment on the fragrant Mrs Shackleton.

Danny had been Shackleton's staff officer for a year and had briefly been the object of their daughter Tamsin's infatuation. She was still at school and persistently dogged Danny with tales of cruelty at home and staged faints beside his car. Every time there was a bizarre incident with the girl, who Danny had decided was unstable, he told her parents. Jenni had always been charming, Shackleton had made it obvious that it was women's business and didn't want to know.

Then Danny's wife decided to divorce him. She was having an affair with an officer at another station and one of his colleagues had thoughtfully pinned a pair of her pants to the noticeboard with a graphic photograph of how she lost them.

She took him for half his house and all his children, leaving him in a spiral down towards the bottom of a bottle. He'd pulled himself back but not before Jenni had decided he was flaky.

'I think there's something just a tiny bit flaky about Dan Marshall,' she had said in passing to HM Inspector of Constabulary.

And though she never said it Danny knew it was because she didn't believe a black man could ever really make it. That there was an inherent weakness. Then he knew that Jenni was as crazy as her daughter. For all her veneer of sophisticated liberalism, Jenni Shackleton was a provincial mind in an elegant body and towards Danny she had always alternated between condescension and suspicion. It had never occurred to her he would make DCC and in her mind he had only done so because the police needed a black face for *Question Time*.

'I'll call round later, to make sure everything's OK?'

Danny dumped the pot plant by the umbrella stand and returned to the front door.

Carter held out his hand.

'Thanks, Danny, there's no need, my wife . . .'

Danny glanced around, up the stairs.

'Is she here, sir?'

Carter suddenly looked quite lost. Bambi.

'I thought she would be. And the boys . . . maybe they forgot it was today. But don't worry. They won't be far away.'

'I could stay, sir, make a cup of tea . . . ?'

Danny saw his boss wanted company but was shy of saying so. Without waiting for a reply Danny opened the living-room door. The noise hit them at the same time as a young boy launched himself at Carter.

'Surprise!'

'Daddy . . . Daddy . . . Daddy.'

'Welcome home!'

Danny saw the whole room and the kitchen beyond was festooned with banners and bunting saying everything from 'We love you, Daddy' to 'Welcome home, hero.'

He also saw Carter's other son rocking from side to side, lost somewhere in an autistic world in which liquid, any liquid, was the only focus. And that focus was obsession. Danny knew no glass, vase or bottle must be left unguarded in case Alexander found it and drank the contents. Whisky, meths and undiluted Ribena all been pumped out of his stomach at one time or another.

He seemed not to know Carter, who greeted the child no differently from the other boy, Peter. Peter's intelligence and love of life was always enough for two, as if he was trying to compensate for his lost brother.

Eleri was trying in vain to attend to the children, kiss her husband and make Danny feel welcome.

'Sit down, Danny. You'll stay for tea, won't you? We've got jelly and blancmange –'

Peter was now sitting on Carter screaming, 'And chocolate ice-cream!!' He turned to Danny. 'That's Daddy's favourite, you're not allowed, it's all for him.'

The boy started bouncing up and down on his father's legs. Eleri saw the pain on Carter's face and quickly pulled the child off, dispatching him upstairs to get the welcome-home offerings Peter had made for their father.

Danny felt awkward and intrusive as Eleri sat on the arm of Carter's chair stroking his suddenly exhausted face. She was an attractive woman with a pre-Raphaelite tumble of auburn hair which she tried to smooth with vast applications of Frizz-Ease. Her face was lightly freckled with prettily tilted hazel eyes and lips that always smiled. She was at once mumsy and sexy but, thought Danny, she'd never make a dirty woman. Not like the mad Mrs Shackleton. What on earth had put that thought in his head?

'No, I'd better go. Thanks anyway. I'll see you in a couple of days then, sir. I'll see myself out.'

'Yes please, Danny . . . Eleri will have given me egg-custard poisoning by then.'

He turned to go and was almost knocked over by Alexander who'd suddenly changed from what Danny had thought was a low-browed zombie into a furious, biting, thrashing animal. Not a sound did he utter as he attacked Danny. Eleri pulled him off so violently Danny was worried the boy's arms might be broken, but he saw quickly it was the only way to deal with him.

'Too much excitement, I'm so sorry. Once he's in one of these tantrums there's nothing we can do – I'm so sorry. Can you see yourself out?'

Danny was only too pleased to go. Guilty though he felt about it he found Alexander's autism repellent. There was something not yet human about the boy. But the Carters loved him. Danny felt rotten that he couldn't detect anything to love.

Peter however was a totally different thing. He was hurtling downstairs with his dad's presents as Danny reached the front door. As always the child paused to spread happiness where his brother may have sown discord. He smiled at Danny and wished him goodbye, apologising for not shaking hands because his hands were full.

Good manners satisfied and Danny gone, he presented Carter with his armful of offerings while Alexander screeched and fought with Eleri in the kitchen. Egg cartons as dinosaurs, paintings on grey cartridge paper and a washing-up-liquid-bottle moon rocket.

Danny, getting back into the car, was still thinking about the family, the two boys who bore no resemblance to their parents. The sons the doctors told Eleri she couldn't have because faulty ovaries had robbed her of her fertility.

She and Carter had met at university, she a fresher as he was leaving. She had fallen in love with his humanity and delicate beauty and he with her capable serenity.

They married quickly and for years they'd fostered children of all colours and abilities then, some time after Ceauşescu when things should have improved, Eleri had gone to Romania and found two lice-ridden abandoned Roma boys. Illegitimate and gypsy, they had no hope. Sharing a rusting cot, tied to the bars and atrophying physically and mentally into some state less than human. Eleri, desperate for kids, and Geoffrey, desperate for her happiness, brought the boys home after two years of fighting domestic bureaucracy. Two beautiful smiling cherubs on whom they lavished love and food in the belief that would be enough to stop the nightmares, stop the rocking and the endless staring at their hands.

Peter responded quickly, miraculously finding himself at the top of his class at age ten and certain to find a place in a good academic senior school. But Alexander, a year younger, stopped smiling at eighteen months and had never spoken. Just noises, noises that sounded to Danny like the screaming of a chimpanzee. Terrified and terrifying screeches.

He had no idea what he would have done if one of his own children had turned out like that. Yes he did. He would have walked out rather than live with that level of damage. He wished he could be a better person but knew himself too well to think he might ever change.

Back in the house Carter was wondering how he'd ever thought they were happy without these two gorgeous monsters. He was the only person who could contact Alexander. Eleri tried, as she tried daily to love him, but she found his lack of response to her devastating. She'd never been hugged by him, never had a kiss or even felt his head asleep on her shoulder; it was like caring for an aggressive un-housetrained dog. But she would never give up trying.

Later that evening the two boys were asleep, tucked into the armchair either side of their father. Alexander, when exhausted, would always find a shelter by his father. Eleri was sitting on the floor sipping a cup of hot chocolate. She was no longer jealous of Alexander's attachment to her husband, but she'd never stop hoping it would be her he curled up next to one day.

She was very quiet. Carter's attempts at conversation had met with monosyllabic replies since tea. He'd asked her what was wrong but received short shrift.

This wasn't what he'd imagined for his homecoming. A bit of hero worship would have been nice. A bit of tender loving care. She'd been an angel up till now, during the aftermath of the siege and in the hospital.

But nevertheless the security of domesticity had settled Carter's doubt and turmoil like a strong painkiller.

He was dozing with his cheek against Alexander's hair when Eleri said, 'Come on. Bedtime. All three of you boys. Upstairs. Now.'

With great protests at Mummy's bullying Peter took his brother up to start the task of cleaning teeth and climbing into their pyjamas. Eleri got Carter to his feet, turned out the lights and checked the front door was locked. They stood together in the hall. Carter put his arms around her, full of quiet love, and content.

Carter breathed in deeply, feeling clean for the first time since the siege. Since being so close to Shackleton. It was as if something in the man had infected him. Ridiculous. He held the soft body of his wife tightly.

'Oh Eleri. I do love you.'

Her response was automatic. But although physically close he could feel her distance.

'And I love you. Did you see the plant?'

'Couldn't miss it. What do you want to do with it?'

'I don't know, Geoff . . . but we can't get rid of it, they might come round and you know what Jenni's like, she's bound to want to see it.' Guilty at being a little less than generous she added, 'But it was a kind thought and she sent me a hundredweight of lilies.' She looked at the triffid. 'We'd better leave it where it is, I suppose. I don't like it though, do you? Looks like something out of a Grimm's fairy-tale.'

'Mmm.'

He wasn't listening but kissing her, burrowing into her generous welcoming flesh. Suddenly she pushed him off. Her face was contorted, trying to stop herself crying. She failed. She was sobbing and shouting and almost laughing.

Carter was completely taken aback.

'Eleri . . . what is it? What's the matter?'

'What's the matter? You . . . you. I hate you . . . I really hate you. No, I don't mean it . . . but how could you? You could have been killed. They wanted to kill you. Look at you. Look at what they've done to you. It wasn't your job . . . you should never have gone in there. You didn't think about us . . . we're your family. But your job, your bloody job always has to come first. It wasn't worth it. Was it? Look at you. How could you? Why? Why? . . .'

She exhausted herself and slumped against him howling. Peter's worried face appeared over the banisters. Alexander started to moan and rock. Carter reassured them.

'It's all right. Mummy's just a bit upset, she'll be all right in the morning. She's just tired.'

'No she's not,' came the muffled voice from his chest. 'She's pregnant.'

Time went into slow motion. And into the spaces between the previously close-packed seconds poured peace, love and warmth. A miracle had happened and there were no words, no whoops of joy or shouts of happiness that could encompass what he felt. It was as if they were suddenly alone in a snow-filled landscape, not a breath of wind, not a cloud to obscure the serenity of the star-filled sky. Muffled silence and absolute perfection. Carter went blank, didn't know what to say. Then he remembered.

'Are you sure? How long?'

'Twelve weeks on the day of the siege. I'd put the champagne in the fridge. I couldn't tell you before. In case. But they say three months is a milestone, don't they?'

Carter couldn't speak. Nothing in his life compared to this. Commissioner, Tsar, nothing. Just that little frog on a string growing inside the woman he was holding far too tightly in his arms. His own child. Their own baby.

He knew it was a girl. A girl whose grazed knees he'd already kissed better, a girl who'd want to tell her dad all her secrets. A girl he'd walk down the aisle on her wedding day. This was the only dream he'd had left and it had seemed as likely as scoring the winning goal for England in the World Cup Final. He beamed up at the two worried little faces squeezed through the banisters. Relieved that everything was all right Peter grinned back and quietened Alexander.

They went upstairs with not a word spoken. Eleri remembered the Virgin Mary had held the news in her heart. It had always puzzled her but now it made perfect sense.

Peter shyly cuddled his mum. Carter pulled Alexander towards him and his embrace encompassed them all. It was the moment he would remember as the happiest of their lives.

Reality would wait till tomorrow. He knew the future was now anything but a foregone conclusion. But tonight . . .

Carter couldn't bear to let go of his family and reached across them to turn out the landing light. He looked down at the plant.

It looked beautiful.

By six o'clock Lucy was plucked and trussed like an oven-ready turkey. She had bought a new shade of eye shadow and kept checking in the mirror that it was all right.

Jenni's flowers were arranged and she had made cups of tea for the caterer who was to prepare the meal.

'Why don't you take your frock off. It'll crease sitting here.'

Gary broke the silence that had settled on them. In Lucy's head there was no silence, though. She was deafened with contradictory thoughts. Wishes. Hopes. And the one word, Tom, repeating over and over.

'Yes. You're right. I'm ready much too early.'

She went upstairs and put on a shapeless dress she'd bought years before when she thought she was pregnant. She could put it on now without even a moment's thought of those few weeks. Was this really the most excited she'd been since then? She tried to think of other times as she re-hung the silk on its cushioned lilac hanger.

Suddenly her life looked poor and mean. An existence on the periphery of experience. In less than a minute she had gone from the intoxication of anticipation to the flat recognition of futility. What hopes did she hold for tonight? Whatever they were they shrivelled as she summoned them up for scrutiny.

Lucy, you are ordinary. You are an ordinary woman, neither plain nor pretty, married to a pleasant man with a progressive disease. Don't make a fool of yourself. Why not? If it's all so written, if there's really no hope of slipping the chain of inevitability, you might as well delude yourself into happiness as much as possible. Yes. Well, why not just take drugs and be done with it.

And of course she knew Jenni didn't really want her there – she was just a cover for Jenni and her politician. Jenni probably didn't know any other women who could come to dinner alone and not be competition. Lucky for Jenni she had someone quite sad and unlikely to upstage even the soup.

Her thoughts were speeding again but now in a downwards spiral. If she didn't stop them she knew she would think herself into the fuck-off, Big Ears position.

She sat on the bed, picked up the stuffed pink elephant Gary had given her for their first Christmas and plaited the ridiculous tuft of nylon hair on its head.

'You see, Noddy wants to borrow Big Ears' lawn mower.' Talking pushed her thoughts away. 'So he leaves his house full of optimism, but by the time he reaches Big Ears' front gate he's thought of a thousand reasons why he'll refuse him and humiliate him so when Big Ears answers the door Noddy says, "Fuck off, Big Ears."'

The pink elephant's expression didn't change but Lucy lay back and laughed out loud at the idea of belligerently banging on Jenni's door and shouting, 'Fuck off, Jenni,' when it was opened. She said it again and it made her laugh more. She said it again and laughed until she ached, clutching the pink elephant to her stomach. The ringing doorbell brought her back to a sort of reality. A reality where there were at least possibilities and the future wasn't written out like a bus timetable.

The nurses bundled into the hall, as always, full of good humour. This particular team, Denise and Mel, were Gary's favourites. They always flirted with him and made him laugh. Watching them with Gary Lucy felt guilty over not being more grateful for what she had. As she put the kettle on for his girls' cup of tea ('Mugs, please, Lucy, mugs, me and Mel only have cups at funerals') she wondered about the workings of her mind – it was always scurrying about trying to find an emotion or a feeling to wallow in.

One minute elation, next depression and anger, now guilt. She looked at her carefully made-up face in the chrome of the kettle: but you'd never know it from that ovine stare, would you? She made the tea and took it through.

Gary was suspended above his wheelchair in a sling attached to a flimsy-looking mobile hoist. It had cost £700 but meant that, theoretically, they could get away on holiday, just booking a local nurse at the destination. Of course they had never risked it. And now they'd bought the hoist they couldn't afford a holiday.

Denise was threatening to leave him hanging there while they drank their tea and all three were shrieking with laughter. Gary so helpless he looked in danger of falling out of the grubby white cradle. Lucy looked at them. If she could only settle for what she had. Be content. Be grateful. If she could just go to the phone and call Jenni, tell her Gary wasn't well, his cold had got worse today, that wouldn't be a lie. If she didn't go to dinner maybe she could start tomorrow without Tom Shackleton, without discontent and this fidgety longing for excitement.

Maybe if she joined the Open University or the amateur dramatics. A nice hobby. Something to take her mind off the great expanse of nothing inside her. That big echoing hole shaped like Tom Shackleton.

'Gary, how's your cold now?'

'Oh, getting worse,' he said cheerfully as he was lowered on to his bed.

'Only I could not go tonight. I wouldn't mind. Really.'

She found she was desperate for him to say yes, stay at home. She panicked. She suddenly saw the evening as a science-fiction window between dimensions; if she passed through she would be unable to turn back. Nothing would be the same again.

Gary was sipping his tea, a biscuit, brought by Denise, held ready for dunking.

'No, you go. I told you, I'm talking wheelchairs tonight.'

'That's his story,' hooted Mel. 'He's got girls coming in, haven't you, Gary? You're having one of them orgies.'

'Ooh, can I come?' Denise's voice was loud, as if talking over the noise of a party. 'I'll bring the baby oil.'

Gary was enjoying himself.

'I think I'd be better with WD40.'

Lucy wanted to be a part of this fun. It might be false, it might be forced, but it was safe. She wanted them to let her in. But it was good for Gary because she wasn't a part of it, this was his. He was the centre of attention for these two women. They knew his body better than Lucy: they were close, they were his. Lucy remembered from her brief youthful sojourn as a care assistant the way the intimacy of illness would exclude wives. The unconditional love offered by infatuated patients to their nurses. The simplicity of affection between strangers.

'Isn't it time you put your dress back on, Luce? Show Mel and Denise.'

Lucy smiled and said, 'I'll just pop over the road and make sure everything's all right.'

Jenni and Tom arrived back from Buckingham Palace at five o'clock. They had eaten their Lyon's Swiss rolls and chatted briefly with members of the Royal Family who had been politely curious about the Flamborough Estate and politely concerned about Tom's burns. Jenni was thrilled when a princess in a hat said she was an avid reader of her newspaper articles. Several junior members of the government paid them court.

Jenni was very satisfied. Her husband was being regarded with respect. And he was, above all, her creation. She let him hold her hand in the car on the way home. Shackleton found holding hands comforting. It was never a prelude to further intimacy. She approved of him and that made his life more comfortable.

Lucy tapped apologetically on the door. A radiant Jenni let her in, pleased to see her, overwhelming her with gratitude and praise. The caterer was pottering in the kitchen and there was an atmosphere of happy anticipation. Tom went upstairs to change. As he did he winked at Lucy, a funny, conspiratorial flicker that made her giggle. Lucy went into the kitchen to see if there was anything she could do, reluctant to go home and leave the memory of that half-smiled wink. When she came out, Jenni was picking up and putting down bottles. Tom was coming down the stairs and the mood had changed. He felt it as cold as the air from an open freezer. Jenni turned on him, two mixer bottles in her hand. Tom winced, ready for her to throw them. Lucy, taken unaware, stood still in the doorway, not daring to move.

'Where's the ginger ale?'

As always Jenni caught him unprepared, the most successful policeman in the country, the darling of the media, the man of achievement.

'What ginger ale?'

'Yes,' she hissed triumphantly. 'What ginger ale? There isn't any. You've drunk it, haven't you?'

He was unsure what the right answer was. He took too long to decide.

'You stupid prat. Don't look at me like that! Why the hell didn't you tell me we'd run out?'

As always he rolled over.

'I'll go and get some. Now.'

The caterer, coming out of the kitchen, was embarrassed by this onslaught.

'I've got some ginger beer in the van.'

'Don't be so stupid,' spat Jenni.

The caterer quailed and went back to her hors d'oeuvres. Lucy, helpless, looked at Shackleton but he could only look away, braced for the onslaught. All he could feel was humiliation, which seemed to hang round him like the smell of unwashed clothes.

'I can't believe you didn't tell me. You're unbelievable . . .'

Jenni was screaming now, incoherent. Her outbursts had been getting more frequent but he didn't want to consider the possibility that she might be deteriorating. That these 'turns' might be a sign of something seriously wrong. While he sometimes hated her he often thought nostalgically – and probably inaccurately – of their early, gentle days together when she was his beloved Jen. Now Lucy was showing him that gentleness but he knew what would happen if he trusted her. He glanced across at her, cowering in the kitchen doorway, willing the carpet to swallow her. Witnessing his cowardice. How could any woman love or respect a man too weak to stand up to his wife? Jenni was destroying him and Lucy was part of the humiliation.

But the pain Jenni caused him concentrated his mind remarkably on his job. Lucy was a luxury he couldn't afford. He picked up his car keys.

'Oh, you can't even walk to the shop – no wonder you're so fat.'

She was still shouting as he closed the door.

He didn't drive to the nearest repository of ginger ale but to a large busy supermarket where he knew he'd have to queue behind families with trolleys of industrial packs of everything from pizzas to nappies. Buying time with a dozen small bottles of ginger ale. Even the wailing of ill-disciplined children was preferable to the screaming of his wife.

When he parked back in the driveway he glanced across the road. He could see Gary laughing, his nurses clowning with the hoist. Lucy, minutes ago holding him in her eyes with a gentleness that hurt, now holding mugs of tea. She couldn't have understood it was her tenderness that caused him more pain than Jenni's onslaughts. Shackleton saw her laughing too. Had she told Gary? Had they had a laugh about poor pussy-whipped Tom Shackleton? She looked so happy. He envied the warmth of the scene. He wanted to be in the picture as he'd wanted to be in Christmas cards when a child. To feel wrapped round with love. He envied Gary his wife and saw no irony in envying a man whose wife was all that was left of a life once as successful as his own.

Once Tom was out of the house Jenni calmed down. While she was changing for dinner she thought about Tom and his inability to take the initiative. It wasn't just the ginger ale, it was everything. She brushed her hair, getting angry again thinking about the way he coerced her by inaction, but then she looked in the mirror. She knew she looked extraordinarily beautiful. Everything was prepared for the evening ahead. Her table was perfect, her house a triumph. Gary had once described it as Yorkshire chic, recalling his own mother's fondness for reproduction grandeur and Franklin Mint objets d'art.

The final pleasure of the day so far was a phone call just now from a broadsheet editor asking her to do a personal in-depth of her husband. She put the tantrum and her dissatisfaction with Tom out of her mind. It was his own fault, he would insist in provoking her.

Occasionally she was tempted to examine why she attacked him, rather in the same way she examined her breasts once a month. She had allowed herself to look inwards once and saw a picture of her mother beating her father with clenched fists. He had just stood there. She never looked again.

When you were beautiful it wasn't necessary to be a nice person. The catechism of youthful indoctrination didn't apply to her. Nice people would inherit the earth, but only after the beautiful and powerful had finished with it.

She scrutinised her flawless face in the mirror. She was still thrilled and surprised by the extraordinary power of her looks. Sometimes she wondered if she should have married Tom so early. Maybe she should have waited, caught a bigger fish.

No. A bigger fish wouldn't have been hers to mould. She was sorry she had shouted at him. But she couldn't say it. Couldn't bring herself to admit she found it more and more difficult to control her outbursts.

'Anyway,' she repeated out loud, watching her lips in the mirror, 'it's his own fault.'

Seven-thirty. She must go downstairs. The Gnome would be here, and Lucy. Hopefully wearing something a little more inspiring than the shapeless tent she'd left in. Poor, dull Lucy. She smiled. She really was quite fond of Lucy – Gary's illness had brought out the best in her. Before, she'd suspected Lucy of being a bit competitive, pitting her quiet intelligence against Jenni's fiery beauty. But now? Lucy was just a sweet, slightly dumpy friend. No threat. She and Tom really must do something for them.

The doorbell rang.

Tom was approaching the front door, the small bottles of ginger ale now nestling by the Scotch.

Aware of the picture she made, Jenni posed halfway down the staircase. He opened the door. It was Lucy. Jenni relaxed and came to kiss air either side of Lucy's cheeks. This was Lucy the guest, not Lucy the staff.

Tom took her coat and Jenni was fulsome in her praise of Lucy's silk dress. Tom noticed how it moulded softly over her breasts and how rounded her buttocks were.

'Would you like a glass of champagne, Lucy?'

Would Lucy like a glass of champagne? The last real champagne she'd tasted, not Spanish Cava or New Zealand Fizz but real, French champagne, was after the 1997 Election. She and Gary had drunk to the new world, the new beginning. She had felt as though they were coming out into the sunshine after two decades in thick fog.

'Yes please, that would be lovely, Jenni. Thanks.'

She took the long-stemmed glass and sipped. The bubbles were tiny, expensive.

'Oh Jenni, what a treat.'

'You deserve it,' said Jenni, squeezing her arm. 'You're such an angel. And look at these flowers, Tom, aren't they super? Lucy did them.'

'Very nice,' said Tom, sharing with Lucy a look that gave her an orgasm of the stomach. She clenched her ribs and diaphragm and took another sip. The earlier scene seemed to have been edited out. This was calm water, no memory of the earlier weir.

'What's your other guest's name, Jenni? I don't think you told me.'

'Didn't I? It's Robert MacIntyre.'

Lucy was impressed. In the *Sunday Times* list of Britain's most powerful MacIntyre had been eighth. Jenni really had landed a prize.

'Tom, hand Lucy the crudités. The dip is gorgeous, do try it.'

As Lucy picked up a piece of celery her hand touched Shackleton's. She would have liked her nails to have been as long and polished red as Jenni's.

Tom thought how nice it was to see a woman's hand without blood-dripping talons.

They sat and chatted about nothing. Lucy remarked on Tom's jacket, very fine wool, very designer label. Expensive. He wore it over a fine silk shirt. The colour of the sea. Or chemical effluent.

At ten-past eight the doorbell rang. Jenni, who had dropped her public face while they sat and talked, immediately re-assumed her diamantine mask. She had been warm and funny, completely re-laxed. Enchanting company. Lucy thought if she were like that all the time Tom would never look at another woman.

Jenni went to the door leaving Lucy alone with Shackleton. Gathering her courage in the awkwardness that filled the pause, she touched his sleeve.

'Sorry about . . . what happened earlier,' was all she could think of to say.

He looked as if he'd been scalded.

'I'm used to it,' he said shortly.

Tom stood up as Jenni introduced the Gnome. Shackleton towered over him looking almost like a different species. Lucy stood too, a little awkward.

'Lovely to meet you,' she mumbled, looking down at the ugliest man she had ever seen.

Robbie looked back and saw a pleasant, unexciting face with a very pretty mouth. A mouth made to accommodate –

'Champagne, Robbie?' Jenni was beside him holding a glass.

'Splendid. Thank you. Sorry I'm late. The PM called me in at the last minute. Couldn't get away.'

They small talked their way through until eight-forty-five when the caterer indicated to Jenni that dinner was ready. Lucy had hardly said a word but had smiled and nodded from her cocoon of champagne confidence. She was nowhere near drunk but the bubbles had gone to the backs of her knees. Jenni unfolded elegantly from an armchair. Lucy just got up. As she did she leant forward slightly. Tom caught sight of her innocent cleavage as her dress gaped. Lucy saw his look and turned scarlet, not the *ingénue* blush of romantic novels but a blotchy beetroot, the way she used to look after hockey.

Jenni was already shepherding her Gnome into the dining room and didn't notice. She was close to him, her hand hovering half an inch from his back. Lucy walked in front of Tom. She could feel him behind her. She willed him to touch her. When she turned to smile up at him she saw he was putting coal on the unnecessary fire. She walked towards the dining room alone. MacIntyre looked back at her and she felt an extraordinary and luckily swiftly suppressed desire to cry. His look had not been pitying or sympathetic but simply understanding. He understood what it was like to be Lucy. And she recognised Robert MacIntyre. He walked away from Jenni as if she didn't exist.

'Lucy, I do beg your pardon, I thought Tom was bringing you through. Allow me.'

And he was next to her, escorting her to the table. Attentive, charming. He moved round the table, a balletic goblin seating Jenni and herself. As he pulled out her chair he looked into Lucy's eyes and again she was terribly moved. She saw such gentleness, such empathy there. She touched his hand in silent thanks. He didn't withdraw as Tom had done earlier but held her fingertips lightly. A tiny gesture.

Lucy had heard of MacIntyre's legendary charm and charisma and had dismissed them as the shallow weapons of the professional politician.

Now she saw how wrong she was.

If she wasn't already in the grip of obsession, she might have fallen in love.

The Gnome had seen the way this poor duckling in the ill-fitting dress looked at Shackleton. He'd read the situation and he'd seen his younger self in Lucy. He gave her a fleeting private smile. For a moment it was as if Lucy was looking at a great work of art. Then with a conspiratorial look, he turned his attention to his hostess.

Jenni's taste veered between the perfect and the appalling. Piles of arranged copies of *Hello!* magazine in the cloakroom, flower prints on the walls. Lladro ballerinas and antique clocks. Good rugs and hotel-style reproduction furniture. There was nothing in the public areas to show Shackleton lived there.

Her table was also contradictory. The glasses were elegant, large, expensive and would have been beautiful in their pure-lined simplicity had there not been a deep border of gold fancywork around the lip of each. The epergne, an old silver gilt confection of inverted dragons and cut glass, would have been understated perfection without the riot of tuber roses Jenni insisted on having spewing out from its crown.

As they sat down she realised it was too big for the table – they couldn't see each other. Without breaking her interest in the Gnome's conversation she swapped it for a small group of candles on the sideboard.

But her napkins and tablecloth were beyond reproach. The cloth was draped to the floor hiding their legs and feet in its embroidered folds.

The small talk was exceptionally small.

'Do you live in London, Robert?'

Lucy heard herself and couldn't believe she was asking such a banal question.

'I have a house and flat there but my home is in Gloucestershire,' said the Gnome, reaching for a slice of olive bread. Why couldn't people just put a bit of plain white bread on the table instead of all this ciabatta and grit-filled brown. 'My wife breeds llamas. Most weeks I'm only there at weekends, though I was there last night, funnily enough.'

'Do you have sheep?'

Jenni looked at Lucy. Why on earth was the stupid lump talking about sheep?

'No. And actually the llamas seem to have befriended the local fox.'

Jenni felt she was losing the thread.

'I'm sorry, Robert . . . sheep? Llamas? Foxes?'

The patronising look she gave Lucy indicated she knew he was trying to include her rather dim friend. If he had only disliked her for being Shackleton's smug wife he now despised her in her own right. He felt a flicker of desire. The desire to . . .

'Yes, Jenni. Lucy's spot on. Llamas are great guard dogs. You put one in with a flock of sheep and it's supposed to see off any predators.'

He'd inflicted just enough of a sting; he applied the balm.

'We could do with a couple in the Commons!'

They all laughed. The tiny frisson was gone.

'D'you know, it only took an hour to get here this evening.'

'That's marvellous . . .' responded Jenni brightly as the caterer discreetly served the main course.

'Thank you.' Jenni was gracious, magnanimous. 'I don't think we'll need you again this evening. You've been marvellous.'

She didn't add, see yourself out and there's a cheque on the mantelpiece but it was in her tone.

Lucy looked at the table. She knew she would spend most of tomorrow clearing up. Loading and unloading the dishwasher. Putting away. Almost immediately the door had closed Tom and Robert started talking politics and police.

'What do you think would be best for London when Ingram retires?'

Tom visibly relaxed. They were on his ground. Without pause he began to speak, a long, well-thought-out unhesitating answer. 'I think London is a unique case. I mean . . .' and he was off.

His hesitations were only for effect, the quietness of voice and sincere seriousness of the tone compelling. The Gnome was impressed. Not with the content of Shackleton's speech, which to his mind was woolly, but with his mesmeric delivery. He sensed in this man who was holding his eyes with a seductive intensity the same power he had himself. But this was more dangerous. He realised this man had no humour about himself. That this mind was narrowly confined within the discipline of his immediate world.

As the evening progressed it was clear there would be nothing in Tom Shackleton's life to distract him from his ambition. To be Commissioner of the Metropolitan Police. He didn't go to the theatre or opera, he had an unsophisticated taste in art and almost no knowledge of music. The Gnome was fascinated. He had never met anyone whose emotional landscape seemed so empty. In a way he envied him. MacIntyre could still be moved to tears by a sunset or a piece of Mozart.

'What are you reading at the moment?'

Lucy was startled. No one had addressed her for twenty minutes and even then it was to request the dill sauce.

'I'm . . . I'm just finishing *The Quantum Theory*.'

The Gnome was impressed.

'Really? I have to confess I've never actually got through it.'

'Neither have I before, but being at home so much . . . I . . .' She was losing confidence. 'I thought I should make the effort. I'm not sure I understand it all, though.'

Seeing her run out of confidence MacIntyre took over.

'I'm particularly taken with the idea of parallel time. One has found oneself there so many times.'

'Oh yes. Since my husband's been disabled . . .' Lucy paused. Maybe this wasn't the sort of thing to talk about at Jenni's dinner party. She glanced across at her hostess. Jenni's smile was encouraging but Lucy thought she saw ice in her eyes. 'Oh . . . well . . . nothing.'

She subsided but MacIntyre wasn't going to let her go.

'I think I know what you're saying, Lucy. Officially I'm disabled, you know.' They made the appropriate noises. 'Oh yes, achondroplasia is a disability. You'd be amazed how many jobs I wouldn't be allowed to do. Police officer, for instance. I could never be a chief constable, Tom – do you think that's a loss? However, parallel time . . . yes, as a cripple, or a spastic as I have often been called, though that is technically incorrect' – Jenni winced – 'you're put outside common time. Disability can put you in not just parallel time but a parallel universe.'

Although he spoke in measured terms with no hesitation, Lucy could sense what an effort it was for him. As it was for her to talk about a childhood long gone. But no one could see her childhood. The words bullies had thrown at her you could throw at anyone; the words that had followed MacIntyre were uniquely and unhappily his own.

'It's not easy, as I'm sure your husband has discovered. I'm sorry he's not here – I've no doubt he and I would have a great deal of common ground. And time.' He was aware of how uncomfortable Jenni was. And Tom? Difficult to tell but MacIntyre thought he was embarrassed. 'But look on the bright side – you can park on double yellow lines.'

Lucy laughed and her napkin slid to the carpet.

The Gnome bent and picked it up. As he handed it back he smiled his extraordinary smile and again captivated Lucy. She wished she could discuss the book further and talk about disability and illusion and . . .

He turned his attention to Tom.

'You ever managed to read it, Tom?'

Tom shook his head, suspicious this was a trap to catch dumb plod. But it wasn't, the Gnome was far too clever for such point-scoring.

'No. Port?'

'Just a small one.'

Jenni was watching the two men circle each other. Weigh each other up. No matter how well her husband did this week she knew he wasn't the intellectual equal of Geoffrey Carter. She had no doubt he'd read *Quantum Theory*. She felt a dagger of thoughts and started to straighten her cutlery. If she could adjust knives, forks, spoon, glasses, napkin without the intrusion of another thought, another stab of hatred towards Carter, everything would work out. No harm done. Jenni clenched her tiny hands, her forearms on the table. She was desperate for Tom to impress this man who had the power of life or death over his ambitions. Her ambitions. She dug her nails into her skin to push the thoughts away.

Robert MacIntyre knew why he was there and was giving no hint that the outcome was already written on a confidential memo in his inside pocket. The Chief Constable's wife wasn't going to get that for a plateful of Sainsbury's mixed vol-au-vents.

Having learned all he needed to about Shackleton's inner man, he skilfully turned the conversation to lighter things. Past experiences, embarrassing moments. By telling, very wittily, some tales of his early days in the Commons he allowed Shackleton to relax into reminiscence.

Now the Gnome was surprised. The serious, convincing policeman turned into a schoolboy. The encouragement of his audience and the wine and port liberated a very funny story-teller whose humour was quite earthy and occasionally risqué. And he had this extraordinary laugh, as if he was doing it from memory and it hadn't changed since puberty.

Lucy heard it and it made her more fond of him. More maternal. Jenni heard it and thought it sounded asinine. She also hated it when he told his crude stories. Especially the one about the Italian PC with the abnormally large member. The tag line always guaranteed a wave of pleasantly shocked laughter. Tales of Tom's beginnings in the canteen culture of the Met in South London. His well-rehearsed party turn.

Lucy was laughing out loud when she felt it. At first she thought it was an accident. Then it became more pressing. Shackleton had put his foot between her ankles. Still listening she turned her body slightly towards him under the pretext of attentiveness. With the help of the alcohol she found the courage to take his leg between her own. She squeezed hard and felt his response, a quick vibration reminiscent of the quick, light rhythm of his love-making. He continued to talk fluently.

The Gnome was delighted. He started to tell a story about one of his parliamentary colleagues that named names and revealed sexual predilections usually reserved for the more lurid pages of top-shelf magazines.

While Lucy held Tom Shackleton's thigh between her legs Robert MacIntyre had managed to rest the fingers of his left hand between the legs of Tom's wife. Hidden by the tablecloth they stroked and probed through the heavy silk of Jenni's designer trousers. With wine dulling her revulsion she squirmed appreciatively and crossed her legs lightly.

At eleven o'clock MacIntyre's driver had been waiting half an hour. But MacIntyre seemed in no hurry.

'So tell me about you, Lucy?'

'Well, I . . . there's nothing to say really. I clean a bit –'

She was astonished when Jenni interrupted.

'Lucy is an incredibly talented artist. She makes stained glass. I'm going to ask her to make us a window. Don't you think so, Tom?'

Tom nodded, smiling at Jenni, for all the world as if they'd discussed this idea.

Mrs Shackleton had surprised MacIntyre. He had her down as a twenty-four-carat bitch but now he suspected she was only gold-plated. Interesting . . . But he could see it would be easy to be magnanimous towards Lucy; she was lead, poor woman, striving to keep up with the glittering Shackletons.

An intriguing evening.

Sometime before midnight the Gnome said he really must go and stood up from the table. Jenni had prepared for them to move into the sitting room but the conversation had been too fluid to interrupt.

Jenni, rising, was pleased. It had been a success.

'Goodnight, Lucy.' MacIntyre took her hand. 'Here's my card – I wonder if you'd give my secretary a ring, I'm sure my wife would love to commission a piece from you.'

'But I don't really do anything any more.' Lucy took refuge in inadequacy.

He pulled her down towards him and whispered, 'Don't let yourself disappear, Lucy.'

At midnight the front door opened and the Home Secretary-in-waiting could be seen kissing his hostess goodnight. In the beam of the security light the driver saw him squeeze her breast. His host, standing the other side, didn't.

'Goodnight, Tom, and thanks again for this evening. Jenni? Terrific. And I'll see you tomorrow.'

She looked surprised.

'We've got a bit of unfinished business.'

Her mind was still a blank. The wine.

'The interview.'

It was as if her brain had stalled and now revved into motion again.

'Of course, Robbie. I'm so sorry. What time?'

'Oh, as early as you like, at my office.'

The office, the House of Commons. My office, the flat off Russell Square.

'I'm sure I've got plenty more to tell you,' he said, getting into the car.

'I'm sure you have,' replied Jenni, blowing him a kiss.

She'd get what she wanted tomorrow. And he knew he would too.

When Tom and Jenni went back into the house Lucy was starting to clear up.

'Leave that, Lucy, you can do it tomorrow. Have another drink. Look, there's some champagne left.'

'No thanks, Jenni. I'd better go home. See Gary's all right. Thank you so much for tonight.'

'I'll see you across.'

Tom walked to the front door abruptly and opened it, standing on the step.

Lucy was confused and began to say her no it's all rights when Jenni whispered to her, 'He wants to go out so he can let off. You know . . . he always does it. Dreadful stink. I won't allow it in the house.'

'Oh . . . right.'

Jenni laughed and gave Shackleton a sort of slap on the arm, rather as one would a smelly but loved old dog.

Lucy didn't know what else to say. She picked up her coat, air-kissed Jenni and went.

Tom walked beside her with four feet of electric air between them: 'I never thought flatulence would come in handy,' he said.

Lucy giggled.

'Back door or front?'

Lucy looked at him.

'Oh, back, I think.'

To get there they had to walk down a narrow alleyway lined with high bushes. It was lit by a single old-fashioned lamp-post. The wall of the next house was blind; no windows overlooked them. Now they were unobserved, both felt shy. He walked with his hands behind his back. They walked as slowly as possible without stopping.

Lucy wished she had put some breath-fresheners in her bag. Her fingers searched through the debris in her pockets for an old mint. They came into contact with a tube of lip-conditioner, guaranteed to soften and add shine, but she could see no way of applying it without drawing attention to the action. Besides, if he did kiss her she didn't think he'd appreciate being smothered in strawberry-flavoured Vaseline. She licked her lips. A bit dry. She licked them again. The conversation between them had ground to a halt. They were now awkward with each other.

'Are your hands all right now, Tom?'

It was the only thing Lucy could think of to say that didn't include: Tom, please kiss me, take off all my clothes and do all those things I've been thinking about since . . .

'Yes. Thank you.'

'Smell the jasmine. It's lovely, isn't it?'

Lucy could hear herself and wished she could just shut up and be silent and mysterious. Make him speak.

Tom, on the other hand, was wishing he could speak. He started to tell her about the policing strategy he intended to implement in the deprived estates in his county. He knew Jenni would say, 'Do stop droning on, Tom – Lucy doesn't want to hear all that.'

But he couldn't stop himself. He didn't know what else to say. He wanted to be alone with this woman but not in this situation. Not in any situation that required talk. He looked at her to see if she'd glazed over with boredom. It was a look that haunted him from his adolescence.

But she was gazing up at him as if he was speaking poetry. She looked soft and defenceless. She wasn't threatening or judgemental. He stopped. She stopped, still looking at him trustingly, her mouth a little open.

'I'm sorry about . . . what happened.'

Lucy was confused. He should have kissed her by now.

'Sorry?'

'In the study . . . I'm sorry. It was . . . a mistake.'

Lucy couldn't believe what she was hearing. The best, most exhilarating five minutes of her recent life dismissed as a mistake?

'I didn't think it was a mistake.'

She sounded reasonable, as if she was talking about having the wrong newspaper delivered. She didn't want to sound reasonable, she wanted to turn into some Mediterranean harpy, screaming at him that he couldn't dismiss her as a mistake.

'I'm very fond of you.'

She offered him the words like a child offering a bunch of wilting daisies.

'Me too.'

Me too? What did that mean? Me too? Tom felt a fool. He winced, ready for the verbal onslaught. But there wasn't one. Lucy was still looking up at him as if he was Gabriel come with glad tidings. Now he was completely at sea. He was prepared for the sharp clever rebuke but not for this adoration. Lucy hadn't known what he meant by me too either but she was in a precious moment, not one for semantics.

'I'd better go.' Tom said it, but didn't move.

'Yes, Jenni will be wondering where you are.'

'No. I don't think so.'

There was a pause. It was the moment for him to kiss her, it was the violins moment when 'The End' comes up in a heart on the screen.

'Goodnight then,' Lucy said.

She looked away, searching in her bag for her key.

Had he been dismissed? He didn't know what to do. He just stood there, confused.

'Yes. Goodnight.'

Lucy found her key but kept her eyes down because they were full of tears.

'Are you all right?'

Lucy couldn't reply. She was now rooting in her bag for a tissue that hadn't been reduced to a rock-like ball by overuse. Her nose was running now and she daren't look up at him. She found the remains of a piece of kitchen roll and blew her nose.

'Fine. I'm fine.'

She looked up again, this time trying to smile through a mask of dimpled floral paper. Her eye make-up was smudged and wet. She looked about twelve. She put away the damp rag of paper.

'It's just . . . it wasn't a mistake to me. I . . . wanted it . . . to happen.'

And then he kissed her. He kissed her not because he was over-come with desire but because he didn't know what else to do. It was a gentle kiss, careful. The first kiss since finding they shared affection. He loved the cosiness of her, the softness. The way she let him be in control. With Jenni he was clumsy. He had always felt she marked him out of ten and he never got past five. The kiss came to an end.

'I'd like to try it again. What happened. In the study.'

Lucy spoke with her face to his chest, his arms round her. She couldn't look up at him in case he said no with that gently implacable tone she'd heard him use before. The tone that implied regret but no possibility of change.

'Me too.' Me too again. 'Yes . . . Lucy, I'm sorry. I've got to go. But I have to see you again. I don't know how. But . . .'

He'd run out of words. She saw him struggling, unsure.

'It's all right. I understand.'

They stood close together for another couple of minutes. He stroked her hair and she held him with her arms around his waist, her hands flat on his back absorbing his warmth.

'Right.' He pulled away from her. 'Goodnight. Take care.'

'Take care . . . Tom.'

He turned away and walked quickly back to the road. She watched him go, happier than she'd ever been in her life.

Tom didn't stop until he got to the gates of his house. He wasn't thinking about Lucy. The gentle meandering daydreams of Lucy he'd been enjoying while he stood with her had been brutally replaced. Instead of her trusting gaze he was seeing the sewn-up eyes of the

African woman. He opened his eyes but he could still see them. The fear he'd felt sitting with the three . . . what? What were they? The three weird council tenants?

He saw the lights were off in the house. Jenni would have gone to bed. It took her an hour to take off her make-up and apply all the gels and creams that kept her so perfect. He was never welcome while she completed this ritual. He wanted to talk. But didn't know how. He knew he could talk to Lucy but sex was in the way now. He couldn't go back and ask for a cup of coffee.

And Jenni never really listened. He hadn't told her the details of his encounter with the women though he'd wanted to. His memory of it was patchy, like trying to recall a dream. He could see the sewn-up eyes again. He tried to look away but they were inside his own eyes, projected on to his lids when he closed them. Fear became anger as he opened the garage and got into the four-wheel drive. The spare keys were in their hiding place. He started it and drove, a little too fast, to the outskirts of the Flamborough Estate.

He parked by the pub and turned off the lights. At first he thought the women weren't there. Then he saw them. This time there were no candles, no deckchairs. The door was closed. He didn't know why he was there and was about to re-start the car when the door opened and the fat one stood there. She was lit from behind and he couldn't see her face, but he heard her call.

'Thomas. Welcome back. Come in, come in. We been expectin' you.'

Why didn't he just pretend he didn't hear? Why didn't he go home? He opened the car door and went over. She was beaming, massively welcoming.

'Come in! Come in!'

He went into the flat, unable to stop himself. The hall was lit by a pink bulb hanging in the centre of a pink, tasselled shade. The walls were covered in calendars. Tom could see some with forties blondes, on tiptoe, smiling over bikinied shoulders, and others showing ladies in bustles. Some of flowers and several of dewy-eyed kittens. One, even older than the others, declared itself 'A present from Norway'. But time had faded the year, making it look like 1400 and something.

He was bundled into the front room before he could look closer.

The other two women were sitting, either side of the coal-effect electric fire. The two bars were on, below them the black coal moulded and painted into a plastic orange cover, behind which glowed a 40-watt bulb over which a small propeller turned, supposedly giving the impression of a glowing, living fire. The flickering light moved across the two black faces, giving them expression where there was none.

'See, Thomas has come back to visit us. Sit down, Thomas. Sit.'

The chairs either side of the fire were elaborate armchairs of red-and-gold-fringed velvet. On the backs and arms were antimacassars of long-necked African heads. Tom sat on the matching settee. All around the room there were cheap souvenirs from all over the world. 'A present from Kampala', 'Greetings from Beijing', and 'Hello from Dublin'. As his eyes got used to the gloom he saw the sewn-up eyes watching him. Again the fear. He looked away. It was oppressively hot. The thin one offered him a glass of sarsaparilla. He didn't want to but he took it.

'So what is it you want, Thomas?'

He felt silly.

'I don't know. I don't know why I'm here.'

'Look into the fire, Thomas. Look . . .'

He looked and saw the propeller move over the bulb. Nothing more.

'Look, I don't believe in all this fortune telling.'

He stopped. In the fire he saw himself in uniform. But it wasn't his force's insignia on the hat or buttons. It was London's. He saw his triumph, felt the satisfaction, saw the recognition, the admiration in people's eyes. He felt happiness. It was better than anything he'd felt before.

'Is that it, Thomas? Will you be content with that?'

The blind shell eyes turned to him again. The hollow sockets of the thin one.

'What else is there? It's the top job.'

'But, Thomas, if it wasn't, would you still be content?'

'I don't understand. What do you mean?'

'Careful what you wish for, Thomas. You're not drinking your sarsaparilla.'

Shackleton shook his head; he thought there may be some drug in it.

The fat one shrugged, still smiling. She squatted down on a fancy camel saddle that had been home to a pile of *Time* magazines and copies of *National Geographic*. The faces of powerful men on the covers of the former and the natural disasters featured in the latter lay exposed on the red fake-fur rug.

'Who are you? You're like . . .'

The fat one exploded with laughter, slapping his thigh in her enjoyment.

'We're like nothing on this earth. Are we, ladies? Nothing on this earth.'

The three of them were now screeching with laughter. The noise seemed to push against him, to stop him from thinking. It got into his mouth and prevented him speaking. He wanted to leave but couldn't get up.

'How long have you been here?' He could check them out on the electoral register, police computer, immigration . . .

'Lord . . . how long? Let's see now, well, I tell you this, we here not just for an age but for all time. Y'understand?'

He didn't.

She put her hand on his thigh again.

'Are you a good man, Thomas? A clean man?'

Shackleton nodded, a little boy again.

'You believe that? Good. Why you so mean then?'

'I . . . I'm not mean.'

As he spoke he heard his mother's voice. Her litany of his faults, her dislike of her awkward ugly little boy.

The great black hand tightened on his leg.

'Put the past down, Thomas. Let it go.'

'I can't. It makes me what I am.'

'Yes, Thomas. It makes you a bear on a chain. Back and forth, back and forth, over and over the same patch of earth. You coming to a cross-road, child. The place they buried suicides, you know. You will have to choose. You, Thomas, no one else. Come and see us again, Thomas. We're always here. But listen to me.' She leaned close to him. There was no laughter in her now. 'Examine your life.'

Tom wanted to ask what she meant. But he knew. His protection was always to think in the concrete. The abstract with its dangerous cousin imagination were to be avoided. If he looked for his soul he found an aerial view of inland waterways. The central canal strong-flowing and clear. But on the lesser canals the locks were rusted, the water stagnant. And further still from that main highway were great pools of stagnant weed-choked water. Foul and opaque through decades of neglect. And that was Tom Shackleton's inner life.

'Make the water flow, Thomas.' She grasped his arm hard. She was strong enough to hurt him. Her powerful fingers dug into the muscle.

He winced.

'And, listen to me. You can have everything you want but take care of the wood. Not the knives or bullets, Thomas, it's the stake in your heart will bring you low. Keep away from the wood.'

When he got home the street was quiet. It was 4 a.m. There was no sign of drama. He couldn't sleep and so sat working on his papers until six when he stood under the shower, the radio turned up loud, closing the door on the night. He hadn't thought of Lucy until the record 'Bright Eyes' was used to trail a news item about rabbits. That's what she was, a small, trusting rabbit. He was comforted thinking about her.

Lucy had waited until Tom was out of sight before she let herself in. She couldn't stop little squeaks erupting like bubbles. She wanted to tell Gary all about it. Wanted to share with him the elation she felt. She did a little conga with herself while she found the bottle of Christmas brandy and poured herself a glass.

She couldn't go to bed. Not yet. She was too excited. She wanted to live and re-live every second with Tom. She could taste him, smell him, feel his arms round her. Quietly she opened the door of Gary's room.

At first she thought he was snoring, then she realised there was something odd about his breathing. As he took each breath he was trying to suppress a cough, then swallowing. Then he'd get a snatch of breath but the back of his throat would close and he was left with his ribcage pumping up and down trying to pull in the air. She turned on the light.

Gary was on the floor amidst the Scrabble set, his pills and the pile of sandwiches she had left for him. His catheter had come away and the bag of urine was empty, its contents over Gary and the carpet. Lucy shouted his name. She crouched beside him and tried to wake him. His lips were blue. By shaking him gently she released the clamp in his throat and he took a long juddering breath.

She picked up the phone, also on the floor, and dialled for an ambulance. Then she sat holding him, trying to ease his breathing and crying at the thought of his lonely suffering. Why hadn't he called her? Because he hadn't wanted to spoil her evening. The thought of him being so thoughtful upset her even more. While she was standing outside the back door kissing someone else's husband, her own was lying on the floor, helpless.

By the time the ambulance arrived she had bargained with God that she'd never see Tom again if Gary could recover. It was all her fault. She should have stayed at home. Her self-flagellation was total. When they arrived at the hospital she knew she didn't really want Tom. It was just an infatuation. A desire for a thrill to relieve the boredom of her life. Looking at Gary's face, covered in an oxygen mask, she swore she'd never want excitement again. At that moment she would have given anything to be playing Monopoly with Gary on a wet February afternoon.

There was no bed for him at the hospital and none of the nursing staff seemed to have experience of multiple sclerosis. Lucy kept telling them he would need a special bed, a ripple bed. One that would prevent sores, keep the blood moving, avoid the necessity of manhandling him so the risk of spasm was minimised. She was smiled at and reassured, but nothing was done. Luckily he was still unconscious and his body couldn't cause him any pain.

The doctor who examined him said it was pneumonia and that he was 'very poorly'. Lucy hated that expression. 'Your cat's very poorly,' 'That geranium looks very poorly,' 'Your husband's very poorly.' But it wasn't in her to be rude, to say something sharp to the condescending child with a shiny new stethoscope in his pocket. All she could feel was misery and regret.

She sat by the trolley on which Gary lay hooked up to tubes, holding his hand and loving him. Not that silly girly feeling she had for Tom but a deep ache, a knowledge that without Gary her life wouldn't be worth continuing. She knew she could never have Tom and even if she could he wouldn't be half the man Gary was. But had Gary been this man before the illness? Probably not. He'd never had to call upon his better self while out there competing, running, striving. Gary was what was left of the man when job and position were taken away.

And if Tom had got MS and Gary had got his dream of becoming an MP? What would be left of Tom? Lucy tried to change her thoughts. Find some that didn't automatically revert to Tom Shackleton. But she was in the grip of a disease and could no more talk her way out of it than out of the flu. She would just have to wait until it passed and hope that, like shingles, it didn't keep coming back.

She'd made her decision. When Gary recovered they would move away – but if Tom got the Met? – they'd move away, never mind Tom! she shouted at her mind. Shut up about bloody Tom. Gary and I will move right away, to Cornwall maybe. The weather's good there. Or Sussex – Gary had always loved Brighton. Yes. That's what they'd do.

'We've found a bed for Gary.' The tired-looking nurse was smiling her professional smile. 'It's about sixty miles away, in Kent. We're just waiting for an ambulance to take him.'

Lucy was confused. She didn't know what to do. If she went with him, she'd have no clothes, no money. But if she left him and he woke up to find her not there. She wanted help but didn't know what help she was asking for.

She had some change in her pocket and seeing the phone down the corridor she loosed her hand from Gary's and followed the coloured lines on the floor towards it. Red for X-ray, Blue for Wards, Yellow for Outpatients. She pushed in the numbers. Five rings and Tom answered. It was eight o'clock.

'Tom?'

'Who's this?'

'Lucy.'

He gave a nervous little laugh.

'Good morning – I'm afraid you've just missed Jenni, she's gone to London.'

'Oh. Right.'

Lucy could hear none of the intimacy of last night in his voice.

'It's just that Gary's been taken ill. Pneumonia. He's in hospital here but there are no beds and they're transferring him to Kent and I've got no clothes or money and I don't want to leave him.'

There was a tiny pause. Lucy knew he didn't want to be involved. That this was irritating.

'I'm sorry, Tom, I suppose you're just leaving for work.'

'Yes, I've got a conference in Birmingham.'

'If you could just . . .' Lucy didn't know where she found the strength to coerce him. 'Get my front door key from the hook in your kitchen and bring my handbag. It's on the fridge. I forgot it.'

She knew asking for clothes would be pushing him too far. She could already feel his reluctance.

'I'm sorry to bother you.'

'Oh, it's no bother. I'll see to it straight away. I only hope Gary will be all right. Anything else?'

Yes, Tom, despite all the promises I've made to God, Gary and myself in the last seven hours, I still want you and I'd like you to come here now and just take me away from all this illness and smell.

'No. Just my handbag. Thanks, Tom.'

After she had given him the details of the hospital he rang off with a brief goodbye and a softly spoken 'Take care.'

She went back to Gary. Well, at least she'd see Tom, if only for a minute. She went to the Ladies quickly. She looked a mess. She splashed her face with water and dried it on paper towels. Immediately the skin felt tight and shiny. She wished she had some moisturiser. A comb. She sighed. What was the point? She went back to Gary who was moaning quietly but still unconscious. Every twenty minutes a nurse checked his vital signs. His blood pressure was low; Lucy told them that was normal for Gary. His temperature though was high.

Lucy saw a policeman come in. One of the many that had passed through Accident and Emergency since she'd been sitting there. But this one was carrying her handbag. She called him over. He gave her the bag and she signed a chitty for it. He seemed a pleasant young man and no, he'd never met the Chief Constable. Lucy couldn't believe Tom hadn't come himself. She was angry and deeply hurt. But within a few minutes she was making excuses for him.

And Jenni would come home to the pile of unwashed dishes and glasses. Her dining room a litter of crumbs and candle wax. Lucy left an apologetic message on Jenni's answer machine. The early years had left their mark; she was still more frightened of losing friends by causing offence than she was fearful of being regarded as a doormat.

The ambulance was ready. Gary was loaded gently into it and Lucy took her place beside him.

*　　*　　*

While Lucy was worrying about the washing up, Jenni was hearing a favourable future told by her hairdresser's medium.

She had arrived at the modern brick-built cottage in a cul-de-sac of similar homes near Tower Bridge a little early. The extraordinary creature who opened the door begged her indulgence while she watched the end of *Star Trek* on Satellite.

Jenni was seated in the 'reading' room which doubled as sitting room. The small television kept the medium rapt while Jenni stared around in astonishment. Heavy curtains framed the double-glazed patio doors leading to a small square of green complete with umbrella-shaped clothes-dryer. The rest of the room was a riot of icons. Virgin Marys jostled with voodoo figures and sinister-looking carvings. Buddhas and Hindu gods were hung with rosaries, and pentagrams fought for space with crosses. The furniture was draped with cheap Indian shawls, and joss sticks filled the air with the smell of seventies student parties.

Star Trek came to an end and the medium, a hefty Danish woman with long blonde hair parted centrally in the manner of a semi-professional folk singer, made camomile tea and sat down to commence the reading. She talked non-stop for an hour saying all the things Jenni wanted to hear. She even summoned up a message from the other side that Jenni identified as coming from her grandmother. As Jenny handed over her £25 at the end of the session she clasped the Viking's hand.

'And my husband will get the . . . promotion?'

'Oh, yes. I'm sure of it. And you'll both be very happy. You wait, you'll be coming back to me in six months saying, "Ailse, everything you told me was right. Everything."'

If Jenni had analysed what she had been told she would have recognised it all as confirmation of what she'd said herself. But she didn't analyse it. She wanted to believe. She wanted to go to her meeting with the Gnome bolstered by magic.

She drove to Russell Square and parked in a fearsomely expensive car-park under a hotel then walked the short distance to the Gnome's flat. It was a beautiful day and London was full of brainless tourists in ghastly clothes drifting along in herds, like wildebeest. Jenni wished the predation that beset the wildebeest on the plains could be visited on these ugly specimens of humanity. She hit an impenetrable wall of French schoolchildren. They were open-mouthed with boredom and refused to part to allow people to walk on the pavement. Jenni did not walk in the gutter for any spotty adolescent.

'Excuse me.'

No reaction.

'Excuse me.'

A little louder, a little less reaction. She smiled and pulled a couple of designer-jacketed sleeves.

'*Excusez-moi. Parlez-vous anglais?*'

There was a surly chorus of *Ouis* and yeses.

Jenni beamed at them and said in the loud tones of English people talking to foreigners, 'Then get out of my fucking way. *Now*.'

As if Moses had raised his rod the sea of horrified young faces parted and Jenni proceeded, triumphant, to the Gnome's block.

She pushed the buzzer and was answered by his voice and another buzz to signal the opening of the door. She went in, paused to repair her immaculate make-up, and got into the lift. He met her as the doors opened and immediately had his hand on her. She felt like a whore who had been ordered like a pizza. She went into the flat and was just preparing to comment on its decor, the view, the weather, when he spun her round and rammed his snake-like tongue into her mouth. There was no trace of Robbie MacIntyre. This was The Gnome.

As quickly as was polite she pulled back.

'Robbie, well, good morning.'

He grunted and started to undress her. It was impossible to recognise the urbane and charming dinner guest of the night before. His strange ugly beautiful face was contorted by determined lust which transformed it into a vicious blood-engorged mask. She wanted to scream. His sweaty hands were leaving marks on the cream silk of her blouse. He had dropped her linen jacket on the floor. Didn't he know how badly linen creased?

'Robbie. Wait. Just a minute.'

He was annoyed.

'Why? I have got something you want and you've got something I want.'

She tried coquetry.

'What have you got for me, Robbie?'

'Don't be a silly bitch, it doesn't suit you. Whatever I have to give you, I can withhold just as easily. There's no such thing as a free lunch, Jenni, you know that.'

Jenni had never been spoken to like this and she considered walking out. A woman less accustomed to her own way with men would have seen the danger signs. But no man had ever dared go further than Jenni allowed; rape and assault were what happened to other women. Not to her. The medium had said she'd get what she wanted but she hadn't asked how. She couldn't afford to walk. She smiled at him from under her eyelashes, a look guaranteed to disarm. He didn't see it. He was pulling at the blouse again. He pushed it up like a doctor preparing to examine her chest. Then he grabbed her bra and pushed that up too so her breasts hung below a tyre of clothing.

He grabbed them.

'Nice tits.'

And then he began biting and sucking at them. Jenni felt such revulsion she had to hold her breath. It was like being eaten alive. At the same time he heaved up her skirt and dragged her knickers and tights down to mid-thigh.

'Tights. Don't like tights. Like stockings. Go in the bathroom and put some on. In the drawer.'

He said it all while chewing on her nipples. Humiliated but glad to be out of pain she went to the door he indicated, pulling up her knickers and pulling down her bra. She thought he'd give her a moment alone, a moment to find the control of the situation, to turn him back into Dr Jekyll, but she was wrong.

'Still like me, Mrs Chief Constable?'

She swallowed. 'Of course, why not? These?' she held up a pair of black stockings and suspender belt.

'They'll do.'

He watched her change in silence.

'Take it all off except the stockings.'

She could see herself in the huge mirror. It covered one wall. She saw him sit in an oriental-style chair and watch her. He was dribbling with anticipation. Inhuman. She stood in front of him.

'Put your shoes back on.'

She obeyed. As she straightened up he flung himself on to his knees and buried his face between her legs. She tried to clench them but he prised her thighs apart and continued on her clitoris what he had begun on her breasts. His abnormal tongue searched further and deeper. She was disgusted with herself when she felt a twinge of pleasure.

It passed quickly when he bit her, hard. She yelped. She had to get out – nothing could be worth this. He stood up and grasped her nipples between his thumbs and forefingers. He pulled so hard her pretty breasts looked like empty bags of skin.

'Do you want your husband to be Commissioner or do you want Geoffrey Carter to be Commissioner? It's up to you.'

'How do I know I can trust you? That you won't give it to him anyway.'

'Because I give you my word. You walk out of here and your husband will get that job over my dead body.'

She looked at him as if that were an option.

'Your word?'

'My word.'

She let the air out of her lungs and gave in. As he continued to treat her body like a plate of junk food she found a sort of detachment. She watched him in the mirror and was fascinated by his absorption. He had no desire for her to react. She just stood there. But she could feel he had no erection. She moved her fingers to check that she was right. He pushed her hand away from him as if she was interrupting.

'Get in the bath.'

She didn't hear him: his voice was muffled by her flesh.

'What?'

'Get in the bath. On your hands and knees.'

She did what he said. She was looking down the plughole. The taps were big, Victorian originals. The bath was cold cast iron. And uncomfortable. Hard white enamel.

She jumped when she felt the warm water on her back. Then she smelt it. The sharp acid smell of male urine. It cascaded over her back and hair. It went on and on and on. A form of shock set in. She couldn't think or feel, she just endured. The shower finally stopped. Silence. She didn't dare move. She closed her eyes. Her knees were hurting. She wondered if Lucy had put the glasses on the right setting in the dishwasher. Then she looked round.

Now he had his erection. Because he was so short it was waving on a level with her eyes. It was enormous, shades of red and purple, utterly repulsive. She knew she would be sick if he wanted to put it in her mouth. But he didn't, he wanted her in the bedroom. Stinking and wet she walked ahead of him. He had taken off his trousers but still had on his shirt and socks. He was encouraging himself with his hands as he followed her.

'Lie down.'

She lay down.

'Turn over.'

The words formed themselves quite clearly in her mind: No. Oh no, please. Not that.

She had once had an internal examination carried out by an Egyptian junior registrar. She had had to lodge a complaint after he caused rectal bleeding. But this was worse pain than she even remembered from childbirth. She knew that pain was worse. But the utter degradation that accompanied this made it the final pit of hell.

She tried to scream and found she couldn't breathe through the pillow her face was now pressed into by his weight. He struggled and pushed and thrust as if he was trying to win a race. Still ramming into her he pushed his long-nailed fingers into her vagina. He rubbed them hard against his penis through the thin skin. Then with a rictus of loud ecstasy he came deep inside her, smashing against her buttocks. She had to brace her hands against the headboard to stop her head smashing into it. With a final grunt he flopped on to her back, murmuring, 'Good fuck, Jenni. Better next time, eh?'

And then he was asleep. Still inside her though she had collapsed on to the bed now with no pretence of enjoyment. Detached from the hideous reality, she unloaded him. She didn't look back at his repulsive body sprawled, snoring, across the bed as she ran into the bathroom. Twenty minutes later she was still standing under the shower and the blood still ran red in the water.

Her hands shook as she dressed and she found she had to sit down to do up the buttons of her blouse. The mirror that had witnessed her degradation showed her a composed and beautiful woman with slightly flushed cheeks. There was no mark on her face to show what had happened to her. But the tearing pain below was more eloquent than a broken nose or black eye.

Jenni went back into the bedroom determined to be controlled, cool with him. As if he had done nothing she had not experienced before. He was lying against the piled-up pillows that were marked with her lipstick, smoking a cigar. His face was once again his own,

129

no longer inhabited by evil. There was even a sweetness in his expression, a gentleness. He was in a fine mood.

'Always have a cigar after a good meal.'

'I've got to go, Robbie. I'm sorry.'

'Aren't you forgetting something, Jenni?'

A kiss goodbye? An affectionate hug perhaps? Jenni looked blank. She couldn't go nearer to him.

He put his abnormally long hand under the pillows.

'This. You could have read it if you hadn't been enjoying yourself so much.'

He handed her a piece of paper:

Memo: Confidential. Re the appointment of next Commissioner of the Metropolitan Police. It is felt that Thomas Shackleton QPM, LLB . . .

Jenni looked at it but couldn't read any more. Her face had rested on this during her ultimate humiliation. This was her payment. This was what she wanted. She should be triumphant. She should be as satisfied as the repellent Gnome scratching his balls on the bed. She smiled a ghost of a smile.

'Thank you, Robbie. I'll see myself out.'

'Yes, Jenni. We must do it again some time, eh?'

He winked at her. He waited until he heard the front door open before he phoned his wife.

Waiting for her to answer he rubbed himself thoughtfully, considering the blood on his penis, and felt disgust. It was as much a part of the experience as the uncontrollable hunger that consumed him as soon as one of these ambitious women decided sex with him was a legitimate route to success.

He felt disgust because he couldn't control himself, not because of what he did. He had always excused himself because he screwed women who were willing. Women who asked for it. Who deserved it. No, his disgust was at his desire being greater than his rational self. For being out of control.

He wife answered.

'Yes, Lizie, I think I will come home tonight. I always sleep better in my own bed . . . yes, see you about eight or nine. Last night? Oh it was fine. The hostess is a bit tight-arsed but I managed to loosen her up. Yes . . . I've got some paperwork but, yes, let's have a quiet night, and how about fish and chips, eh? Pretend we're young and poor again, shall we? . . . I love you too, Lizie. But God only knows why you love me. Bye.'

The phone call hadn't stopped his train of thought. He remembered seeing a young woman walking ahead of him one day and the overwhelming urge he had for her. Long slim legs, skirt a little too tight, riding up a little at every step. Great arse. Round and high. Small waist. Confident. Too confident with her lap-top briefcase and telephone earpiece. He remembered the urge he'd had to grab a handful of her hair and force her to her knees. To see her lipsticked mouth encompassing him. To watch her choke and cry . . .

Then, feeling him too close, she'd turned and said, 'Hello, Daddy, what are you doing here?'

He'd convinced himself all fathers had a moment when they saw their daughters as women and were disturbed at the desire they felt. To realise you were stirred by the sight of their breasts, the closeness of their bodies. But what MacIntyre had felt wasn't fleeting. He had lingered over the thoughts of what he wanted to do to her. But, he'd consoled himself, he only did it to a certain sort of woman. There had been nowhere for him to hide when he realised his little girl was now exactly that sort of woman. He was now, when not in the grip of it, fearful of his appetite for the extreme.

But he hadn't been extreme with Jenni. Extreme had once cost him a great deal of money and almost his career but in those days the police had little patience with women who cried rape and certainly none with women who were pragmatic enough to take a couple of thousand pounds to keep quiet.

He turned on the CD player and Beethoven engulfed him. Standing naked at the huge window he looked down on Bloomsbury, then further afield towards the river, St Paul's and the flashing beacon of Canary Wharf in the distance.

He longed for the comfort of the confessional but knew that would be self-indulgence. If he really wanted redemption it would be harder than three Hail Marys and a Glory Be.

Tom Shackleton would never be overcome with desire, with the need for degradation and bestiality. But neither would he stand naked consumed with the beauty of great music, moved by the fragility of the London skyline. His was a soul on Prozac.

Lucky man, thought MacIntyre.

When Lucy got home it was dark. Gary had slept all day but he was no better; in fact she had sensed from the nurse's attitude he was worse. She was still wearing her little silk dress, which hung like a rag now. She was exhausted and felt as if she hadn't washed for a week. She was too tired to eat or go upstairs for a shower.

The house was exactly as it had been when the ambulance arrived. No reason why it wouldn't be but she felt as if there should be a difference. She was different but the evidence of Gary's crisis was unchanged, still reproaching her neglect. She sat on the edge of his bed. The room felt cold. There was nothing so bleak as the deserted equipment of disability. The empty wheelchair, the ridiculous hoist, the cumbersome bed with its primitive press-button controls.

Ten o'clock. Lucy decided to have a few hours' sleep, then drive back to Kent. Take some clothes. Then she saw Jenni.

She was standing staring out of the window towards Lucy. Lucy waved. There was no response. Maybe she was angry because Lucy hadn't cleared up. Lucy reached for the phone. It was ringing, ringing but Jenni didn't move. Jason answered.

'Jason, I'm sorry to bother you. Can I speak to Jenni?'

Jason sounded awkward, reluctant.

'Um . . . yeah . . . I'll see if I can find her.'

It sounded as if he had put his hand over the mouthpiece. Lucy waited. He must be in his room. She sat watching Jenni.

'Sorry, Lucy. She's not about. Maybe she's gone to bed. I . . . don't disturb her when her door is closed.'

'Thanks, Jason. Bye.'

Jenni hadn't moved.

Jenni had been too busy after leaving MacIntyre's to think. She didn't want to think, to re-live what had happened. By six o'clock she thought she was all right, she'd go home and take off these clothes. She would never wear them again. She would have a bath, wash that filthy little man away. She got home and felt quite good, confident. Nobody would ever know about it. It was as if it had never happened and although it was a high price to pay it was worth it. That memo was worth it.

She walked up the stairs to the bathroom almost happy. Unbuttoning her blouse as she went, she opened the bathroom door. She saw the lavatory bowl, the bidet, the shower, the mirror.

The bath.

Her hand was over her mouth but it couldn't smother the sound that forced its way out of her. Never in her strictly controlled life had she sobbed uncontrollably but now she slumped against the bathroom wall and screeched. The noise she made was so foreign to her it seemed to be coming from someone else.

She slid down the wall until she was a crumpled heap on the floor. She threw her head back trying to shake off the images that her mind was ruthlessly replaying. She banged her head. The pain seemed to help. She banged it again. And again. And again, against the cold tiles. The noise and the pain filled her head and blocked out the Gnome's leering face and the searing smell of urine. Screaming now she started to rip her clothes away from her body. She stood and clawed her bloody knickers off.

The sight of the dried browning stains made her freeze. This wasn't a scene from a movie. Screaming and crying wouldn't clean her. Now completely controlled she dropped the remains of bloody lace into the bath and walked naked into the bedroom. She started searching the drawers for matches. Her calm was being drowned in panic. She emptied the drawers on to the floor. Nothing. Jason's room. There would be a lighter in Jason's room. She slammed open his door. Bedside table. Nothing. Bookshelves. Nothing. Anger took the place of hysteria. Now she was talking, a stream of swearing and blame.

Tom and Jason were as culpable as MacIntyre. She was the victim of male ego. Tom would do nothing for himself. It was left to her. As her righteous anger rose she turned it to violence. She ripped Jason's room apart, smashing his sound system, ripping clothes and stamping on the keyboard of his computer. After throwing her son's personal CD against the wardrobe she paused.

There, in the middle of the floor, was a Zippo lighter. Jason's pride and joy. He never took it out of the house it was so precious to him. On one side was a picture of Humphrey Bogart in *Casablanca*, a present from his father. Jason was always teasing him about 'rounding up the usual suspects'. Jenni picked up the lighter and ran back to the bathroom.

The soiled knickers were lying with the stains hidden. She picked them up and flicked the lighter open. It had a good big flame, big enough to burn the ugly remains of her humiliation. The lace and silk caught quickly and flamed dramatically. She dropped them and watched the extravagantly expensive scrap of underwear writhe and curl in the heat. The flame died away leaving a black patch of sticky nothing.

Jenni calmed down, tore off a strip of lavatory paper and picked up the remains in it. She dropped the lot into the pan and poured most of a bottle of bleach on top. Then she flushed. Little specks of black were regurgitated. She flushed again. She could still see black specks after the ninth flush. After the tenth, twelfth, twentieth, again and again . . . After the fiftieth flush she saw the water run clean.

She was sure the water was clear.

Peace. No daggers in her mind.

Calm now she set the shower at its hottest and stood under it, her skin turning livid red as it was scalded. She scrubbed herself with a nail brush and raked her hair with her fingers, emptying a bottle of almond-scented shampoo over her head. The nail brush didn't seem to be harsh enough. She reached across to the cabinet and took out a pumice stone. Rubbing her already red-raw skin with it she saw the fine hair and skin of her arms and legs being sloughed off. She reached round to her back, determined to scrape off the skin contaminated by the Gnome's urine.

While she was flaying herself Jason came upstairs. He'd had net practice after school and had come into the hall like a hungry Labrador, dropping his cricket bag where he stood. He dashed into the kitchen and made himself a doorstep sandwich of cheese and pickle, then bounded up the stairs to his room.

He was expecting an e-mail from his virtual girlfriend. He saw his door was open from the stairs. Then he saw the room. For a second he thought there had been a burglary. Then he heard loud music from his mother's room. Maybe the burglars were still here. He opened his wardrobe door, trying not to register what was destroyed, and took out his old cricket bat. Heart pounding he crept towards her bedroom, bat held ready for attack or defence.

The room was undisturbed. The mirrored door of his mother's bathroom was open and he could see her misty outline, naked, in the shower. The music was coming from her stereo, tuned to some unaccustomed station pumping out repetitive, trance-creating music. His mother was responsible for the trashing of his room; she'd come close many times before.

On the floor by the bathroom door was his Zippo. The top had been ripped off. Its innards littered on the carpet. He picked up the pieces gently. Like his father he invested his affection in things rather than people; inanimate objects were less unpredictable. To hurt his precious things was to hurt Jason. He cradled the lighter in his hands and quietly left his mother's bedroom, closing the door behind him.

Then he sat in the ruins of his little world, unmoving until the phone rang and Lucy asked for Jenni. He had heard his mother moving about, going downstairs, but couldn't face her. He didn't want to speak to her. He wasn't sure he ever wanted to see her again. He and his sisters had always made excuses for her odd outbursts but this, this he couldn't forgive. He couldn't take any more of her. He had been her punchbag and confidant all his life, sided with her against Shackleton, but now he saw he'd just been an extra, used as a weapon against the father he idolised.

Jenni was staring sightlessly out of the window of the living room when Lucy tapped on the glass. As if called back from a great distance, she was startled. Lucy. What was Lucy doing there? She found she couldn't move, she just stared at her. Lucy lifted her keys and mimed coming in. Jenni didn't react. A minute later she heard Lucy open the door.

'Jenni? . . . Jenni, are you all right?'

There was no sign Jenni'd heard.

'Have you come to clear up?'

Jenni's voice was formal, she kept her back to Lucy.

The woman Lucy had never seen without make-up, whose hair was always picture perfect, was standing, shoeless, wearing a towelling dressing gown and her hair was matted, unbrushed after washing. Every now and then Jenni would take a handful, sniff it, then pull it rhythmically. After six pulls, reassured, she laid it back over her shoulder. Then a moment later she did it again.

Lucy gently went behind her and took her elbows. Jenni didn't resist so Lucy guided her to a chair. As if relieved of a great sorrow Jenni started to cry quietly.

'Oh Lucy . . . Lucy.'

Lucy squatted down in front of her.

'What is it? Jenni? What's the matter?'

But there was no reply, just the sad, muted crying. Lucy put her arms round her and rocked her gently. Jenni didn't resist.

When her sobs subsided a little Lucy said, 'Jenni, tell me what's wrong. Please.'

Jenni just hicupped a couple of times trying to control herself, then she pulled away.

'Nothing. Really. Time of the month.'

Lucy knew she was lying but didn't press it.

'Do you want a drink?'

Jenni nodded, still finding it difficult to speak.

Lucy poured her a large Scotch. Jenni hated Scotch but she drank it.

'Sorry I didn't come in today. It's Gary. He's in hospital.'

She could see Jenni wasn't listening. The Scotch worked quickly and Jenni's rigid tension gave way to a floppy sleepiness. Lucy coaxed her to her feet and slowly guided her upstairs. In the bedroom Jenni sat docile on the edge of the bed while Lucy closed the curtains. Lucy tried to help her off with the dressing gown but Jenni clutched it round her and Lucy gave up. Even in her distant state Jenni knew she wanted nobody to see the teeth marks and love bites on her breasts and back. Lucy swung Jenni's legs up on to the bed and pulled the satin cover up under her chin. Without her make-up Jenni looked young and vulnerable. She was whispering something; Lucy leaned close.

'Sleeping pills. In the drawer.'

Lucy was about to object then thought better of it. She got out the pills and went to the bathroom for some water. Soaking towels were thrown everywhere. She picked them up and dropped them into the bath. As she filled the glass with water she saw the mirror had been smashed with the heel of a Manolo Blahnik shoe that now lay, ruined, in the sink.

When she returned Jenni was already asleep, frowning slightly and restless. Lucy put a pill and the water on the table, then, leaving a small light on, quietly left the room.

As she closed the door Jason was coming out of his room carrying a bulging rucksack. Lucy thought he was crying. He was obviously in a hurry and didn't want to talk.

'Are you all right, Jason?'

'I'm going to stay with a friend. I'll leave a note for Dad.'

And he clambered down the stairs, all big boots and student greatcoat. Lucy followed slowly and heard the front door slam. She wasn't sure what she should do now. Jason's note was on the hall floor, blown off the table in his haste to escape. She picked it up and put it back.

The light switch needed a damp cloth run over it. There were finger marks on it. What to do? She supposed she could do the washing up and went into the kitchen. There was something comforting about loading the dishwasher and scouring the saucepans. The activity stopped the wheel of her thoughts of Gary and Tom, the ifs and if onlys. Insidious images of Gary dead and the possibilities beyond. She had almost finished when she heard the front door open discreetly.

Tom.

Her stomach did its usual flip. Why wouldn't it stop doing that? This wasn't the time for desire. It was gone midnight; she had wanted to get back to Gary as quickly as possible. But she'd have to tell Tom what had happened. She couldn't just walk out. It would be rude. Wouldn't it?

'Jenni?' Tom called apologetically. His voice was always apologetic towards his wife, anticipating his fault.

'No, Tom, it's me. In the kitchen.'

Seeing her rubber gloves she whipped them off but dropped them in the sink. She watched them fill with greasy water and sink sadly through the tepid soup.

'Oh blow,' she said ineffectually.

He came in looking tired and a long way from being lit up with pleasure at seeing her.

'Lucy. What are you doing here?'

'I was just finishing the clearing up and . . . I don't think Jenni is too good. I've put her to bed.'

He turned quickly.

'I'd better go up.'

Lucy felt a twinge of jealousy at his concern. No, concern was what she and Gary felt for each other. Tom Shackleton was simply anticipating a scene and was anxious to contain it.

'She's asleep. I think it's better to let her rest. She seemed very upset.'

'She's always upset about something.'

Lucy was surprised. He'd never let the mask slip in front of her before; whatever he'd said about his wife had always been expressed with regret, not bitterness.

He went to the fridge and poured himself a beer, then, without asking her, he poured Lucy a large glass of white wine. She followed him into the living room. He sat on the sofa.

'How's Gary?'

Lucy imagined throwing herself into his manly arms and sobbing out the events of the day while he stroked her hair and made the sorts of noises vets make to elderly dogs with bowel problems. She saw he was only asking out of politeness.

'Oh, you know,' she said.

He barely nodded. Lucy pulled the curtains, not that anybody was likely to peep in and even if they did there would be nothing to see.

'Jason went to stay with a friend. He left a note. Shall I get it?'

Lucy was hovering awkwardly by the door.

'No. Come and sit here.'

He put his arm along the back of the sofa. Lucy sat down. If he wanted a kiss or more, would she want him to? She hadn't cleaned her teeth since when? Before the dinner party. She probably had gum disease by now. And just how sure could you be of a twenty-four-hour deodorant? She sat on the edge of the cushion.

'Oh . . . Lucy . . .'

She turned to look at him: he was grey with tiredness. He put the backs of his fingers to her face and lightly rubbed the down on her cheek. There was no sex in the contact, just comfort. Perhaps his mouth tasted like the inside of an army boot too. Well, if he wanted to kiss her maybe she could hold her breath. She put down her glass and sat back. His eyes were closing. He was struggling to push off his left shoe with his right foot. Having managed that he did the same with his socked left foot. The wool kept slipping on the leather. Lucy automatically leaned over and helped him.

'Smelly feet. Sorry,' he murmured.

The only thing she could smell was expensive shoes. Long sight and innocuous feet were the rewards of age.

She sat back and picked up her wine.

'Cheers.'

She said it quietly turning to look at him with what she hoped was a seductive half-smile. His head had slumped on to his chest. He was sound asleep. Lucy watched him while she sipped the rather good Sauvignon. Jenni had abandoned Chardonnay when women who wore Giorgio perfume started to drink it instead of rum and Coke. He was snoring slightly. Lucy thought she might have fallen in love with him as this just seemed to make him more attractive. She wondered if she should wake him up, pack him off to bed, remind him to clean his teeth. She wished she could, that this was the end of a normal day for Tom and Lucy Shackleton in their lovely home . . . She sighed a small polite sigh, put their glasses out of harm's way and left the house.

PART THREE

The election had dominated the news since its date was announced. The pundits were talking themselves round in circles, trying, for the sake of keeping it alive until the poll, to convince the public there was a chance of the government being defeated and the removal van fetching up at Number 10 on the morning of 22 November.

Behind the scenes the jockeying for position was absorbing everyone who thought they had a future and quite a few who knew they only had a past.

Jenni was finding herself more and more in demand to write sympathetic features about various hopefuls, most of whom seemed to be earnest young women who wouldn't know an original thought if it got up in their fat-free yoghurt and bit them. Jenni had recently turned her back on the broadsheet left and was concentrating on her natural constituency, the female readership of the *Daily Mail*.

She was sitting in the Ivy with a particularly irritating first-time MP from Birmingham. She hadn't meant to waste a good lunch on this earnest, shining young thing but the seasoned battleaxe with whom she was to have lunched was called to a crisis meeting at the Treasury, so rather than waste the booking Jenni threw out her line and reeled in this ambitious girl who was, according to the press office, 'a bright hope for the future'. God help them, thought Jenni.

They were sitting facing the entrance, side by side on one of the rather awkward banquettes that lined the room. The sun was making pretty lights through the coloured diamonds of the windows and the Lovely of London were grazing with confident noise. The bar area was busy with people, some eating at tables by the door, the poor corner. She watched them coming in, influential, famous, all on first-name terms with the maître d'.

The girl by her side was droning on about the importance of being 'on message'. An expression Jenni thought had fallen into disrepute after Labour's first term in government. Perhaps it had only just filtered through to the Black Country.

Then the swing door opened and Robert MacIntyre walked in with Geoffrey Carter. Jenni hadn't seen MacIntyre in the weeks since the encounter in his flat. The bite marks had faded but she could still feel him forcing entry . . . She controlled the expression on her face but had to put down her fork because her hands were shaking. They paused by the maître d's desk, MacIntyre surveying the room, making sure he was seen, checking who would be paying court to him before he left. Then Carter saw Jenni and pointed her out. The Gnome's face lit up. They came straight towards her. She felt sick. The idiot child next to her was almost wetting herself with excitement.

'Jenni, what a lovely surprise. How are you? And your husband?'

Jenni gave the right responses, smiling.

'And of course you know Geoffrey Carter.'

'Yes. Oh Geoffrey, congratulations, wonderful news. A baby Carter! You must be so thrilled, and looking forward to more time at home, I should think. There really is nothing like watching them grow up in the first few years. It really does go so quickly. Do tell Eleri I'll drop in later in the week.'

'She'd appreciate that. I'm afraid she's not having the easiest time. She's a bit mature to be having her first. Thank God men only have to put up with shaving, eh?'

Jenni laughed.

'But you're looking very well. Are you recovered? Oh, I'm sorry, may I introduce Belinda Sharrow?'

The Gnome was instant charm, overwhelming the silly ninny simpering on Jenni's right.

'Belinda, of course, one of our fastest-rising stars. Keep an eye on her, Jenni, she's got a very bright future come the election. Now, we must sit down. I tried you a couple of times but your son, was it? said you'd gone to a health farm . . . I long to hear all about it. I'll give you a call – we must get together again soon. I so enjoyed our last meeting.'

'Mmm . . . me too.' She sounded gratifyingly genuine but her hands were shaking and she felt herself sweating.

Belinda hadn't noticed a thing. She was twittering.

'God, how can someone that ugly be that attractive? Don't you think so? He's asked me to go and see him a couple of times – do you think I should?'

Jenni looked at her silly simpering face.

'Oh yes, you should. It'll do your career no harm.'

'It's not my career I'm thinking of. I've heard a rumour that he's got the most enormous thingy, you know.'

She laughed, looking across at the two men. MacIntyre raised his glass. Carter smiled.

'He's gorgeous, isn't he? Geoffrey Carter? But I hear he never plays away. Such a waste.'

'Yes,' said Jenni, wishing she'd shut up or be hit by a falling chandelier.

'Your husband is a chief constable too, isn't he?'

Jenni didn't like the way she made it sound as common a job as bus driving and no mention of his good looks. She might not want him herself but she liked other women to desire him.

Belinda continued while attacking her galette inelegantly.

'I thought he was very good on *Question Time*. But Carter is very impressive, isn't he? No wonder they want him for this new thing.'

Jenni was still distracted by MacIntyre. She wiped her hands on her linen napkin.

'What new thing?'

The question was automatic. Jenni's mind was back in the 'health farm' from which she'd recently emerged. A celebrity refuge for neurotics and addicts. Jenni had gone in as one and come out the other.

'Oh, I thought you'd know . . .'

Belinda had spilled the crumbs of her bread across the tablecloth.

Jenni placed a translucent fingertip on one of the larger pieces. She wanted to pour the girl's glass of mineral water over her badly cut hair.

'No, I don't know, Belinda. Do tell me.'

'Well, I don't think I'm telling any secrets . . . no, I know I'm not. Apparently he's favourite to head up a new force.'

Jenni still wasn't hooked.

'What? Are they creating a new county or something?'

'Oh no,' said Belinda, eagerly accepting her Caesar salad from the waiter. 'It's a new national thing – like the FBI. You know . . . they'll handle all the big stuff all over the country. I believe he'll even have jurisdiction in Northern Ireland in some cases. He's going to be a very powerful man. The most senior police officer in Britain. The Crime Tsar, they're calling him – there's never been anything quite like it. Bit of a risk if you ask me, mind you we've anointed more tsars than the Patriarch of Moscow and most of them are as much use as chocolate fireguards. Oh please, don't write that. Strictly off the record!'

The waiter put another plate between them.

'Ooh, what gorgeous chips. Here, Jenni. Dig in. Are you all right? You've gone as white as a sheet.'

Jenni couldn't speak. She shook her head, picked up her handbag and, with deliberate care, walked from the table, behind the wooden barrier where the waiters busied themselves, to the carpeted stairs. Up the stairs past pictures of louche women smoking cigarettes and into the Ladies.

A large black woman in a nylon overall was arranging yellow flowers in a bright vase. Jenni nodded. The woman beamed back. Sitting behind her by the open window was an older woman, also black, but skeletally thin. Jenni felt panic. She was desperate to be alone, to rebuild herself.

She locked the door of her cubicle and sat down. In her bag was a bottle of pills. The bag wasn't large but she couldn't find them. In her frustration she tipped the contents on to the floor. But she couldn't see the bottle. She scrabbled through tissues, filofax, perfume, cosmetics. There was no gap under the door. It must be here. It must be. It wasn't. In a fury of frustration she smashed the door open into the dividing wall. The surprise of what she saw almost made her laugh. A third black woman, this time well over six feet tall with a scarred face and sightless eyes, was standing there, her nylon overall too short and the arms reaching barely below her elbows. Like the Goon friend of Olive Oyl she blocked out the light and was compellingly abnormal.

She was holding the bottle of pills.

Jenni was too taken aback to wonder how she'd got them.

Her hand reminded Jenni of the enormity and delicacy of a gorilla's. Suddenly Jenni was embarrassed. Could the woman see she had mentally compared her to a great ape?

'Thank you so much,' said Jenni with a sufficient smile, taking the bottle.

She closed the door. The lavatories seemed a little overstaffed – she'd have to mention it when she left. She took the top off the bottle. One pill? Two little pills? They were only tranquillisers after all and she really needed one – two – now. She swallowed the two little pieces of magic and sat with her eyes closed watching them take effect.

She had woken up in the middle of the night after Lucy put her to bed, alone and surrounded by demons forcing her to feel him again, ramming his way into her, chewing on her. Whimpering, she ran downstairs. By the time she reached the foot of them she was screaming, fighting off Robert MacIntyre. With the logic of the insane she thought she could cut him out of her. A knife, a carving knife.

She was in the kitchen when Tom was woken by the noise. Lucy was no longer beside him. After years of Jenni's hysterical outbursts he didn't hurry to find out the cause. As he crossed the hall her words became clearer. She was screaming a rosary of obscenities. He thought there must be someone with her. Lucy. She must be attacking Lucy. He opened the door. For a moment he was confused; he could see blood and his wife attacking someone or something with a carving knife but he couldn't see Lucy. Then he saw it was her own body Jenni was slashing into, it was her own blood sprayed across the kitchen cabinets.

Jenni remembered him grabbing her, the knife skidding across the floor and his arms round her holding her as he might have done a lover or a violent criminal. She wanted to pass out but her mind wouldn't let her. The ambulance attendants, young people who shouted her name as if she was at the other end of a tunnel, loaded her on to a wheeled chair. She was smothered in a green blanket.

She would never forget the way her husband looked at her. With pity and revulsion. An odd thought struck her as she was pushed out into the street, lit by the silent blue strobe of the ambulance light: Tom would never willingly touch her again, not with anything like affection and certainly not with desire. With one look . . . wasn't that a song? With one look he told her she was the other side of repulsive.

He didn't travel with her in the ambulance. He said he'd follow in the car. When she saw him again he was distant, unable to find words in his limited emotional vocabulary for her. She had been stripped of her dressing gown and put into a backless hospital shift.

She knew he had seen the marks on her. She turned her head away from him. There was no point trying to explain to Tom Shackleton; the time for talking had gone soon after they married. The time for listening before. She was too complex, too frightening for him to want to tackle. And in her frustration with his limitations she had been cruel to him too many times to find his compassion now. Never complain, never explain. An unbelievably stupid maxim that had come to symbolise their marriage.

During Jenni's lost weeks in the clinic to which she'd been transferred after initial psychiatric assessment, she had been surprised not to receive a visit from Lucy. She had decided to be hurt by this until she discovered Tom had told Lucy Jenni didn't want visitors. Even Tom only dropped in occasionally, awkwardly and not for long, delivering and replacing clothes and flowers. They had little to say to one another that wouldn't open an unacknowledged wound.

Tom felt uncomfortable around so many people whose grip on reality was fragile or non-existent.

Lucy had phoned to say Eleri Carter had been on wanting to send her some flowers. Would she like them? During their conversation it became clear Tom had been very economical with the truth of what had happened, and very few people knew Jenni was 'ill'. Indeed she was surprised and annoyed that Eleri had found out.

Jenni didn't know how much Lucy knew but maintained the fiction of a health farm, being wrapped in seaweed and drinking carrot juice. She assured her she'd be home soon and that it wasn't worth coming all that way to visit. Lucy, dear docile Lucy, seemed satisfied and rang off promising to clean out the cutlery drawer.

The next day, while Jenni was sitting in the vast conservatory surrounded by subdued, white-gowned patients, Eleri appeared. Jenni was initially embarrassed and angry to be found so, so far from herself, worse, unmade up. But her aggressive reaction was soon soothed by the serene good temper of the other woman. She positively glowed with pregnant happiness, wearing what looked like a cast-off circus tent in case anybody didn't notice her condition.

Eleri's quiet Welsh voice and calm presence really helped Jenni. They talked about things Jenni hadn't thought of for years. Morning sickness that in Eleri's case went on for twenty-four hours. Piles, varicose veins, sagging pelvic floors and the chances of Carter getting anything approaching conjugal rights ever again. They laughed at the lack of dignity and downright humiliation of childbearing and found after an hour together they'd really enjoyed themselves.

Jenni didn't object when the other woman said she'd like to visit again and soon Jenni was looking forward to the increasingly rotund figure waddling in, always carrying flowers or fruit or silly magazines.

It soon became their habit to sit with a box of chocolates reading out the horoscopes and the problem pages and shrieking with laughter. All the jagged sophistication fell away from Jenni and Eleri was rewarded with the revelation of a very funny, wonderfully attractive and totally natural companion.

But then Eleri had never seen her as anything else. She had touched a part of Jenni no one else had ever realised was there. A small good heart arrested in development by sex, envy and mistrust. And now, twenty-five years after that little heart stopped, a late girly flowering had restarted it.

It was raining the afternoon the conversation turned to husbands and lovers. They were playing an endless game of Monopoly and working their way through a box of Harrods chocolates. Jenni liked Harrods, Eleri found it rather vulgar, having been brought up to dislike conspicuous expense, but she battled through sprawling tourists and the loud-voiced wealthy for her friend.

'Were you a virgin when you met Geoffrey?'

It wasn't the reply Eleri had expected when she asked for rent on Leicester Square but she just said, 'Nearly. That'll be ten pounds.'

Jenni burst out laughing.

'What do you mean nearly?'

Eleri tilted her head coyly.

'Well, it didn't really count because he was wearing a condom.' She paused. 'And he lost his erection. So I don't think that counts.'

Jenni nodded and handed over the money.

'I never tried again till Geoff. What about you?'

Jenni laughed.

'Oh, I don't think I was ever a virgin. Tom was.'

Eleri threw the dice. Five.

'Why do you ask?'

Jenni sat back, elegant even in a towelling dressing gown.

'I've . . .' She stopped.

Eleri waited.

'It's stupid, all this crap they put you through here. We do what we do.'

She stood up quickly and toppled the game board off the low table between them. Eleri automatically put her hands out to stop it falling. Jenni didn't seem to notice.

'It was his own fault. Tom had only himself to blame. He made me feel trapped. I can't tell you how he used to look at me. God, it was horrible, like a fucking dog. He worshipped me, followed me around. If he'd stayed at home that night . . . it was his own fault. These fucking psychiatrists . . . there's nothing behind it.' She was arguing with a voice in her head. 'No fucking trauma. It's a weapon . . .' She was angry now, impotently furious.

Eleri, far from being shocked at Jenni's language or savagery, saw a desperately unhappy child she wanted to calm and comfort.

'Sleeping with men has got nothing, fucking nothing, to do with self-esteem. It's crap. Total crap.' She was talking not to Eleri but at the walls, the door. 'I'm beautiful, you ugly, ugly bastards . . . I'm not like you. I'm different . . .'

She stepped backwards and caught her leg on her chair, causing her to sit down suddenly, comically. But Eleri wasn't laughing. She reached towards her friend and, at the touch of her fingers on Jenni's hair, Jenni calmed down but she was coldly angry.

'Tom thought I was some porcelain doll. It was his own fault. Sex is just something men want, that's all. That's all it is. It doesn't mean anything. It's like money, Eleri, you spend it. It gets you things.'

'Oh Jenni . . . come on. Shh. You don't really think that.'

Eleri stroked her hair. Jenni allowed the other woman to comfort her but she was out of reach, somewhere in her head.

Eleri spoke very softly, her accent taking any judgement out of her words.

'I think sex is the most precious part of yourself. I . . . I couldn't imagine . . . well, just doing it, like, like animals. I couldn't do it without love, Jenni.'

Jenni looked at her.

'Does it really mean that much to you?'

'I mean that much to me.'

Jenni wasn't really listening.

'Tom has never done it with love – he can't. D'you know that? Sex is something he does to you, but he doesn't like it, Eleri. None of our children was any more than a fuck to him.'

'And what about you? What did it mean to you?'

'He doesn't like women. Not really. Oh, he likes tits. But you know what he does? He grabs you by the scruff of the neck. That's how you know he wants it . . . No. No, I've never felt what you do. Christ. I wouldn't want to. Sex isn't about being sentimental and love really isn't enough.'

Jenni said it with such contempt Eleri was upset. She knew her love-making with Carter was probably a bit staid, a bit dull, that maybe he'd prefer something more exotic. She wanted to leave, get away from the thought of her modest sexual vocabulary not being enough. That love didn't change everything.

She stopped herself but changed the subject.

'What did the psychiatrist say?'

Jenni reached for a cigarette. Eleri was surprised; she'd never seen Jenni smoke before. It was, as she might have guessed, extra long and extra thin. Lit with an incongruous throwaway lighter. Jenni took the cliché deep inhalation, bent her left arm across her body and rested her right elbow on it. She pushed her hair back with her little finger, holding the cigarette between index and middle. Suddenly the picture of forties Hollywood sophistication.

'He said I have poor self-image and asked me if I'd ever heard of borderline personality disorder.'

'What did you say.'

'I told him he was a cunt.'

Eleri didn't visit again for ten days but then guilt and her genuine fondness for Jenni had her making the journey to the clinic again. Her pregnancy was beginning to tire her and she almost collapsed into the easy chair opposite Jenni. Jenni, seemingly recovered from her previous outburst, brought her a cup of tea and fussed over her. Eleri thought it better not to mention it; after all, it may just have been a side effect of Jenni's medication.

That afternoon Eleri told her Geoffrey was thinking of taking early retirement to spend time looking after her and to watch this miracle baby grow up. She was sadly serious when she talked about the impossibility of caring for Alexander and a newborn. Apart from the possibility that Alexander might attack the baby.

Jenni appeared shocked at the thought but Eleri just said, 'I know, Jenni, it's awful and I didn't want to think about it but it's something we've got to consider. You know he hates change. He'll attack anything new. It frightens him, poor dab. Everything frightens him, poor little boy.'

So it seemed the choices were: a full-time nanny, residential care for Alex, or Geoffrey staying home. He could of course take the statutory thirteen weeks' paternity leave but . . . was a chief constable an employee? And would thirteen weeks be enough for her to find some way of coping? Her worries were beginning to overwhelm her.

'But I don't want to put pressure on him because the Home Office has dropped some heavy hints about another job. Something bigger.'

Not a hope, thought Jenni. She waited for her to finish, watching the mobile, attractive face shadow with barely suppressed panic. Eleri was the only person Jenni had ever met who was transparent.

Jenni's enthusiasm for Geoffrey to retire took Eleri aback. Jenni told her in no uncertain terms that it would be for the best.

'After all he's been chief of a large force – what else is there? I mean, London's not really a challenge, is it? Not in real terms. More money and a higher profile, yes, and of course you get a knighthood, but really it's just bigger. And you'd have to move. Or he'd have to commute. I spent far too long trying to keep a marriage alive with Tom doing all that. No, Eleri, it's ridiculous. He has to resign. The baby's far more important.'

Eleri was touched. She assumed it was because Tom had missed so much of his own children's early years.

'And, darling. I'm not being funny, but you are forty-one.'

'Forty-four.'

Jenni managed to control her look of horror. A first baby at forty-four? The woman needed psychiatric help more than she did.

'Well, you don't look it. But, Eleri . . . you're already wiped out, aren't you? You can't do this on your own. You need his help. I mean, when I get out of here I'll do what I can – come and sit with the boys to give you a break. Now don't argue. I really don't mind Alexander at all. I'll just remember to leave the Versace at home. Oh . . . and of course you've no family here, have you? And even if you did they're usually more trouble than help. No, you're going to need him at home. You tell him: this is far too important to miss.'

'I think you're right, Jenni, I know you're right but I've got to let him make his own decision.'

Jenni, convinced the future was clear and the recent past was merely a bad dream, dropped the last vestiges of her ever-present suspicion and wariness; so for a brief time Eleri became the best friend she'd never had.

But now, sitting in the lavatory at the Ivy . . .

She wished she could claw back all the trust she'd given. All the naive belief she'd put in the hands of a stranger. She wished Carter dead. She wished his gypsy bastards dead and especially she wished dead Eleri and her unborn baby . . .

The pills kicked in. She found that place that didn't hurt, a little above and a little to the left of real life. Where revenge was just a pleasure, not the only thing that would keep her from screeching like a banshee through the restaurant.

She was ready to go back to the awful Belinda and get the whole story. She opened the loo door. There was no tall black woman. They seemed to have gone as she could hear nothing. She walked out to the washbasins and was startled to find the three women there. She smiled at them quickly and bent slightly to wash her hands, watching herself, and them, in the mirror.

'You look like you need a little sleep, girl. Thinking so hard about all those little chickens.'

Jenni wanted to tell the fat woman to shut up and mind her own business. The pills and good manners stopped her.

'Thank you . . .' she murmured.

'Sleep. Balm of hurt minds. You think so, Mrs Shackleton? The balm of hurt minds?'

The three black faces were smiling at her. Standing behind her.

Too close. Jenni felt panicky, even through the cotton wool of the tranquillisers.

'Who are you? What are you doing in here?'

The women continued to smile.

'You gotta knit up that ravelled sleeve of care, girl. Knit it up, I say!'

It was the thin woman speaking, her voice in the decayed cadence of the very old. She laid her bird's-claw hand on Jenni's arm. It was like thin dry paper. She peered with her bloodhound eyes at the others. They were not smiling now, but serious, nodding and agreeing with one another that this was the only way she could save herself. Then, as if a prayer meeting had ended, they went, the fat one skewering a hat to her head as she left.

Jenni was desperate to get out but didn't want their company on the stairs. The door opened, she jumped. Belinda came in.

'You all right, Jenni? You've been gone ages.'

'Yes . . . I was talking to those women.'

'What women?'

'The three . . . black ladies – cleaners, I think . . . you must have passed them on the stairs.'

'No. I didn't see anyone.' Belinda looked at her, through the mirror, with pity.

Jenni recognised the look from hospital. Jenni the Sad Case. Oh no, that's not how Jenni Shackleton saw herself. She turned and looked at Belinda, unblinking, daring her to repeat that look.

'They must have gone the other way, into the function room.'

Belinda looked doubtful.

'There's a private room. Have you never been in it? Oh it's lovely – Tom and I were there for a party a few months ago . . .'

And still talking, Jenni led the way back down to the restaurant.

It was almost eleven-thirty when Tom got home that night, announcing himself in his usual 'don't be angry with me' tone. Jenni was waiting for him. Normally she went up to her room when he was late, leaving him to creep round, careful of disturbing her and provoking an attack. But since she'd been in hospital something had changed between them. He hadn't mentioned the marks on her body; she didn't know whether to be angry or hurt. What if she'd been raped? But he'd found something to keep him working late almost every night since she'd come home.

'Tom . . . in here. I'm in the living room.'

There was a moment's pause, then he came in. She was surrounded by notes and press cuttings, preparing a piece for one of the Sundays for their regular column, 'Making Dreams Come True'.

'You're up late, Jenni. Everything all right?' He asked as if they were flatmates.

'Fine. Look, I heard something today . . . yes, I'll have a vodka tonic. Thanks.'

Tom prepared their drinks. He didn't really want a drink but then he didn't want to have to sit down and talk to Jenni either. He handed her her glass and sat in an armchair. Not beside her.

'I had lunch with one of the Follics today.' 'Blair's Babes' had changed their name to celebrate the *nouvelle entente cordiale* with Europe. 'She said there's going to be some sort of national police force and Geoffrey Carter's going to run it. Well?'

She looked at him as if he had kept the secret from her.

'Well what? It doesn't affect the Met. He's thinking of putting his ticket in anyway but if it puts him out of the running, what's the problem?'

'The problem, you prat, is that he will be higher up the evolutionary scale than you. Don't you see? This Crime Tsar —'

'Oh God, not another Tsar. They'll have a Tsar's Tsar next —'

He saw she was within a hair of losing control.

'He'll have the power to coordinate police crime strategy. The chiefs and commissioners won't be autonomous any more. He will be more senior than you. He isn't going to sit at home changing nappies if they're offering that kind of power. He'll be the fucking king. Do you see?'

A pause. Tom saw very well. He'd come second. Again.

'Yes. I see.'

There was a silence between them. Not emptiness occasionally flooded with antipathy but a companionable quietness full of thought.

'You're sure Geoffrey's's got it, are you?'

'No, I'm not absolutely sure. It may just be gossip-mongering. But I am sure you're getting the Met.'

He knew he didn't want to know how she knew. Tom sat with his elbow on the arm of his chair, his little finger stroking his eyebrow. When he spoke it was quietly, reasonably.

Jenni watched him and knew he wasn't speaking to her but to himself.

'I heard a long time ago there was a plan to make a national investigation team. They wanted to see if NCIS took off first. But I didn't think . . . I thought it would be . . . I didn't think it would be for another couple of years. I spoke to MacIntyre about it at dinner –'

'I know you did, I was there.'

Tom didn't hear her.

'He said not yet. He said there'd be plenty of time for that . . .' Tom stopped. He looked at Jenni. 'When did they decide?'

'No idea. I'm going to look into it tomorrow.'

She spoke his feelings.

'But there's no point in getting London if you have to answer to that long streak of piss.'

He watched her gather up her papers, watched her feed her anger.

'He might turn it down.'

She laughed. 'Oh Tom, Geoffrey Carter might seem to have his mind on higher things but believe me, he's as ambitious as you. He'd no more walk away from this than you would. For God's sake, this isn't just a job, this is the crown.'

'What are you going to do, Jenni?'

'We are going to fight.'

He knew better than to ask who or what.

'But if we lose –'

The ice cubes hit his face before he realised she had thrown the drink at him but it was the look on her face that really shook him. He had never seen such undisguised hatred and contempt.

'We won't lose.'

She put her glass down carefully on an embossed silver coaster, turned and went upstairs. She hadn't wanted to get angry but waiting up for him had been torture because she couldn't take her pills, the little bits of heaven that knocked her out for the night, stopped her dreaming, thinking, but let her sleep, a good deep dreamless oblivion. The companion she craved. And if she took them more and more often with vodka, what did it matter?

Downstairs Shackleton went to the kitchen and used a tea towel to dry his face. Since seeing another man's territory marked out on her skin he'd found himself outside the prison into which he was first put by her casual callousness. He looked in the mirror – the impact of the ice had bruised his cheekbone. He could hear Janet saying, 'Ooh, Mr Shackleton, have you been in the wars again?' And himself blaming the car door or his grandson's exuberance. He must make sure it wasn't an excuse he'd used before for the damage Jenni did.

Through the mirror he looked back on himself and on their past. It used to make him wince but now he could watch it all like an old film.

No one then could understand what Jenni saw in such a tongue-tied lump as Tom Shackleton. He was a policeman and he was a virgin. Jenni pretended he wasn't but as he was so paralysingly shy no one believed her.

But in the place where they were brought up, a wind-blown village long since concreted into suburbs by estates of cheap bungalows for newly-weds, everyone knew Jennifer's reputation. All the neighbours knew she'd had an abortion at fifteen. Those that didn't relish that piece of tittle-tattle enjoyed the memory of her seducing the father of a child in the same class as her younger brother. And the fine sight of the boy's mother throwing a bucket of paint over her at the school gates. She'd moved in with the man for a while but left him when the money ran out. Further scandalising northern sensibilities.

By the time Jenni was eighteen she had the face of an angel and the reputation of a prostitute. But Jenni wasn't stupid, she'd decided to go to college – she barely scraped the necessary exams – and she'd decided to get married and get away from the minty women who'd found a lifetime's hairstyle and sprayed it with Locktite. Those disapproving wives for whom possession was nine-tenths of a marriage.

Unfortunately there was no one left in the village who didn't know her reputation. None of the 'nice boys' would marry her; she'd had sex with most of them in almost every place except a bed and there was nothing more conservative than a provincial stud.

But there was always Tom Shackleton. He was a huge shy twenty-two-year-old who had been brought up by his mother in a house by the canal, at the end of a short, ugly terrace. His mother was an enigma in the village; she had little to do with anyone but had always had Tom. Son, husband, lover. His father had made an early exit and Tom's unwanted arrival had been the reason; so little Tom had to pay for spoiling her life.

Tom had always been alone with her unpredictable aggression and it had made him withdraw into his schoolwork and then his police studies. His ambition, the warmest place in his heart, took the place of love or shared humour.

His mother's only reaction to his announcement that he was joining the police was: 'Well, your feet are big enough.'

And she laughed. As always, at him.

Then one day he was walking his beat and there was Jenni. Pretty, tiny Jenni. Bused in from estates called villages to a vast comprehensive in the next county the children gazed out from their barred concrete playground longing for something to excite them. She was nearly fourteen and she looked up at him as though he was a prize, something to be desired, like gold hoop earrings in a Saturday-afternoon shop window.

When she was sixteen and taking a break from the repercussions of teenage copulation she let him kiss her and was gentle with him, stroking his hair and listening to his hopes for the future. He fell in love easily. He brought her bunches of wild flowers and put them on her rendered wall. He enjoyed turning scarlet at her quiet flattery. He was proud that people looked at them together, thinking they were impressed at his catch. But most of all he remembered being happy, more than happy, to have found a female who was kind to him, who was predictable and supportive. And who laughed at his jokes.

Two years later, when he was a young fast-tracking sergeant, he proposed.

The only thing he found awkward was sex. The first time they fumbled in the darkness of the cinema he thought they had done it. She was patient with his ignorance and clumsiness. Pretended not to notice when he climaxed before she'd released him from his clothes. He didn't dare tell her he had never gone further than fantasy – and had no friends to tell him she had.

The day of their wedding was fixed but his mother didn't like her. At the time it didn't occur to him it was because they were too similar. His mother's tongue had plenty of exercise in the weeks running up to the wedding, her son's stupidity being the main subject of her onslaughts. She often said 'his girl' was nothing more than a prostitute without even the sense to charge for her services. Tom, as usual, looked at the wall and disappeared inside himself.

He started work on his degree. Then came the night before her hen night and his stag night, to which he'd begged colleagues to come. He had no friends; even his best man was from the station, an old PC who remembered his father. That night Jenni said she was going out with the girls.

He'd worked all evening at home, reading and re-reading his law books, trying not to listen to his mother talking to the television. Eventually he'd had enough. He decided to go into work for some peace but then, restless, walked round to Jenni's, although his station was in another area, young police officers not being trusted in their own communities. It was raining. A fine drizzle. Loud teenagers were swearing at each other for lack of anything more interesting to do.

When he arrived at Jenni's house, he wasn't sure if he should ring the doorbell. Maybe it wouldn't be right. Her parents would be embarrassed, feel they had to ask him in. The television would be turned down but not off . . . He stood, unwilling to go home. Drizzle turned to rain.

A car pulled up. The lights were out. The rain made it impossible to see into the car. He stood watching for ten minutes. He didn't know if Jenni was in the car but he was dully sure she was. Dull. His mother said he was dull. Everything about him was dull. He was looking forward to moving away from her. To starting again with his lovely Jenni. She didn't think he was dull. She loved him and he loved her like he'd never loved anything in his dry life. And now, at almost twenty-six, thanks to her he was a success, envied and disliked for his beautiful fiancée and obviously glittering future.

The passenger door opened and Jenni's legs appeared: her skirt was rucked up high under her thighs. As she leaned forward to get out of the car the driver's hand reached round and pulled her back. She hung half in and half out of the car, he watched her kiss the unseen man. Straining to satisfy him she stretched herself the better to accommodate his tongue and hands.

Tom watched.

He watched, no less dull than before. There was no move in him to pull her out of the car, to punch the man whose tattooed hand he could see slipping under her skirt. He just stood, dully staring. Finally she got out, a little bit tipsy, a little bit giggly. She waved to the unseen driver as he roared off, fuelled not by petrol but testosterone.

She balanced, stork-like, searching for her door keys. Tom walked across. She was standing under a street lamp, the better to see past the contents of her bag. She was startled when he said hello and she looked up at him. The same pure green eyes as when she was thirteen. He remembered the shining admiration then and saw the alcoholic resentment now. Her blouse was open and he could see the lace of her bra. And on her skin the pattern of the driver's teeth, the red-brown blotches of his sucking lips. Her smeared face smiled at him above a collar of love bites.

'He's more of a man than you'll ever be.'

She was drunk and the words were spat out in angry self-defence but nothing could have hurt him more. He turned away and walked up to her front door. His love was left to die on the rendered wall as so many of his flowers had been before. The evening was never mentioned again. They married and moved away; they had children and created an image of success and confidence.

The children came quickly and Tom was separated from his family for the first time after four and a half years of marriage. A posting to another area, a place Jenni didn't want to live in with a gaggle of fractious under-fives.

A female officer saw him alone in the canteen and took pity on him, the lonely handsome giant. The same pity got him into the beds of numerous women over the next five years. Then he stopped. Stopped sleeping with all the women who wanted to nurse his shyness or who perceived in him a lack of need. There was no point. He had never been close enough to anyone to find out that all women would not, in time, metamorphose into his mother or his wife.

But each time he bedded a woman he'd ask the same question: 'You won't hurt me, will you?'

And each one would cradle him and reassure him. But he never waited to find out. Always got his retaliation in first and left them puzzled and angry at his sudden indifference. His withdrawal and denial.

Eventually, disgusted with himself and their easy availability, he just stopped having any contact with women. It was easy in the police force, in the days before it became a police service, easy to deal only with a uniform. Sex was a form of release to him and now he was being promoted quickly through the hierarchy he didn't need that release any more – he was no longer frustrated. So ambition took the place of affection and his marriage was founded on the common ground of wanting to escape upwards from the mud of the past. It was a way to live. He'd never known any other. Until he saw the love bites on Jenni again and found the comfort of Lucy.

Examine your life . . . He kept hearing the women. But it was uncomfortable, painful. And it was frightening. For the first time he felt fear. Fear of failing, fear of allowing a woman in, the real fear that there was nothing for that person to discover. He had looked into himself and found nothing looking back: no garden, no morality, no soul. And Lucy wanted to love him. Love what? There was nothing in him to love. He was afraid he didn't exist. With Jenni he was safe.

When the doctors told him of Jenni's mental condition they said one of the symptoms was 'an inability to introspect'. Shackleton had thought he'd been blessed with that gift too, until now.

He changed the channel of his thoughts to Geoffrey Carter and the new force. He would have to refuse the Met now, when, if, it was offered. He could not be seen to be subordinate to Carter. Soft, sentimental Geoffrey. Then what? Retirement? Ultimate failure. He dismissed that thought and changed the perspective. He must make it known he wanted the new force. But what would be the point? It was a political appointment, a political creation – they would have decided on Carter from the beginning. Shackleton knew his strengths but he knew Carter's just as well. He couldn't fault his intellectual ability or his political skill and administrative flair. Old-fashioned coppering hadn't counted since the Sheehy Report.

Who was it that had put his wife over the edge? Who had she allowed to write his signature in her flesh? He shook his head. The thoughts were intrusive, unwelcome. He had never had difficulty controlling his thoughts before: control was a pleasurable vice. But in these few weeks rogue thoughts had leaked in, emotions, jealousies, affections. He found himself missing his son in the house, becoming sentimental. No, feeling sentiment.

Geoffrey Carter. He was the problem. He'd thought maybe there could be a friendship there, nothing too close, nothing that might expose Shackleton as an alien. Carter had told him that now Eleri was pregnant he no longer cared if he got any further in his career. Then why didn't he just throw the towel in? Why was he forcing Shackleton to compete against him? He had everything he wanted, more. Why was he being greedy? What was it those women had said?

He didn't want to think about them. He had felt a fool after re-visiting them, as if their fairground voodoo meant anything.

Jenni would have an idea. Jenni always had a solution. He went to the fridge and took out a piece of cold chicken. Jenni didn't like him eating with his fingers. He stood with the fridge door open, something else she detested, for fear of flies. Flies sneaking into an open fridge and laying their eggs. Sluggish maggots in awkward corners. He ate the chicken without tasting it. He would wait. Carry on as usual. He closed the fridge and washed his hands. Cleared away every sign of his presence. Yes. Just wait. Wait for Jenni.

Lucy looked at the luminous numbers on her bedside clock. As always she couldn't see what time it was because the hands weren't luminous. She thought she might get some of that tape cyclists wore on their jackets to prevent them becoming organ donors and stick it on. But it would be fiddly and she wasn't good at fiddly jobs.

Lucy turned over.

She switched the light on. It was four o'clock in the morning. Working out the logistics of making her alarm clock visible at night had followed counting sheep, calculating the amount of feet on a mixed herd of sheep and ducks and trying to remember what stopped a legless lizard being a snake.

She lay on her back wanting to touch her breasts, resting her hand on her pubic hair, wondering how it felt to someone else. To Tom. Wondering if it was soft. She'd doused it in conditioner the morning after their first night together. It was so unexpected she hadn't had time to moisturise her elbows. She had caught sight of them as they undressed, like her knees, ten years older than the rest of her. Mercifully, he switched the light out.

Tom didn't like making love in the light. She was quite grateful really although she would have liked to have seen him. But that was silly because she always closed her eyes during intimacy. It was an automatic reflex.

She lay staring into the dark wondering why. Predators closed their eyes when killing prey to protect them from the thrashing of the dying.

Lucy knew if she allowed her fingers to start to move, if she brought herself to a climax re-enacting scenes with Tom, the exquisite pleasure would end in gulping sobs. She'd read in a magazine about women whose orgasms were so intense they resulted in uncontrollable crying. How silly, she'd thought. And now it was happening to her. Tom had been taken aback when it happened and then tender and protective. Holding her while she bathed his chest in her tears. She had clung to him and whispered, 'I think I've fallen in love with you.'

He hadn't said anything, just held her a little tighter and put his lips against her forehead. She wanted to believe he was unbearably moved but suspected he was just embarrassed at being so far from love himself.

Once Gary was out of danger she had come home, and commuted to visit in the afternoons, between his waking and falling asleep again. She enjoyed the train journey which was, against all expectations, fast and efficient.

He was out of danger but the pneumonia had left him frail and depressed. As always he tried to be the cheerful patient, not wanting to be any trouble.

'The man's a saint,' said the large Irish staff nurse who shifted him about on his bed with no thought of the silent pain that made his face a rigid, vein-raised red.

Lucy hated being in the house alone, with Gary's disability hardware. The rooms reminded her of ships' graveyards, with their strange, malevolent metal hulks abandoned and accusing. An empty wheelchair was not a versatile piece of furniture. The frames and pulleys had only one use and without Gary they seemed to be waiting for something. Or someone.

Lucy wondered if a Chippendale or Rennie Mackintosh would ever design for 'the disabled', that strange place where sex, colour and religion didn't count. To take her mind off the emptiness she had spent more time across the road, cleaning, and having cleaned, finding more behind, above and below to polish, wipe and lather with sugar soap.

It wasn't until two days after Jenni was taken to hospital Lucy realised she was away. Tom left a note for her. It was brief, formal: Jenni was away and Jason had moved out. Please hoover his room.

Lucy had finished her cleaning and sat down in Jenni's showroom kitchen with a cup – no mugs, Jenni didn't like mugs – of instant coffee. Jenni wouldn't have instant in the house. 'Ugh, ghastly!' she'd cry in her actressy voice. So Lucy brought a little jar across in her bag. Lucy didn't much like real coffee, and she preferred evaporated milk to cream. She and Gary had a Saturday-afternoon treat, in front of the football results. Tinned peaches and evaporated milk, with slices of bread and butter. Comfort food.

Gary.

Always a fighter. Never a loser. But now, home from hospital, the fighter was just a shadow boxer. A winner only on points. But still no complaint, no whisper of defeat. And still laughing. He'd heard a joke on the radio: Centurion goes into a bar and asks for a Martinus. The barman says, 'Don't you mean a Martini?' The centurion says, 'When I want a large one I'll ask for it.' He'd laughed so much he'd needed the nebuliser. When he realised it was true he was put on pure oxygen. Laughing, faith in God and Lucy kept him sane. Kept him alive.

Her hands moved to the no man's land of her belly. She tried to concentrate on Gary, downstairs, asleep. But Tom kept pushing him out. Think about Gary's love for you. Unconditional devotion. It was no good. She gave up and let the last few weeks take her towards sleep.

When she had realised they were both alone she had decided to seduce Tom. Lucy automatically recoiled from the idea of seduction. Lucy was not seductive. Affectionate yes, cosy, reassuring but . . .

She had gone and bought two salmon en croûte from Marks & Spencer, some ready-washed salad and a bag of new potatoes. She hesitated by the fruit flans but thought individual crèmes brûlées were probably sexier. And a bottle of wine. Did Tom prefer white or red? She wandered the aisles agonising over Beaujolais and unoaked Chardonnay. She settled on a sparkling New Zealand nearly champagne. It was three pounds more than the wine but he liked champagne and this, according to the assistant, was just as good.

Once she got the food home she felt she was about to make a fool of herself and left the bags in the hall, where they challenged her until she had to leave for the station.

She had been to the hospital and visited Gary who was too ill to talk. He smiled weakly when he saw her, then slept until she left.

When she opened the front door the bags toppled over. What should she do? Just put the stuff in the fridge and pretend she'd bought it as a treat for herself? Pretend she never intended to go over the road and force herself on a chief constable in his own home while his wife was in a clinic? What if his driver came in? He did sometimes. Or if he had someone with him. Another woman. Maybe he already had a mistress. The local papers never stopped putting him on 'best-looking' and 'sexiest' lists. What on earth would he want with Lucy? Well, hopefully exactly what he'd wanted before.

Oh, for goodness sake – Lucy was irritated with herself – just give it a try. What have you got to lose? Your dignity, your pride. All right, just offer to cook him supper because you're both alone at the moment. Just a neighbourly gesture. No hint of being desperate for him. No whisper of the aching desire that obsessed her. No. Nothing like that. Just dear old Lucy being nice. Making the right gesture. Good.

Having decided on her strategy she waited until eight o'clock, made herself watch a soap opera, then put on her jacket, just her ordinary jacket over an ordinary skirt and rather clingy jumper that showed off her bust. Nothing special, as the pile of discarded outfits on the bed testified. No lipstick but a light gloss that wouldn't mark if. . . . If. . . .

She picked up the carrier bags and went across the road. She let herself into the empty house and turned off the bleeping alarm. Then she wasn't sure what to do. Sitting in the living room would be too forward, too intrusive. The kitchen then but not to look as though she was waiting. She thought if he found her cleaning out the cutlery drawer that would strike the right note. As if she'd been working away and just lost track of the time. And then she'd produce a splendid supper as an afterthought. 'Oh by the way, Tom, I happen to have this salmon en croûte I made earlier on . . .' Who was she trying to kid? Herself.

She jumped as she heard his key in the door. She strained to hear voices. He was alone. There was a pause, then she heard him cross the tiled hall. She concentrated on polishing a fork. The door opened.

'Hello, Lucy, what are you doing here at this time of night?'

'Oh, is it that late? I hadn't realised.'

'How's Gary?'

'Still very poorly.' That awful word again.

He nodded sympathetically.

'And Jenni?'

He shrugged. 'About the same.'

As mad as a bag of stoats, you mean, thought Lucy.

'I . . . er . . . I thought as we're both on our own. I wondered . . . I got some stuff to eat. If you'd like to. It won't take long to cook.'

He did that smile, the shy one with the little head-dip. She clenched her fists to stop herself reaching out and touching him.

'That'd be nice,' he said. 'Can I do anything?'

She opened the fridge and handed him the ersatz fizz.

'Open that if you like.'

He took off his suit jacket and his tie, hanging them on the back of a chair. Lucy was surprised – he was always meticulous about his clothes.

'Don't tell Jenni,' he said, smiling conspiratorially at Lucy. 'She doesn't like clothes hung anywhere they shouldn't be.'

Lucy smiled back happily.

The meal was well received. He ate everything and, when the nervous flutterings of her stomach prevented her eating her potatoes, he reached across and took them from her plate. She was thrilled with the gesture. Thrilled he felt he could do things with her disapproved of by Jenni.

Jenni became the absent headmistress and they giggled like kids at a forbidden midnight feast. They finished the champagne and opened another bottle, real this time. He talked about his young days in the job, nothing daring, nothing private. Lucy listened, not realising how much more powerful an effect on him her trusting adoring eyes had than any amount of femme fatalism. She made him feel protective, masculine, attractive, and it wasn't just the bubbles that made him lean across and kiss her, pulling her on to his lap.

They kissed for a long time, for the first time with no hurry, no fear. His hands moved over her clothes and then under them. She rippled and squirmed at every caress. The intensity of her pleasure was painful. It was almost a relief when he took her nipple in his mouth; the feelings that produced were familiar and deeply satisfying. He explored her breasts slowly with his lips and tongue then, as if having made a decision, he settled on to her left nipple and started to suck. He sucked with the rhythmic intensity of a baby feeding.

At first she found it disconcerting, looking down on his famous profile buried, oblivious, in her flesh, watching his jaw move as he fed on her. Then the feelings deepened, as if a sensual door had opened and she passed on to a different, more intense plane of pleasure. She groaned. He pressed his fingers into the muscles low on her spine, a slow explosion of feeling, nerves deep inside overwhelming her with waves of ecstasy she thought were more intense than any orgasm she'd ever had.

She almost wanted him to stop, but his lips went on pulling at her. No wonder breast-feeding Madonnas had that irritating look of private ecstasy on their faces. She started to laugh at the thought. All her emotions were jangled and jumbled; the intensity of it forced a relief. And she laughed. He released her and looked up. His eyes were almost the colour of violets.

She put her hand on his hair, not knowing what else to do. She moved on his lap and felt the wetness between her legs. He moved his hand up under her skirt. She breathed in sharply as he gently pushed his finger into her. His thumb moved lazily through the lips of flesh, seeking out the hard little tongue which twitched at his touch. He murmured something – she wasn't sure if it was 'Lovely' or 'You're lovely'.

He led her upstairs and into his bedroom. He didn't undress her and she stood for a moment rather awkwardly as he started to strip off. There was a shyness between them. They undressed like a married couple. He neatly folded his trousers, then caught himself and let them drop on the floor.

Lucy slid into the bed, anxious for him not to see her imperfections. He turned out the light and got in beside her. Lucy leaned across and started kissing him. Apart from his chest he was almost hairless, smooth, a little overweight, a little out of condition, but still the shape youthful sport had given him. She kissed his neck, chest, arms and was delighted to find him agonised by her gentle nips at his nipples. She took them between her fingers and manipulated them gently at first then a little harder. She was gratified by his excitement. Glad to be able to reciprocate.

She moved down, her tongue licking and exploring. She let her cheek give the first stroke to his penis. It lay straight and hard against his belly. The sharp clean smell excited her; she adjusted her position but he stopped her.

'No. Not that. I don't like it.'

Lucy was disappointed. She wanted to taste him, feel the size of him in her mouth.

She couldn't know the feel of lips on him made him almost

physically sick, churning up the silt of memory. Of Jenni's cruelty and his naivety. Whimpering in the dark at the mercy of her unseen mouth.

He seemed to make a decision and pushed her on to her back. He kissed her again as though that was an important thing for him. Lucy loved the hardness, the sharpness of his tongue. Again he caressed her and brought her so close to orgasm she thought she might lose it. Then, as if knowing how close she was, he let his fingers rest. She held him in her hand, slowing her movements and lightening her fingers so they barely stroked him. Then, with great care, he moved on top of her.

'It's all right, I won't break,' she whispered.

She felt him aware of his size and weight. His care not to hurt her. She moved to accommodate him and felt the blind probings before he slipped inside her. He was bigger than she had remembered. She tilted her hips and felt the weight of his balls on her . . . what? Small expanse of skin between vagina and anus. Perineum – was that it? Her mind screamed: Shut up, Lucy! You're not doing the *Cosmopolitan* crossword now.

She reached down and took his balls in her hand. She felt them tighten and harden. His fingers found her nipple again. The pleasure was almost too much, she wanted him to stop, not to reach the end, but he went on and she could hear gasping and sighing. It was her. Quiet, undemonstrative Lucy. She tensed, trying to keep quiet, and cramp paralysed her right hip. She couldn't believe it – this wouldn't have happened if she'd kept going to Keep Fit. She raised her leg and the pain shot down into the bones of her foot. Mistaking her rictus for pleasure he redoubled his efforts. Miraculously her muscles relaxed and the spasm of agony was replaced with a plateau of pleasure, the moment almost better than fulfilment. She wanted to stay there, in perfection. He felt the new change in her and slowed his movements. He almost stopped and she could feel his involuntary pulses inside her, and then she couldn't hold it any more, she raised her legs and gripped him, pulling him further inside her.

And then the release came and with it a sound she had never heard before and she was making it. He arched up, his thrusting faster and faster, like an animal balanced on its back legs, and as they shuddered and gasped with the glorious intensity of the rare simultaneous orgasm, Lucy started to sob. Uncontrollably from the depth of her being, she sobbed in his exhausted arms.

The last thing he heard before slipping into that sleep that's like no other except, hopefully, death, was her love for him. Too late to argue or reject. He slipped into unconsciousness.

Lucy lay listening to him breathing, enjoying the almost forgotten discomfort of seeping wetness.

Lucy had gone when Tom woke up. It was still dark. He felt disorientated. He groped for his watch and the light. Half-past three. Maybe it had just been a dream – he felt more relief than disappointment. Then he saw the earring. The cliché earring. It was caught on the edge of the pillow, clinging on like a tick.

And she had said she loved him.

He closed his eyes and winced. The spartan simplicity of his inner life suddenly felt cluttered, grubby. He didn't want her love. He didn't want any kind of commitment from anyone.

He showered, trying to leave feeling in the bed. Washing her away. He wouldn't see her again until Jenni was back. He felt a spider's web across his face, felt his fingers caught in the drain at the bottom of a swimming pool: the childhood fears of being trapped, unable to escape. How could gentle quiet Lucy make him feel like this? She should have known better than to cry and talk about love.

He shaved. He wanted to put on his uniform and just be the sum of that uniform. He felt oddly angry with Jenni for leaving him exposed to this. He was irritated with himself, these bouts of uncontrollable thoughts, the involuntary need to see Lucy, to hear her voice. Like a small boy kicking against his mother he resented her love, didn't want that feeling of ownership directed towards him. Why did she have to love him? Why did she have to say it? He didn't want to hear all that. All they'd had was sex. Love was a gift he didn't want and couldn't reciprocate.

When Gordon arrived at eight-thirty precisely Tom had defeated Lucy. She had got what she wanted and he had had some relief. That's all it had been. He would make sure he was not similarly distracted again.

By the time Jenni was discharged Tom had slept with Lucy eight times. Every night his self-contempt choked him after she'd slipped out of his bed and padded downstairs. He listened for the front door closing and gave himself up to an orgy of self-hatred, but by the time he returned home from work he ached to be with her, to bury himself inside her.

When Jenni walked back into the house her husband had discovered self-doubt, uncertainty and a sort of love. And between him and Jenni an unbridgeable chasm filled with mutual accusation. And, worse for Tom, the unspoken accusation of the clinic staff.

Jenni wouldn't say where her injuries were from or who had inflicted them – she just looked pale and wounded when asked if it was her husband. Her brute of a husband. And benzodiazepines became her new best friends, her quiet companions protecting her against the violence of men. Tom as always had no idea how to react to Jenni in need and withdrew into cautious formality.

Lucy was hoovering Jenni's fluff-free carpet one morning when Jenni called her from the hall. Obediently Lucy went out to her. Jenni was wearing a light tweed suit, cut by a master. Since her spell away she was more fragilely beautiful than ever, almost translucent, thought her lumpen friend. How could Tom not find her attractive? How could he have preferred Lucy's dimpled thighs to the gazelle legs of this creature?

Jenni, for once, noticed her mood.

'What's the matter, Lucy?'

Lucy smiled, a horizontal tightening of the lips.

'Oh, I was just thinking about Aristotle Onassis missing Maria Callas's thighs when he was married to Jackie.'

Jenni laughed.

'I doubt it, Lucy. She could have played for Arsenal. Now, you remember I've got to go to Vienna today? I should be back tomorrow night – just have to do a piece on some actor who's been elected to Parliament. Too boring. Keep an eye on Tom for me, will you? Oh . . . and how is poor Gary?' She turned to pick up her elegant overnight bag as she asked.

Lucy moved to open the front door for her as she said, 'He's no better, thank you, Jenni. But no worse either.'

Jenni wasn't really listening as she waved to the taxi driver waiting patiently, watching the fare tick up.

'Good. I must get him a healing crystal. They are fantastic. See? I've got one on now and I feel fantastic.' She fished inside her Armani shirt and pulled out a lump of faceted glass on a silver chain. 'It deflects bad radicals. Frees you to be strong, Lucy. Maybe I'll get you one too. Bye.'

Jenni was in the taxi and gone. Lucy stood on the front doorstep. Although they had not discussed Jenni's illness, Lucy sensed she was only maintaining her mental balance, but whatever Jenni was feeling neither Lucy nor anyone else was going to know.

Lucy saw Jenni was taking more and more refuge in New Age claptrap. Everything from colonic irrigation and feng shui to aura readings and sea-shell tarot.

She should finish the cleaning then go back to Gary. Gary with his rock of belief. His inner strength. She mentally contrasted Jenni with him. What did Jenni believe in? Her divine right. And Lucy, what was her faith? She wished she had one. She realised she was bobbing about on a poisoned sea just as Jenni was. Only it was a different sea. And Tom? What did he believe in? The inevitability of death. Nothing more. Gary, believing in the inevitability of life, was, she knew, a better person than any of them. But it was too late. She'd joined the church of hopeless love. Lucy could see the light and longed for its warmth but couldn't stop herself walking into the cold shadow of Tom Shackleton.

She put the hoover away and went upstairs into Tom's bathroom, blocking out the wave of nostalgia she felt walking through his bedroom.

Jenni had asked her to change the bedsheets when she came out of the clinic, not knowing Lucy had changed them almost daily since she'd gone away. But changing them that day, holding his pillow cases to her face and smelling his soap on them, had nearly broken her heart. Nearly broken the heart she'd only found she had in the last two weeks.

Lucy, trying to feel determined, picked up his hairbrush, an old silver-backed affair, no doubt a gift from Jenni. Taking tweezers from her pocket she pulled out a few black hairs, carefully dropping them into a tiny envelope. Then she went downstairs. In Jenni's bookshelf of recipe books she found what she wanted: *The Herbalist's Book of Remedies and Traditional Spells*, between *Buddhist Nutrition* and *Eating to a Better You*.

She opened the book and laid it on the kitchen table, studied the page for a moment then took an apple from the dish in front of her. She sliced it open. Studying the spell intently she took the hairs she'd taken from his brush and placed them on a piece of tissue paper. Then, cutting a few of her own, she laid them on his. She looked at the book again:

> Fold the paper seven times concentrating on your loved one's face, then place it on one half of the apple covering it with the other so the apple is complete again. Bind the apple with a green ribbon and plant it close to your desired one's house. Love will blossom in the untouched heart for you.

Lucy followed the instructions, substituting green electrical tape for the ribbon, and planted the apple between the lavender bushes by the back door. She needed faith in something to stop her sliding into despair over his change since Jenni's return. The withdrawal of his affection was eating away at her sanity. She knew she was not treating Gary well. Nothing in her life had any flavour or joy without Tom, so here she was, sensible, practical Lucy, casting a spell. A love spell on a forty-eight-year-old married policeman.

She set the burglar alarm and left the house quickly before she could dig up the apple and throw it in the bin. It might, just might, work and she would have Tom Shackleton's love. It didn't occur to her it hadn't been invented yet.

Jenni took the train into London. She disliked the city now. The heaven of her parochial childhood had become a dirty, aggressive place populated by people whose lives seemed squalid and pointless as they rushed around in cheap shoes eating out of bags, smoking in doorways and pouring inanities into mobile phones. But there were still pockets where the dream survived, Bond Street, parts of Knights-bridge, tea upstairs at Fortnum's. But today she was in Baker Street and her excitement was as great as when she'd been brought to Madame Tussaud's at the age of six.

Her flight wasn't until late afternoon but she was so keyed up she kept checking her watch. She loved the feeling, the adrenalin released by ambition. The thought of being an also-ran stimulated her more than the brief certainty of victory had.

She withdrew £200 from a cashpoint, as she had regularly since the day of the Ivy lunch. Then she walked up Baker Street until she came to a plain glass-fronted shop. The lettering on the windows indicated that within was held everything a modern spy could want in the course of his or her job. Jenni was wearing large designer dark glasses and a headscarf tied under the chin and behind the head. She looked like Audrey Hepburn as she pressed the buzzer for admittance.

The man who greeted her was a squat version of her husband. His face though was completely unlike Tom's. The skin was darker and the features coarse in comparison. After their mutual good mornings Jenni could see no resemblance. She had him completely spellbound as she asked him to show her his 'bugs'.

She was, she explained in a shy little voice, writing a spy novel and she hoped he'd forgive her using him for her research. He was captivated and happily showed off his polished-wood presentation boxes containing small black cubes. Out of the cubes grew matt black aerials.

'And what are these called? They're exactly what I'm looking for. How exciting!' She gazed up at the man adoringly.

Like a seal thrown a fish, he performed.

'Those, madam, are UHF room transmitters. What the public would call bugs.'

'I see.' Jenni gazed at these small objects of her desire. 'And are they what the CIA use?'

He laughed, charmed by her naivety.

'They are certainly developed from an original used by the intelligence forces, yes. What you must avoid are the cheap imitations – they're aircraft-frequency transmitters. Hopeless. Everybody can listen in. You can probably call minicabs on them. No. These are what you need.'

She held one in her hand: discreet, matt black body, stumpy black aerial. Perfect. She wanted to buy it. Now. Cash. Her bag was heavy with used notes, the fruit of weeks of quiet withdrawals. Risk it. Before she could give in to the temptation she handed it back, then dimpled and fluttered her way out of the shop, promising volumes in the literary future and certainly an autographed first edition. Patience, Jenni. Do nothing that could be traced back to you.

She was all but sweating when she went into Marks & Spencer. Passing the sensible blouses she put her headscarf and sunglasses in her bag and emerged from the front of the store to hail a taxi which took her to the airport.

The ride was an enjoyable hour of picturing the future; by the time she checked in at the Lufthansa desk she was glittering with excitement. She had a plan and that plan would lead to the implosion of Geoffrey Carter and a clear path for her husband. Who was it said if you want to kill a man don't use poison or a gun?

She sat back in her business-class airline seat, and sipped a glass of wine. With it she took one of her magic little pills. By the time they landed she was feeling invulnerable with only a nagging whisper of the paranoia that had begun to dog her. Before disembarking she checked her appearance, though the admiring glances she had been getting from the sweating businessmen near her told her more than her small mirror.

The air hostess with poor skin had looked at her with undisguised admiration and envy for which she had been rewarded with one of Jenni's secret conspiratorial smiles. For want of anything better to do and in the mood to enjoy the girl's attention, Jenni chatted with her. If there was time Jenni always encouraged disciples. The girl had been warmly pleased when Jenni asked her what tights she used. They were obviously expensive, with a high sheen. Enthusiastically, bubbling about how they were her one extravagance, the stewardess produced some packaging and Jenni copied down the name. The girl couldn't know she was doing so to ensure she was never tempted to try them. Shiny Lycra would make a snake look fat.

That evening Jenni, relaxed and preened, sat in her hotel bar in Vienna waiting for the man she was to interview. He arrived an hour late, but she was charming, gracious in putting him at his ease. He had not expected his interrogator to be a great beauty or someone who, apparently, believed in his cause. He was a square-jawed giant originally from some obscure story-book town in the Czech Republic. A film actor of some distinction, often playing honourable U-boat captains. A man who always looked full tortured imagination and compassion. He was in fact as unintelligent as most actors but with more than the average capacity for self-deceit.

Jenni had initially been reluctant to undertake this interview. She had no interest in obscure European political wranglings and certainly didn't care if the people of Austria wanted to race headlong after their fascist past. It seemed almost fashionable in so many European countries.

She was about to tell the editor to find someone else when she saw a way of turning the trip to her advantage. A way to prove Jenni Shackleton was nobody's victim and nobody's fool.

The actor was soon captivated by her and sure she was going to write a loving portrait of him and his views on national borders and the movement of asylum seekers within Europe. But he'd been misquoted too many times in his life not to have in place some insurance policies. He had been surprised to discover who her husband was but, as a politician elected on his strict law-and-order stance, had not been as bothered as some of his left-wing colleagues might have been. But he had learned to be wary of everyone, especially journalists. And journalists more beautiful than any of his leading ladies? Impossible.

He watched her closely, as closely as the plain-clothes policeman in the corner was watching him.

The interview would have been so much more stimulating had she known her subject was the object of police interest due to his enormous but mysterious funds and his close but secretive friendship with several Libyan and Saudi businessmen. Fiscal prudence made strange bedfellows.

She asked if he would like another drink, at the same time, out of habit, being girlishly impressed with his capacity for alcohol.

When the waiter had gone leaving them another inch closer together Jenni said, 'Dieter – such a lovely name.'

'It was my grandfather's. He was from Munich.'

What a surprise, thought Jenni.

'And was he a contemporary of . . . um . . . ?'

'Adolf Hitler? More or less, yes.'

'How fascinating . . .'

And under her adoring and unblinking gaze he talked endlessly into her recorder. Lots of colour, lots of background, while, for his own security, the tape he wore turned silently under his shirt. He'd been misquoted and misrepresented too many times not to keep a record of every encounter.

While he talked her mind roamed around the idea of having sex with him. There could be few women in Europe who hadn't seen his body displayed to great advantage in at least a dozen films. His pure-lined face and lazy dark eyes were cold, a little haughty, under a disciplined wave of gold-blond hair. He was the model of Aryan perfection from art works *circa* 1939. It was a look he had deliberately developed with the help of cosmetic surgery and hair dye transforming the squinting, dark-haired drama student who was too plain to be a leading man. It had cost money, time and pain but he had bought perfection.

He was a challenge. The body at all angles had looked smooth and beautifully muscled. The body of a dancer. Why not?

'Of course we are operating under very bad circumstances. We are continually attacked by anarchists and communists –'

'Good Lord, are there any left? I thought they'd died out with tank tops.'

Dieter did not smile.

Jenni left polite humour bleeding on the coffee table between them and continued.

'How do you deal with them?'

'By due process of democracy.'

Touché, thought Jenni.

She was riveted by his eyes. Dark green, flecked with tiny lines of amber. Too sharply defined to be hazel, too variegated to be brown.

I must have drunk too much, she thought, but it felt good, warm, and made her companion all but irresistible.

He was asking her to have dinner with him. But that wouldn't be all, would it? For him sex came with the bill. She tilted her head back, looking at him through half-closed eyes. What would it be like to bed a legend? A man who had been consistently lusted after for twenty years. Was this the bicycle she should re-mount after her fall? She was certain of a smooth ride. His technique was widely reported in glossy kiss-and-tell magazines.

Why, though? What was in it for her? And that was what decided her: there was nothing riding on this encounter. If she couldn't do it, if she was repelled at the sight of his erection and ran screaming from the room, she had nothing to lose. But if she didn't, if the next time she called upon her body to pay the way and found it unwilling or incapable there might well be a great deal at stake. So why not? He'd be doing her a favour. Another drink, a couple of pills, no problem. And he was increasingly gorgeous.

He'd covered her hand with his. Long, slim and pale. Strangler's hands, she thought.

He nodded as though reading her thoughts.

'You don't mind me finding you attractive, do you?'

What an exceptionally stupid thing to say, she thought.

'But maybe you are happily married woman. You don't need me.'

She rather liked his humility. His lack of assumption. Of course it was an act. Did it matter? No.

'My husband . . .' Her luminous eyes seemed to fill with tears. He moved his hand up her arm. It felt very nice.

'He is bastard, yes?'

'Oh yes,' she breathed. 'How did you know?'

Dieter raised his eyebrow, waiting.

'I'm sure he has . . . a mistress.'

Jenni almost cracked at this. The idea of Tom Shackleton willingly being intimate with anyone was just funny. Hilariously funny. She started to giggle.

'He finds me repulsive. He hasn't made love to me for years. It's awful. Sometimes he beats me . . .'

The graceful arm was now round her shoulders. The hand proprietorial, protective, and, as Jenni noticed, slightly grubby.

He was suitably but quietly outraged.

'Bastard!'

Good, that was the right effect. She looked up at him and her eyes stung with tears. To her astonishment they were genuine, as was her whispered plea.

'I don't know if I can. I . . . I was hurt, badly. I would need you to be patient. Gentle.'

Nothing could have made him desire her more.

When they got to her room the coverlet of the double bed had been turned down and the table lamps lit the room romantically. Gold-covered chocolates on the pillows.

Dieter was convinced by her nervousness that she rarely took men to bed. Her awkward response when he had tried to kiss her in the lift. He liked that. It was nice to know she wasn't easy. It flattered him.

He sat down in an armchair watching her fluttering about, opening the minibar, reluctant to come back to him. She reminded him of a virgin. Good body too for her age. She handed him a brandy.

She'd made her decision but her mind was arguing. What's to lose? Another man, another bed. She'd been to bed with worse for less. Yes . . . but the Gnome. The Gnome. Fall off the bike, get back on. This was the night to get back on. But what if . . . ? What if?

'Have you got protection?'

'Always.'

He produced a neat triumvirate of condoms. Why had she asked? She had let MacIntyre – shut up, shut the fuck up. The noise in her head was deafening. She was shaking now. She felt vulnerable. She felt like the fearful girl she'd been before she invented Jenni. Scared by everything.

He was captured.

'Here, don't be frightened. I have a little of this. And by chance I have two of these. I must have known we would be here maybe.'

His accent and quaint constructions made him less threatening, a little comic. He put a tiny box and something that looked to Jenni like a small suppository on the low table.

'You call them poppers in English. You don't know them? Amyl nitrate, yes?'

'I don't know,

I don't take drugs,' said Jenni primly. 'And I'm surprised you'll risk it in front of me. How do you know you can trust me?'

He shrugged. 'I don't. But you have more to lose than me, yes?'

She watched, fascinated, as he set out his stall and prepared what she took to be cocaine. She had only seen it done in television serials about city whiz kids and was fascinated despite herself.

'I . . . I don't . . .'

She trailed off lamely. Inside she was screaming for another pill. Maybe this would do. Lift her away from this sordid room, sordid spreading of her legs for yet another stranger. Lift her into her dreams, to the place where success made her untouchable.

She walked towards him. He saw in her a reluctant desire, like that of a squirrel approaching a hand outstretched with nuts. He found her enchanting. Seeing she didn't know what to do, he placed some of the chopped and prepared white powder on the back of his right hand and reached for her with his left. She wanted to object, ask for a rolled-up twenty-pound note and the mirror. She knew the way it should be.

He caught her gently round the back of her neck reminding her of Tom's prelude to foreplay. She bent towards him. He placed the cocaine close under her nose. Pushed it firmly against her nostrils then closed one with his thumb.

'Sniff in now. Good sniff. Big. Good.' He closed her other nostril with his index finger. 'Other side. Yes.'

Obediently she sniffed it all up. It reminded her of when she was a child and her father had made her sniff salt water for a cold. The kindly paternal hands. He wiped the residue from her nose with the top of his index finger then lifted her upper lip and rubbed it on to her gums. She felt like a horse having its teeth examined. Nothing, nothing, was happening but a numbness in her gums. A lot of fuss over a local anaesthetic. She watched him doing the professional line-dance sniff with a rolled note. Still nothing.

He stood up and started the sex. That was the only way she could think of it. He'd done his drugs, now he was doing his sex. Then it kicked in. She felt the mass of energy: the picture in her head was, for a second, an innocent stick of uranium, a scene from a news programme. Then she saw, heard the radiation. Had an impression of atoms colliding, splitting and exploding their energy into her head.

And she started to talk. And she couldn't stop. What was she talking about? Power, the power invested in her. The overwhelming confidence she felt lifted her away from everything that had dragged her down. The man busying himself with her clothes was funny. Really, really funny. Jenni couldn't stop laughing. She had never in her life laughed like this, until the tears ran and her ribs hurt.

He was undoing his trousers now, pulling down his Calvin Kleins, releasing the bouncing, waving resident. Then he took more white powder and rubbed it on to the ugly, shiny, expectant face below. It looked like snow on the roof of a Masai warrior's hut. The thought of it, the sight of it, set her off again and she fell back on the bed, helpless with laughter. She couldn't think when she'd enjoyed herself so much.

And there was the freedom. The clarity. The release. She hardly felt the sex at all. She was still laughing, not at him but at her fear. She was free of the fear of MacIntyre. A man pumping away inside her as if reaching for a lost coin was nothing. It was just funny. Her mind was not a part of it. She was not there, she was with her ambitious dreams, barely disturbed by the rhythmic pushing against the bones of her open pelvis. The manipulation of her body had been skilful, considered, masterful and completely wasted on her. It was all a joke. A very funny joke.

He lay on his back and pulled her on to him, astride him. She let him guide her wherever he wanted, and what he wanted was her sitting on his face. Again the bubbles of hysteria, shaking her with laughter: 'Sit on my face and tell me that you love me, sit on my face and tell me that you care.' How many times in the early days had she heard Tom's cronies singing that as they brought him home too drunk to stand.

His tongue was nothing like the Gnome's: it was soft, gentle, not unlike water lapping against her. Very comforting. She was no closer to orgasm than when she unloaded the dishwasher. She altered her position, carefully impaling herself on him. She moved automatically, her hands on his ribs. Look at me, I'm riding Dieter Gerhardt. Look on, you harpies, and despair. She was laughing again. Threatening to expel him. Concentrate, Jenni. She frowned slightly. Eyes closed. She was enjoying herself. Yes. Not the sex, no, that was no more or less than it had always been.

No, she was just enjoying being free. But now she was tiring. She tried a few fancy moves to bring him closer to a finish, having no idea the cocaine on his penis had numbed it more than the brandy she had been pouring into him all evening, making him able to go on and on – and on.

She moved him on top of her, behind her; she moaned and gasped and manipulated his flaccid balls but nothing seemed to bring him closer to a climax. Now she was beginning to be bored and uncomfortable. The drug was wearing off; she clenched her inner muscles more rhythmically trying to squeeze him to an end. But nothing worked. He was in his own sexual fantasy.

Then he gasped, 'Talk dirty. Say dirty words. Now. Quick.'

Jenni's mind went blank. The only German she knew was '*chemische Reinigung*', dry cleaner's. In English all she could think of was an anecdote told her by a media colleague about a news reader caught in flagrante who had screamed 'Fuck me till I fart' at the moment of ecstasy.

She tried it.

It seemed to do the trick and he speeded up to a rictus of pleasure accompanied by grunts and strangled cries of, 'Oh God, *Mein Gott. Gott.*'

Then, 'Take me now!'

In all her sexual encounters Jenni had never heard anyone actually say that. It set her laughing again as he yelled it like Henry V on the eve of Agincourt.

Spent, he was apologetic she hadn't come. He insisted on manipulating her until she did. How could he know in all her life Jenni Shackleton had never had an orgasm. After a decent interval she shuddered and moaned and sighed convincingly enough for a man who'd already been there. She knew it was with some relief he kissed her and sighed into sleep with her head on his chest, his arm under her. She got up carefully and looked at him, naked and spreadeagled in the foam of sheets. He really was stunning. Every hair on his body a fine uniform gold. She appreciated how much work that must have taken. Looking down at him she thought there was nothing more satisfying than having something coveted by others.

She went to the bathroom, showered and felt fine. She still couldn't face the idea of a bath but it hadn't been so bad getting back on to that bicycle after all. The poppers lay unused on the table. She put them in her bag. They might come in useful. A little more magic to help her through the mire of life. There was a little white powder left, scattered. She fingered it up and rubbed it on her gums. Nice. Very, very nice.

Lucy had waited as long as she could for Tom to come home. Her excuse was Jenni's request that she should look after him. But he didn't come so she went across the road to give Gary his hot milk and biscuits before the nurses came to put him to bed.

Since leaving hospital he hadn't been strong enough to use his chair. Going to bed was no change of scene for him. Lucy knew he was depressed but couldn't find the words to help him. The feelings she'd allowed to grow for Tom as a defence against what seemed the inevitable early death of Gary had got out of control. Now more real than her love for Gary.

'Did you see Tom?'

Lucy felt guilty at his question. An urge to defensiveness.

'I came back as quickly as I could. Jenni's away – she wanted me to make sure he was OK.'

Gary's eyes, the only part of him that still seemed fully alive, followed her movements as she fussed around tidying. Keeping her back to him. Avoiding him. He knew something had happened while he was in hospital but wanted to avoid the truth. He didn't want to hear how often she talked about Tom. How difficult she found it to say 'Tom' in front of him. The way she called him the Chief, or His Nibs, or him over there, because the word 'Tom' had become sacred, too powerful to speak aloud.

Gary had never felt so lonely and for the first time wanted to die. He had once been water skiing and although the ride, being dragged across the water by grimly holding on to a rope attached to a speed boat, was exhilarating, the most pleasurable part was letting go and sinking into the sea. It had been warm and welcoming, a Greek sea full of dolphins and sparkling light.

Lucy handed him his baby cup of warm milk.

He wanted to let go now.

Since the ambulance had brought Gary back Shackleton had avoided Lucy. He knew she wanted to talk, women always wanted to talk, to analyse, but his instinct was to walk away. As if it had never happened. His brief addiction to Lucy's willingness had woken in him a vicious self-dislike. For his weakness and his betrayal of Gary. He had never had friends, but in his mind Gary became a friend betrayed. Tom saw himself hanging in the ruined garden of his own pleasure. Pleasure was bad. The threat of happiness undermining. Lucy the serpent of temptation. He desperately wanted to be free again, not to feel, just to be. Not to be scalded by her gentleness or burned by his need for her.

He came home that night to an empty house, grateful for the silence. He felt her watching from across the road as Gordon said goodnight and he unlocked the front door. He went into the kitchen. On the table was a salad and a note from Lucy. A small chocolate egg beside the plate. He put the lot into the bin. The note unread.

He poured himself a drink and took his briefcase into the living room. It was filled with papers that would occupy him until the early hours. An evening of their uncomplicated intimacy would be a relief. The curtains were open; he went to draw them and saw Lucy in the window opposite. He didn't hesitate to shut her out.

Gary saw and said nothing. There wasn't anything to say. He

turned his face to the wall and prayed like a man trusting to a note in a cracked bottle.

A few days before Jenni straddled Dieter and Tom rejected Lucy, Geoffrey and Eleri were returning home from a reception in London. A charity bash with a discreetly A-list donor core. And at the centre of that core? Robert and Lizie MacIntyre. They had been more than friendly to the Carters. The two men had discovered they had something in common when they lunched together, though Carter had for years been at pains to hide it: they were both intellectual snobs.

Mrs Ismay from next door had looked after the boys for them. She didn't cause Alexander to panic so was one of the few people they could leave him with without risking the Wedgwood. When they arrived back she was sitting in the living room knitting; Alexander was curled up on the rug in front of the fire chewing a piece of coal. It was a warm night but Alex was obsessed by fires as well as liquids so, to guarantee a quiet evening, a fire had been laid and lit.

While Eleri said goodnight to the old lady after listening to every detail of the evening's events, including who had read the news and what the weather forecast had in store for her agapanthus, Carter carried the boy up to bed. The child was floppy and unresponsive though wide awake. Carter was glad – better this than hyperactive and the rest of the night spent following him from room to room trying to protect him from the hardness and sharpness of the furniture. He didn't try to take the coal out of his hand: that would only bring on a screaming fit and guarantee nobody in the street would sleep.

Peter, as always, didn't wake through the disturbance as Alexander was put to bed. Carter leaned over and kissed him, savouring the smell of warm sleeping child. Peter smiled and put his arm round Carter's neck. He gently disentangled himself and tucked the child's arm back under the duvet. He turned to go but was stopped by Peter's sleepy voice.

'Daddy . . . I love you best in all the world.'

'I love you too, Peter. Best in all the world.'

It was their joke.

''Cept for Mummy and Alex and the Bump.'

'Yeah, 'cept for them. Night, Petey.'

Downstairs the night-time peace every parent craves settled on them as they sat in front of the fire. The room was long and thin, filled with books, toys, Peter's violin music, magazines and, on one of the radiators, a pair of striped socks. The light from the table lamps made the mess look cosy. On the shelves, high enough to be out of Alexander's way, expensive crystal shared space with Christmas cracker novelties and CDs parted from their covers.

'So what did he say?'

'MacIntyre? Nothing much. Nothing he didn't say at lunch.'

Eleri was sitting cross-legged on the floor, her growing belly resting on her heels. She rubbed it for the fiftieth time, as she had every day since finding there was an occupant within. She sat back against his chair, tucking her shoulders under his legs.

'Talk me through it.'

'Well . . . he says they're determined to make me change my mind. Apparently the Prime Minister's decided there's no one else for the job.'

'What about Tom?'

'No, they want him for the Met. They don't think he's got the . . .' He paused – what was it MacIntyre had said? Clever but not an intellectual giant. 'Mental capacity for the job.'

Eleri laughed. 'Don't let Jenni hear you say that. She thinks her husband is in direct line to the Almighty. You don't think he's dim, do you?'

Carter considered his drink. 'Not dim, no . . . but . . . he's not an independent thinker. And he's not an innovator.'

'What about the siege?'

Carter shook his head.

'That was a stupid risk – I should never have gone along with it. Pure ego. But that's the thing about Tom. He has an extraordinary instinct for self-promotion but basically' – the killer blow – 'it's not a first-rate mind.'

And Carter's was. Neither he nor Eleri had to say it. At university he had shone but in the police service he was a mental colossus and Tom was clever. For a policeman.

Eleri's sympathy was genuine. It was never anything else.

'Poor Jenni – I'm sure she'd rather be married to a Tsar than a commissioner.'

Carter smiled. He was quite sure she would but she could surely never imagine Tom would be considered for such a job.

He'd been surprised and not entirely comfortable with the new closeness that had grown up between Jenni and Eleri. His wife always saw the best in everybody. She was always getting hurt, bounding up to people like a Labrador puppy trailing loo paper and getting smacked on the snout for its trouble.

He knew his wife needed the company of another woman now, one that could make the pregnancy ordinary, natural, nothing to worry about. But Jenni Shackleton? She had never struck him as the earth-mother type.

'Is she coming over tomorrow?'

'Yes, she said she'd look after the boys every afternoon this week so I can get some rest and start getting the baby's room ready, then she's going to Vienna to interview Dieter Gerhardt, lucky thing.' She paused, hating to do anything he didn't approve of. 'I know you don't like her much but she's been a good friend, Geoffrey. I don't know what I'd have done without her these last few weeks. I think that breakdown she had changed her. She's not nearly as brittle as she was.'

They talked about the Shackletons because neither of them really wanted to broach the subject of The Baby versus The Job. Carter had been quite determined to quit, but that was before he'd known exactly how big the government's challenge was. MacIntyre had talked budgets and aims that were far beyond anything he'd envisaged. This was not to be another slice of gesture politics. This Tsar, unlike those for drugs, homelessness and various cancers, would have some real power.

Carter had become very excited – but he'd promised Eleri, so the chance to shape policing in the twenty-first century would have to pass him by. Every day he put the thing out of his mind and every night before sleep he couldn't stop planning his team, forming his strategy, imagining the future. He ached to be the first anti-crime coordinator, not the billionth father.

Eleri broke the silence.

'You've got to take it, you know.'

'What?'

'The Tsardom. Oh Geoffrey . . . you'll never forgive yourself if you don't. I can't watch you torturing yourself over it any more.'

He was ashamed. Was his desire really so obvious? Defensively, Carter became entrenched in moral certainties. He was adamant: the baby came first. He owed it to Eleri, he owed it to the family. But even as he spoke he felt as if her words had released him from a prison of domestic duty. No man had ever wanted a child more than he wanted this one but it wasn't his body it was growing in, and it wasn't the focus of his every waking moment. But stubbornly he continued to argue logically, illogically and logistically until Eleri was exhausted.

The question hung unresolved between them.

Eleri, like a chastised but determined child, spoke quietly.

'Geoffrey, I can't tell you how much I want you to stay home with me. You know how frightened I am but . . . if you do give it all up I won't be married to Geoffrey Carter any more. I'll only have a bit of you. The little tiny bit that isn't your job. And do you know what? It's for me I want you to go for it. I don't want to be grateful and guilty and married to a man who'll always be thinking: What if . . . No matter what you say, somewhere, deep down, you'll always resent me and the baby if you give it up.'

He knew she was right. He was nothing without his job, any more than Eleri was without her family. And, he realised, he didn't want to be anything without her.

She watched him thinking it over. His face was serious, his eyes fixed on the dying fire. Yes, it would be enough of an upheaval making room for one stranger, let alone two, as there was no question of not having someone to help with the child. But if you took emotion and sentiment out of the argument it was obvious that he should become Crime Tsar; it was what he'd spent his life preparing for. Her face shone up at him as she realised she was winning. She spoke with the fervour of Saint Joan.

'We'll move down to London – I've found a school that will take Alex and a choir school I'm sure Peter could get into and I've registered with a place that supplies Norland Nannies. We can do it, Geoffrey. I know we can. There's no rule that says you can't have it all . . .'

That night they clung to each other so closely they could have slept on a razor blade. The future was the Promised Land and tonight they were on Egypt's border.

Despite Geoffrey telling her not to say anything, Eleri greeted Jenni with the news as she arrived next day.

Eleri was overwhelmed with the warmth of her congratulations and assurances of support. The Shackletons would always be there.

Jenni was in her bathroom when there was a knock on the door. Dieter had gone soon after she had demonstrated her skills at fellatio: always keep a tune in your head, she'd been advised by a school-friend, something with a strong beat. She remembered they had sniggered over everything from the National Anthem to 'The Flight of the Bumblebee'. For Dieter she had chosen '*Deutschland Über Alles*', speeding up towards the end, of course.

When he'd gone she fell asleep without help but woke with vague nagging fears and her nerves writhing like worms just under her skin.

Robert MacIntyre persisted, like drizzle, at the edge of her mind. She took a pill. Then another. She drank coffee. She showered and sat down to apply her make-up. This ritual always calmed her but still there were the jitters, the anxiety. She took a third pill and felt better. She knew it was stupid to take more than two but . . . just this once. Just this once.

Then there was the knock at the door. It made her jump. She opened it and was handed a package by a dumpy maid in an ill-fitting uniform. Or perhaps not, thought Jenni. Maybe it's the body that doesn't fit. She shoved a piece of paper at Jenni and a cheap blue biro. She signed without thinking. The maid said, '*Danke*,' and waddled away down the corridor.

Jenni closed the door and opened the brown-wrapped box. Inside was a charming marcasite brooch. Perfect for Lucy, she thought. 'From Dieter with thanks for an enjoyable interview.' And beneath the unwearable brooch? A neat packet of cocaine.

Jenni smiled. It had been worth it. She could tell the world that Jenni was herself again. Oh, the glorious power of beauty. There was not a man born she couldn't seduce or manipulate. How did plain women manage with just intelligence to carry them through? She laughed. That was not a question to which she'd ever have to discover the answer. She took a little powder, just a tiny buzz, finished her make-up and made her way to the nearest metro. At the deepest level modified but unchanged by experience.

*   *   *

187

When she was in Vienna before she had been shocked at the literature displayed openly at the news-stands at the mouths of the metro stations. On the ground were laid out pornographic magazines, and it had been a Sunday. A church-going day. Jenni smiled at how much she'd altered.

It was a glorious sunny morning and the walk past the old buildings made her feel clean and new. She recognised the feeling as happiness. She was getting what she wanted. Passing a fine old baker's she decided to take back a Sachertorte for Lucy and Gary. After all, Lucy had long since given up watching her figure and the thought would count. Poor Lucy. She had neglected her since coming out of the clinic. Concentrating too hard on the two-faced Mrs Carter. She'd always disliked the Welsh. Her mother said they were like fog: they were dense and you couldn't touch or trust them. And Eleri Carter had proved the rule. But she'd make it up to dear old loyal Lucy. Maybe she'd take her shopping when she got back, buy her some new clothes. That thing she'd worn to dinner must have looked nice on the hanger, she supposed. Ten years ago.

At the metro she found a spectacularly well-stocked pavement and searched the covers for one particular perversion, but what there was was too tame. She picked up a couple anyway and went to the shaggy individual in the booth. He took the note she offered without looking at her. His grimy mittened hand passed back her change.

'Excuse me . . . do you speak English?'

There was no one else at the stall, just a few people scurrying down the escalator into the metro.

'A little. *Ja*. I speak a little.'

Jenni didn't waste any charm on him.

'These magazines, do you have more? Different? More . . . serious?'

He looked at her for the first time.

'You want young? More young?'

'Yes,' said Jenni.

'More young. Girls? With adults, grown-ups. Anything.' He looked at her again.

She applied a dimpled smile.

'Yes. But boys, not girls. For my husband. You understand. It is not possible to get in England.'

He nodded, sucking the nicotined ends of his moustache.

'English men like little boys.'

'And girls sometimes,' added Jenni, as if they were talking about a choice between pork and lamb.

'*Ja*. Girls too. But not so much.'

He reached under the counter and produced a magazine.

It was hard-core homosexual paedophilia and sickeningly graphic. She looked at it briefly.

'Only in German?'

He pulled at his nose.

'*Nein . . . Ich habe* Dutch and . . . Wait . . .'

He rummaged under the counter.

'American. But with American a little of dogs too.'

'Oh good,' said Jenni sweetly. 'My husband loves animals.'

She took the two well-fingered magazines. They were horrifyingly explicit.

'How much?'

The figure he named was ridiculous and she knew he was ripping her off but was in no position to haggle. They looked as if they'd been used as part of a lending library they were so soiled. But she gave the money for them and for three other equally disgusting publications then put them quickly in her bag.

'Wait,' the man in the booth said.

She stopped.

'You like video? Not gay stuff. Men, women with little boys. One only three years.'

'How much?'

He held his fingers up.

She did a quick calculation. Almost £80. He must have seen her coming. But she handed over the money and put the video in the carrier bag without looking at it.

As she turned to go she didn't notice the leather-jacketed young man with the camera.

The confidence that had surged through her an hour before was gone as she packed to leave. She had never been stopped at customs but now snakes of fear made her shake. She wished she had some of that magical white powder to give her that glorious feeling of untouchability again. She decided to go back to the hotel for just a tiny bit more of the magic powder. Dieter had sent a bottle of vintage Krug up to her room, and a note: 'One more night . . .' Well, she could do with a little more time, a little more cocaine, and if that meant having to sleep with one of Europe's most enigmatic sex symbols again, well, she'd manage.

There were two more jobs to do before she could relax. Jenni, for all the adrenalin and risk, regarded the destruction of Geoffrey Carter as something that had to be done, like removing the giblets from a chicken. It was a job. She didn't dislike him – he caused her no more emotion than a car parked across her gates. It was the driver for whom she nursed her hatred. And that was Robert MacIntyre.

She was sure, beyond sure, that he had known Carter was to be Crime Tsar when she rolled over for the Met. She was not stupid, as she never tired of telling Tom. She knew, if challenged, MacIntyre would say she'd never mentioned the other job, that she had wanted London for her puppet of a husband, and he'd got it for her. She had made a payment. He wasn't telepathic, after all. It was business, wasn't it? A messy business and unfinished . . .

Jenni fingered her crystal amulet as she left the hotel room, placing the 'Do not disturb' sign on the door.

She was pretty sure where she was going; she'd seen it when visiting Vienna with Tom. He'd brought her for her birthday last year. But only because he was attending a symposium in the city. Another spoiled gesture of empty generosity, another shared bed undisturbed by their frigid bodies. People looked at them and saw enduring romance. But Tom and Jenni never looked at themselves, only at each other, and always with suspicion. Barcelona, where Tom was about to take her for another birthday, would be another such exercise, but this time she would shop. Her husband, she thought, was always the master of the inappropriate gesture.

As always, Jenni had seen everything and stored the images away like picture postcards. The one she pulled up now read Friedrich-strasse. The taxi dropped her at the end of the road and she walked up it, not quite sure what she was looking for.

There it was, exactly as she'd remembered it, a small dingy café, very old and very picturesque. She went down the steps holding on to the iron railing, her slim coltish legs and soft leather shoes, toned perfectly to the shade of her subtly gleaming legs, appearing first in the view of the men in the café. The door was heavy wood with small leaded glass panels. She pushed. A bell tinkled and the door opened into a splendid pre-war expanse of polished wood. Music played loudly from a system behind the bar. For a moment she thought she'd made a mistake, then she saw them. The computers, as grey as wood lice against the dark sheen of the panelling.

The three men who had watched her come down the steps made no sign they'd noticed her come in, beyond a brief friendly nod from the barman. In the corner sat a dreadlocked Viennese whose blond braids were matted together at the roots and whose red neckerchief matched that of his dog. On the end of a piece of string it slumped in dejected neutral, staring at the wall. The second man was reading *El Pais* at the bar and was obviously a student of Spanish as he was discussing an item in the paper with the barman and doing grievous harm to that language with his Germanic accent. The three men, carefully indifferent, each glanced at her.

She liked the way their looks became appreciative as the full subtlety of her loveliness revealed itself to them. There was nothing obvious about her and men always had a feeling of private pride that they had spotted her. She somehow made men feel they had discovered her, like a rare flower. It was a skill she'd developed after marrying Tom.

Tom's view of Jenni hadn't changed since the night he'd seen her come home with – Jenni shook her head to dislodge the picture of Tom's hurt eyes in those early days. The awkward virgin Tom thrusting at her like a rabbit. Unable to arouse her and embarrassed by her practised fingers.

Their marriage had been a glorious Gothic arch of disaster followed by years of mutual ambition punctuated by public triumph and private grief. One pregnancy had ended as it had begun, quickly and without joy. Tom had bought her a card. It was inappropriate: 'In Sympathy', the sort of card you'd send for someone's granny's funeral.

The death of her first child was her grief, her tragedy, and she always loved that barely formed unborn baby above all others. Jenni could only give love to something that didn't exist.

If she had allowed herself to love Tom, not deliberately wreck her nascent feelings on the rocks of promiscuity, she would have laid herself open to fear. The fear of losing him, the fear of illusions shattered. Sometimes the thought of what might have been, if she'd been kinder, curled up like white smoke. But she always pulled away, blaming him for her anger. The anger that came out of a hurt he'd never inflicted.

Tom. Jenni had given up wishing for him to take charge in the house, in the bedroom, but couldn't, even after decades of marriage, see that she was responsible for his impotence. He seemed to cease to exist as he walked through the front door. Like that dog down there, staring at the wall, no more than the table leg, a part of the floor.

Jenni went to one of the computers, ordering a cream-laden Viennese coffee as she passed the bar. A young man came in and sat at the other computer. She didn't give him a glance.

She sat down and opened her bag; in a box she had two floppy discs of different specifications. She smiled, the more widely used of the two was compatible. She slid it in. She smiled. This was the maraschino cherry on the outrageous cocktail of her plan. And its consequences had no more reality for her than a video game.

She began surfing the net. An obliging young sub on one of her newspapers had spent a besotted afternoon close to her, guiding her mouse through webs and sites. She had rewarded him with a probing kiss and the pressing of her unfettered breasts against his polycotton shirt. Jenni always liked to express her gratitude where it would be appreciated.

She worked quickly, dipping in and out of various sites promising photographs, names and contact addresses for children, then found what she was looking for, an American paedophile site of such depravity Jenni had to sit stunned for a moment staring at the words and pictures. It would not make sense to her brain that this was real. For the first time she paused. The weapon she was about to use against Geoffrey Carter would split him apart as surely as the man would the boy on the screen in front of her.

If Jenni was ever to stand outside herself this was the moment to do it. And she did, she looked down on herself and prayed for cruelty, prayed to have Tom's ability to see people without compassion. The world related to Tom, he did not reciprocate, and that, watching this parade of filth, was the dislocation she wanted. Please God, let me not care. For a moment the mother in her hesitated. What if they were her children . . .

She pressed the keys and without drama or a finger of forked lightning from the sky the degrading and defiling of children was downloaded on to her innocent disc. It was done. She moved on to another five sites and made a note of them. They were all more disgusting than anything she'd ever seen before but now she was in control. She cut herself off from the reality of the images moving jerkily on the screen in front of her.

She paid for her undrunk coffee, smiled at the three men and the indifferent dog and left. She needed to get back to her room, get her bag and go to the airport gently infused with one of her little pills. The man at the other computer pulled his jacket across his camera and drank her coffee.

Just one more thing to do.

The taxi stopped outside a disappointingly ordinary building situated in an area of Vienna that looked like an opera set. Jenni was speaking into her mobile as she struggled to find the money to pay the driver. He gave her her change and offered her back the scrap of paper she'd given him with the address. She waved it away. The page of the Vienna phone book that began with Speer and ended in SpyMeister. Subtle. No doubt during the cold war they'd been run off their feet.

'Janet . . . could you tell the Chief I've been held up and won't be back till tomorrow? Yes . . . I know he's got a conference today.' I'm his wife, you stupid woman, I have his diary. 'Just let him know, when you have a chance. Oh . . . and how's your mother?' Was that a ladder in her tights? Damn. Never mind, she had spares at the hotel. 'A stroke? Oh dear, I am sorry . . . You're breaking up . . . No, I'm losing the signal . . .'

Jenni pressed the button and Janet was gone, still saying, 'I can hear you, Mrs Shackleton.'

Jenni checked her scarf and sunglasses – no need to take any risks – and went into SpyMeister. The assistant was a polite young man – couldn't possibly be a Viennese, thought Jenni.

'Do you have any VHF room transmitters, please?'

His English, like his manners, was immaculate.

'Of course, madam.'

Simple, straightforward, as easy as buying shoes. Normally she would have expended charm on the young man but the urge to get back to the womb of her hotel was becoming too strong to ignore.

Her heart seemed to have developed an extra beat which tripped it into a disturbing flutter. It had happened occasionally in the past but since the clinic she'd noticed the irregularities becoming more frequent. Something to remember the Gnome by. She shuddered.

'Let me see them.' She checked that they were identical to the ones she'd seen in London. She loved the feel of them, the shape, the smooth surfaces. Perfect. 'I'll take five.'

The boy was surprised and started to question her. She snapped at him and he wrapped them up in an unmarked but elegantly designed carrier bag. She opened her shoulder bag, careful not to reveal her purchases, and paid him in cash. This, however, did not surprise him.

A man who'd come in after her waited patiently until she'd been served, busying himself looking at the miniature cameras.

By five-thirty she was back in her room, her purchases laid out on the table in front of her. Her little bottle of pills was by her glass of champagne – just a half-bottle from the minibar, to celebrate – and the cocaine ready on her make-up mirror. This time she'd do it the way they did it in the films. God was in his heaven and all was right with the world.

She picked up the phone and languidly pressed Dieter's number.

'Dieter . . . is that you? Now about tonight – you *are* still free, aren't you? Why don't you come here for dinner? . . . Good, about eight . . . Oh and Dieter . . . I *did* appreciate your sweet present. Where did you get it? I'd so like to buy some for myself . . . well, if you can spare it . . . how lovely. I'll see you at eight. Bye.'

Jenni sat back. This was happiness.

PART FOUR

'**S**o you've heard the rumours then?'

Carter was smiling as he asked the question. He and Tom were standing at the improvised bar set up after the conference. Behind the white-draped trestle table comfortable middle-aged women in black-and-white served drinks while other, even more mumsy types mingled with trays of canapés. Tom was more relaxed than Geoffrey had ever seen him. Jenni had got held up in Vienna and would be away an extra night and Tom seemed like a different man. A very likeable one, too often held rigidly in control either at work or under his wife's always watchful eye.

Tom surveyed the scene with some pride. He liked hosting the occasional gathering of his peers and was proud of his force's headquarters, a building of some history. They had dealt with the thorny question of decriminalising underage prostitution and now they were relaxing, some faster than others.

Tom looked at Carter; he noticed how white his teeth were. He noticed because Jenni had mentioned them. She had something of an obsession with teeth.

'They must be caps – or he bleaches them, yes, that must be it. He uses that stain-removing paste.'

By the time she'd finished Geoffrey Carter had had every tooth in his head out and dipped in hydrochloric acid so he could be Crime Tsar, soundbite- and photo-friendly. Anything to get one over on Tom Shackleton.

Tom looked again. They were real and they were natural. He smiled, looking out across the room, aware they were even more subjects of speculation than Carter's dental ware. His own smile was constructed to conceal his teeth, not that they were bad or misshapen, just a little crowded at the top causing him to draw his upper lip down and turn the corners of his mouth up giving him that shy appearance when he smiled. Women found it devastatingly attractive, men just thought he wasn't much given to smiling.

'Yes, it's me for the Met and you for the Crime Tsar, I hear.'

Carter looked at him over the rim of his glass; his eyes were sparkling with conspiracy. He raised his eyebrows.

'Well?'

Shackleton was friendly, easy, non-competitive.

'Well what?'

'Happy?' Carter asked, and Shackleton saw it hadn't even occurred to him that Tom might want the Tsardom.

He saw himself as he imagined Carter saw him, someone who'd done well, risen beyond his roots, a man who'd be more than proud to achieve the position of Commissioner. A man with little imagination, a policeman's policeman. He saw in Carter's eyes he wasn't even a threat, not in the same class. It had never occurred to him, or the shadows behind him, to consider Shackleton.

Tom suddenly felt like a child who's performed his tricks and been patted on the head. Now the grown-ups would go about their business with no further thought of his precocity. And that's what really bit, that no matter how high he got he was still just Tom. Oh, Tom'll do that. Oh, give that to Tom. That's good enough for Tom. No, Tom's good enough for that.

'What do you think?' Carter asked.

Did he want an answer? Was he asking through politeness or was this a fishing trip?

'Well, I haven't been appointed yet. As far as I know it's just the Serious Rumour Squad working overtime.'

'Sure. Sure,' Carter nodded, dropping peanuts into his mouth.

He had only once looked at Shackleton, the rest of the time his eyes roamed the room, benign, smiling, watching over their flock. Shackleton watched too, his midnight eyes alert, cold, the eyes of a predator.

'What about you? The Tsardom, you've been approached?'

'They haven't officially asked yet. Presumably they have to advertise. Go through the motions.'

Shackleton nodded, envious of Carter's smooth nonchalance. Carter didn't have to look at him for the next question, he knew Shackleton didn't have a choice.

'Will you take the Met?'

They were aware of the other chiefs' awareness of them as thoroughbreds. But only one winner.

A waitress drifted past carrying a tray of unidentifiable mouth-fillers. Shackleton stopped her, a delaying tactic. He picked up something soft and pink on an inch of biscuit. Automatically he half smiled his thanks to her. She frowned back at him and sucked the air through her lips and teeth.

He was confused, unexpectedly off balance.

It was the big one, the voluptuous one, the one that made him feel inadequate. He involuntarily made a little giggle, incongruous in a man of his size and position, a leftover from the awkwardnesses of his adolescence.

'Hello . . .' he said. He had a way of saying the word that sounded at once intimate and apologetic. Like his diffident smile it charmed women and irritated men.

It had neither effect on the waitress, she just turned her great body towards Carter and stared at him. Despite himself he was shocked by his quick response to the sheer sexuality of the woman.

'You watch him, Geoffrey, cos for all your big brain you don't have what he's got.' She laughed loud enough for people to look round.

Two women chief constables were amused by the appearance of reverse sexual harassment. Both Carter and Shackleton looked very uncomfortable. She laughed and sashayed off with her tray. The tension between Carter and Shackleton was palpable.

Carter broke it.

'Care in the community, eh?'

Shackleton laughed, relief making Carter's comment very funny.

'Want another drink?'

Carter had turned to the bar; Shackleton looked at his relaxed, well-tailored back. No pearl handle there and he was surprised to find himself thinking how little he wanted to see one. He liked Carter. He recoiled from the feeling. His spotlessly empty soul was becoming cluttered.

He had once had an apartment in Los Angeles – another conference, was it armed police or zero tolerance? He couldn't remember. He'd made his way from the bedroom to the kitchen for a glass of water in the middle of the night, without turning on the lights. At the sink he groped for the switch and pushed it. The satisfyingly clean metal surface of the sink was a moving, glittering mass of cockroaches. They scattered in the light and disappeared. He had examined his interior landscape not long before and seen only his own reflection in its stainless surface. Now? A mess of emotions, feelings, unwelcome compulsions. The pain before the birth of conscience.

'Just a mineral water – Gordon's driving.'

Carter appreciated the joke. There was a bond between them. The two most envied men in a room full of disguised ambition and well-cultivated indifference.

'How is Gordon?'

Shackleton was again impressed by Carter's ability to smooth over, move on, while he was still screwed on the black woman's warning.

'Gordon? He went fishing last week and brought us some of his catch.'

Carter handed him the mineral water. His expression was encouraging, interested. Again Shackleton pulled away from liking him.

'Good eating?'

'They were goldfish. In a bag. From the petshop.'

Carter registered just the right amount of quizzical amusement.

'Was it a joke?'

Shackleton laughed. It was a real laugh and he enjoyed the feel of it.

'Geoffrey – you've met Gordon. Did you find a sense of humour?'

The chief of one of the more rural forces came towards them. He was a 'lucky to get it' chief. The word in ACPO was Shackleton had done everything in his power to get the man a force when he was Shackleton's deputy. That he had been pulled into the Chief's office to be told what the Chief was going to do, not because he was good, as gossip never tired of telling, but because Shackleton disliked him so much and thought so little of his abilities he simply wanted him off his patch.

And Jenni hated him.

Of all the irrational dislikes she took to people her antipathy towards this man was the most implacable. Her youngest daughter – Tom's contribution was always overlooked unless as part of an accusation – the later sensible Jacinta, had been caught with an early-vintage Ecstasy tablet in her pocket and had been taken into custody, aged sixteen. The Shackletons were at a dinner and unaccountable.

Barnard, the object of Jenni's special loathing, had been phoned. He could have let Jacinta off with a caution, used some discretion, but instead insisted on her being charged and had not contacted Tom through his pager. Jacinta had spent four hours in the cells and was hysterical by the time her screaming mother arrived. Barnard was, as always, an uninspired follower of rules and utterly unaffected by the beautiful, if highly strung, Mrs Shackleton. This stoked Jenni's hatred of the tall, grey-minded man whose vowels were as flat and unprepossessing as his policeman's feet. The girl was found to be in possession of a class A drug and Barnard's days as Shackleton's deputy were numbered in the hastily quieted flurry of press interest.

He stood in front of Carter and Shackleton, a tall man inclined to arch his back slightly, and looked down his long undistinguished face.

'Hello, Tom, Geoffrey. I hear congratulations are in order.'

He was regarding Carter as a stork might an interesting clump of grass. Carter widened his eyes in a charming cover-all expression. Barnard took it as confirmation.

'Crime Tsar, eh? Good.'

He looked at Shackleton with a thin wisp of a smile.

'Best man for the job, eh?'

His words were intended to slap like the glove that calls for a duel. Shackleton just nodded.

'Still, no doubt you'll get the leavings. Your New Labour bone, eh? The Met, I hear. Well, you know what they say, to be a copper you only have to be able to read and write, but to be Commissioner of the Met you only have to know someone who can read and write.'

Even though all three men had known this joke since training he still had to cross every T and dot every I. Barnard never made a leap of imagination where a route march of pedantry would do. He laughed his desiccated laugh and wandered off, satisfied, looking forward to telling his wife of Shackleton's discomfiture over a medium dry sherry.

Carter remembered the stories about their enmity and thought he'd never met a man as inept at knowing who not to offend as Tom Shackleton. Amongst his peers no one really liked or trusted him; he seemed to have no friends and was altogether too exotic for many. The expensive suits, the overly well-modulated voice, the costly home and wife, but most alien and envied was his ability to climb the greasy pole with never a glance back at those that had helped him or down at those on whose shoulders he stood.

Cold bastard, thought Carter, himself the acceptable face of blind ambition.

He was careful not to pick up on Barnard's pleasure. His innate good manners and public-school conditioning made him avoid any subject that threatened contention or unpleasantness.

'How's Jenni?'

Safe ground. No man's land.

'Oh, you know, too busy, too popular –'

'Too beautiful,' broke in Carter.

Shackleton was surprised, off balance again. Did Carter find Jenni attractive? Shackleton searched for the right reaction. None came.

It was Carter's turn for confusion. He did it disarmingly.

'Oh, I'm sorry, I didn't mean . . . I do apologise. I meant no offence.'

Shackleton was magnanimous.

'None taken. Look, Geoffrey, I can't live on bits of decorated cracker. I think I'll go for an Indian – Jenni's away – what about you?'

Carter looked briefly round the room. Was there anyone he needed to talk to? No. And it could be useful for the future.

'Yes, why not? I haven't had a curry in years.'

Across the room Carter's deputy had been standing with Vernon, Shackleton's number two, each making a show of not watching their chiefs and both studiously avoiding the subject that obsessed everyone else. It was a room filled with two sorts of people, those who'd stagnated and those who were still moving. Vernon realised Danny was still rising, while he was stuck fast. And the greyhound-sharp faces of the still ambitious were alert to any whisper of advantage. Chiefs were wooed, higher chiefs were stroked by those lower down the pecking order and in all the elaborate dance everyone was watching Carter and Shackleton. With these two out of the regions two circlets of power would be available. The smell of desire in that room was like rancid sweat.

Carter and Shackleton made their way to the door. Their progress was slow because everyone wanted to have a word, a touch, a smile, and they were as gracious as monarchs blessing scrofulous petitioners. Danny and Vernon, without a word, moved to be close to their chiefs, reflected influence falling like fairy dust on to them. It wouldn't hurt the courtiers to keep in with the deputies, particularly Carter's. After all, the future could well be black.

Certainly Danny's immediate horizon was, black and carrying a tray of canapés.

She beamed at him and said, 'Nice to see a dark face outside the kitchen here. You with Mr Carter?' She was nodding, answering her own question.

'He's a nice man, eh? And you too? You a nice man? I think so. Too nice. Watch the lady, not the birdie. You like these? Fish, little eggs from a fish. Take it. The lady's going to mash him up. Mash up his life.'

She put a handful of lumpfish-caviar-covered Doritos on his paper plate. He wanted to push them away; he felt he should question her but felt odd and distant as if mildly hypnotised. By the time he blinked his way back into focus she had gone and for all her bulk, he couldn't see her.

Vernon was being poured a drink by a couple of young ACCs keen to impress. Vernon, amused by the futility of their efforts with him, was telling stories. '. . . apparently a woman phoned Sussex police and reported she'd found a hole in the road – they put her through to lost property.' The men guffawed.

Danny looked at them and realised they hadn't seen the waitress. In a hot room overfilled with people he felt cold. He looked at his watch. Twenty to eight. The devil flew at twenty to.

'So, Danny, you applying for Chief when the musical chairs start?' Barnard asked, still watching the triumphal exit of the heirs apparent. Relieved, Danny smiled and turned on the charm.

Tom, as always, had Gordon standing by armed and ready. Shackleton's brief secondment to the anti-terrorist unit, known to the unreconstructed as the raghead department, made him vulnerable to attack. The unit had worked closely with intelligence departments busy since the Middle East replaced the Soviet Union as the barbarian at the gates.

The Irish had never had Shackleton on their lists but domestic Islamic fundamentalists had more than once expressed a wish to end his life, despite arguments and objections from the moderates. Since the war, notwithstanding their reassurances, Gordon always carried a gun and had been glad to become the Chief's driver, as the late nights and long engagements kept him away from both his shrill wife and shrill girlfriend.

Back at the house Shackleton installed Gordon in the kitchen with the television, his biryani and an invitation to help himself to mineral water.

In the living room the chiefs took refuge in whisky, beer and curry camaraderie. They talked about the election, carefully avoiding what it meant to both their futures if the unthinkable happened and the government lost. Jackets off and ties slack, the two men were really enjoying themselves. Each was a prince politic, perched on a platform of achievement, but neither was satisfied. Sitting eating vindaloo out of foil containers, watching highlights of Manchester United thrashing Arsenal, was a taste of the fraternal past neither had had.

Shackleton brought in another couple of beers, no glasses, by the neck. Whisky chasers in tumblers. Jenni would not have approved. He stopped, looking down at Carter hunched over his curry, watching television intently. Was it the beer? Jenni not being there? He felt a further encroachment of reluctant softness. A warmth towards Carter. What did it matter if he was Crime Tsar?

'A fuck of a lot.' Jenni's clear voice was loud in his head.

'Beer?'

'Thanks.' Carter looked up, taking the bottle.

Disney, pure Disney, that face, the big eyes and tremulous mouth. No face for a chief constable. And the voice, beautifully modulated though light, the words rapidly formed and fluently delivered. It had the diffident confidence of class and education. There had been a piece in the local papers when James Bond was about to be re-cast, with pictures of likely candidates, and among the actors and models was Geoffrey Carter: 'Our Own Chief Constable', darling of grannies on housing estates.

Shackleton could see why Carter was so popular with the public and the politicians but he knew damn well he wasn't as good a policeman as *he* was. But what did that have to do with anything?

Carter was a lucky pretty boy. Shackleton was relieved to feel the poison seeping back into his soul. He felt exposed without it.

'I mustn't be too late, it's not fair to Eleri, and tomorrow's going to be a long day.'

Carter was ACPO spokesman on drugs and had been invited by everyone from gay daytime presenters to heavyweight news Rottweilers to comment on the government's new approach to drugs, to be announced the next morning.

'Anything new in it?'

Carter laughed.

'Sure. Free heroin for pensioners on the NHS.'

Carter wanted to be indiscreet, wanted to make a waspish comment at the expense of the latest Home Office minister to be given responsibility for the great plague, but discretion had always been his better part. He concentrated on the football. Shackleton felt the sting of being put in his place.

By half-time both men were slightly pissed. They were so used to the self-discipline of moderation in all things that the alcohol took hold quickly and unexpectedly. They found themselves talking about sport, cars and work with passion and sentiment. Carter became expansive about Shackleton's ability and the transformation of his force since taking over. Shackleton in return wanted to tell Carter that it would be all right, they'd work together, he would persuade Jenni to leave well alone. That this was men's business and her scheming was surplus to requirements. Had he ever been there before he would have recognised his mood as alcoholic fondness, the forerunner of morning regret. Shackleton suddenly felt angry with Jenni, determined to put her in her place.

Carter was looking at the framed photographs of the children. He picked one up of Jason.

'Your son?'

Shackleton nodded.

Carter contemplated the handsome young face through a haze of memory and drink.

'Have you ever done anything you're ashamed of?'

Shackleton didn't understand the question.

'I don't mean little things, like . . .' Carter thought hard, swaying slightly. 'Peeing on next door's dahlias, but something unforgivable.'

Shackleton thought then shook his head.

'Why?' he asked.

'Because I have and I'm desperately afraid I'll have to pay for it. Eleri's pregnant, you know . . .'

How could he not know – Jenni had spent more time with her than at home since it was announced.

'. . . and I'm afraid. We were never supposed to be able to have children of our own. You couldn't understand what that means. It's as if you're on a round earth and I'm on a flat. You will never fall off into obscurity, your descendants will just keep circling the earth, safely bound by the gravity of fertility. And now? I feel like a man, like I've joined the human race . . . But I did something and . . . I'm frightened, really frightened. Does this make sense?' Carter looked at him, searching for forgiveness and protection. Shackleton, liberated by the drink, wanted to help. He waited. Carter seemed to have forgotten what he was saying, he was staring at the photo of Jason again.

'Your son. I'd always envied you for him. Your generation of a dynasty. Shackletons stretching down the millennia to the crack of doom.'

He paused, serious again.

'I have to pay for what I did. What if I have to pay with this baby?'

Shackleton struggled for words.

'Life's not like that.'

'Hubris . . . I want the job as much as I want the baby.'

Shackleton took refuge in bluff dismissal.

'Don't talk daft.'

'Yes, daft. Yes . . . those whom the gods wish to destroy first they make mad.'

Shackleton didn't know where to go.

'So what was it? What did you do?'

Having asked the question he was interested in the answer, although Carter's soul-searching made him uncomfortable. Not embarrassed but inadequate, as if they were involved in an emotional You show me yours and I'll show you mine.

Shackleton was shocked to see Carter was on the verge of tears, his face contorted with the effort of keeping them back. A Canute of salt streams. Not having a handkerchief Shackleton offered him his beer. Carter nodded and gulped at the bottle.

'I killed someone.'

Shackleton was shocked. Suddenly sober. Not because of Carter's sin but because of his own, lying untouched in his subconscious. He saw Leroy, his eyes. Then no eyes, no face.

'Do you remember Trevor Percy?'

'Child killer.'

'Yeah.' Carter had found an earlier voice, the accent of the Police Federation, the way he'd had to speak on the way up. 'Little girl, Melanie Tustin, nine years old, raped, strangled, dumped naked in a layby on the A3.'

'You worked on that?'

'Proudest day of my life when he went down. Fat pasty bastard. Looked like a child killer. Bit backward too. Thirty-two and still lived with his mother. We wanted him . . . we really wanted him to be the one. So he was.'

'I remember. What happened?'

'He did his time. Sixteen years. Mainly on the nonce's wing at Maidstone – didn't stop him getting beaten up though, stabbed a couple of times, and he lost an ear when some avenging angel bit it off. He got out on an unsafe conviction, a technicality. Went back to live with his mother. She'd stayed in the same house, never gave up telling anyone who'd listen her son was innocent. I saw him one day walking back from the shops, shambling along carrying a string bag full of potatoes and a cabbage. That's what they lived on, cabbage soup and potatoes.' He paused.

The two men drank in silence.

'He was found in a kiddies' playground. Beaten to a pulp and castrated. Bled to death. Nobody saw anything.'

Shackleton shrugged imperceptibly. Carter didn't see, he could only see the past.

'When Melanie was found she had a pair of men's pants tied round her neck, plenty of semen on them. Enough to get a conviction. But they were damaged, contaminated. Big problem. We had the body, we had the killer but no concrete evidence. Trevor Percy was going to walk and the police would be a laughing stock . . .' Carter took a breath as though trying to find clean air. 'He was always playing with himself – that was what had led us to him in the first place, schoolgirls saying he'd touched his thingy in front of them. I've never told anyone this before . . . oh God.'

He pushed himself on.

'I was a DC, cocky, trying to make friends among lads who thought I was a bit of a ponce. Proving what a good bloke I was. But most of all I wanted to impress my DCI. He was absolutely sure it was Percy, all the circumstantial pointed to him. He was seen in the area, he knew little Melanie, he'd given her and her friends sweets and, damning evidence, turned their skipping rope when she and her friends were playing in the park. And he was always drinking Coca-Cola, important point. So we rounded him up and he went in with my DCI. Admitted he'd done it. Christ, after four and a half days with that sadistic bastard I'd have admitted shooting J.F.K. Anyway, we got our statement . . .'

Shackleton couldn't see the problem. If the man was guilty, what did it matter how the verdict was reached. The Police and Criminal Evidence Act was, at the time, just a figment of hopeful imagination.

'I shouldn't let it get you down, we've all bent the rules, but as long as the outcome's satisfactory . . .'

'Oh yes, more than satisfactory. Gold-plated textbook conviction. DCI got a commendation and finished up a Chief Superintendent. But Percy didn't do it, Tom. He didn't do it.' Carter leaned forward, desperate for Shackleton to understand. 'There had definitely been intercourse but the killer poured the girl's Coca-Cola into her. OK, points to our Trevor. The scientists couldn't identify the vaginal semen. One or two hairs were found but forensics weren't what they are now and they couldn't get a definite match. But there had definitely been penile penetration and definite ejaculation.

'But . . . Trevor Percy couldn't orgasm. And according to what he said to me he didn't even know what an erection was. I believed him. He was telling the truth. He'd never had an erection. I was on nights while he was in the cells and he was so scared, so pathetic, I talked to him. All the time we talked he'd have his cock out and be stroking it, like a pet. It comforted him, I suppose. He never got it hard. Never. But he didn't tell his brief, never said a word. He had the mind of a child, he didn't understand what was going on. When I asked him about his penis he just kept saying it was bad. That his mother had said they got boys into trouble . . .'

Carter paused. Shackleton saw his jaw open and set at an odd angle, his tongue pressed against his bottom teeth. When he spoke his voice was a little too high, a little uncertain.

'I went to the DCI. Old was his name. I'll never forget him, fortyish, round eyes and a long crew cut. God's chosen own. He took me into one of the interview rooms. Sat me down. I remember I had a bar of chocolate, I offered him a bit. He didn't sneer exactly, he was a genius at never quite doing enough for you to accuse him of anything . . . but he made me feel as if I was trying to bribe him. I told him about Percy. Told him he couldn't possibly have done it and that there was one more thing, his mother bought all his underwear at British Home Stores. He wore BHS knickers, like girls' knickers. The pants round the child's throat were Y-fronts. From K Mart.'

Carter stopped again. Shackleton gave him another whisky. Carter looked at it but didn't drink. He controlled himself and continued.

'Old stared at me. I'll never forget those round blank eyes. Like a surprised bird. And that ridiculous lavatory-brush haircut . . .'

Shackleton smiled.

'Yes, it's always that or what Jenni calls bouffant with moustache.'

Carter tried to laugh but it didn't come.

'He said if I wanted to stay a detective constable for the rest of my life I was quite welcome to repeat my story outside that room but if I'd just forget it as it wasn't really evidence, just hearsay, the future could look quite bright. I was a fast-tracker, like you. It wasn't the future looking bright I was worried about, it was the possibility of it turning dark. I wasn't so naïve I didn't know what he meant or that membership of his Lodge wouldn't be useful. I caved in. No contest.

'I should have spoken up but I didn't. I couldn't. I could have gone to the creeper squad . . . maybe I should have told his defence . . . I don't know. I thought I had more to lose than Trevor Percy. I thought maybe I'd feel better talking about it. But I don't. I didn't just kill him, I tortured him and his mother for sixteen years first.' Carter made one last effort to control himself. 'I had a look at the autopsy report. Undeveloped, non-functioning sexual organs. Bit late then . . .'

The tears were now running down Carter's face. Shackleton wanted to dismiss this display as self-pity but he couldn't. He put his hand on Carter's shoulder. He had no belief in poetic justice and related Carter's fears to a sort of superstition. Leroy had never haunted him nor any other, lesser, ruthless action he'd taken. Leroy had died before he'd had a chance to kill. It was a form of justice. And Trevor Percy? The world was not a poorer place without him. It was sad but not a tragedy.

'Geoffrey, come on. Nothing's going to happen to your kid. Everything'll be fine. Young coppers make mistakes. You're sorry, that's enough. There's nothing you can do about it now.'

Shackleton's hand on his shoulder and the brief paternal words undid him. He cried as Shackleton had only ever seen a woman cry. He tried to staunch the flow.

'Look, you're not the only one who's ashamed of something in the past. But that's where it is. The past. There's no payback – you're carrying your punishment with you.'

So where was his? No, it was just words, verbal bandaging. He didn't believe what he'd just said. Shackleton did what he did. Regret scratched but had never dug deep.

But what would he feel about the destruction of Carter? What if Jenni's plan was to do what had been done to Trevor and Leroy? What was the difference? No, this was too confusing; it blurred the lines of his certainties. Carter was an obstacle to his ambition. Need like his justified any means.

The doorbell rang. Automatically Shackleton looked at his watch. Apologising to Carter he went to the door. The disturbance was enough to make Carter pull himself together.

'Tom, I'm so sorry. I've lost my cheque-guarantee card. It's in my driving-licence folder and I remember I put it down on the coffee table in the living room. I'm so sorry, may I fetch it?'

Lucy. What on earth was she talking about.

'Sure. Go through.'

She was suprised to see Carter – she knew him immediately. He was a *Newsnight* pin-up. Polite introductions and pleas to be excused replaced emotion. Shackleton was relieved. Everything was back to normal.

'Are you all right?'

Lucy, always alive to misery, reached out and touched Carter's arm.

The unexpected tenderness of the gesture completely undermined his self-control. He was sobbing and apologising. He reeked of whisky and beer but to Lucy he was a lost soul. She rocked him as she'd rocked Shackleton and he felt a shaft of jealousy. She was murmuring a litany of comfort and even managed to produce a crumpled tissue from her pocket. Shackleton half expected her to lick it and wipe Carter's face. In a minute she'd given more comfort than he had in a whole evening. But that was what women did. Especially this woman. He didn't want her to be holding another man. He couldn't bear her giving his affection and gentle reassurance to someone else. Like a child with its mother he couldn't bear to share her. How could this plain, ordinary woman get so far inside him?

What was she doing now? Carter, having pulled himself together, was trying to leave, gathering as much dignity as he could find. Lucy was standing behind him and seemed to be trying to say something.

Shackleton recognised what she was doing and almost laughed with relief. She was making the same faces his mother had made when she collected him after a crucifying children's party.

'Say goodbye, Tom. Give him a hug, Tom. Be nice, Tom, he's your friend.'

Shackleton was seven again, in short trousers and red bow tie. He walked towards Carter and put his hand out exactly as he had forty-one years before.

'Bye, Geoffrey. You all right?'

Carter shook his hand, as lost for the right words as Shackleton, but his eyes were swimmingly grateful for the contact. The forgiveness.

'Yes. Right. Yes.'

And without thinking the handshake became an awkward, heart-felt hug and Lucy was fussing Carter into the Jaguar and telling Gordon, who Shackleton had summoned from the kitchen, to drive carefully. Then they were gone leaving Lucy and Tom waving like fond aunts on the doorstep.

They went into the house. Lucy stood close to Tom in the wide hall as if waiting for her reward. She put her arms round him and kissed him very tenderly, very gently, but he pushed away, holding her shoulders.

'Not tonight, Lucy, eh?'

Lucy felt foolish. She thought she had misread the signs. She had in a way, but it wasn't indifference that was making him reject her, it was the pain of feeling. Like blood surging into a frozen limb.

She was quick to make it look as if she'd expected no more.

'Yes. Right. I've got to go anyway. Is everything all right? Jenni's back tomorrow, isn't she?'

She was at the door now, opening it before he could.

'Shall I see you in the morning?'

Tom looked down at her with that infuriating expression of regret.

'I don't think so, Lucy.'

She couldn't stop herself.

'Shall I . . . see . . . you again?'

He shook his head, giving her a 'This is hurting me more than it's hurting you' look.

'I don't know, Lucy. I really don't know.'

She was now in so far she couldn't go back.

'Do you want to be with me again?'

He didn't pause.

'Yes.'

She felt a surge of hope and joy.

'So what's the problem?'

'You know I can't make that kind of commitment, Lucy. Neither can you.'

She knew she had to settle for that and went home before the delicate web of her fantasy was completely ripped to pieces.

Tom closed the door behind her. Why had he rejected her? Why did he feel such an urge to hurt her? He wanted her body. Yes. But didn't want the ugliness and implications of the rest of the baggage that went with a 'relationship'. He was strong and Lucy was the only person who could undermine that strength.

Lucy put the kettle on. When Jenni was home they always had a coffee and a chat at about eleven. Nothing so common as elevenses, of course, a cafetière and organic coffee, perhaps some *biscotti*.

Jenni came into the kitchen. She seemed more hyper than usual, somewhere near an edge. She had been very affectionate towards Lucy since she got back from Vienna and had given her a lovely brooch. Lucy had almost cried but she wasn't sure if it was the brooch or the mess her life was in that had caused the surge of sentiment.

The phone rang. Jenni answered. There was delighted surprise in her voice.

'Jason . . . darling.' She winked at Lucy. 'Oh it's lovely to talk to you . . . yes, darling boy, but I'm better now . . . I understand. I know you do, Jason . . . Of course you can come home. I don't know why you went in the first place . . . It's all right, Jason. I forgive you, of course I do. Bye . . . yes, Lucy'll give it a dust and a hoover.' She looked across at Lucy. 'Jason's room – you'll spruce it up, won't you?'

Lucy nodded. Tom was back in the impregnable bosom of his family.

'Whenever you like, Jason. Bye.'

Jenni was triumphant. She didn't need to say anything; that small conversation had put the constellations back in place. She gave Lucy's arm a little squeeze.

Odd. Out of character. Lucy thought she looked like a consumptive heroine with her glittering eyes and flushed skin. She'd be the sort who would still be devastatingly lovely even in the final stages of tuberculosis.

Lucy handed her a cup of coffee.

'Nice for you Jason's coming home.'

'Don't you just love it when things work?'

Lucy searched for an arrangement of her face that said rueful.

'Don't know – I can't remember when anything last did.'

Jenni gave her the silvery bells.

'Oh, come on, Lucy, things aren't so bad, are they? You've got Gary.'

Lucy thought that was like saying you've got plenty to eat but it's all infected with botulism.

'Yes, but he seems to have given up. He just doesn't seem the same since he came home from hospital. Sometimes I feel it's all getting too much. I feel so dowdy. I feel life's going past and I'm standing watching it from behind a fence. Do you understand?'

'Mmm? Sorry . . . what was that?'

And your husband doesn't want to sleep with me any more, Jenni.

'Nothing. Wasn't important. Well, I think I've done for the day. See you tomorrow, eh?'

'Yes. Yes . . . Oh Lucy.'

Suddenly Lucy had Jenni's full attention. She turned the full candle-power of her eyes on Lucy and despite herself Lucy was again struck by her beauty. What would she do without it? When would she? At fifty? Later? Jenni wouldn't let her looks go any more than she released anything that belonged to her. Like her husband, her most valuable possession.

'Would you mind doing a big clean while Tom and I are away? You remember we're going to Barcelona for a few days – it's our wedding anniversary. Too romantic. A full day if you could. The living room is beginning to look a bit dingy – I just need you to have everything out and give the place a good going over. All right with you?'

The extra money would be welcome.

'Certainly. Yes.'

'And Lucy . . . I, I want to apologise.'

Lucy had never heard Jenni say the A word. She'd often wished she had but now she didn't know what it was for. Not knowing what to say she said nothing.

Jenni was gratified by the look on her face. It acknowledged the rarity of the moment.

'I haven't treated you very well lately. And I'm sorry. You're a loyal friend and I've neglected you. But I want to take you out for a huge shop and maybe some pampering to make it up to you. What do you say? My treat, of course.'

I say you're a patronising, condescending cow and you obviously want something.

'That'd be really lovely, Jenni. I'd love to.'

Jenni was pleased. She had excised Eleri and restored Lucy. It hadn't been difficult to say sorry and Lucy seemed so grateful. Life was taking on a pleasing symmetry again.

Lucy, feeling herself dismissed, was at the front door, her hand on the catch. She opened it as Tom's car pulled up. No, she screamed with no sound, no movement. No! You shouldn't be home. You shouldn't be getting out of that car looking so handsome, smiling at me like a stranger. Worse, smiling at me like the cleaning lady. Smiling.

'Morning, Tom. Are you well?'

'Fine, thanks, Lucy. You? And Gary?'

He looked at her and was ambushed by a need to protect her. She looked so threatened, so exposed in the glare of his wife's perfection. She was carrying her rubber gloves and a pile of dusters for washing. It would be so much easier if she wasn't there.

He closed the door. When he got the Met he and Jenni would move. Jenni would insist on it – there may be less money to lavish on her pleasures at London prices but her pleasures would be closer, she would be inside them. They'd move away from Lucy. And Gary. And the discomfort of emotion. And love. Where had that come from? It

214

had grown, like buddleia in the cracks of prison walls. Yes, they'd go away. It would be sad, the end of an era, but better for everyone in the end.

'What are you doing home?'

Jenni's question was not accusatory. That made a change.

'My neck's playing me up and the Home Office meeting finished early so . . . I've got nothing much on this afternoon. Just a discipline starting in the morning . . .'

'Good. I wanted to tell you – I don't think Geoffrey is going to be a problem.'

'Geoffrey who?' He saw the flash of irritation too late.

'Geoffrey fucking Carter. Who did you think I meant? Geoffrey Boycott? Geoffrey Howe?'

His mouth poured oil.

'Yes, yes, of course. I'm sorry, I wasn't thinking. It's my neck. Sorry.'

'Take a painkiller and go to bed.'

She said it without affection or tenderness. Take a meat cleaver and cut your head off.

'Yes, I think you're right. I will go for a lie down.'

Tom had injured the bones in his neck during an armed robbery when he was twenty-five and the condition had deteriorated as he'd risen through the ranks and become more deskbound, causing intense, nauseating pain, not frequently but regularly.

It was his first big stake-out. He'd long since forgotten the laddish excitement of that night, replacing it with a sanitised memory of a job well done. He had been praised and decorated for his bravery in saving the life of a fellow officer, his neck injury proud proof of that bravery.

No one on his team had told the truth of that night and the only witness was a corpse without a face.

Officially Leroy Chandler had held a sawn-off shotgun to a young PC's head. Shackleton had tackled him using skills learned on the rugby field and in the scuffle the gun went off killing Leroy. Shackleton had injuries to his face and neck sustained during the fight. An inquiry was held and Shackleton was found to be not only blameless but a hero. Leroy's death caused little furore, possibly because he was a recidivist of some magnitude, but more probably because he was a single black man with no family to challenge the police version of events, all those years before Stephen Lawrence and Michael Menson.

The truth was that Leroy, cornered by Shackleton, had given up the gun after being tackled. Shackleton, carried away by the heightened mood, turned the gun on the now gibbering robber. They were alone. Two young men awash with testosterone.

The rest of the squad had hared off after Leroy's accomplices. Shackleton had never thought about the events that followed until the night with Carter. Then he'd seen himself squeezing the trigger, not intending to shoot but unable to stop himself. Fascinated, hypnotised by how far that trigger would pull back and, as if in a dream state, convinced it would just click and the film would continue along familiar lines. But the slow-motion scene exploded in blood, bone and brains. Leroy's face disintegrated over Shackleton, and the gun, held in Shackleton's left hand, like a revolver, jumped on being fired, as any older, more experienced officer would have known it would. It jumped high and hard, smashing into Shackleton's nose and whipping his head back. When he came to his colleagues had surrounded him and a legend was created.

Maybe the painful bones in Shackleton's neck were a manifestation of guilt, as Carter's pain was over Percy. But he lived with it more comfortably than Carter lived with his. A damaged body was easier to deal with than a soul in turmoil.

No more macho heroics tackling armed thugs now though: a chief constable was simply a politically astute accountant. It wasn't the thing to be a policeman any more.

He turned on the stairs.

'Jenni . . . ? What did you mean about Carter?'

Jenni came to the bottom of the stairs and looked up at him.

'Do you really want to know, Tom?'

He felt awkward, he wanted to say yes and to tell her he wanted nothing to do with it. Whatever it was. He wondered what she would do if he said he wanted to retire from the police at the end of his seven-year turn as Chief. That the scheming and climbing were over, that he just wanted to let go of it all and walk dogs on the South Coast. To give in gracefully within sight of the winning post if it meant treading on one more person, making one more enemy.

But someone had once said to him that he had no rival in making enemies. It was a talent. No one did it better. His face was always turned to the sun. To turn away now and look down the greasy pole at the desolation on which it rested, to see all the people they'd hurt and neglected on the way to this place. Was it worth it? But now, what else was there? It was too late to make friends – he's proved that in his inadequacy with Carter – he didn't have the vocabulary. There was no one in their lives who was for decoration, for pure aesthetic pleasure. Just for use. Use, abuse and rejection. It was easier that way. No commitment, no obligation.

'What about Lucy?'

Jenni's voice was hard. Her eyes harder.

'What?'

'Lucy. You just said Lucy.'

Tom felt his face getting hot.

'Did I?'

He was confused. Had he said her name out loud?

'I . . . er . . . I thought she was coming in to clean today.'

Jenni relaxed into contempt.

'Tom, you've just watched her walk out – the dumpy female in the baggy leggings. God, you're hopeless.'

He took refuge in humility.

'Sorry.'

'Shall I bring you up a cup of tea?'

Jenni never ceased to surprise him. He was expecting vitriol, not tea.

'That would be nice. Thank you.'

In the bedroom he stripped off to his boxer shorts. Brown silk, expensive. He preferred ordinary pants, the ones he'd worn as a boy, snug, reassuring. But Jenni insisted on these. He remembered bending over to put a log on the fire shortly after they'd married. He was wearing his best trousers, pale-beige slacks, fashionable then, bought by Jenni. She had screamed at him for the visibility of the elastic of his underwear as the trousers tightened. How could he? Didn't he know how gross it looked? Visible panty line – what did he know about it? She had prescribed boxer shorts and he'd suffered in their insecurity ever since.

She came in with his tea and sat on the edge of the bed. He froze, lying on his back, embarrassed.

'You're getting fat,' she said with no malice. 'Do you ever think about sex?'

He didn't know what to say. They hadn't discussed sex for years.

'No. I don't. I might get frustrated.'

He tried to make light of it, unsure what she wanted him to say. He dreaded the idea she might want him to perform. He knew he couldn't. Not with her. Not any more.

'Good,' she said, as if he'd passed a test.

She put a slender finger on his reluctant penis.

'I don't want you getting distracted.' She was watching his face.

'Oh, I forgot to tell you –' The beady vigilance was replaced by a radiant smile. 'Jason's coming home. Isn't that wonderful? I think he missed us.'

Shackleton was genuinely pleased but slightly thrown by the 'us'. It was usually 'me' in anything to do with the children. But his pleasure was genuine.

'That's good. I'm glad. I've missed him.'

There was a rare moment between them of contented peace. They each in their own way savoured it.

He sipped his tea. The pain in his neck was so bad he was feeling sick; bending it to drink the tea was too much. He put the cup down. She was still sitting by him, watching him, but her look was gentle, almost sympathetic.

'Saturday. We're dropping in on Geoffrey. In the afternoon. About three o'clock. Nice surprise for him. All right?'

Shackleton was struck by how sure she'd become since Vienna. Confident. More so than she'd been since before the breakdown but jagged now, like a sliver of glass. And translucently beautiful. Now, as she sat with the sunlight making a halo of her hair, he could see the delicate veins beneath her skin. She was like a fairy, a delicate figment of his imagination. He felt an almost forgotten desire to touch the perfect blonde hair.

'Why?'

Again her manicured nail wandered along the shy outline of his genitals. Her voice was as sharp as the nail.

'Because. He'll be alone in the house looking after the autistic child. Eleri's taking Peter, the normal one, to a film. Starts at two-forty, something about alien dinosaurs, apparently. So while you chatter away to Geoffrey about boys' things I'll take Alexander upstairs to play. They've got Sky so you can watch the football, do some bonding, eh? What do you think?'

'I think you're a witch. What are you going to do?'

Although his voice was as measured as always, she could feel, under her continually moving finger, the first stirrings of interest.

Shackleton was horrified at the twitching response she was getting. He wanted to push her away – he did not want to have any intimacy with her. Not now, with this pain, in daylight, with nowhere to hide himself . . .

'Stop it, Jenni. Please. Stop.'

It was his penis he should have been speaking to. Jenni was thrilled. After all this time she could still give her husband an erection, even when he didn't want one. She looked down at the object of Lucy's fantasies as if it were a rather disappointing chop.

'I remembered it bigger. Do you remember you used to say "make it hard"?'

He winced.

She held him in her hands as though praying.

'Save it for me, Tom. I want you to pour all your gratitude into me when we're . . .' She paused, a predatory smile spreading from her perfect lips to her frosted eyes. 'Just don't let me down on Saturday, my darling.'

She kissed the end of it. He winced at the touch of her soft mouth. She got up, smiling.

'God, you look like Moby Dick. You really have let yourself go.' As if this was a well-considered compliment. 'Get some sleep. I'll see you later.'

And she was gone.

He lay looking at the ceiling longing for the clinging warmth of Lucy's flesh. And the cold release of loneliness. And Carter? He didn't want to hurt him. He didn't want to hurt anyone any more. But what was the alternative? Non-executive director of the local department store and a timeshare in Marbella. No. It had to be all or nothing. He winced. His erection had quickly subsided but his neck was still agony.

He found some relief in thinking about the new recruitment strategy. About the progress he was making with his community initiative. The dry stone walls of policy excluded imagination. Provided a screen against the chaos of feeling. Just as he fell asleep, his neck numbed by the latest in painkillers, he saw the faces of the black women, laughing at him. He fell into a dream of them, defenceless against his own subconscious.

They showed him Geoffrey Carter's funeral, and himself speaking the eulogy. And he was good. So quietly sincere. The church littered with politicians, their faces shining with approval. He felt the women dressing him, placing his medals in order, QPM Jubilee, Long Service, others he couldn't see. Jenni in a hat. An investiture. Cameras and Buckingham Palace. The three black faces pushed against the railings, laughing. Telling him not to fall.

He walked towards them to hear them more clearly; he didn't see the hole, the black echoing nothingness into which he fell, his stomach churning over and over, sweating fear, and the faces looking down at him from the rim far above him. And this was hell. The wages of sin is death. No hope or suspicion of another chance. Blackness. Emptiness. As if they'd never been. He and Jenni. Obliterated from life and no one to speak a word for them. No flowers. No headstone. No memory of his achievements. Where was Lucy? She'd speak for him. Pray for him. Hope for his eternal life. The sewn-up eyes stared blindly at the dust that had been him. A breath blew the dust into a landscape of nothingness.

'We were at an auction just down the road. We didn't buy anything but we thought we might pop round to see you.'

Jenni swept in, past Geoffrey, trailing Tom behind her. The two men hadn't seen each other since the night of the curry and, vaguely shamed by the memory, behaved as if it had never happened. Carter was surprised to see them but was warmly welcoming and showed them into the living room.

Alexander was pacing up and down, absorbed in the mysteries of his fingers. Shackleton watched him while Carter and Jenni chatted about Eleri. Those fingers, too long, too tapering, weak caricatures of Christ's praying hands. For Shackleton, as for Danny, there was something even less human about them than about the boy's too thick, low-growing hair and empty eyes. Looking at him he understood Carter's fear. But, unlike Danny, Shackleton felt no guilt at the discomfort the child caused him.

Carter offered coffee and Jenni insisted on making it. She brought in the tray, the drinks alone, no cafetière, no milk, because of Alexander's obsession with liquids. While picking up the bowl of brown sugar she had looked at the bowl of white. It made her think of the tiny sniff of cocaine she'd promised herself after this visit was completed successfully. Having served the coffee Jenni suggested she take Alex up to his room so the men could talk. Alex could show her his collection of batteries.

Now they were alone there was the possibility of awkwardness, but Carter picked up his newspaper and handed it to Shackleton.

' "Labour Mouthpiece Made a Fool by Educated Archie".'

Shackleton laughed.

'I thought Archie was a ventriloqist's dummy.'

'I believe that's the point. As the government's anointed one it was assumed I'd be exactly that.'

Shackleton read the article.

'Any feedback from Whitehall?'

'I'm sure there will be. They've got an election coming up – they don't want any gaffes.'

The drugs debate that had been dragging on since New Labour's ascendancy had been enormously enlivened by Carter's complete devastation of a badly briefed junior spokesman the day before. The new strategy had been published but instead of it being a one-day wonder the media had decided, in the absence of a natural disaster or train crash, to whip up the controversy always surrounding the subject. Carter had in the past couple of weeks been a fixture on every news programme, becoming less and less on message as the days passed. But last night he'd surpassed himself.

Shackleton had watched, admiring and envious of Carter's ease and fluency.

The junior minister, flabby in body and mind, said, 'Well, of course it would be ludicrous to legalise the whole gambit of drugs.'

Carter dismissed him so effortlessly Shackleton almost didn't register the sin he was committing.

'I'm not about to shoot you down in etymological flames, but nothing this government has put in place has allowed police officers continuity. We're still in a situation where individual chief constables are left to decide the ferocity or laxity of enforcement, rather than . . .'

He then climbed off the political fence with a show of verbal and mental gymnastics which left the official spokesman looking, at best, a fool.

Shackleton, reading the newspaper, felt Carter had made a mistake in pitting himself so blatantly against the government. Would they really want a Crime Tsar who was so unpredictable? He smiled and handed the paper back.

'What do you think of Villa's chances this afternoon?'

Carter was surprised at the change of subject. He had never had Shackleton's acute antennae for the sensibilities of his superiors.

'I don't know . . . I'll put the telly on.'

Alexander, once occupied with his batteries, was guaranteed to be quiet for between five and ten minutes, so Jenni had quickly laid out the thousand-strong collection on the carpet, waited until the boy was crouched over them, then slipped out of the bedroom down the stairs to the first landing. Off this small carpeted square was one room which, during her many visits to the house, Jenni had discovered was Carter's study.

She was shaking as she pushed the door open with the back of her hand. Although what she saw was what she'd hoped to see, the shaking worsened, making it awkward to put on the thin latex gloves she took from her pocket. She paused a moment, listening to the sound of the television and the men's voices below. Three deep breaths.

In the study everything was neat, books, files and papers. She'd been in there before. In fact there wasn't a corner of the house she didn't know. During her respite visits to Eleri she had patiently examined and assessed every nook and cranny and, like a parasitic wasp, had laid her eggs. Behind rarely disturbed books in the living room she had placed one of the bugs, in Eleri's chaotic kitchen another and, when Eleri went out for an antenatal appointment, a third behind their bedhead.

The videos she left among the vast collection of Disney and cartoons in the rarely opened hall cupboard. The magazines she was unsure about until, using the bathroom one afternoon, she looked at the fascia enclosing the bath and saw the perfect hiding place. The next day, prepared with gloves and screwdriver, she removed the tiled board, watched by a solemn, silent Alexander, and pushed the magazines under the bath to the wall. She replaced the fascia and swept up the debris. Alexander silent witness throughout. The floppy disc she had taped to the back of a drawer in Carter's study. Everything, thanks to her patience and planning, was going to be perfect.

Jenni sat in front of the computer. Carter's computer. The screen saver twirled lazily. She'd discovered he always left it on when he was in the house – apparently it was bad for the mechanism to be switched off frequently. Not as bad as leaving it on, Jenni thought with a smile. She'd discovered a lot during her baby-sitting sessions. It had been worth every boring, irritating minute with the two boys when Peter had told her Daddy used his name as a password for his computer. She remembered her automatic reply of 'How sweet'. It wasn't until later that little seed germinated and grew.

Later she'd mentioned how slow her laptop was when filing stories and Eleri had said yes, that's why they'd got ISDN and Broadband, it was on all the time. No more dial-up. That had been a relief, the noise of the modem would have wakened the dead, even the dead watching football.

Her hands were wet now inside the surgical gloves. Downstairs the television still roared, the husbands shouted encouragement. Upstairs Alexander was standing watching her, shifting from foot to foot in agitation. She recognised the signs: any second he'd start that inhuman wailing, the screeching expression of isolation she'd come to dread. She spoke to him calmly, quietly. Asked him to come down and see what Auntie Jenni was doing. The screams were building up inside him.

In desperation she said, 'I'm finding some batteries for you.'

He didn't seem to understand but stretched his neck and threw his head back against the wall. Jenni ran up the stairs to him, grabbed his wrist and pulled him, tripping and falling, down into the study. Inside she closed the door. Alex was petrified. He started to whimper. She knew she had very little time before he exploded into uncontrollable screams.

She quickly typed in the password. The screen revealed itself, ready at the home page. She carefully put in the coordinates of one of the paedophile sites she'd found in Vienna. It was bone-achingly slow in coming up; she browsed its contents for a minute, then visited another. This requested credit card details to proceed. She took a breath, calming herself to remember the numbers she'd taken from Carter's Mastercard. He was so vain he'd never carry a wallet when in full dress uniform, might spoil the line, so one morning while he and Eleri were out at an official function she'd copied it down. Halfway through keying it in she realised Alexander was almost at the boil, then she saw, down by the waste bin, a half-finished bottle of mineral water. She reached down with her free hand and picked it up.

'Alex, look. Look what I've got.'

The boy dived for it, instantly obsessed by the fluid within. While she continued her visits he tore at the cap. By the time he'd got it off and sucked out the contents she had returned to the home page and restored the screen saver.

Jenni was now shaking so badly she could barely find the keys. Her pills were downstairs in her handbag. She felt a handful of them wouldn't be enough to tranquillise her but she also felt triumphant. She'd downloaded the first images that came up after payment then returned the computer to its dormant state. Originally she'd thought of using the Trojan virus as a conduit for the material, but that would be easily found out. Then she'd planned to alter the time and date to make it look as if everything was done after she and Tom had left the house, but after thinking about it decided it was better not to. If there were alterations to the clock forensics would find it sooner or later when, hopefully, there was an inquiry. But if the material was downloaded while she and Tom were in the house, well . . . It would be word against word. Why would she or her husband do such a thing and, more to the point, how could they? She knew a man would have altered the time but then the female was more deadly than the male. She'd always liked that line. It was the only poetry she carried with her.

The shakes were getting worse. She controlled herself, took the empty bottle from Alex, pushed him from the room and closed the door.

She took off her gloves and looked at her watch: the whole exercise had taken less than twenty minutes. Perfect.

Alexander burst into the living room with Jenni.

'Oh God, Geoffrey, I'm so sorry, I've just remembered I've got the washing-machine mechanic coming round. I'm so sorry, it completely went out of my head. Tom, we must go. If I miss him I won't get him again for days. He's doing us a favour coming out on a Saturday anyway.'

'Can't you phone Lucy and get her to let him in?'

He thought for a moment Jenni was going to hit him. Even Carter couldn't miss the anger on her face even though it was erased as quickly as it appeared.

'She's out,' said Jenni. 'Geoffrey, I'm so sorry. Do forgive us, and you and Eleri must come over for dinner. Soon. Bye, Alex darling. Give me a kiss.' He seemed as repelled at the idea as she was but she hid it better. 'No? Oh well then, never mind. Give our love to Eleri, Geoffrey. Oh and doesn't my plant look lovely there, just perfect, look, Tom. Isn't it gorgeous? Bye.'

She was down the steps by the car, the two men trailing behind in a wake of confusion and disappointment. They'd been enjoying themselves.

Geoffrey waved them off and closed the door. Alexander seemed very disturbed and tried to drag Carter upstairs. His father resisted and managed to distract him with an unopened twelve-pack of double-A batteries.

Carter felt as if he was in shock – the effect of Mrs Shackleton up close and in overdrive was exhausting. He had been thinking of mowing the lawn but he decided, using Alexander's mood as an excuse, to give himself up to paperwork and the remains of the Villa game instead.

Tom and Jenni were silent on the drive home. He knew she had done something. Something he wouldn't like, but if he didn't know what he was innocent. The brief opening up of tenderness between the two men had healed over with no scar.

'Why don't men ever want to know what goes on?'

Jenni's voice was sharp. She often seemed to read his thoughts.

He knew where this was going but, out of habit, he avoided the destination.

'I don't know what you mean.'

Jenni was too triumphant to be contemptuous so she just laughed at him, almost affectionately.

'Oh come on. You know I wasn't admiring his low-level avocado bathroom suite up there.'

'I thought you were playing with Alexander.'

The words 'No you didn't, you spineless liar' lay between them unspoken for once.

'Don't worry, Tom, I've got you this far without you knowing how, I'm not going to spoil your little fantasy that you did it on your own.'

She turned to look at his profile. More handsome now than in his twenties. He concentrated on his driving.

'You really think you could have done it without me, don't you? You'd have had as much chance as a sperm swimming up the Thames.' She laughed. As always she'd managed to hurt him. 'Oh, can we stop at Tesco, we need some more Scotch. You really gave it a hammering while I was away. Couldn't get through a few days on your own, eh?'

He stopped the car on a yellow line and she got out. He didn't watch her go into the shop. Should he ask her what she'd done? Then what? Tell Geoffrey. Sacrifice Jenni and implicate himself? Maybe she hadn't really done anything or perhaps what she'd done wasn't too extreme. The only way to find out would be to ask or wait and see. He knew he wouldn't ask.

Lucy had returned to her house after Tom's regretful rejection. She had the feeling she'd outlived her usefulness and, like many women before her, had mistaken the passion of a powerful man for love. She had made a fool of herself over men before but not since her teens.

Gary was very much awake when she let herself in, hoping he'd be sleeping.

'Everything all right?'

His question was innocent but she felt it to be accusatory.

'Of course. Why wouldn't it be?'

She regretted her sharpness but did nothing to soften it.

Gary had hoped her infatuation with Teflon Man would wear off. He had reasoned the situation from every angle. He understood what Lucy's needs were: he saw, more clearly than anyone, that his condition was impossible to come to terms with, physically or mentally. He had even managed to convince himself that this was best for Lucy, that it would make it easier for her when he was gone. But now he could see whatever had happened between his wife and Tom was hurting her and he couldn't bear it.

'Lucy?'

'What?'

'Come here a minute, will you?'

Lucy stopped her tidying and sat on the edge of his bed. He took her hand; there was no response.

'What's the matter, Luce?'

'Nothing.'

She pulled her hand away and went to get up.

'Is it Tom?'

She reacted as though stung.

'No. Why? Why should it be him?'

Gary had nothing more to lose.

'Because you're sleeping with him.'

Lucy wanted to defy the truth and face Gary out. Just deny everything that had happened – who could contradict her? But she had wanted to tell Gary for weeks. Not in the way of a spouse offloading the guilt on to their partner by cathartic confession. No. Lucy wanted to share it with her husband as she would with a brother or a close girlfriend. She had never been in this situation before so didn't know if it was normal to regard her husband as a repository for the joys and miseries of an affair. The pause between them had gone on too long for her to deny the accusation. She just made a tiny movement of her head. Guilty as accused.

Gary felt strangely calm, as if he was just an actor in a well-rehearsed play.

'Are you still sleeping with him?'

Lucy shook her head miserably.

'He's dumped you?'

The use of this adolescent expression made her cry.

He put as much of his arms round her as he could now move and felt comforted himself by the quiet tears soaking into his pyjama jacket.

'There there, there there. He's not worth this, you know.'

Lucy snorted, the result of laughing and crying at the same time. The contents of her nose were projected on to his sleeve.

'Don't tell me. I'm too good for him. Oh God, I'm sorry, take it off and I'll wash it.'

'Never mind that. Lucy. Lucy, come on. Come back here.'

Lucy sat down again. Gary stroked her face.

'Why are you being so nice to me, Gary? I don't deserve it.'

'No, I know you don't. I mean, if you were going to play away, couldn't you have picked someone better? Something part of the human race would have been nice.'

'It was just sex,' mumbled Lucy.

'It's never just sex with you, Lucy. Maybe the first time but after that you want to be knitting him jumpers and tidying his sock drawer. I know. You did it to me, remember?'

Lucy tried to smile.

'Yes. I suppose you're right. I've just got into a mess over it. Not him. I don't really feel anything for him. You do believe me, don't you?'

No, thought Gary.

'Yes. Of course I believe you. And it's my fault anyway. I haven't been much of a husband recently . . . I always said you should take a lover, didn't I?'

'Oh Gary, I'm so sorry. I'm so sorry. Can you forgive me? I wouldn't blame you if you couldn't.'

'What am I going to do? Leave home?'

Suddenly Gary didn't want to talk about it any more. The Gary with MS who was saintly and understanding was giving way to Gary the unfulfilled thug, the man who knew violence didn't solve anything but was prepared to give it a go.

He took refuge in the banal.

'Go and put the kettle on, will you, Luce? All this emotion has parched me.'

Lucy turned to go.

'And, Luce . . . ? You won't be going over there again, will you?'

'What do you mean?'

Gary's tone was harder.

'What I said. You won't be cleaning there any more, or popping over for coffee with the lovely Jenni.'

'But, Gary . . .' Lucy scrabbled round for the right words.

'If we don't talk to them any more, it'll seem strange, won't it? And I've promised to do a big spring clean while they're in Barcelona.'

Gary knew then that it wasn't over; she was still besotted by Shackleton and, like an addict, petrified of letting her fantasy go. What was she hoping? That he'd leave Jenni? That they'd live happily ever after? No. Probably not. She was just hoping he'd change his mind.

Gary's anger with Shackleton was far greater than anything he felt for Lucy: his main emotion towards her was pity. He wondered where the love had gone, or was this love from a different angle? He felt strangely detached, able to see the situation objectively: if he forbade Lucy to go there again, what hope would he have of being listened to? And if she did stop seeing him what kind of Lucy would he have to live with? Some miserable ghost drifting round the house twitching the curtains every time his car drew up.

If he knew Shackleton as well as he thought he did, Lucy would have served her purpose and Shackleton would be doing a fair amount of self-flagellation now. Less likely to want her again if she was always there than if she suddenly went from his life and he built up an image of her as the Lucy he lost and missed. Good psychology, but was it right? Was Shackleton as utterly incapable of sacrificing his ambition for affection as Gary thought he was? Yes. Gary knew the answer was yes. Lucy had been a fling, an exercise, probably just a biological release, and his rejection of her must be because she was becoming a threat to his equilibrium. Or simply something more interesting and less troublesome had come along.

Leaving her there, accusing him by her presence and reminding him of his slip-up would be better than keeping her away. Her availability would be guaranteed to keep Shackleton away from her.

He hoped.

For all his clinical approach to the problem it was just lack of a viable option that made him say, 'OK, Lucy. But no more socialising, eh? All right?'

She agreed quickly.

'Of course, Gary. I understand. I think you're right. Yes. But I'll carry on cleaning, but maybe only go over after he's gone to work. Yes?'

Gary was tired, he wanted to close his eyes and forget it all.

'Put the kettle on, Lucy.'

'Right. Right. Yes.' She went.

She knew all the things she should feel but as she stood, her hands on the work surface, waiting for the kettle to boil, the groan that built up inside her was released in the words, 'Oh Tom . . .'

She hadn't heard the fat lady sing. But she suddenly saw and felt Gary as he'd been when they met. The first time they made love. As she poured the boiling water on the bags – Gary had always been fond of organic Darjeeling but now it was almost always supermarket own-brand sweepings – she remembered the surprise she'd felt when she first touched Gary intimately. She couldn't believe what her fingers were feeling. It was enormous. Well, enormous in her limited experience, no not enormous in girth, but very long and with an inclination to one side in its final, triumphant two, or was it three, inches. And his stamina . . .

She added milk and two sugars for Gary. Black for herself, still dieting for the Chief Constable.

After the first two hours he'd asked if she minded if they took a break. A quarter of a glass of cheap chilled white wine and a cigarette. Then two and a half more hours of what the magazines of the time had coyly called foreplay. Sometimes heavy petting. Sounded like two overweight poodles. Then he'd asked her if he might put on a condom. As if asking if she'd mind him tuning in to the cricket. She hadn't watched as he expertly rolled it down that extraordinary length of enthusiasm – it had seemed slightly rude to look. And then . . .

'Any chance of that tea before Christmas, Lou?'

She hadn't come on that first occasion; not because she wasn't excited by him but because she was watching him, enjoying the mounting surprise on his face, the pleasure building and bursting inside that strange rubber bag clinging to him closer even than her own flickering muscles.

Then he talked and they laughed and finally slept, together, entwined.

As she took the teas through she felt again the happiness she'd had watching him sleep. Maybe that's where her maternal feelings had been channelled, into watching men's sleeping faces as she held them close after they had emptied themselves into her.

'What are you smiling at?' Gary asked as she put down his baby mug.

'Was I? Nothing. Just thinking back.'

Gary watched her. He recognised the redness of her face and the base of her neck. She was thinking about sex. He doubted it involved him.

The hospital doctor, consultant, all loud voice and Garrick Club tie, had been bullish about Gary's chances of continuing to 'satisfy the little woman'.

The MS specialist, a quietly spoken man with unpolished shoes, was more realistic and offered Gary a selection of pumps and pulleys and magic pills. But it wasn't just the body's mechanics for Gary. His mind had made him impotent. He was revolting in his own eyes: how could anyone still want him? So the glory of his teens and twenties cowered in a wrinkle of skin under the eternal cotton of his pyjamas. And even though she sometimes, rarely now, pushed herself against him, lay down beside him, he couldn't let his fingers roam over her. He couldn't give her pleasure.

And now his hands weren't capable.

He wondered if he should be grateful she hadn't been shagging everyone from the milkman to Mr Chawla in the corner shop.

'What are you thinking about?' Lucy's tone was gentle, nurse-like. She knew exactly what and knew she deserved his anger for asking.

'Fuchsias,' he said. 'I think I'd like some outside the patio doors. So I can see them from here.'

'Yes. Good idea,' she said, dipping a low-fat chocolate biscuit into her tea.

The Gnome was listening to *Don Giovanni* when the phone rang. Listening to Thomas Allen he remembered the impact of the singer's sexuality when he'd seen him perform the role. The Don's obsession with the chase and Allen's obvious understanding were the perfect partnership. It was, without doubt, Robert MacIntyre's perfect opera.

He'd been dealing with his red boxes. His beloved and most satisfying red boxes. The reward he'd waited for for so long.

The run-up to the election had lacked tension other than that generated by the media. The opposition had been in such disarray it was almost embarrassing to talk them up as a threat. Of course on voting day everyone had had an attack of the jitters in case the hand of fate misdealt, but the landslide remained, even if it was from less than 30 per cent of the electorate. MacIntyre didn't mind – he saw nothing wrong in apathy if it worked to the government's advantage.

The day after the result the Prime Minister called him to Number 10 to offer him Home Secretary. He accepted and experienced the first perfect day of his life.

MacIntyre had known the idea of satisfaction, he'd had a taste of completion, but nothing prepared him for the rolling orgasm of power that the position gave him. Home Secretary. He loved it. It was, he felt, what God had made him for. Not Prime Minister, he didn't want that: the vulgar showmanship now required wasn't his style at all. No, he'd found his niche and felt almost mellowed by the experience.

'PM's on the phone,' Lizie called.

He picked up the handset on his desk. The voice on the other end was, as always, colloquial without being at ease.

'Hi . . . Robbie . . . I've er, I've just seen the broadsheets. This guy Carter, what's he up to? What do you think? Bit of a loose cannon possibly?'

MacIntyre had realised that when he'd watched the interview but wanted to see to what extent the press would pick up on it. No point in overreacting if the media had something to distract it, but as usual the PM wanted control.

'I don't think his views on decriminalisation necessarily make him a danger, Prime Minister.' MacIntyre detested first-name familiarity. 'Why don't I have a word with him on Monday?'

'Good idea. I mean, Robbie, this bloke's going to have to be with us as Crime Tsar, isn't he? On everything. Anyway, he's your man so as long as a word's enough. I don't know. Maybe we should think again. Look, I've got to go. Just give it some thought, eh, Robbie? Oh and all the best to Elizabeth.'

With Us. On Message. Singing From The Same Hymn Sheet. The mantra of contemporary success.

MacIntyre walked over to the window. The llamas, comical creatures, were jumping about like cartoons. He could see problems ahead with Mr Carter. It had been widely reported that he was to be the Crime Tsar, though not officially announced. He was respected by press, radio and television as an individual thinker. The government had garnered praise from usually critical areas for selecting someone not regarded as a Party poodle. But . . . MacIntyre realised there could be no but. No going back unless the PM and his advisers wanted to unleash a tornado of contemptuous criticism from the media. And that criticism would be deflected from Downing Street and on to him. The Home Secretary was responsible for this appointment. If a mess was created it would be seen to be his even though the decision to give Carter the job was made before his time.

A rock and a hard place.

He knew Carter would not be passed over without adding his own well-focused thoughts to the furore which would, inevitably, follow.

No, Mr Carter was, irrevocably, the first Crime Tsar, but a word in his ear would not go amiss. Not of warning exactly but simply advice. Yes. Just a little guidance. But he would always present a threat. That was not something the Gnome relished.

The door opened and Lizie came in carrying a tray. On it was a pot of tea, two cups and a freshly made Dundee cake.

'Cup of tea and a slice of cake!'

They said it together, a juvenile chant, emphasising alternate words. Comforting and childish. The Gnome leaned across the dispatch box and kissed her cheek.

'God, you're a temptress! Oh all right then, just five minutes, then I must get on.'

Jenni was more than usually on edge as they drove to the airport. She hadn't been sleeping properly since their visit to Geoffrey Carter and had taken to hoovering at 3 a.m. or packing and re-packing their luggage.

Shackleton broke the silence.

'We need petrol. I'll stop at the next services.'

Jenni didn't react, he couldn't see her eyes behind the expensive sunglasses she wore. They went on in silence, Jenni twisting and untwisting a silk scarf between her freshly manicured hands. Shackleton drove into the green-canopied petrol station.

'I need some water. And the loo.'

These were the first words Jenni had spoken since getting into the car.

He was anxious to please.

'I'll get a bottle – oh, the toilet's out of order.'

'For Christ's sake . . . toilet? Toilet? You're not at Kingsley Mixed Infants now. God!'

Shackleton continued to fill the tank. He recognised the rising hysteria in her voice and wanted to find a way round the looming confrontation.

'Sorry,' he murmured.

'Drive over to the restaurant.'

He paid for the petrol and then quietly obeyed.

Suddenly her mood lightened.

'Come on, I'll buy you a sticky bun. There's plenty of time.'

She smiled at him.

He was pleasantly surprised by the evaporation of the thunder clouds but too wary to abandon his caution. They got out of the car and Jenni set off for the entrance. Shackleton paused to lock the car.

She turned back.

'Where's your jacket?'

'In the car.'

'Aren't you going to put it on?'

He was confused.

'No. It's a nice day. I don't need it.'

'You look like a second-hand car salesman. Put your jacket on.'

'No, I don't think so, Jenni, I don't need it. We'll only be five minutes . . .'

And then she snapped. The elegant, silk-clad woman six paces ahead of him suddenly transformed into a screaming banshee.

'Why don't you respect me? You put your jacket on if you're with someone that matters. But I don't matter, do I? I'm just your wife. Put your jacket on. You're humiliating me! You bastard! You arrogant bastard!'

And with the half-dozen mums, dads and kids picking chips out of cardboard cones in the car-park watching, she threw herself at him with the mad strength of total fury. Her red-painted nails found no resistance in the skin of his cheeks. They pulled down his lower eyelids, making him look for an instant like a sad Saint Bernard. When she turned her back on him there was dark blood oozing from the wounds on his face.

He heard her say, 'Put your jacket on,' as she disappeared through the automatic doors advertising family meals for £4.99.

Acutely aware of the stares from the puddingy children nearby, he bent to retrieve his jacket. He followed Jenni into the plastic restaurant. She held out a cup of tea to him.

A fat man tattooed with the key influences of his life, Mum, Evelyn, Love, Hate and 2 Para, walked up to Shackleton ignoring Jenni.

'I'd smack 'er one if I was you, mate. Give 'er a good hiding. She'll not do that again.'

Shackleton looked at him, took in the gold neck-chain, rings and bracelet. The stale smell of cigarettes.

'I can't do that. I'd kill her.'

The tattooed man could respect that. He nodded.

'No jury'd convict you. What a bitch.'

With no further glance at Jenni he wandered off, satisfied with his world and his wisdom.

'What did he want?' Jenni asked. Sharp, glittering.

'Coins . . . for the cigarette machine.'

If Tom Shackleton had been accustomed to using the word symbiosis he might have found it useful when he tried to find some reason for their staying together.

Jenni maintained her silence until they were installed in the Hotel Sobrino in one of the more picturesque back streets of Barcelona.

The room's long windows opened on to black wrought-iron balconies which Jenni declared 'sweet' in her first utterance since the jacket incident. This was Shackleton's cue to return to normal – punishment over.

They passed the day sightseeing with Jenni being caustically funny about every sartorial mistake they saw. On this level they enjoyed each other's company and they certainly enjoyed the admiring looks they drew.

By mid-afternoon of the second day all Tom wanted to do was get away from her, find a bar and get drunk. But that would have only caused more violence, more abuse.

'Would you like to go out for dinner?' As always his tone was conciliatory.

'Later. I'm going to have a rest. Why don't you go out? Find a bar. But –' She smiled her gentlest smile at him. 'Don't get drunk. And, Tom . . . ?'

He saw the glint of danger again.

'Take your jacket.'

And don't forget to leave your balls on the bedside table.

She went on to the balcony and watched until he was down the narrow road. He didn't look up. She then went back into the pleasant white bedroom and sat on the edge of one of the mahogany beds.

'Tom, don't forget. Twin, not double. I can't bear you sweating and snorting in all that heat.'

She picked up the phone and dialled Lucy's number. Gary answered after eleven rings. Jenni always counted the amount of rings. Nine was usually her limit.

'Gary, darling. How are you? Sorry, silly question. Is Lucy there? Thanks . . .'

She heard him call to Lucy. Probably liquidising something for his tea, Jenni thought. Poor Lucy – she'd treat her to a day at the Sanctuary when they got back. Not that a day's beauty treatment was going to make huge inroads into Lucy's problems.

'Hello, Lucy. Everything all right? I'm just phoning to let you know our number here. You will phone, won't you, if anything happens . . . Like what? Well, nothing really, but Tamsin, Tamsin and little Kit, said they might drop in to have supper with Jason if he's about, and you know the chaos they can cause. The kitchen will look like a nuclear-testing zone.'

Lucy laughed because it was expected.

'But do feel free to call . . . And you won't forget to do a big clean, will you? I shall be checking under everything when I get back, so no slacking, eh?'

Jenni's idea of light affectionate banter had Lucy grinding her teeth. She wanted to say their son had come back and ransacked the house before setting fire to Jenni's wardrobe but she just said, 'Fine. No problem. Have a lovely time.'

After she'd hung up Jenni sat for a while. She felt jumpy and oddly fearful. There was a cure for that, a medicine she had found pleasurably easy to acquire in the loos of good restaurants. She reached over and picked up her handbag, a neat square of expensive leather discreetly stamped with the name of a designer never considered by the women guided by mass magazines. This designer never allowed himself to become a one-season must-have.

She slid her hand into it and pulled out her powder compact. Under its disc of translucent dust was a tiny paper envelope. Inside it a comforting amount of cocaine. She knew it was a stupid risk to bring it but no sniffer dog could have detected it past the industrial amounts of perfume she was wearing. Besides, her husband was a chief constable: nobody stopped him.

Jenni prepared it, taking pleasure in her new skill, and took a 50 Euro note from her purse. She rolled it up and inhaled the drug through it from the polished surface of the coffee table. The numbing effect of the fingered powder on her gums was still her favourite sensation, a prelude to the flood of confidence that followed. She cleared away the evidence and prepared for dinner.

Prepared for the next few crucial days.

It didn't take long for Lucy to find the transmitter once she started the big clean, but she had no idea what it was so she dusted it and put it back on the shelf.

It wasn't until breakfast the next day she thought of it again and mentioned it to Gary. Just in passing.

He was immediately interested.

'Bring it over,' he said.

'I can't do that. I don't even know what it is. It might have something to do with the security.'

Gary was amused.

'What, a burglar alarm in a cupboard? With all that stuff they've got? No chance.'

Lucy shrugged. But Gary didn't let it go and eventually she picked up her keys and went across the road to fetch it. She tried not to look at the photograph of Tom on the side table in the hall. As she had been trying not to think about him since her dismissal. But with distance she was beginning to convince herself she had misinterpreted what he said and how he'd said it. Maybe when he got back things would be all right between them again.

She handed the transmitter to Gary. He turned it over, examining it with disbelief, feeling he was a bit player in a Bond movie. He knew exactly what it was – the books he absorbed in large print from the library were full of spies and the hardware of espionage. He'd long since given up struggling with the literary novel, its convolutions further removed from his own reality than even SAS mavericks saving small African states. Gary almost laughed.

'It's a transmitter. A bug. Was this the only one?'

'I don't know. I haven't looked for any others.'

His hands couldn't grip it and it fell to the floor.

'Gary . . . be careful. You'll break it. Are you sure it's a bug?' She felt silly using such a B-movie word.

'I think so. I watched a documentary about MI6 a couple of weeks ago and they used this sort of thing.'

Lucy picked it up looking for a clue as to its use. All she saw was a small black box with a bit of black rubber sticking up from one side. She wanted it to be tiny and made of space-ship metal, small and sexy.

'Maybe it's theirs. I don't know, a memento or something from Tom's time with . . . sorry.'

She saw Gary's expression and knew he thought she just wanted an excuse to speak to Shackleton. She changed tack.

'You could speak to them. You know what it is.'

Gary nodded.

'Yes. All right.'

Lucy dialled the number, reading it off the teddy-bear-decorated pad by the phone.

'Hotel Sobrino ¡buenos dias!'

Lucy always froze when calling abroad. It was something about the single rings and the abrupt confidence of the people that answered.

'Er . . . hello. Mr Shackleton, please. Room one two six.'

'Ciento veintiséis. Gracias, Señora.'

Again the single rings. Three rings. Then Tom's voice with that quiet, three-syllabled 'Hello'. Her heart did what hearts do. Or was it her stomach? She handed the phone to Gary.

'Tom? It's Gary, Lucy's found something in your house . . .'

Shackleton put down the receiver. Jenni was in the shower. He didn't move when she emerged swathed in white towels.

He looked middle-aged and saggy out of his immaculate suits and uniforms. Slightly foolish. His passivity irritated her even more now they were alone together with nothing to distract them. But they were here for the image of their marriage, the golden couple. Two people who'd got through life never beached or wrecked on the rocks of endless intimacy.

'What's the matter with you?'

Jenni thought it must be his neck or his stomach or another nameless ache, the debris of stress and age. Jenni felt if she never showed sympathy his symptoms would eventually give up and go away. Or he'd stop demonstrating the pain in front of her.

'That was Gary –'

She cut him off.

'On the phone? Why didn't you call me? What did he want? Is everything all right at home?'

'Lucy found a transmitter while she was cleaning.'

Jenni was controlled. She picked up a brush and gently teased it through her wet hair.

'What are you talking about?'

Jenni listened with satisfaction as her husband, in full Chief-Constable mode, phoned his deputy, arranged for the house to be minutely examined by the special operations unit.

Jenni turned on the hairdryer.

'Is it serious?'

'Of course it's bloody serious.'

Good, she thought. About time too. What had Lucy been doing not to find it for so long? Stupid woman.

'Does this mean we'll have to go home early?'

'Yes.' He picked up the phone again. 'Turn that thing off – I can't hear.'

Jenni wasn't remotely annoyed but saw her opportunity. She slammed down the dryer knocking an ashtray on to the tiled floor where it shattered.

'You always spoil everything. You bastard! You apology for a husband! We've never had a break you haven't ruined. Don't try and change the tickets on the phone, you'll only cock it up. Go down to reception. Get them to do it. Go on! Get out! Get out! Leave me alone.' She was screaming now, pleased with the effect she was creating.

As usual he quailed and collapsed under her expert attack.

'Jenni, calm down. Stop shouting. All right, all right, I'll go. Just calm down.'

She didn't let up until he'd gone and closed the door behind him. Immediately she went to the phone and pressed the numbers of Carter's home. Eleri answered quickly; Jenni was tearful, a small voice of vulnerability in her ear. Eleri was immediately solicitous.

'. . . and she found some sort of transmitter. A listening device. Oh God . . . Someone must have got into the house. It makes you feel so awful, violated . . .'

Eleri tried to calm her, unsure why Jenni had called her.

'Well . . . you could have them too.'

Like mice, thought Eleri.

'Yes, I suppose we could, but I don't see why.'

Jenni wanted to scream: 'You stupid great pregnant cow, your husband's a fucking chief constable, that's why.'

'Why? Eleri, Geoffrey's going to be the Crime Tsar, Tom's going to be head of the largest and most controversial police force in the country, they're both higher profile than most politicians. Don't you see? Anyone from MI5 to the *News of the World* could have planted them. And after what Geoffrey said on television, well, they'll be watching him now, won't they? God knows how long they've been there. We've had workmen in the house so many times this year.'

'Oh . . . funny you should say that, we've just had replacement windows –'

'Were you there all the time?'

'Well, no . . . the next-door neighbour let them in sometimes.'

Jenni knew when to stay quiet. Let thought do the work.

Eleri's baby-soaked mind was slow but finally she said, 'I'll have a look, Jenni, really. I promise. But your friend might have made a mistake. We should wait and see. I'll tell Geoffrey when he gets home but he's terribly busy today and I've got to take Alexander to see his new school. They do conductive education and we've waited ages to get him in . . .'

Jenni wanted to scream at Eleri's hormonal serenity but she kept calm and rang off. She would have to wait, bide her time and wait.

She was too tightly wound up to relax; she needed a release. What to do. Where was Tom? She felt as if small claws were scrabbling round the inside of her skull. She could hear them scratching. It was difficult to breathe. She felt a wave of panic. She needed more of the magic white powder but had none left. She had had a couple of little handmade envelopes in her dressing table at home but had made sure they were gone before they left for Spain. If the house were to be searched for any reason while they were away . . . Jenni smiled. Two of her pills and a large vodka might take the edge off her craving. She poured the drink, swallowed the pills and dialled the Gnome's direct line.

'Jenni, what an unexpected pleasure. How are you?'

One of the new girls came in with his coffee. As she turned to go he noticed she didn't shave her legs. He briefly wondered about her armpits. Laziness or naughtiness?

'Robbie, I'm so sorry to bother you. We're in Spain and Lucy just rang to say –'

The story tumbled out and the Gnome listened. He really didn't have the time for this but he had rather a soft spot for Mrs Chief

Constable. She had been so deliciously disgusted by him. He rarely revisited the scenes of his triumphs but he rather liked the idea of dipping into that particular honeypot again.

'. . . and poor Eleri's expecting so I don't want to alarm her, but I'm afraid with the business of the siege and Tom and Geoffrey being so high-profile – I'm sure you understand, I hope I'm not being paranoid but well . . . I'm so sorry to drag you in but Tom's not here and I'm dreadfully worried.'

He reassured her and promised he'd look into it but she could hear in his voice he wasn't quite convinced.

'Robbie, thank you. I'm so grateful.'

Oh, you will be, you will be.

'And, Robbie . . .' Did she dare? 'There was something else.'

His silence invited her to go on.

'I've visited the Carters' house a lot lately and . . . well, this is very difficult, I think Geoffrey Carter may be . . . may have . . . Oh God, Robbie, I don't know how to say this but I think you may find more than bugs in the house. I really can't say any more.'

What on earth was she twittering on about?

'Stolen goods, Jenni? Illegally imported rolling tobacco? What?'

'Some sort of pornography . . .' Jenni stopped. Had she gone too far?

'I see.' MacIntyre paused.

Jenni rushed into the silence.

'Alexander, their autistic boy, he found a video in a cupboard. I didn't watch it but the cover, the title – I think it was . . .'

'What, Jenni?'

The Gnome's voice was hard. She hesitated. What was he thinking? Did he believe her?

'Something involving children.' She rushed on. 'Look, I could be wrong, it may be perfectly innocent. Maybe I shouldn't have said anything. I haven't even told Tom. I didn't see it properly. I'm sorry . . .'

MacIntyre frowned. Was Carter going to prove more trouble than he was worth?

'Don't worry, Jenni. The matter of the transmitters will have to be looked into and if anything else turns up –'

Bingo!

'Thank you, Robbie. I hope you don't think I'm being hysterical.'

'Not at all, Jenni. Not at all. And, Jenni, when you get back we must find time for a meeting. I so enjoyed our last encounter.'

'Me too, Robbie.'

You're a bad liar, Mrs Shackleton.

'Right . . . let me know when you can get away from your husband. And thanks for the call. I'll look into it.'

Jenni Shackleton the broken flower panicking in her husband's absence was a hard act to swallow but she sounded genuine enough and the snippet about Carter's sexual preferences was extraordinary. He wanted to know more but gossip wasn't his style. An accusation like this needed to be shot down immediately. Unless of course it was true.

After a brief series of phone calls a man called Trevor Hemsley was put in charge of the delicate matter of searching the Chief Constable's house. He found it vaguely irritating, as it was his day off and he was reconstructing *The Mary Rose* out of a balsa kit, but he put down his glue, put on his coat, and went to work.

Jenni was dressed and reading a tour guide when Tom got back with the new tickets. He looked hot and exhausted. He was sweating and his face was red, not with sun but exertion.

'Darling, when did you last have your blood pressure checked?'

Shackleton never ceased to be amazed at the mood and subject changes his wife was capable of.

'I've got the tickets. The flight's at eight-thirty tonight. OK?'

Jenni was sweetly surprised at his question.

'Of course, Tom. You do look awfully hot, you know. Come and sit down, I'll get you something to drink.'

She gave him a bottle of too cold sparkling water from the minibar and stood behind him running her cold fingertips, like cobwebs, across his forehead. He didn't dare move. He didn't like the feeling of her mortuary skin on his but knew better than to shrug off her attentions. He glanced up at her but she wasn't conscious of him – she was looking into some distance that contained pleasure. A look that didn't include him.

'Are you worried about this bug?'

Her voice had a softness, as if she wanted him to say yes. Wanted to be able to comfort him.

'No. But I'd like to know who put it there.'

'Maybe it was the security services. Making sure you're sound before you get the Met.'

'Doubt it. That lot haven't much time for the police. They think we're not bright enough to get up to anything that could remotely be a security risk. Anyway, they're too sophisticated for that sort of hardware – they tend to go in more for phone tapping.'

Jenni continued to soothe his troubled brow. He wished she'd stop.

'What about the press?' Jenni asked.

Tom didn't say anything for a moment; he was beginning to realise why Jenni wasn't doing an impression of a Komodo dragon that had stepped on an anti-personnel mine.

'Jenni . . . has this got anything to do with you?'

She squatted down beside him, her delicate bird hands on his arm.

'If it had it would be for you. You know that, don't you?'

He touched her hair. Yes, he knew that was what she believed and there was no point in trying to inflict reality on her. He wasn't even sure he could withstand the onslaught of naked hatred that would provoke. This oasis of peace and gentleness was so rare.

'I know Jenni, I know.'

For one awkward moment each thought the other was going to attempt a kiss. Jenni had never really liked kissing, tongues and teeth awkwardly and messily in conjunction. She saw the panic in his eyes, those innocent eyes that had looked so hurt so often.

An image she hadn't thought of for years came into her mind: Tom on their first date, when she'd reached up on tiptoe to kiss his cheek as they said goodnight. The same look of panic. But then she'd gently touched his lips with her fingertips and asked him what was wrong. Looking at him there in the Spanish hotel room she could hear his soft, sad voice from that night. 'Nobody ever touches me.' She remembered wanting to hold him and protect him.

Then the fear.

The fear it was a trick.

She was quite happy to give him her body but anything else would come at a price.

'Don't you want me, Tom?'

Abruptly he was on his guard again. What he'd thought was companionship was something far more threatening. He preferred

243

her when she was telling him how much she hated the thought of sex with him. He didn't understand this playful kitten act and he certainly didn't like it.

He looked at her face: there was something strange, different, about her. As if she was slightly out of focus, blurred.

She mistook the intensity of his look for desire. Had she been without drink, without drugs, she would have seen the revulsion there but all she saw in those still beautiful eyes was the twin reflections of herself. She wanted to feel her power over him again. The altered state of her mind hid the reasons for their frigidity with each other. Dieter had given her back her magical powers and she was invincible.

Tom froze as she undid his shirt, expertly slipped the buckle of his belt and undid his zip. Her sharp red nails disappeared from sight and reappeared as she eased his penis free. She held the limp troglodyte in the sunlight. She kissed it. Shackleton looked down at her. He felt like a character in a sci-fi movie whose wife is replaced by an alien. Attempts at oral sex had been abandoned early in their marriage. The idea repelled him. Nevertheless her tongue and lips were expertly manipulating him when the phone rang. For a moment he thought she would continue while he answered it but the phone was on the other side of the room. He stood up, hating having to gather his trousers around him as he picked up the receiver. She stayed kneeling on the floor, not looking at him but still wrapped in dreams. She reached across for her vodka.

Tom kept talking as long as he could. It was Vernon who'd simply called to reassure his boss that everything was under control. Most chiefs would have resented the intrusion but Shackleton was grateful as well as relieved. Vernon's fussing had never been so welcome.

After a minute or two Jenni got up, picked up her handbag and reapplied her lipstick. Tom could see she had completely forgotten what she, moments before, had wanted so badly. Relieved, he rang off and suggested they pack.

She turned and beamed at him.

'Why not?'

Two Special Branch men arrived at Carter's house with Hemsley from MI5 at the same time as what looked like a regiment of Royal

Engineers descended on Shackleton's, where Lucy hovered clutching her keys, on the verge of self-accusatory tears. They went through every nook and cranny of the house with her trailing from room to room begging them to be careful and replacing everything precisely after they'd examined it. They were pleased to find a second transmitter in the hall-light fitting.

In the middle of all this Jason opened the front door.

Lucy scuttled out to reassure him but he didn't seem very interested. He had a car waiting outside full of friends, and the promise of a party later. He just wanted to dump his bag and be away.

At Carter's house three discreet men waited in their discreet car until he arrived to let them in, Eleri being in London with Alexander. All he had been told, by the Gnome's disinterested assistant, was that there was a possibility his house had been bugged by a person or persons unknown.

The men thought he seemed nervous when he opened the door, miskeying his burglar-alarm code and causing it to contradict him angrily, giving him another ten seconds to get it right. He pushed the buttons again. Silence.

The largest of the men asked politely, in a voice that suggested urbanity and education, if they might look around. Carter nodded. He was sweating – a greasy sheen covered his nose and upper lip. The men could smell the fear. They were not curious by nature or training; they knew they'd find out why soon enough. One man went to search the top floor, the second the mezzanine floor study, and the third, the urbane one, took the ground starting in the kitchen, where Carter was clumsily filling the kettle and attempting to plug it in.

It didn't take long to find the bug behind the Coalport teapot. Carter was by this time sitting at the kitchen table staring blankly out at the garden. The next thing to be found was an envelope. The second faceless man brought it into the kitchen, careful of possible fingerprints and ready to bag up the evidence. Nothing was said. The man opened the envelope and displayed its contents. Photographs of young men in artistic poses of physical splendour, photographs of younger men entwined in each other's arms, laughing, and finally three photographs of teenage boys arching their naked bodies as they were caned by stern uniformed men. Carter barely nodded when the educated tones asked if they were his. There was a faint tut.

He put them on the table. Carter reached across and turned them over, face down.

A few minutes later the other bug was found and a small pile of magazines was brought in. The atmosphere was by now poisonous. Judgements had been made.

'Behind the bath. Nearly missed them. Not what we're looking for though, are they?'

'Can't ignore them,' the urbane one replied. Hemsley worked on a need-to-know-only basis.

Carter, hearing they'd been found behind the bath, turned to look.

'These yours too, Mr Carter?'

Carter saw the provocative poses of the children.

'No.'

He was so surprised at the images he didn't think to say anything else for a moment then the full horror of the images hit him. His explosion of anger took the investigators by surprise.

'No. No, my God . . . They're not mine. I'd never . . . No. What's going on?'

One of the men restrained him, but too late to stop Carter's fingerprints being left on the evidence. The only fingerprints that would be found. The third searcher had found the hidden floppy disc. He wanted to take Carter's computer so they could examine the contents of the files. Back-up was called for. The evidence neatly bagged up.

By now Carter's fury had subsided into shock. He was mumbling, 'That's not mine. It's not mine. It's filth . . . not mine.'

Just before the video was found the doorbell rang. Carter was allowed to answer it.

His deputy stood on the doorstep.

'Jesus Christ. What's happened, Geoffrey?'

Carter stared at him.

'Come in. Danny, I've . . . I've got some visitors.'

The Gnome was intrigued. Hemsley was in his office presenting the results of the search.

'So . . . let me get this straight. The Chief Constable had three transmitters in his house, a quantity of questionable photographs and an amount of illegal material with paedophile content?'

'That's right, sir.'

'But he's denying some of it is his?'

'Yes, sir. Says the pictures are his but that he's not a paedophile. Very emphatic about that, sir.'

The Gnome looked at the colour laser copies on his desk.

'Believe him, Hemsley?'

'I wouldn't want to say, sir.'

MacIntyre nodded.

'And the transmitters?'

'The police tell us they're the same as those found at Shackleton's house. Obviously an amateur planted them, sir – they weren't even switched on – possibly someone with a grudge. None of the agencies would use anything so crude. The whole thing feels a bit odd to me, sir.'

'Hmm . . .' The ugly little face scowled with concentration. 'Thank you, Hemsley. Keep me informed. Oh . . . one thing . . . where is Mr Carter now?'

'At his office, sir. We've handed everything over to his force. His ACC Complaints is forwarding the details to the Home Office.'

He left the room.

Nothing had surprised the Gnome since he failed Music O level but this puzzled him. He reached out and spread the photocopies across his desk.

Homosexual sex had never appealed to him but the images before him were intriguing: domination and degradation, flesh as food. The youths concerned quite old enough to know their own minds and, more to the point, bodies. On the very edge of popular morality of course but quite appealing. MacIntyre smiled. So this was what the urbane Mr Carter had learned at public school.

He looked at the magazines and any sexual interest he'd felt evaporated. Children.

He turned on the video and saw a small boy being woken by a naked man. From the weary misery in the boy's voice it wasn't the first time. He clutched a small threadbare teddy in his right hand.

MacIntyre watched what followed with tears running down his face. He had controlled his emotions until he realised the tune he could hear playing in the background was 'Away in a manger'.

The cattle are lowing,
The baby awakes,
But little Lord Jesus, no crying he makes . . .

The childish voices so full of Christmas. He could taste ginger and feel the paper tearing from his presents.

He stopped the video. When was the last time he'd cried? At the sight of the magnolia in his garden. Beauty made him cry but this kind of ugliness tore him open. He had fought his way to where he was because of bullies and this suffering of little children roused a kind of righteous anger in him. Whatever the evil in him he knew it was not this, never this.

He blew his nose. Emotion was a distraction, certainly in this case.

The procedure was clearly laid out. The Assistant Chief Constable Complaints would contact the Home Office and they would appoint an outside force to investigate. It would be premature to arrest or suspend as there was no de facto evidence that the illegal material belonged to Carter.

The chief of the investigation would have to be senior to Carter, Commissioner of the City of London, the Chief of Greater Manchester, the Chief of West Midlands, the Chief of Merseyside or an ACC from the Met, or of equal rank. MacIntyre thought for a moment about going against the rules and giving it to Shackleton. No. Too cruel. Too personal.

If the City of London took it they would serve a Notice of Complaint No. 1 but numbered 39 next door in the Met. And the investigation into Geoffrey Carter would be under way. He would continue in his job, under suspicion, under a cloud. He could alert his legal representative but until prosecution was decided on there would be nothing more he could do. Stalemate.

MacIntyre knew it was imperative for him to accelerate the investigation, to establish the truth before Carter could move on or face prosecution. The news would soon hit the press and minds would be made up. Shit would stick no matter what the outcome.

There could be no shadow hanging over the Crime Tsar.

He looked again at the evidence. Something was wrong. The bugs, Jenni's phone call, the contradiction of almost art-house pictures and hard-core child pornography, not necessarily mutually exclusive, but . . . an unlikely combination?

If it was a set-up, if Carter was simply the victim of an unfortunate combination of his own bizarre tastes and a vendetta, the truth could be quickly established. But did the Gnome really want a quick conclusion to the matter? If there were second thoughts from on high about Carter's reliability this could be the perfect opportunity to put his life on indefinite hold. By the time the facts were established the hand of time would have moved on and lifted someone else into the limelight. No messy court case, a quiet fading away. A safer Crime Tsar in place. Good.

The total destruction of Carter's life was merely the answer to a small but nagging problem when seen from a different perspective.

MacIntyre thoughtfully tidied away the photocopies and facsimiles. The video was placed in a drawer. Perhaps, in this case, it would not be expedient to expedite matters.

When Eleri came home with Alexander that day, the day that contained the end of the world, she was flushed and excited. The school was perfect and Alex had liked it.

'Well,' she said as they bustled through the front door, 'he didn't scream the place down so he must've loved it. Hello, Danny, what are you doing here?'

Carter and Danny were sitting in the kitchen. Each had a cup of undrunk coffee. They were silent. Carter had had the conversation with his deputy.

'I'm not a paedophile. I swear to you, I'm not a paedophile. That stuff must have been planted at the same time as the bugs. You believe me, don't you?'

He looked at his deputy whose steady gaze flickered just enough for Carter to know he didn't.

'The photographs, they're mine but they're not illegal.'

No, but you're going to be finished whatever happens. The thought was so loud in the deputy's head Carter heard it. Or was it the echo of his own mind?

'Danny, this is really difficult, but . . . those photos, they're – they were something I used to think about. Not now, not for years. But I, I was the boys not the men. Do you see? I wanted to be the boys, not have them.'

He wanted to be able to explain his teenage fascination with the strength and domination of older men but saw his deputy's expression. There was no understanding there.

'What was the kiddie stuff doing mixed up with your stuff then?'

This was where it became confusing. Where his story sounded thin and unreal.

'It wasn't, they found it somewhere else. Not with my . . . photographs.'

Danny didn't know what to say; he was profoundly uncomfortable thinking Carter was gay and suspecting he was a paedophile.

His deputy looked away, ashamed to be so visceral in his reaction.

He wanted to believe in Carter's innocence but was too disgusted by the images skulking round his head to say anything. The deputy was confused; he wanted to get out but Carter was talking.

'I've never . . . done anything, you know? Not physically, with a man. Too scared, I suppose. And . . . I didn't really want to, it was . . . I don't know. A sort of fascination. A part of a fantasy left over from my adolescence.'

He paused.

'The press will have a field day, won't they?'

His deputy thought he was missing the point. As far as everyone else was concerned Carter would be a trader in kiddie porn. The modern witchcraft. He'd be put on a stake and burned.

'That stuff was planted in the house. I swear to you –'

'Listen, Mr Carter . . .' That seemed harsh, somehow judgemental.

'Geoffrey.' Carter tried to smile.

Danny went on not wanting to be trapped by emotion or obligation.

'I must go. I'll give you a call tomorrow. Have you got on to your solicitor yet?'

Carter was suddenly angry.

'No. Why should I? I've done nothing wrong.'

'You had that stuff in your possession, Geoffrey – it doesn't look good . . .'

Danny realised the inadequacy of what he'd said but Carter had turned back to stare out of the window.

His deputy knew he shouldn't leave him alone but he had football practice and anyway he really didn't want to stay. That would be Eleri's responsibility, poor woman. He felt somehow dirty being there. He didn't know what to believe but kept thinking this murky stew of perversions would be too strong to escape from odour-free. He longed to get home and take a shower. He didn't want to pre-judge, especially not his friend and mentor, but revulsion and self-interest were getting the better of him.

That's when Eleri and Alexander tumbled into the house and Danny made his way out with smiles and apologies.

He closed the front door quietly and breathed in deeply as if he'd been saving his lungs from contamination.

He didn't know what his feelings were towards the man who had been his hero and his friend only twenty-four hours before. Anger, disgust and the desire to walk away and erase the man jostled with doubt, affection and disbelief.

He decided he wouldn't see Carter tomorrow. He needed time to find a single emotion to carry him through. More than that he needed to distance himself from his fatally flawed chief. The future mustn't be diseased by the past. He disliked himself for his brutal pragmatism but no one reached the top by being sentimental.

Eleri didn't notice her husband's mute misery while she was dealing with Alexander.

'He loved the school, didn't you, Alex? Hello, Peter, how was your day . . . ?'

Peter bounded through the back door dropping his school bag and demanding a sandwich and his jeans. Eleri wanted to know what on earth he'd spilled down his uniform trousers and Alexander was jumping up and down with excitement.

There was no good time to speak. Carter felt like a ghost, an invisible observer, no longer of their world.

It wasn't until the boys were in bed that Eleri said, 'What's the matter with you? You've got a face that would stop a clock.'

Carter moved the muscles that had recently made smiles.

'There was a search today. Here. They found some transmitters and –'

Eleri was loudly remorseful.

'Oh Geoffrey, I'm so sorry. Jenni phoned me to say something like that had been found at their house. I'm so sorry. It went right out of my head. Is it serious?'

'Yes. Quite serious.'

And then the evening shattered into images of pain. Eleri curled over their hidden waiting child, rocking back and forth, protecting herself and the baby from its father. His own face caught in the mirror, so much like the face he'd had that morning. The mouth moving, emptying itself of words that drove nails into the mind of his wife.

Which to start with? Homosexual? The desiccated remains of his childish fantasies. The near forgotten fascination with the hardness of male flesh, the strength of men's arms. Or paedophile. How could he explain there was a grain of truth in one and a silo of lies in the other?

He started with his admission. The distant, half-remembered dreams of being dominated, protected, punished, fathered.

Eleri rocked the child inside her, comforting herself.

'Wasn't I enough?'

Carter wanted to say this isn't about you but he didn't, he told her she was all he'd ever wanted. He put his arm round her shoulders.

She shook him off. She wanted the time to find her Christianity. To find the other cheek, to put down the stone she longed to throw. She saw vividly their love-making and searched his remembered face for any sign of indifference. She judged herself dirty, pendulous, and too, too rankly female against his ascetic beauty. No doubt everyone but her had realised years ago.

But she couldn't stop loving him, could she? She looked up. He was still talking but she didn't hear what he was saying. His face seemed to have changed. It was like the one she loved but different, the face of a stranger in a crowd, fleetingly alike but on examination no resemblance.

Carter lost all his smooth assurance, the sophistication that had draped him so elegantly for all his adult life, when he saw the revulsion in his wife's eyes and felt her flinch from his touch.

No matter how many times he said he had never been with a man he couldn't stop the pictures in her head. He stopped talking. Her breathing slowed. Two people isolated in a bath of misery, each unable to reach out and comfort the other.

Eleri thought it was finished but Carter knew he had to go on.

'They found some other material. Things I swear were not mine. Things I found – find – wicked, evil. That I would never, ever look at. I swear. Eleri, please, you've got to believe me. They found sex . . . magazines, a video, a disc here. They involved children.'

Eleri was staring at him. She seemed completely calm.

'Boys?'

Carter wasn't expecting that. He tried to think of what he'd seen. 'I think so, yes. I'm not sure. I didn't really look.'

Eleri pulled herself into the moment. Shut out the past and not consider the future.

'You swear to me –' She took hold of his hand and placed it on the swelling of their hope. 'On our baby, you swear? You have never thought about children' – she wasn't sure of the words to use, there weren't any kept apart for these occasions – 'like that.'

'I promise you. Eleri, I promise I have never. Never. I couldn't. I promise you.'

Nothing seemed adequate. He looked completely broken, defeated.

Eleri found her strength again in his vulnerability.

'So . . . the pictures were yours, but whatever I may think they weren't illegal.'

'No, they weren't.'

'But the other stuff has been put in the house by someone who wants to damage you – us. Probably at the same time as the transmitters.'

'Yes.'

'Well, the investigation should soon establish the truth of that, shouldn't it?'

He looked doubtful – she seemed to be clinging to the wreckage of order and logic while he was drowning in a sea of uncertainty.

'I don't know. I hope so.'

She looked round the room. The day had started so well with breakfast in the chaotic kitchen of their cosy home, which now looked ugly and shabby. This was now the house of a man who'd made his wife a fool in the eyes of the world. A man who craved male beauty but had stayed with her female craving for procreation. And now she was a silly pregnant woman in her forties who'd got what she wanted but would never know why. Her certainties were now all doubts. But she couldn't, wouldn't allow herself to think the worst. Yes, she could, if she controlled and blocked her imagination, continue her life with Geoffrey. Time would ease the pain. Their baby would dull it, deafen her ears to it. But the other thing? The maggot of doubt was wriggling at the back of her mind.

They talked as if their mouths were full of thorns until Eleri could decently say she was tired and going to bed. Life would continue normally. She would find understanding. He would be innocent until proven guilty. But they both knew, Eleri lying awake, staring into the darkness, and Geoffrey hiding in the darkness downstairs, drinking, that paedophilia was the one crime that contaminated simply by being spoken.

Jenni was in her bathroom. The search of the house had, according to Lucy, been disturbingly thorough. But Lucy had ensured that everything was put back in exactly the right place.

She was kneeling on the tiled floor, naked. On the sink surround was the pale dust of a cocaine hit, waiting for a slim finger to wipe it up. Her eyes were bright, caterpillar green, glazed with the drug. She was concentrating on a picture of Geoffrey Carter in the paper. He was captioned simply 'ACPO spokesman on drugs'. She spat on his handsome face and wished him dead. A curse for all seasons.

Nothing had been said about Carter since they'd got back from Spain. The papers were a sea of international misery, the radio and television news silent. So her mood swung between supreme confidence and shaking fearful doubt but this . . . this must catch him. Trip him up on his confident stroll to success.

She reached for a tissue. Tom had asked her if she had hay fever; she'd said yes but she knew it was the coke. Small price to pay for such power. Now all she had to do was find patience and wait.

There was a knock on the bathroom door. Her heart did a strange manoeuvre that seemed to involve engorging with blood and then expelling it by a contraction sideways. It felt like the cumbersome discharge of a loose bowel.

'Who is it?'

'Lucy . . . dinner's ready.'

Jenni arranged her voice on the edge of an emotional precipice.

'I'm not hungry, sorry. It's just the shock. I know I should but I can't get over it – I can't bear the thought of those things being found in our house . . .'

Lucy retreated, unsure whether to offer a tray or a boiled egg. Downstairs she stood confused for a moment, in the hallway. She knew Gary would be watching for her, that he'd have seen Shackleton come home.

When Jenni phoned to plead with her to come over and keep her company Gary had wanted her to say no but Jenni sounded almost hysterical. Almost out of control, talking rapidly and breathlessly, she begged Lucy to sit with her. Knowing Shackleton was at work Gary eventually told her to go over but to be back before he was due home. Lucy, nodding obediently and wearing her most ovine look, went. Gary stared at the house opposite until it started to get dark.

Lucy rang and said Jenni had asked her to cook dinner and she hadn't the heart to say no. Gary couldn't stop his arm going into spasm as he put down the phone. It lay on the floor whining at him for a while, then went silent. Should he press his emergency button?

'Hello, Gary dear? Hello? Have you had a fall, dear? Are you all right?'

'Oh yes, sorry, I'm fine, I just set off my alarm while trying out position one hundred and three of the Kama Sutra.'

No, he didn't press the easy-size-for-cripples-to-use red button hung round his neck, he just sat staring at the blind house opposite, waiting for his wife.

Lucy had cooked the lamb strips with couscous and red pepper. She didn't know what it was supposed to look like when it was ready so she just did her best. It was already drying up when Jenni decided she didn't want it but that didn't surprise her – Jenni's behaviour was even more odd since Spain. Lucy thought psychotic but suspected herself of wishful thinking.

She stood in the hall knowing she should go and simply leave the food. She'd done what she was asked to do and Jenni had given her £25 for the extra time. What else was there? She opened the front door as Shackleton's car drew up. She knew Gary was watching but didn't look across at the gaping uncurtained window. She went back into the house and waited. It seemed for ever until he came in.

'I've just cooked dinner. Jenni asked me to, but she doesn't want any. She's upstairs.'

He put down his attaché case.

'Thanks.'

She followed him to the door of the living room, unwilling to go in, in sight of Gary.

'Shall I warm it up? And serve it?'

'No. No thanks, Lucy.'

She knew he wanted her to go.

'Do you want me to go?'

He was stung by her accuracy.

'No. No, of course not. Have a drink. It's just been a long day.'

She still hovered by the door.

'Any news on the bug?' she asked.

He shook his head.

'Are you all right . . . Tom?'

When he looked up at her he seemed to have tears in his eyes.

She frowned, trying to see if he did without going further into the room.

'Tom, what's happened? Tell me. Come into the kitchen.'

Shackleton hesitated then, picking up the decanter of Scotch, followed her. They sat down either side of the kitchen table.

'You remember Geoffrey Carter?'

'Yes.'

'He's being investigated for possession of paedophile material.'

Lucy didn't know what to say. So she waited.

'Lucy . . . oh Lucy . . . I don't know what to do.'

The tears in his eyes blinded him but they couldn't fall. There was no release after a lifetime of control. She wanted to put her arms around him, to take away the pain, but there was something . . . an anger? Some violence in him that kept her away. He stood up and wiped his face with a piece of kitchen roll.

'You'd better go.'

'Can I help, Tom?'

He shook his head. She ignored her instinct and crept up behind him, putting her arms round his waist, resting her face against his back.

The pain in her wrist was so unexpected she was almost distant from it for the moments it took for him to twist round and put her arm up behind her, the back of her hand against her shoulder blade. He slammed her, face down, on the table an inch from the couscous and leaned his weight on her.

She couldn't breathe.

She felt him push up her skirt, felt him put his hand on her knickers, thumb inside the elastic, ready to tear them.

'Is this it? Is this what you're after, Lucy? Is this what you want me to do?'

He turned her over again, on to her back, grabbing her arms and pulling her close to him. His face was contorted. He stroked her hair back from her face.

'I'm so sorry, Lucy, I'm so sorry. I'm not worth this. Believe me. I can't give you anything. I told you I couldn't give you anything –'

'I never asked you for anything –' Lucy managed to say.

'Please, Lucy. I'm so far into this, I can't get back. Go home. Go home to Gary. Please. There is nothing in me that deserves you. Jenni's right, I am a bastard. Go back to Gary, please. I've made my bed, Lucy. I've got to lie in it.' That mantra again.

'What's happened, Tom? Let me help you, please.'

He let go of her and took a deep breath.

'You can't, Lucy.' He stepped away, formal again. 'I'm sorry. I'll see you out.'

They walked to the front door in silence. He opened it and Lucy went out turning to speak to him but the door was closed, silently, as she turned.

Gary watched and was glad.

Shackleton drank half the whisky before he found the courage to go upstairs. Jenni's light was out, he couldn't see it under her door. What would she say if the door opened and he went in? That used to be the signal he wanted sex. She'd get up and put a towel on the bed. He winced at the memory. The light was never turned on and he left her immediately after. She had never asked him to stay. Not like Lucy, clinging to him, her body pressed against his in sleep. Needing him. He shook his head.

He opened the door and listened for her breathing. Silence. Blackness.

'Come in, Tom.'

She turned on the bedside lamp. He was struck afresh by her extraordinary delicate beauty and was astonished to think of his bulk crushing her. Making babies. Thrusting and gasping. Seemed like a long time ago. Thank God it was.

'Carter's being investigated. They found kiddie porn in his house.'

At last. The devil had more patience than any damned saint. Jenni's stained-glass eyes were wide with disbelief.

'God, how awful. Have you spoken to him?'

'No.'

257

He didn't know what to say next.

'Jenni . . . ? Did you . . . were you . . . ? It's too much, Jenni, you've gone too far. Carter's no paedophile.'

Jenni was sitting up now as straight as a cobra before striking.

'Well, you'd better tell everyone then. I'm sure they'll believe you. Whoever "they" are.'

She was cold and still; he knew he couldn't win against her.

'You put that stuff in his house, didn't you?'

'What stuff? What are you talking about?'

She watched his fatal weakness and embryo moral courage raging in him.

'You can't do this, Jenni. You'll destroy him.'

She was scornful – to her the idea of Tom Shackleton developing a conscience was laughable.

'What are you going to do then, Tom? Call a press conference and tell them you and your wife framed him so her rather dim husband could get his new job? Grow up.'

Suddenly the strength went out of him. He visibly slumped.

'Oh God, Jenni, what have you done?'

'What have we done? We have simply moved an obstacle. Look, I'm sure it'll sort itself out. Might make him a stronger person.' She thought this was terribly amusing. 'We all need a challenge. Oh, go to bed, Tom – it'll all look better in the morning.'

She turned out the light and her husband was dismissed.

All night Shackleton sat drinking and thinking. What could he do? Tell the world his wife planted those magazines? Say he'd done it? Say nothing but stick by Carter? Drop him and hope they'd never meet again? For the first time in his life someone else's pain was hurting him.

Jenni slept sweetly, without drugs, for the first time in months.

Carter hadn't shaved or washed or slept. It was three weeks since the destruction of his life began. At first he went in to the office, a combination of defiance and innocence giving him strength. But this was a new Tuesday, the day after judgement. Strange it should be a Tuesday, an insignificant little day, tucked away under the lowering ledge of Monday.

Suddenly his calls were not returned, the investigation was not to be fast-tracked, the phone had stopped ringing. And Eleri was gone.

He sat in the kitchen watching the rain, surrounded by if onlys. It wasn't the depressing drizzle his mood required but a vigorous sunlit downpour.

If only Eleri had called him after she'd spoken to Jenni. If only he'd stopped himself keeping those pictures. What did he want them for? He'd long since stopped looking at them, long since stopped needing to reassure himself he didn't find them attractive. If only he'd thrown them out. But now the waters were muddy. The mind of the public would make no nice distinctions. If only he'd denied all knowledge. If only.

Yesterday he'd been told the hard disc of his computer had revealed its secrets and there was irrefutable evidence of visits to child sex sites. Knowing his innocence Carter demanded to know when. Grudgingly the date was given. A Saturday. His work diary gave no clues as to where he was that day. He had to wait until he got home after a day of uncertainty and doubt about his movements that day. The satellite football game. Jenni and Tom.

In his struggle to maintain a veneer of careless normality he hadn't had the energy for home life and had begun to shut Eleri and the boys out, sinking into introspection every evening. But his wife, with a strength born of desperation, pulled him back to life.

On Sunday, only two days before but seeming like a distant mirage, Eleri had insisted he and Peter spend some time together. The papers had begun to carry small, carefully worded pieces about the investigation and Peter was becoming very agitated on his father's behalf. They decided to go fishing, leaving before dawn. Both felt excited, Carter the child and Peter the father in the darkness.

'Dad . . . stop it, behave yourself.'

Carter was drawing a stick man with his finger on the opaque windscreen of a neighbour's car.

'And do up your coat, it's cold.'

Carter laughed out loud and put his arm around the slight shoulders of his son. He squatted down suddenly under a cherry-pink street light, taking the boy's hands in his.

'Peter. I'm sorry if I've been a bit . . . funny with you this last couple of weeks. I don't mean to be grumpy or anything. It's just I've got a lot on at the moment, at work.'

The boy pursed his lips, frowned and looked down, his black curly hair veiling his expression. This was his serious face: Carter knew better than to smile at its desperate earnestness.

'Is it because of the investigation?'

Carter was so surprised he just nodded.

'Have you done something wrong, Dad?'

'No, Peter. How do you know about the investigation?'

'Freddie said his dad said it was in the paper that they'd found some stuff at our house. But I don't understand why that's bad. Is it bad?'

He wanted to reassure, he wanted to be a proper father and deliver his son from evil. But the Almighty could no more intervene for Christ than Carter could now for his child.

'Yes, it's bad, Peter. But I promise, whatever you hear, I haven't done anything wrong.'

'Cross your heart and hope to die?'

'Cross my heart and hope to die.'

Peter arranged his features into an approximation of adult reassurance.

'That's all right then,' he said, nodding solemnly.

Carter wanted to put his arms round him and hug him until the boy's childish warmth thawed his frozen soul, but this was men's stuff and men didn't get soppy.

They walked towards the river.

'Peter?'

'Yes, Dad?'

'I love you best in all the world.'

'Except for . . . ?'

'No. No except for.'

That Sunday was perfect. After, it seemed to Carter, it had been perfect for a reason.

On Monday morning the phone rang as Carter was leaving the house. Alexander was being particularly difficult and it was taking all Eleri's skill to keep him under control. Peter had gone to school so Carter signalled his driver to wait and answered.

'Mr Carter?' The voice was Scottish, very polite.

'Yes?'

'Good morning. My name's Jimmy Mackay from the *News*.'

Carter knew this was going to happen but it didn't make him feel any less sick. He made himself sound cheerful, interested. Innocent.

'Good morning, Mr Mackay, how can I help you?'

Mackay's voice was full of apology, his tone implying this was all a horrible mix-up and he'd rather be doing the fish prices than making this phone call.

'Mr Carter, you're obviously aware, and, please forgive me, but the rumours are growing.' He said it again with weary emphasis on the 'are'. 'The rumours are growing. Do you not think it's about time, now, for you to actually set the record straight, one way or the other –'

Carter wanted to slam the phone down. He controlled himself, even put a little regretful laugh into his voice.

'Mr Mackay, I understand your question but I'm about to get into my car. Why don't you ring my press office and if you give them your questions, I'm sure you'll get an answer.'

Mr Mackay sounded a little more hard-edged.

'But would those answers be satisfactory to the questions that are being asked?'

Carter was angry now. As angry as any of this had made him. He took a deep breath, afraid of what he might say. When he spoke he was the Chief Constable.

'Mr Mackay, I've given you enough time, I'm late for a meeting at Headquarters –'

Mackay was immediately solicitous.

'Oh, I beg your pardon, I quite understand, of course. My apologies.'

Carter was pleased; the man had backed off at his official tone. Carter relaxed.

The voice went on. 'One last question. Are you a paedophile or not?'

If the reporter said any more Carter didn't hear it as he dropped the phone. Dropped it, almost threw it away. As if the voice coming out of it was some infection. Then he realised he was the infection in other people's minds.

He replaced the phone on its cradle. He could hear a faint Lilliputian 'Hello? Mr Carter? Are you there?' as he did so.

The perfection of the day before was already as distant as the Boer War.

He knew the whispering about him was building steadily and he was finding very quickly who his real friends were. They were pathetically few.

Arriving at police headquarters he was glad to see Danny. After his initial flicker of doubt the deputy had put on a fine show of solidarity. Carter was grateful but aware that it was good politics. If, when, he was cleared, Danny's position would be questionable if he was seen to be judging his boss now. No, Carter knew it was as much pragmatism as belief. Probably more.

The day dragged on with meetings and the minutiae of running an empire. The supportive phone calls had dribbled away to nothing after the first week. It was just suspended animation now. He had suspected he'd been abandoned by the puppet masters but when the call was put through by his carefully neutral secretary it was still a shock.

'I'm afraid the Home Secretary hasn't made a decision about the fast-tracking of the investigation as yet – I'm sure you'll understand the pressure . . . perhaps next week.'

The smooth uncaring voice spoke on unheard. Delivering just one of many life-altering messages. Unaware of its impact. Maybe it didn't belong to a person at all. Perhaps it was just a voice.

Carter closed down another cell in the honeycomb of his self, retreated a little further into himself. Then hope flared briefly when he was told the hard disc had given up its secrets. He immediately phoned Eleri and told her the date and the times. Once he'd checked his diary everything would be fine. He was in a discipline all afternoon so would sort it out when he got home.

His looks and elegance had seemed very slightly dulled by the stress of the last weeks but that afternoon everybody commented on the reappearance of his old sheen of confidence. Carter was certain proving he had never visited a paedophile site would drive a coach and horses through the whole ridiculous nightmare.

Eleri, unable to wait, opened his diary and fumbled to find the day. All it said was: 'E. & P. film'. Yes. Yes. She remembered perfectly. It seemed her baby did too as it delivered a healthy kick to her kidneys. She laughed out loud – even Bump was fighting for its father.

Think. Remember.

She sat down, pencil and paper in hand. Forced her way back to that day. Geoffrey had spent it alone with Alex. Could Alexander have done it by accident? No. She tried the idea on several times but it wouldn't fit. What else? The window cleaner, but he didn't do inside.

Then she remembered: 'Oh, Tom and Jenni dropped in for a cup of coffee. They didn't stay long.'

It seemed a bright light was turned on. Jenni would remember what happened while she was there – she had total recall. Eleri grabbed the phone. In her desperation she pushed the wrong numbers three times. Finally it rang. Jenni answered.

'Jenni, it's Eleri.'

'Oh Eleri! How are you? And Geoffrey . . . I'm so sorry we haven't been in touch but we've just been so busy. Is everything all right? The whole thing's ridiculous of course but such a pain. Do you need anything?'

'Yes.' She realised how abrupt she sounded. She didn't care. 'Do you remember the afternoon you dropped in for coffee? Geoffrey was here with Alex.'

Jenni went on red alert.

'Of course. We had a super time.'

'What time did you arrive?'

'Gosh, er, well, I suppose it was somewhere around two, two-thirty. Yes, there was some football match on that afternoon. Tom and Geoff watched it.'

'Were you still there at half-past three?'

'I'm not sure. Possibly. Why?'

Eleri paused for a second. She knew she should be careful, wary, but desperately needed to talk. And Jenni had been a good friend. She knew she should be filled with suspicion, always alert to the possibility of betrayal, but she was desperate and very much alone.

Jenni opened her arms to Eleri and she fell straight in, like a friendly bee into a deadly flower.

'The hard disc of the computer shows there were visits to paedophile sites while you were in the house.'

Jenni was shocked. She measured out her surprise and outrage as if following a recipe.

'Did anyone come to the house while you were there?'

Pause for considered thought.

'No . . . no, I don't think so. But I wasn't downstairs for long – I took Alex up to his room, to play with the batteries.'

263

There was usually an indulgent laugh when Alexander's odd collection was mentioned. Today, nothing.

'I'm sure no one else visited, though. Tom would have mentioned it.'

'So Geoffrey and Tom were together, watching the television all the time you were with Alex?'

'Yes. Absolutely. Oh, hang on. Geoff went to the loo. Tom only mentioned it because in the football half-time they turned over to watch the rugby and Geoffrey missed a superb try and a missed conversion. Apparently the chap that scored the try was knocked out cold, they had to stretcher him off. It wasn't a foul or anything, just an unfortunate accident. No wonder they wear those awful hats and tape their ears down.'

'So there was injury time?'

'Gosh, I don't know, we didn't stay till the end.'

'No. When the injury happened.'

'Oh . . . well . . . I suppose so. I hadn't really thought about it. Why?'

'No reason, Jenni, just trying to gauge time. There's obviously some mistake.'

'Probably, I mean I've had cashpoint withdrawals notified when I haven't even been in the country. You really can't trust computers, you know. But . . . Tom did say something about Geoffrey being gone for ages.'

Eleri sat unmoving for quite some time after their conversation. Alexander watched her and seemed to catch her mood of stillness. He squatted against the wall gently banging his head on the heel of his hand.

There had been four people in the house. No matter how Eleri tried to make sense of what she now knew, her mind kept hitting an obstacle as unyielding as a wall. She could not be certain of her husband's innocence without accusing Tom or Jenni. Or Alexander, poor broken, useless Alexander. But Geoffrey was innocent, he had to be. While her loyalty doggedly believed in him her doubt kept showing her images of him in homosexual embrace with younger and younger lovers. He'd left the room for longer than it took to empty even a full bladder.

But why would he do it while there were people in the house? It didn't make sense. None of it made sense. So if all avenues were explored and discovered to be cul-de-sacs the impossible must be the answer. It was Tom or Jenni. Why not? Why? It didn't make sense. She didn't want any of the answers to make sense.

The back door opened. Peter was home. Eleri pulled herself up both physically and mentally and prepared to hear about the day. He was very quiet, she thought, probably already attacking the contents of the fridge. She was right that he was in the kitchen but he wasn't eating. He couldn't eat. His lower lip was a bloody mess, his front teeth loose or missing. His school uniform, so smart that morning, was ripped and paint-covered. He clutched his blazer to his chest. His thin immature body was vibrating with fear and anger. She saw the earring he'd been so proud to wear as a symbol of his Romany inheritance had been ripped out leaving a ragged hole.

'Peter, oh Peter, what's happened?'

The boy couldn't speak and she found she couldn't either. It was the moment that both child and parent realise they are impotent in the face of violence. She gently took his jacket. It was ruined. She examined it to see if there was anything to be salvaged, then she saw why he'd been clutching it so hard. On the back was painted: *PAEDO SON*.

Eleri didn't want to cry but couldn't stop herself. She hurt so badly for Peter and the hopelessness of their situation.

The wind had blown the feathers of truths, half-truths and lies a long way from their doorstep and any sin but this sin was venal. Rape and paedophilia, once accused never acquitted.

In great sobs Peter told Eleri what had happened. The end of anything in his childhood that could be dismissed as 'just boys being boys'. Just lads beating up another lad. Nothing serious.

'They said Dad had done things. They said he did things to me. They said he did them to other boys too.'

His voice was quiet, old.

'Peter . . . your father has never touched you, has he?'

'No. I told them that. I told them.'

'Good boy. They won't do it again.'

'No, not them. The teachers. I had to tell the teachers.'

Eleri felt the horror grow like a malignant cell.

'Let's get you cleaned up, eh?'

In the comforting familiarity of flannels, plasters and TCP he told her he'd been called to the nurse's room. There he was questioned by her, the head teacher and his form teacher.

Yes, sometimes he sat naked on his father's lap. No, they weren't related by blood. Yes, there were two boys. No, his brother couldn't speak. Yes, his father used to bath him but now he was too old for that. No, his father didn't necessarily put his dressing gown on in the morning. Yes, he'd been curious about his father's thingy and yes, he'd touched it. But only sometimes. Was his father angry? No. He'd just laughed. And he'd touched Peter's too. But it was ages ago. When he used to blow raspberries on our bottoms and tickle us underneath. Me and Alex. It was just playing. It was our private game. We called it Willy Waggling Time.

Eleri listened and saw the ground open and fall away revealing a pit of writhing worms. If hell existed it could be no worse than this.

When Carter got home the house was dark. Cold. It didn't take him long to find Eleri's note. It seemed she no longer knew who to believe or what to think so she thought it best, for the good of the boys and her own sanity, to go away to her family in the sheep-clad wastes of West Wales.

He didn't collapse then. To have done so would have been to acknowledge how utterly alone he was.

Under her note was a scrap of lined paper, torn from a school book: 'Best in all the world Dad.'

He had suspended emotion so completely he couldn't react. He saw the washing up hadn't been done before his wife fled his house with his sons, carrying his baby. His baby. He almost laughed. It was written then. For what he'd taken away so it would be taken from him. Justice.

Carter loaded the dishwasher with surgical precision, every rack filled with plates in descending order of size. The utensils separated from the cutlery, glasses from cups. The mundane job helped but it was soon over. What else was there to keep him from thinking? Nothing.

He poured a large brandy into a lemonade glass. The small defiance of correctness pleased him. As it did on Mediterranean holidays when wine was served from a rubber hose connected to a bucket.

His diary was open as Eleri had left it. He remembered the day. The rugby, Tom, Jenni. Jenni.

His mind was immediately clear. The layer of woolly insulation that had protected him lifted and he saw precisely what had happened. It was so bloody obvious he couldn't believe he hadn't realised before. She'd had every opportunity to plant the magazines, the video, the floppy. And then she'd gone one step too far. Too clever by half.

He was triumphant. He poured another drink. Everything was going to be all right. The enormity of what the Shackletons had done – he had no doubt Tom must have known what his wife was up to – was impossible for him to come to terms with. He needed to talk to someone. He wanted to tell Eleri. It was late, gone midnight, they'd be in bed. Her judgemental parents had no doubt tutted them to sleep.

'Eleri?'

'No, it's her mother. Have you any idea of the time, Geoffrey? . . . No, I don't think she needs to speak to you now, not when you've been drinking. Perhaps in the morning. When you've had time to recover . . . Oh and her mobile is switched off. Goodbye, Geoffrey.'

He tried again. Ringing. Ringing. The bastards had disconnected the phone. Bloody Methodists. More brandy.

Should he phone Danny? Why not?

Answermachine.

The part of Carter that was still sober told him to go to bed; he would need to be more in control tomorrow than ever before in his life. He was going to accuse a fellow chief constable's wife of a serious crime. And then he would calmly take up the threads of his life again and effortlessly assume the Tsardom. Happily ever after.

But most of him was drunk – the confusion and tension he'd been under mixed with the brandy and relief unbalanced him. He was in the throes of madness and thought himself sober and sane. He didn't smoke but had a box of Don Ramos half-coronas in the sideboard. He pulled out the boxes of Monopoly and Cluedo, spilled cards and dice in his desperation to get to them.

Tonight he would smoke and drink and leave his self-control in shreds. Tomorrow he'd fight back and win.

*   *   *

Tuesday morning. The paperboy's battle with the letterbox woke him. His mouth was lined with kapok, his head with drills. For a moment he was lost, then the layers of realisation formed. Today was judgement day. A shower, shave and a handful of painkillers.

He stood up carefully, swallowing to control the waves of nausea. The papers were on the mat. Bending to pick them up was agony. He staggered into the kitchen and switched on the kettle. The clock on the cooker said six-thirty. He opened the *Daily Telegraph*. The phone rang.

'Geoffrey?'

Eleri's voice sounded small, more distant than miles would make it.

'Eleri, it was Jenni. I'm sure of it. She had every opportunity . . .'

He realised he was shouting but he didn't care. He had to make her understand. She had to come home. He couldn't fight this without her help.

In the middle of his loud elation he suddenly broke. For the first time he just fell apart, whimpering and begging his wife to come home as he collapsed to the floor. She listened to his ranting in silence.

'Can you prove it was Jenni?'

Her voice was cool, calm, far away.

'I'm sure I can. I don't know how, but it must be possible.'

'Can you prove it wasn't you?'

He couldn't understand why she was talking to him like a solicitor. He lost his temper, started shouting at her. When he stopped she'd hung up. He rang back. No answer. He tried again. She answered.

'I'm sorry. I'm sorry. Look, I'm going to –'

'Peter's told me what you did.'

Carter stopped.

'Told you what?'

'About your secret games. About what you did to him.'

'Eleri – what are you talking about? This isn't you. Stop this. I haven't done anything.'

He heard her start to cry.

'Please, believe me. I haven't –'

'Geoffrey? It's Bryn here.'

Eleri's father. Carter was relieved, he was less ready to jump to the worst conclusion than her mother.

'This is very serious, you know.'

His ponderous stating of the obvious almost made Carter laugh.

'Young Peter's story is very disturbing –'

'But –'

'No, Geoffrey. No buts. We've talked this over, all night we've talked, and we think it would be better if you didn't see the boys again. Peter is very upset –'

'Let me speak to him.' Carter was desperate, unwilling to believe the tightness of the noose round his neck. 'This is ridiculous.'

'And Eleri is in a very bad way. We're calling the doctor to her. We just hope this hasn't affected the baby. Oh Geoffrey . . . how could you do this wickedness?'

The voice offered pity for the fallen but no hope.

'Let me speak to Eleri.'

'No, Geoffrey. You don't understand. She doesn't want to talk to you any more. She called you to tell you she will be wanting a divorce and she will be having the boys examined –'

'You can't do this. I love her –'

'And I think she still loves you, but she'll get over it.' The old man paused. 'I am sorry for you, Geoffrey, but I can never forgive you.'

The conversation was over.

Carter screamed, 'No! No! Please God, no!'

He thrashed and kicked and smashed everything he could find, exhausting himself in a blizzard of despair. His paper lay open, serene in the chaos. Silence settled and he saw the small, discreet headline tucked away at the bottom of page three: 'Police Chief "Dropped".' He read the neat column inches as if they referred to someone else:

A Home Office source last night gave a clear indication Chief Constable Geoffrey Carter was out of the running for the job dubbed 'Crime Tsar' of Britain. Sources close to Robert MacIntyre indicated that while the probe into 'certain allegations' concerning Mr Carter's private life was still ongoing no decision could be made about his future.

An Association of Chief Police Officers source admitted there was concern over delays in the inquiry into the allegations against Mr Carter: 'It is in the Home Secretary's power to accelerate this process but he has signally failed to do so. From this we can only draw the conclusion that the government is having serious doubts about his suitability for advancement.'

And so, on a Tuesday, an innocuous day out of seven, he sat in his living room and laid out the facts as he had been taught so many years ago as a young detective constable, calm now being his only option.

The whispering campaign against Carter gathered momentum over the following weeks. The tabloid hyenas under the waiting eye of the broadsheet vultures closed in, certain of a feast.

Carter appeared little altered by events. He lost a stone in weight and was perhaps less ready to laugh than before but, said his staff, he seemed to be bearing up very well. Bearing up after the long sleepless nights when hope died at 4 a.m. and despair occupied him until he could get ready to join the world again.

His accusation of the Shackletons had met with polite assurances from the investigators that all avenues would be explored. Anyone who had visited the house would be traced and eliminated. They seemed very sure they would be eliminated. Through each night Carter wrote out lists, plans, ideas. Every tiny detail that might be relevant was scrawled in a notebook: somewhere was the key to his innocence. But the nightly search was taking him closer to the edge of insanity.

Every day he phoned Eleri and finally she agreed to speak to him. Her pregnancy continued uneventfully. Alexander was settling down but Peter was behaving in a very disturbed manner.

'Of course he is – you've dragged him away from his home and made him feel like a criminal.'

Eleri remained calm. It was one of the most infuriating things about this stranger, his wife. She seemed insulated by some psycho-babble cotton wool. Everything he said was met with the pitying implacability of a social worker.

'Geoffrey, your aggressive attitude isn't helping.'

'Let me speak to Peter.'

'I don't think that would be a good idea. We've managed to get him seen by a child psychologist and' – she had the grace to falter in her born-again assurance – 'and it seems he has some repressed memories which are only now being uncovered.'

She was talking like an automaton: there seemed no resemblance between this voice and his wife.

'Eleri, I swear, I promise you, I have never touched Peter or Alexander like that. I couldn't.'

There was a hair's breadth pause.

'Geoffrey, Peter has been examined by a paediatrician and we're taking Alex to the hospital tomorrow.'

He knew she wanted him to assume the rest, to make it easier for her. He knew what he was going to hear but wanted to feel the knife as it went in, not to find the handle between his shoulder blades later.

'Well?'

'Peter shows physical and psychological evidence of abuse.'

Carter had thought it would be a stab but it felt more like the smashing of his skull. What part of his denial would make her believe him? He had only one word.

'No. Eleri. No. Those people have made mistakes before. Cleveland – what was that bloody woman's name . . . ?' He went on, desperate, thrashing around for some sort of sense. 'What about Romania, before they came here –?'

She had found a reservoir of courage and didn't falter.

'My parents are advising me to have you prosecuted but I'm not sure I want to put Peter through that. Of course, you know Alex could never give evidence.' The way she said it implied she knew paedophiles often targeted the disabled knowing they could never legally accuse.

'I've got to talk to them, Eleri. Peter would never say I hurt him. Never.'

'No, you're right. Peter won't admit anything but he has nightmares, screams out, "No, Daddy, no, don't." ' Her anger got the better of her. 'What the hell do you think that means, Geoffrey? You liar, you bloody filthy liar, what did you do to those boys –'

'Eleri –'

She was screaming now, hysterical. He could hear her mother in the background trying to calm her.

And then Peter, he was shouting, shouting as loud as his desperation would allow him: 'Dad . . . Daddy . . . I want to come home! Dad. I haven't told them anything. Dad, please. Come and get me!'

Eleri's voice drowned everything else out. There was no vestige of wife or lover left in her. No trust or love. She was a mother who had betrayed her sons with a monster. She would never forgive him because she would never forgive herself.

'You'll never see those boys again. Never. I'm divorcing you. And, Geoffrey, I'm changing my name back to Morgan. The baby will be a Morgan and if I could stop it ever knowing who you are I would. You're nothing to us. Do you understand? Nothing.'

Carter understood. Everything was clear and that clarity gave him peace. He would continue to work. He would give every impression of being a person. No one would know that he'd been hollowed out.

Days later, alone as he always was now, he sat in front of a television which provided noise but not company, and watched a horse fall into quicksand. For minutes it struggled, desperate to find a foothold, then, exhausted, it let its strength go, and gave in to the inevitable. The camera closed in on one of its eyes. There was no peace there, no wise acceptance of God's Will. All Carter saw was confusion, incomprehension and a desperate sadness to be leaving life.

He was looking into a mirror.

Jenni was pleased to be getting more invitations to political gatherings. But frustration woke her every day Carter wasn't officially finished. She knew the new interest in Tom was because Carter was under suspicion but the longer the matter remained unresolved the more she could see the possibility of their being implicated. While Carter paced his empty house in misery she spent every sleepless night going over and over her actions. She knew Tom wasn't sleeping either but his door was closed and the one time she went into his room he wouldn't look at her. She was on the edge of total exhaustion when Eleri rang.

'Jenni?'

She sounded as if she was on the other side of the world.

'Eleri? Where are you?'

'Wales. Reception's terrible here, but I wanted to talk to you away from the house. How are you?'

They spent a few minutes in polite conversation before Eleri said, 'I'm divorcing Geoffrey.'

'Oh Eleri . . . no.' Jenni went on to automatic 'Are you sure? I mean, nothing's proved. It's probably all a horrible mistake.'

'One day I'll tell you everything, Jenni. One day. But I just wanted to thank you for what you've done for us. For the boys and me.'

'Oh, I'm so sorry. Is it really too late?'

'Jenni, believe me I don't want it to be but yes. I told him a month ago.' She paused, ambushed by an image of Carter as he'd been before all this, when she still worshipped him. 'I just wanted you to know, it's official now. I think he's going to contest it so it'll drag on. For God's sake, how could he?'

Jenni thought this was good. The government was distancing itself from Carter and now his wife was too. It could only be a matter of time before Carter resigned. Surely he'd want to follow Eleri and try to re-claim his family.

'Maybe you should give him a second chance.'

'Jenni, you just don't understand.' Then, again, 'One day I'll tell you everything. I promise.'

'Oh, Eleri, I can't tell you how sorry I am. Tom will be so sad. After all, there's no evidence, is there? Don't be too hard on him, Eleri. Maybe if you just had time and space to yourselves you could work it out . . .'

'Jenni. You don't know the facts. You don't know.' She stopped, unable to go on.

Jenni heard her but wasn't listening – she was anxious to speak to Shackleton.

'No, well, whatever happens, stay in touch, won't you?'

'Thanks, Jenni. I really appreciate that. I can't tell you what this has been like. It's like someone has picked us up and dropped us in a sewer.'

Jenni automatically made the right noises, said the right things, until she could end the call without seeming rude.

Once she'd put the phone down she called Tom. He was in a meeting. She wanted to scream at Janet. But she didn't.

'Janet, this is important.'

'I'm sorry, Mrs Shackleton, the Chief Constable said he wasn't to be disturbed under any circumstances.'

Jenni was vibrating with fury.

'I am his wife. I am not any circumstances.'

There was a pause.

'Hold the line, Mrs Shackleton.'

It was less than fifteen seconds before Shackleton came on the line.

'Hello.'

Jenni was disproportionately irritated by the low-voiced sing-song way he said the word.

'It's me. Eleri's divorcing Carter.'

She waited.

Tom, in his office with the Police Federation representatives, didn't know what to say.

'I see,' was all he could think of.

She was sharp.

'No, you don't see, Tom. He might cling on while he was just being investigated but . . . well, don't you see? He'll have to make a choice; if he wants his family he'll have to resign. She's gone. He'll have to go after them. I mean she's started proceedings but he's not going to accept it. He'll fight, and to do that properly he's got to follow her.'

Carefully, mindful of the others in the room, he said, 'Well, thank you for letting me know.'

Jenni was exasperated.

'God, you're a prat.'

'Yes. Thank you. Goodbye.'

Shackleton put the phone down and turned back to the business of unhappiness and unrest among the rank and file.

While one of the representatives talked he looked sympathetic and let himself think.

He didn't know how long Carter'd been alone but he knew Jenni was right: Carter would fall apart without his family. Shackleton was relieved. While Carter clung on they were all in limbo and the weeks were dragging on. The signs were that Whitehall was turning its face towards the Shackletons but nothing had been said. Nothing was sure.

Tom felt almost happy. Carter would resign, Tom Shackleton would be Crime Tsar, the investigation would turn up nothing and Eleri would take her husband back.

It would all work out.

Lucy was washing Gary when she heard the news. Geoffrey Carter had been found dead in his home three months after the start of a police investigation concerning paedophile pornography found at his home . . . There were no other details. Lucy was shocked. Gary cynical.

'One less neck for Shackleton to step on.'

'Oh Gary, don't . . . it's awful.'

'Yes, you're right. I'm sorry – one fewer neck.'

She continued to wash him, making sure her flannel soaked the sheet. A small revenge but her own. She'd comforted the man, they'd shared a tiny intimacy. And now he was dead . . .

'Come on, Luce, you'll give me nappy rash.'

She sighed. What could she do? Nothing. But she felt she should.

Wanting to talk about it, she went over to see Jenni as soon as she could.

Tamsin and her little boy were just leaving. There was noisy laughter, the child shrieking and waving to his nice granny. Lucy felt like a ghost walking into a happy family scene.

Lucy went into the house with her, Jenni still smiling, relaxed.

As soon as the pleasantries were out of the way and Jenni had poured out another coffee Lucy said, 'Have you heard? About Geoffrey Carter? He's dead.'

She would never forget the look on Jenni's face. Surprise and pleasure hastily covered by sadness and regret. It was such a quick transformation Lucy wasn't even certain it had happened.

But then Jenni said with an undisguised eagerness, 'Are you sure?'

Lucy nodded.

'Oh dear. How sad.'

And that was it. But Lucy could still see the triumph behind the modestly downcast eyes. Not long after, she went home and tried to explain the incident to Gary.

Shackleton was in meetings all morning so it wasn't until one-thirty his secretary had the opportunity to tell him.

'Mr Shackleton?' Her voice was even more melodious and quiet than usual. 'It's Mr Carter, sir, he's been found dead. Possible suicide. Don't forget you've got the Police Authority at two o'clock. Would you like a sandwich?'

He shook his head and closed his office door. The walk to his desk seemed unreal. He looked out of the window. Uniformed police wandered across his view coming and going to lunch. The words free will and personal responsibility, hitherto meaningless mantras trotted out by development gurus, swirled round his head.

No matter how fast he ran round the corridors of his mind the rat-tailed words 'You killed him' kept up. There was real terror in the reality of it. This wasn't part of the scenario. He wasn't responsible for Jenni. He hadn't known anything about it. But it was too late for that. He'd changed. He'd joined the human race. He was infected with weakness for the first time. The weakness of conscience. Geoffrey Carter wasn't an abstract obstacle, he was a man who was dead.

No, who he had killed.

But Jenni did it . . . no, not Jenni. Me.

Only a fraction of the reality was being allowed to filter into his mind. He knew imagining the pain Carter had experienced would destroy his control, would eat away at him until he couldn't function any more. Guilt. Responsibility for your brother. No man is an island. Carter being cleared away in a black plastic bag as they all were. Suicides. The dramatic gesture that always finished in the back of the body men's grubby van. A discarded body bagged up, like any other rubbish. Then the slab and the unknown fingers probing and turning the naked dead body. The body that had been a friend, a fellow chief constable, a known success not a month before. Being sliced up and weighed for disease and legal requirement. The organs put back in any order. Brain in the stomach and newspaper in the skull. That's what you did to him, Shackleton. Why? For what? Nothing's worth killing for, is it?

'I didn't kill him.'

He said it out loud. The phone rang and Janet said, mindful of the tragedy, that Mrs Shackleton was on the line.

'Tom? Tom?'

He didn't want to speak to her. Ever.

'Yes, Jenni?'

'Have you heard?'

'Yes.'

'Well?'

'It's tragic.'

She snorted.

'For who? Not us. Mind you, I didn't think he'd go that far – bit melodramatic after all.'

276

She paused.

'I think it just proves he was a paedophile. Why would he kill himself otherwise? I mean, he still had his job, he hadn't actually been prosecuted. They must have found something against him, don't you think?'

Shackleton put down the phone. He felt the ties that had bound him to Jenni dissolving in the acid of self-hatred. What she had done was no worse than many of the things she'd done in his name before. But no one had ever died before. His eyes were staring, unseeing, out of the window, but something wanted to be seen. His eyes found focus and saw the three black faces.

They weren't smiling now. They carried a heavily filled black plastic sack, and it lay, like a body, across their arms. A pietà triptych. The woman who frightened him, the African woman with the blind seashell eyes, lifted her hand to him. Its white palm was red and wet with blood. Slowly, deliberately, she smeared it across her face and opened her mouth in a silent ululation. The other two stretched their lips wide too. Then the sound – it seemed the only sound in the world – filled his head. The wild, high, rippling cry of grief. The three voices invoking misery for the dead and the living.

He didn't know what prayer he made but when he raised his face from his hands there was silence. The women had gone.

Danny Marshall went to the house immediately the call came in that Carter had been found by the local beat bobby. The window cleaner had raised the alert.

When he arrived the place was quietly full of scenes-of-crime officers, CID, police photographers and the soberly dressed men whose job it was to take away the body. The body, unaccompanied by anyone who had known or cared for its inhabitant, was just a sad mess to be cleared up.

He asked what had happened. The first officer he approached shrugged, embarrassed.

Down the stairs was the lumbering Inspector Davidge. Danny had served under him when he'd been starting out. Davidge was a very good copper. Three commendations for bravery, lived in Essex and collected Minton sugar bowls. His girth was remarkable and his off-white shirts always had a triangle of pale stomach peeping out from under his tie which lay, stranded, halfway down his vast belly.

He spoke with the intimate dodginess of a second-hand car salesman.

'Sorry for your loss, sir.'

He stepped respectfully across Carter's body which was still being measured and photographed as it lay at the bottom of the stairs, any dignity it had had in life dispelled by violent and surprising death.

'What happened?'

Davidge nodded at the question and led the deputy into the garden. Danny looked at the stone sculptures Carter had brought back in his hand luggage from Zimbabwe, pretending his bag weighed nothing, and remembered they'd talked about Danny's ancestors who had been taken as slaves from Ghana. They'd laughed at Danny's description of a ship-load of artists being dumped on Barbados because they were only good for housework. The tough ones went to Jamaica.

Davidge lit up a Rothmans. The deputy thought if he made retirement without a heart attack there was no justice, but although he wheezed and waddled and drank for Britain his blood pressure and cholesterol gave no cause for alarm. Bastard, thought Danny.

'What happened, Bob?'

Davidge took a long pull on his fag and looked at the apple tree from which hung a child's empty swing.

'He's gone up to his study, right? And he's writing a letter. Fond farewells, I suppose. We found the hoover hose taped to the car exhaust and he's taken enough aspirin to fell an ox. So far so good. Anyway his pen runs out. Nice Mont Blanc fountain, black ink. Not realising how far gone he is he tries to get downstairs to refill it – we found a new bottle of ink in his briefcase. But . . . he gets to the top of the stairs and loses his footing – the nib of the pen went through his eye into his brain. And he died. Quicker than carbon monoxide. Lucky, I suppose. A paedophile's life is not a happy one.'

Danny looked down the garden.

'He wasn't a paedophile.'

Davidge looked at his cigarette end.

'No, sir. Of course not.'

Danny felt like the disciple who had thrice denied his master. Only evangelism would make up for betrayal.

'He told me. Swore he was innocent.'

Davidge thought about this for a few moments.

'Well, whatever. Doesn't make him any less dead, does it?'

He shook his head and put another Rothmans between his lips. An acutely intelligent man, he had great respect for his instinct and his instinct told him Danny was telling the truth. The atmosphere between them shifted. Davidge had no taste for witch hunts and that is what Carter had been put through.

'I'll light a candle. By the way, sir, I found this upstairs. The letter he was writing. No point in it going through official channels, eh?' He handed him the sheets of paper addressed to Danny in Carter's hand. 'Well . . . I'd better get back in there.'

With the unlit fag in his mouth he shambled into the house.

Later that night he went into his local church and lit a night light under the statue of St Francis of Assisi. It was the only candle lit for Carter in the darkness surrounding his death.

Danny caught sight of Carter's body just before the door closed. If he'd only come round. Had faith. Been there. He read quickly:

Danny. Why does the truth seem more true when the speaker's dead? I don't know and it seems more and more stupid to die just to be believed. But it's too late now. Not too late to make sense, I hope. It's getting dark, round the edges, like looking down a 'what the butler saw'. What do I want to tell you? What must you believe?

I've thought about every option I have and this is the only one that makes sense. Whatever happens I'm finished, there's no future. I can't prove my innocence and whatever the law says, in this, you're guilty even if found innocent.

I believe Tom and Jenni Shackleton planted that stuff but I am too tired now to find any way to prove it.

I could cope with the doubt and whispers if it wasn't for my children. Danny, I can't have them carrying me through their lives. Is it cowardice? Maybe.

I swear I have committed no crime but I can't live like this. I won't be an unwelcome spectre in Peter's life.

Try and find out the truth, Danny, for Peter and Alex and Megan. Did you know I've got a daughter? She was premature, too small for life, but I'm told by the divorce lawyer she's a fighter. Megan Morgan.

If the truth does involve J and T would the government want to hear it? Tabloid headlines

The letter finished there. The final words thin with starving ink.

Danny wanted to go home, to get away from the sordid sadness. He went back into the house. The body was gone and Davidge was ready to leave. Upstairs were two men who didn't offer their identity or condolences.

When Danny looked he saw all Carter's personal papers had gone. The men each carried large briefcases. One of them was just packing away Carter's desk diary.

Danny waited outside the house until they were gone then let himself back in with the spare keys still kept by the neighbour, Mrs Ismay. She had been keen to talk but Danny made it plain he was on police business and not at liberty to comment, or hear comment, on the events surrounding the tragedy.

What did he expect to find? The unquiet shade wandering from room to room, unable to rest till he, Danny, had hewn the truth from the unyielding granite of lies?

Danny despised himself for being so noble now Carter was dead.

He sat on the stairs. There was a small spray of blood on the wallpaper. Pretty, like a small brown fern. He had placed just enough distance between himself and his contaminated chief to ensure his own future well-being. But at what cost of guilt?

When he left the house he was determined to clear Carter's name, and in the process his own conscience.

PART FIVE

The ACPO autumn conference was held at Warwick University in an area cordoned off from the rest of the campus. The three days of police business finished with a formal dinner to which wives were invited.

The guest of honour was the nearly new Home Secretary, the Gnome, in glory now.

Jenni hadn't seen him since just after Carter's funeral, a bleak affair attended by no one of note and only two elderly aunts of Carter's representing the family. Danny Marshall had organised it, inviting everyone who should have been there had Carter died a hero. Most declined, some didn't reply. Eleri's solicitor sent a fax.

The Shackletons had been modest, seating themselves halfway back in the small crematorium chapel. Danny saw them and did nothing to encourage them forward. Jenni was incensed and made sure she spoke to him afterwards, outside in the windy courtyard.

'It was tragic. We were very fond of Geoffrey. My husband worked with him closely – I don't suppose you realised that?'

The deputy was smooth, polite, impenetrable.

'Oh yes, I knew. He was particularly touched by the visit you paid him just before he died.'

Jenni was shocked, the accusation felt so naked. For a moment she was lost for words.

'The press were very cruel. After all it's a disease, isn't it? They can't help themselves.'

'The only disease Geoffrey Carter suffered from was the envy of other people. That's what killed him.'

Jenni wanted to slap that look off his face.

'Yes, yes, of course.'

She wished Tom would come and rescue her.

'I wonder why he had that awful stuff in his house then?'

Her transparent peridot eyes met the undisguised hatred of the deputy.

'He had that stuff in his house because someone put it there. Someone who wanted to destroy him. To stop him going any further.'

'Oh God . . . Who?'

She knew she should stop this and walk away but she couldn't.

'Watch the Internet, Jenni. Conspiracy websites are very popular. And anyone can put any crackpot theory on them.'

'Conspiracy, Danny?' She laughed. 'What conspiracy? He died in a horrible accident. Isn't that the official line? You're being ridiculously overdramatic.'

Shackleton joined them.

'Tom, Danny's just saying he thinks Carter was, oh what's the term, framed, is it? Yes, that's right, framed.'

'I didn't say that, Mrs Shackleton. But Geoffrey mentioned you at length in a letter to me. Sorry, that was a non sequitur. Forgive me, I'm very upset.'

'Of course.'

Shackleton was now standing beside her but he said nothing.

'Excuse me,' said Danny. 'I must go and look after his aunts.' He dropped his head in a sort of bow. 'Mr Shackleton.'

As soon as he was out of earshot Jenni rounded on her husband but something had happened. He was different. She was like rain on a windowpane to him now. Since Carter's death he'd hardly been home and when there he'd hardly spoken. The children, now encouraged to fill the house with company and noise to insulate Jenni from rollercoaster feelings of paranoia, were worried about him. But whenever they tried to talk about anything more than family trivia he withdrew behind that shy smile they knew was as impenetrable as a thorn forest.

The day after the funeral Tom had been summoned to London, to an audience with the Gnome, a government adviser, and the PM's representative on earth, the real thing being somewhere in Italy having a people's holiday in a people's palace, closed to the public.

Jenni had been excited, more excited than she'd been at the deluge of filth proven and unproven printed about Carter since his death.

His personal life, sexuality, history and family were discussed and dissected in everything from the *News of the World* to the *Financial Times*. Pictures of his wife and sons, snatched images of Eleri carrying the premature baby home from the hospital. The contradictions in evidence against him turned over and over like well-mulched manure. Jenni had hoarded every article, every picture.

If Tom had had fear left in him he would have feared for her sanity. But there was a part of him that was dead now too. The man lying at the foot of his stairs with a pen sticking out of his eye socket had been the spectre that woke Shackleton's humanity. But the pain of that, the vicious agony of guilt and conscience, was incomprehensible in a life hitherto so protected, lived with such a lack of self-searching rigour. Shackleton felt a new emptiness, not the clean minimalist lines of his life before Carter's death. He felt guilt and could taste ashes, as if the ghost of Carter's despair had found a home in him.

He allowed himself no thoughts other than those concerned with work. His mind was a blank in which pain and pleasure were equally meaningless. Jenni could no longer reach him and the small happiness he'd felt with Lucy seemed never to have happened. It was a story told about another Tom Shackleton, a man he now despised.

He'd seen her with Gary in the street, pushing him to the park in a parody of a proud young mum with her first baby.

Shackleton found himself envying the clean inevitability of Gary's disease. The one eating him seemed even more insidious than MS, and more profoundly incurable. There was nothing to alleviate his symptoms.

And Jenni? She had thought once Carter was out of the way they would be strong, invulnerable, bound together. But now he couldn't look at her, couldn't touch her, hear her. She screamed, cried, attacked him, but he wasn't there. And he saw she was more frightened than she'd ever been. At night he heard her crying, talking, shouting out, but he never went to her. She was on her own. And so was he. Now he was part of the hell he'd seen in his dreams.

The wages of sin is Death.

That's what he was learning. He was being paid in absolute nothingness. For him there was no life after death. And still he didn't have the courage to say, It was me. It was my wife and me. Never having found catharsis through confession he couldn't see the blessed relief of honest culpability. So he felt the weight of the sin grow, like a rotting living thing on his neck.

At the meeting they had talked with restrained regret of the waste, the sadness, the loss, then they moved effortlessly on to asking whether Shackleton would mind giving up thoughts of the Met to become the first Crime Tsar. Over the weeks of the investigation he had been sounded out, advised not to make any announcements about his future even though it had seemed sealed. But this was the official proposal, the ring was in the bridegroom's pocket.

Tom was suitably modest, properly reluctant and finally persuaded. The greatest moment of his life was within his grasp and it meant nothing. He tasted ashes. The ashes of Geoffrey Carter. He said nothing to Jenni. She would find out when it was announced.

But the Gnome had already told her. He seemed keen for her to express her thanks when the dust had settled. Again under the pretext of her writing a piece on him she'd made her way to his flat, but this time he made her tea and sat across the table from her, talking.

He had looked at her with some distaste. She had lost weight and was suddenly old and stringy. The bones, so delicate and fine when covered with firm flesh, were sharp and hard under the thin stretched yellow skin. The great eyes now burned too deep, too desperate. And her beautiful hair. Still her crowning glory but incongruously young now around her ageing face.

Then there was the sniff, the constant sniffing.

She sat talking small talk, waiting for the move he'd make, planning the revenge she'd take on him when her husband was Crime Tsar. When all the computers, all the lists, all the information in the country would be at his service. Then she'd see. There would be some financial irregularity, some youthful indiscretion – there had been rumours of a hushed-up rape in his past. She'd find it all and then, in time, no hurry, the Gnome would fall on his rod.

His bleeper chirruped, he read its message, then with a perfect show of regret he said, 'Jenni, my darling – it's been glorious to see you but I have an emergency meeting. I have no choice, I have to go. Will you forgive me? Another time perhaps?'

Jenni was ushered out by him without once realising she was

dismissed and that the interruption had been caused by MacIntyre discreetly pressing the button on the side of the pager.

All she took away with her were the words: 'Ah, Jenni, how is my little Tsarina? Think you'll be up to the role? Tom Shackleton's such a lucky man. Dead men's shoes, eh?'

That's how she found out. Before Tom knew, as was only right.

Briefly she was elated, beyond the reach of Carter's dead hands in her nightmares. Every night he came to her, sometimes as a dead and rotting lover, at other times naked and accusing in a restaurant or supermarket. Jenni tried to talk to Tom about it but he was haunted by his own devils.

At night she walked around the house, endlessly padding up and down the stairs, round and round the hall.

Sometimes Jacinta came to the house and held her, forcing her to be still.

Then Jenni sobbed, but never told her daughter why.

In the weeks before the ACPO conference, Shackleton was inducted into the mysteries of Whitehall. In his absence Jenni felt herself slipping away from reality into a grave of depression at the bottom of which was the body of Geoffrey Carter.

She went to her beloved hairdresser, thinking the mercenary caress of his hands and those of the masseuse and manicurist would bring some warmth into her. She sat in front of the mirror. An old woman looked back at her, the glory of her hair undimmed.

Clyde, luckily, had seen her come in and registered no surprise at her appearance when he kissed and greeted her. He pampered her and offered her tea or coffee.

'Oh Clyde, I need something more. Much, much more.'

He looked conspiratorial.

'I'm sure we can find you something.'

Jenni was pathetically grateful.

'Oh Clyde could you? Just for today, you understand . . . I'm just feeling a bit low.'

'I'll see what we can do. Have you an appointment downstairs after?'

She nodded.

'Good,' he said and made as if to widen his eyes but the Botox toxin he'd had injected into his forehead to remove the lines had paralysed his face into a glassy, expressionless cartoon.

When Jenni walked into the subterranean treatment room there was a girl in a gleaming white beautician's uniform and Nayman, the eccentric Malay stylist who worked at the next stall to Clyde.

He was exceptionally tall with his hair worn in a queue. He was twenty-eight and lived his life in a confusion of spiritual prêt-à-porter, anything that fitted his mood and provided no challenge to his hedonism or varying sexuality. He was, as always, overwhelming in his certainties.

'Jenni, my darling. You are Leo, yes? Of course. You need royal treatment. You're a queen. My dear, you look ghastly, tired, I give you something. You feel frightened of the world, don't tell me, I know. I am Leo too. Difficult to be in a world of ugliness for us. This makes the world look better and the people in it a lot more pretty. We hate ugliness, don't we, Jenni darling?'

The girl had gone quietly, and while he spoke Nayman had created a strange new sight for her. He took some foil and moved his fingers over it, dropping something on to it. Jenni couldn't really see.

'Oh darling, let's put some music on. We can't chase even the tiniest dragon listening to pneumatic drills digging up the Northern Line.'

His voice was high and queeny. The type that made S sound like a slow puncture. Jenni pressed the button on the CD. Music filled the room that only those who went to the right clubs would have a name for.

'You want an E, darling? It's just the best as a little taster.'

Jenni shook her head.

'No, Nayman, really. I don't want anything too strong. I just need' – she corrected herself – 'want something to help me relax now and again.'

'Oh . . . darling,' he shrieked. 'You're so coy! I love it. Tell you what, take a couple for later. It's so nice to have when you're coming down. God, you're so beautiful. You could be a drag queen, you're that perfect.'

Then he passed her a kind of straw. She didn't know what to do with it.

'You're such a diva, darling,' he said and demonstrated the best and most fashionable way of smoking heroin.

Jenni copied him carefully, anxious to get it right for her teacher. He was so pleased with her. Again she breathed in the smoke. Perfection. Life became perfection and Jenni a living embodiment of that flawless state. She had never felt a happiness so complete. This, she knew, she must do again. Soon. And although it was naughty, it wasn't bad. After all she could control what she took; she wasn't lying in a gutter like a drug addict. She didn't need anything more than her prescription tranquillisers, no, anything else was just, well, just for relaxation.

From a distance Jenni heard Nayman talking about the inadvisability of injecting heroin. From the insulated distance of Jenni's mind the idea of injecting was silly. Ludicrous. Why would anyone but the dregs of society do that? She had her white powder and now this glorious smoke, an enveloping mist of reassurance and happiness. Recreational drugs, no worse than tobacco or alcohol. It was glorious to feel so in control. Who could want for anything more?

Lucy had kept her word to Gary and their life had become a strange Indian summer of love. The MS, though not fully in remission, had loosened its grip enough for him to spend some time in his wheelchair.

Tom and Jenni had become distant and unreal, ghosts who came and went silently from their now discreetly guarded house. Pulled further away by unstoppable success. Lucy still cleaned but there was little to do. They were never there and when they were Jenni tended to call on the children to provide white noise against the silence that had settled on their lives. As the weeks passed and the furore over Carter's death gave way to other news and scandals Lucy found herself in a pleasant purgatory at one remove from the hell of obsessive love.

She still thought about Shackleton, spoke his name, doodled his initials twined with her own, but it was becoming habit now. She felt like someone recovering from a serious disease, weak, yes, but with a new inner strength and determination to enjoy life.

Gary had sensed the difference in her and one evening suggested splashing out on a bottle of wine and a Chinese takeaway. Lucy found herself getting quite excited at the idea. She locked herself away in the bathroom, making sure the mirror was steamed up before she undressed. As she sat on the edge of the bath passing the razor carefully from ankle to knee she felt a vague anticipation of sex. Could she enjoy Gary touching her again? Distracted by the thought, she cut herself. Maybe they should get two bottles of wine then she wouldn't care who it was.

No. That was cruel. She knew, given her present state of physical frustration, it would take very little to satisfy her, but how could she stop herself seeing and feeling Tom? She couldn't and she knew she wouldn't try. She shrugged. It really didn't matter, did it? If it made Gary happy and it made her happy what was the point in honesty. The truth was not something to be used carelessly. She stuck a piece of tissue paper on her bloody shin.

Gary didn't take his painkillers that day. He wasn't really supposed to take more than four Coproximal in twenty-four hours but he'd recently been swallowing twelve, though he never drank with them. So today was worth the pain, the payment for an evening as a normal man. Just Gary. Not Gary with MS and a secondary spinal tumour. For one night he'd put the disease down with the pills.

At first they were shy with each other. He complimented her on her perfume. She said how much he made her laugh. He didn't see her catch herself as she heard herself saying what she'd said to Tom. But had she originally said it to Gary and it was second-hand for Tom? Who knew? And after another glass of Pinot Grigio, who cared?

Lucy sat close to him while they chose from the menu. She stayed next to him while she phoned through their order. He rubbed her back while she spoke. By the time the spotty seventeen-year-old on a scooter found their address with their order he had kissed her breasts for the first time in two years. They seemed bigger, softer, older and somehow a little sad. He wanted to gather them up and bury his face between them but his arms weren't working too well, so she held them for him and he felt himself melt into the smooth warm skin.

The doorbell rang. The spotty adolescent was at the door.

They laughed and tacitly fell into the pattern of endless love established all those years before in a seaside hotel. They ate and drank and kissed and caressed and talked until, in the early hours of the morning, Gary brought Lucy to a climax. More skilfully than Tom he kept her on the very edge, unable to breathe lest she tip over into the glorious chaos of orgasm. Finally it was too much and she gave herself up to the gulping, heaving, sighing pleasure. Then she lay still in Gary's aching arms.

His feeling of triumph was more satisfying than any orgasm he'd ever had. To play his wife's body like an instrument made him feel like a man again. And she'd whispered his name, over and over. Was it to block out Shackleton? He physically moved to get away from the thought. As he did his penis touched Lucy's hand. She was almost asleep but felt the pressure. She opened her eyes in the darkness. It was hard. Well, no, not hard but not the soft plum she had become used to. She moved her hand almost imperceptibly. He didn't move away. She turned it so palm and fingers could encourage the timid life nudging against her.

Lucy didn't have a huge repertoire of stimulation but she found herself determined to, at the very least, help him maintain his erection. She was astonished at her own inventiveness. Had Gary not been concentrating just as hard on the matter, literally in hand, he would have wondered if she'd used these techniques on Shackleton.

And then it came, out of nowhere, as if someone had switched on the electricity, a surge of excitement, a magnificent tightening and then . . . and then . . . Gary was taking air into his lungs but couldn't release it. The veins on his neck and chest stood out, his face was a mask of determination. Lucy, without relinquishing her iron grip on him, straddled him and placed the tip of him inside her where her lips kissed him with tiny contractions. He shuddered, every muscle tense, rigid, still. She did it again, taking him deeper this time. He groaned but still didn't breathe out. He was focused as if on the tip of a pin. Then she impaled herself fully, savouring the half-forgotten length of him. He reached up for her breasts, she bent towards him. And then the explosion. The massive ejaculation of unhappiness, illness and impotence. A fountain of glory pumped out of him. He was still a man.

He could hear his voice as if from a distance: 'Oh God, oh bloody hell, oh God. Oh Lucy. Oh yes.'

Almost the same litany as for a winning goal.

Lucy bent down and kissed his face. Her hair felt cool. It was comforting, maternal. Gary smiled, Lucy the whore in bedsocks.

He felt himself drifting off, warm and shrinking safely beside her. He was murmuring as sleep overtook him.

Lucy put her ear to his lips: 'Fuck you, Tom Shackleton.'

She rolled off him.

'I wish,' she said quietly as she sat on the side of his cripple bed.

Jenni and Tom dressed in silence for the ACPO dinner. Warwick University campus was hardly the home of haute couture but Jenni wasn't going to let her standards slip. Especially not this year.

Tom hadn't looked properly at his wife for weeks but tonight he did. She was standing in a peach satin thong preparing to put on her perfectly selected evening dress. She had always been slim, like a greyhound or a thoroughbred horse, but now . . . every bone jutted out, her ribs arced round and were topped by a ridge of sharp vertebrae. Her once fine bust hung down as she bent over, flapping, empty. And the skin hung off her buttocks leaving her profile flat and sexless. Tom looked away.

'Ready?'

She obviously wasn't.

'I'll see you in the bar.'

A few months before he wouldn't have dared go without her for fear of the vitriol that would follow. Now he didn't care and she knew it. A few times she'd tried tantrums that, to an outsider, would have warranted police intervention but not now. She knew she no longer had any power to cow and control him.

He went downstairs, indifferent to Jenni's parting shot. In the bar were two country chiefs, good-natured men with comfortable, good-natured wives. People he was finding it easy to envy now. Unburdened with ambition, intelligence or good looks they'd got their jobs by default, simply by being the least worst solution. And they were happy, they'd never expected to get so far.

The older of the two called over, 'Drink, Tom?'

The other chipped in, 'Don't do that, Terry – people will think you're crawling. Is it true, Tom? You're the new Tsar?'

Shackleton smiled his slowest, most seductive smile.

'What can I tell you, George? Thanks, Terry, I'll have a malt. Islay if they've got it. Thanks.'

The wives were keen he should join them but he stayed at the bar. The two old chiefs stood with him.

'Well,' said Terry raising his pint, 'if it is true, congratulations. You'll do well. Best man for the job.'

Shackleton was unexpectedly touched by the sincerity in the older man's voice. Tom searched for an appropriate response and found the cupboard bare. He nodded and sipped his drink. They discussed the recent police review in a desultory manner until George told a fairly off-colour story about HM Inspector of Constabulary and a mushroom omelette by which time the bar had filled up and Tom was the object of focus. Nobody in the room doubted he was getting 'the job' and those with more than a year to serve were keen to make a good impression.

Tom's eyes missed nothing, the insincerities, the fear, the resentment, and despite the dullness that had taken over his mind he felt a tingle of pleasure. This was the first stirring of real power.

And now the wives were flirting, putting in a word for their chiefs. Inviting him to their regions with promises of well, almost everything.

And then there were the ones who he'd never win over. Who were powerful enough in their own bailiwicks to think he wouldn't be able to touch them. He lowered his eyes in case they saw how wrong they were.

There was a time when he'd been careful of his many enemies, wooing them and, if that didn't work, making himself as inoffensive as possible. But now, not only did he not need any of them any more, he had dealt with the ultimate threat. It had been removed. And he had suffered the pain of the damned for that. The removal of subsequent hurdles would cause him no distress. He was as low as it was possible for a human being to be and that knowledge gave a certain security. But he wouldn't forget George and Terry's small kindness. They didn't know how little he deserved it or how little unconsidered kindness he'd ever been given.

While he was considering the future with a glimmer of pleasure Jenni made her entrance. She was breathtaking. The dress disguised her excessive thinness, her make-up was flawless and she sparkled with something more than happiness to be in the company of bores.

Immediately she was surrounded by courtiers and she was magnificent. A vodka tonic was put into her hand by Suffolk (or was it Norfolk?); she rewarded him with a lightly blown kiss. Manchester wanted to monopolise her but had to give ground to Northumbria who wanted her to open a young offenders' centre in Byker. She bestowed looks and words like gold and honey, raising the temperature of the room several degrees.

In retaliation the wives surrounded the handsome Tom Shackle-ton, eager to make this shy man smile, triumphant when he said, 'That sounds nice,' to a mooted visit or trip.

Tom and Jenni were indisputably reigning monarchs patiently watching their subjects jockeying for position in the new order.

Just outside the bar was an ante-room with a couple of tables at which the dissenters sat talking quietly. They had gathered round Barnard, the tall grey man whose mission in life it was to see Shackleton crash and burn.

The City of London Commissioner and the Police Service of Northern Ireland Chief Constable were diplomatically silent, listening with no sign of approval or disapproval while Barnard spoke.

'I think we all agree it's a good idea to have a national liaison officer, if you like. I mean NCIS has been good and no one wants the kind of balls-up we had over the Yorkshire Ripper with no bugger knowing what any other bugger was doing –'

He was interrupted by Sussex.

'Yes, liaison and national databases are fine, but we're looking at an FBI situation here and if we get a J. Edgar Hoover running it it'll be worse than the Stasi.'

The City of London was gently patronising.

'I think you'll find, Eddie, the liberal lefties won't let anyone get away with that any more.'

Eddie was sharp.

'If you can find me a bleeding-heart liberal in any position of influence I'll stop worrying.'

Barnard jumped in.

'Carter would have been damned good in the job.'

They all murmured their agreement. After all, nothing had been proven and he was dead. Rumours of dirty tricks had found popular favour in all ranks.

'You could be damned sure all he was interested in was a better police service. But this shyster . . .'

Barnard seemed at a loss for words to express his contempt.

'He'll be burrowing away into all of us. And he's got a lot of scores to settle.'

'What was that you were saying about the website?' Sussex asked.

'Oh yes.' Barnard was in his element now. He paused to light a cheap cigar. 'My daughter was doing her homework the other night – got a place at Oxford if she can get three As –'

'And will she?' asked the Irishman who, everyone knew, was a Jesus man, as Carter had been.

'Quietly optimistic, Kieron. Anyway, she was surfing the net and found a website called Rumour Room. Come across it?'

The other men shook their heads.

'Well, there's a section on Geoffrey Carter, it seems. All about his life and death, then it says: "Did he fall or was he pushed? *Cherchez La Femme*. Not all little birds that lay eggs are cuckoos." Would be great but . . .'

He stopped.

The faces around him showed no comprehension.

Sussex spoke.

'But what?'

Barnard was irritated.

'That's it. That's all there is. It's from *Macbeth*, Janey said.'

The Irish man was cautious:

'It's Lady Macbeth. She's saying how her husband would like to be the top man but lacks the will to get there. For "will" read "ruthless determination".'

'Good evening. Nice and quiet out here.'

Tom Shackleton stood in the doorway. They looked at him as if he was an apparition, then he said, 'Don't let me disturb you.'

The men created conversation. City of London asked Northern Ireland how things were over the water. There was some cautious teasing of the ostentatiously Catholic chief constable. They continued their conversation until Shackleton was, after another stiff round of pleasantries, safely back in the bar.

Sussex, a heavy, red-faced man, whose one distinguishing feature was that his blood was AB rhesus negative, was eager to get back to the subject.

'So what have cuckoos got to do with it?'

Barnard shrugged.

'Not sure. I'm not sure about any of it. But it's interesting that there is speculation.'

The Northern Ireland man, who enjoyed a good pub quiz and had, in his younger day, had quite a crush on Irene Thomas, spoke.

'It means a bird that isn't a cuckoo planted that stuff in Carter's house and waited for it to hatch out destroying – need I go on?'

Sussex was stumped.

'So what's the bird?'

The Northern Ireland man's voice was so quiet his words were almost, but not quite, missed.

'My guess is a wren.'

The Gnome had been held up and arrived only just in time for the hors d'oeuvres. He was seated at the top table between Jenni and what looked like a badly stuffed sofa. The sofa had a tiny, high-pitched voice and he had to lean close to her massively creased bosom to hear her. He couldn't stop himself imagining the vast padding of slack flesh beneath the yards of flowered silk. It was a mesmerically horrible vision. He would have preferred to be placed between two of the few female chiefs and not just for sexual reasons.

Of all his duties as Home Secretary it was reform of the police that interested him most and his private passion to re-integrate the police with the communities they served included a theory that female-led constabularies were more likely to be sympathetic to the social pressures that caused young men, in particular, to fall out of the social equation. And, of course, there was the question of ethnic minorities, or the lack of them in senior ranks. He looked down the tables for Danny Marshall. He was surprised to find the young man staring at him, the expression on his face unreadable. The Gnome raised his eyebrows questioningly.

Danny made a small gesture towards the door and mouthed, 'After?'

The Gnome, after a second's consideration, nodded.

Jenni turned her attention to him after the main course, as was polite. The Gnome noted her slightly slurred speech and glassy expression, thinking she was drunk, then he noticed she was drinking mineral water. He leaned close to her – no smell of alcohol. He frowned slightly, a certain amount of high-stringing was acceptable in a wife but this was something he hadn't seen before. He glanced across at Tom Shackleton – he was deep in conversation with one of the female chiefs, lucky man.

'Are you all right?' he said to Jenni.

'I'm fine. Fabulous. Couldn't be better. Why?'

'No reason.'

He concentrated on his pudding while Jenni chattered. She had, in his experience, been prone to chattering in the past for effect and he could always detect the rapier beneath but now what she was saying seemed to have no point. He made a mental note to have a word with Shackleton after the meal. Couldn't have a suspect wife, too risky.

He was relieved when it was time for the speeches and he was in sight of his official car and home. The evening had been a disappointment. No, Jenni Shackleton had been a disappointment. Her early vivaciousness had given way to a sort of lassitude and, occasionally, she seemed about to go to sleep.

'I'm sorry. I took rather a lot of stuff to ward of the flu. I think I may have overdone it. But I did so want to be here tonight, for Tom.'

The Gnome was relieved, an overdose of Night Nurse he could cope with. The chairman – husband of the sofa – announced him. He stood up to sufficient but not overwhelming applause.

Five minutes later he came to the important part of his speech: '. . . And now, it is my great pleasure to announce' – he looked at his watch – 'just too late for anyone to catch the deadline for the last editions.'

Polite laughter.

'But coinciding with a Downing Street press release, which, I think means full coverage on *Today*, and we all know what that means to the spin doctors.'

More polite laughter, but now with an edge of anticipation.

'I would like to announce to you all the appointment of the first United Kingdom Anti-Crime Coordinator. On behalf of the government I would like to say how pleased we are that Tom Shackleton has accepted the post for an initial period of five years. Ladies and Gentlemen, Tom Shackleton.'

Tom rose and did not look round the room to see who was applauding wildly and who was sitting on their hands, he simply nodded to the Gnome and touched his lips – it could hardly be described as blowing a kiss – to Jenni. She sat as if she hadn't heard. Away with whatever fairies were now colonising her head.

After the dinner it took the Gnome several minutes to get to the door. He had had a brief word with Shackleton, repeated his congratulations and quietly mentioned Jenni's apparent ill health.

Tom was quick to read the subtext. Don't allow your wife to appear like that in public again. Good note, thought Shackleton, who was quickly swallowed up in a press of well-wishers and favour-seekers.

MacIntyre had forgotten Danny but Danny had not forgotten their silently proposed tryst. They walked together to the car.

'What did you want to see me about, Mr Marshall?'

Danny was too personally involved to be careful or diplomatic.

'Geoffrey Carter, sir.'

The Gnome stopped and looked at Danny. Danny ignored the warning in his expression.

'He wasn't a paedophile, Mr –'

The Gnome cut him off.

'I admire your loyalty but it's rather an academic question now.'

Danny stood in front of him.

'I believe someone planted the magazines and those bugs in his house. Someone who needed him out of the way.'

The Gnome was ice cold.

'And are you anything to do with the Rumour Room, Mr Marshall?'

Danny felt the blood go to his face and was grateful he was black.

'I think I know who planted that stuff in his house and I think I –'

'That's enough, Mr Marshall. I'd hate to think of you compromising such a bright future for the sake of speculation. Geoffrey Carter was, sadly, a flawed personality. But now he's dead we must let him rest in peace. Now . . . why don't you come and see me, we'll have lunch. Strictly confidentially, we're thinking of a caretaker for the Met – give you the time to work up some muscle. A black commissioner is something, I think, London could do with within the next – what? Three years? Four, perhaps . . .'

The schoolboy in Danny wanted to go on regardless of the carrot and the veiled stick but the first black commissioner of the Met won.

'He left a letter. For me,' he said, lamely trailing off.

'Really?'

Few people could invest that word with such honest interest as the Gnome.

'Perhaps you might let me read it?'

Danny had it in his pocket. He handed it over like an illicit comic to the science master.

'I've marked the relevant passage.'

'I'm sure you have,' murmured the Gnome. 'Well, goodnight, Mr Marshall. And be assured. The dead will always find a voice. But we can only speak for ourselves. I shall take good care of this and . . . I'm sure we'd all like to surf the net in future without risking our shins on rocks in the shallows.' He tucked the letter into his inside pocket. 'Goodbye, Mr Marshall. I look forward to our meeting again and giving some thought to your future . . .'

With that he slid into his car and was gone.

Danny stood looking at the place the car had been, disgusted with himself but unable to quiet the voice in his head that said: Commissioner of the Metropolitan Police. After all he'd done all he could to clear Carter's name but he was dead. Danny Marshall had a whole life ahead of him.

Tom put Jenni to bed at about three o'clock in the morning. She had been so strange he'd thought it better to get her home than risk another night at the university, where the walls were none too thick or soundproof. She was barely able to keep awake in the car but too agitated to sleep. She seemed frightened of what was waiting for her if she slept.

When they reached the house it was deserted. Jason, hating being alone there, had gone off to stay with friends in the country for the week. He was learning quickly that his good looks and public-school manners made him an ideal house guest and were the passport to a life away from the tensions of life at home.

Shackleton laid Jenni on the bed and went to her bathroom cabinet. The shock of what he saw was so great he didn't react at all. He simply stood and looked at the instantly recognisable array of tranquillisers and drugs undisguised in front of him. Small packets of cocaine and wraps of heroin. He didn't know how long he'd stood there before he heard the chink of bottle on glass. He turned – Jenni was pouring vodka into her bedside water glass.

'Bring me one of the little yellow ones. Come on. Bring it now!'

She was so far gone she didn't even know who it was she was commanding. He looked for the yellow ones. They were tranquillisers in massive doses. He knew she couldn't have got these from their doctor, and the rest of the powders, crystals, and tablets owed more to a chemistry set than the prescription pad.

As Shackleton stood there, almost unable to move, he felt the beginnings of a deep cold anger. The anger and bitterness that he'd suppressed so completely since the night he saw Jenni with another man in a nameless car under a whorehouse-red street light. The feelings he'd turned in on himself so completely they'd fuelled his career now threatened to run out of control. And then, just as suddenly, he shut them down, frightened of what such unleashed emotion might do. Not to her. To himself. To all he had made of his life.

He closed his fist over the bottle of pills and took them to her. She was sweating now and clutching her stomach, mumbling she couldn't sleep and that she was hurting. He sat on the edge of the bed and almost tenderly pulled a strand of hair from her face, laying it across the pillow. He had always liked her hair, its smell had reminded him of . . . what? Tenderness? Kindness? No, those were just imagination.

Except with Lucy.

Lucy seemed in all this like a dream of what might have been. Jenni reached for the pills. He took off the top and gave her the bottle. Greedily, like a child with Smarties, she emptied them on to her hand. Then, delicately, she selected one and washed it down with the watered vodka. The effect was instantaneous.

Knowing relief was coming she relaxed and smiled at him.

'Thank you. Don't leave me.'

So he sat there holding her hand, watching her drift off to sleep, not wanting to stay and not wanting to go. Thinking of what might have been if they hadn't both been so damaged and determined not to let that damage go. He didn't know how long he'd been there when he heard a 'tink'. The smallest press of the doorbell. He looked at his watch. Four o'clock. Automatically he went downstairs and opened the door.

Lucy, frightened and wrapped in an old jacket, looked up at him.

'Oh, I'm sorry, Tom. I saw the light. I didn't think you were coming home tonight . . . And Jason said he was . . . I didn't want to call the police before I'd made sure . . . I'm so sorry.'

She turned to go.

'It's all right, Lucy. Come in.'

She protested for a moment then stepped into the hall. He closed the door.

'Jenni's not well,' he said.

There was an awkward moment, then Lucy said, 'Would you like a cup of tea?'

And at that moment he thought there was nothing he'd like more than a normal cup of tea with a normal woman in a normal home. He nodded, pursing his lips.

Lucy bustled about the kitchen in a comforting, mumsy way while Shackleton sat at the table watching her. She put his tea down in front of him with a few biscuits on a plate. And that was too much. That was the image that broke into him. Her ordinary, unmanicured hand putting down a plate of digestives.

'You can dunk them if you want, I won't tell,' she said.

He put his face against her soft, untoned belly and tried to cry but his sobs were dry, the comfort of tears denied him. And she, who'd dreamed of him one day doing this, held him in silence. Afraid of losing the moment.

She held him close and whispered in the same voice she'd used to comfort Carter, 'I love you, Tom, don't cry. Don't cry. Sweetheart, don't cry.'

And she rocked him, like a child, until they were both silent and still.

With his face against her, he said, 'Don't love me, Lucy. There's nothing to love. There's nothing in me, nothing. You're warm. Alive. And I'm dead.'

She squatted down beside him and stroked his face so gently it hurt.

'Don't, Lucy. Don't. Please . . .'

But his words had no force and his eyes looked to her like the eyes of a child. She was where Lucy had been born to be, mother and lover, the only one for whom he'd ever been the best.

He offered no resistance when she led him up to his room. He stood by the bed making no move to lie down or undress, lost in his unhappiness.

Lucy, always mindful of duty, went along the corridor and looked in on Jenni. The light was still on and Jenni lay asleep, like a waxwork breathing gently, sound asleep. Quietly Lucy went over to her and turned off the bedside light. Jenni muttered and found her way back into her dreams.

Lucy went out and closed the door.

Tom was still standing by the bed when Lucy reached up and kissed him. As if returning from a great depth he responded then held her to him as if his life depended on it. He wasn't gentle with her that night. He struggled to get inside her, trying to escape the demons in his head. Not trying to fuck her brains out but his own. And still she said she loved him.

After, he was reluctant to withdraw and lay on top of her, holding her for comfort. He was breathing fast, his heart beating through her own chest. She held him and soothed him, kissing him, comforting him. Knowing she'd betrayed Gary and not caring.

Stroking his hair she said, 'You're not dead, Tom. Hold on to me, my love. You're not dead. We're alive. We are, we're alive . . .'

Eventually he fell asleep, her chin resting on his head as she held him, his right hand holding on to her left shoulder, his right leg across her. She held him as if carrying him.

Lucy dozed but knew she had to go. The birds were starting their day and Gary would be waking soon. Softly she tried to move away from him. He let her go immediately. She wanted him to stop her, to say something, but she knew that wasn't part of the deal. She had something of what she wanted; it had to be enough.

'Lucy?'

He held her wrist lightly.

'If I could love you, I would. Only you.'

And that was it. Lucy had the heart, the inarticulate, unformed love of Tom Shackleton. She knew those words would be with her for the rest of her life. Nothing he could do or say, nothing that parted them, would be able to take those words away from her. As she went across the road to her house and her husband, she knew, for the first time in her life, what unqualified happiness was. And all because a man had said he couldn't love her.

Tom woke after three hours of dreamless sleep, the first since Carter's death. For a minute his mind was clear, undisturbed, then he saw his clothes scattered on the bed and floor. The sight of his underwear crumpled on the bedside table, with his tie, depressed him, and opened the door to the greyness that had dogged him for so long. It was as if fog had settled in his bones. On the bedside table was a folded piece of paper, his name written on it. He picked it up. Inside was a small Russian wedding ring, the one Lucy wore on the third finger of her right hand.

He read the note: 'If you're going to be a Tsar then this will bring you luck. I give it with my love and hopes you will give it back one day in different circumstances.'

He was embarrassed by the gesture, knowing how little he deserved it. He picked it up, its three rings lay in the palm of his hand, then put it back on the table. It fell into interlinked solidity. A wedding ring.

He got up and put on a dressing gown. Coffee, shave, shower, dress, the reassuringly mundane. He was cleaning his shoes, putting off the moment of waking Jenni. The small, circular, particular rubbing in of the black polish was soothing.

He allowed himself to think about Lucy. Life would be so easy with her, so ordinary. What if? What if? He tried to imagine what it would be like to be married to Lucy and saw only his life with Jenni. It would only be a matter of time before Lucy turned into her. It would be inevitable, it was what he did to people. Women. They always wanted more than he had to offer and their disappointment at his inability to respond made him withdraw into himself, made them hate him. There was no point. No point in thinking about Lucy.

He had the family. Maybe he could start again with the next generation, the uncritical love of grandchildren.

He put on his shoes and tied the laces. He watched his hands, strong and quick, to his eyes ugly. Square, so unlike the priest's hands of Geoffrey Carter. Abruptly, to dislodge the thought, he stood up and poured a cup of coffee. Carefully, so as not to spill a drop into the saucer – she couldn't stand that – he took it up to Jenni. He stopped at her door. What if?

What if she'd forgotten the pill he gave her and had taken one more. Two more. The whole bottle. What if he opened the door and she was dead. Why had he left those little yellow tablets so close to her? Because he hoped she would take them. Because he hoped he'd be free this morning. Free to start his life again. In less than seconds she was buried and he'd moved to London, away from the memory of his wife and from the body of his lover. If he could open that door and find her life had ended . . . what could he offer to the devil in exchange for that? His soul was already gone: there was nothing left to bargain with. He opened the door.

The bed was empty and the bathroom door shut. He could hear water running. The disappointment was tempered with surprise.

'Jenni? . . . Jenni? I've brought you some coffee.'

He put it down on her dressing table and turned to go. The bathroom door opened and Jenni slumped against the jamb. She stared at him.

'I had a dream last night.'

Shackleton didn't want to hear about it, he had enough of his own, the vivid repetitive images of Carter pleading for mercy.

'No. Not about . . . that. About you.'

She pushed herself upright and walked towards him.

'I dreamed Lucy came in here. She woke me up. But I couldn't speak to her, I wanted to ask her about something . . . what? I don't know. Making pastry, I think. Stupid. So I got up, I was going to follow her. I went down the hall and your door was open. Just a crack. I pushed it. I couldn't see anything, it was dark. Pitch dark. But I heard you. Listened to you humping Lucy. She made silly gurgling noises, like a blocked drain.'

He felt he'd stopped breathing. What did his face look like?

'And?' was all he could say.

'Nothing. Nothing else. I went back to bed. Strange dream. But it was a dream. Must have been. She said she loved you and you said, "Oh, that's lovely." What a stupid thing to say. "Oh, that's lovely." Why would I dream that, Tom?'

He looked as blank as he could.

'No idea, Jenni. Look, I must go, Gordon'll be here in a minute. Will you be all right? Do you want me to phone Lucy and ask her to come over?'

Jenni snorted.

'Not after last night. I couldn't look her in the eye.'

'It was only a dream, Jenni.'

She was angry.

'I know that. But the dreams I have are more real than life. You don't know what I'm talking about, do you? It must be so nice to have no subconscious. Even dogs dream! But not you. Not Tom Shackleton, oh no, he's superhuman. No weakness there.'

Her voice was rising, the sound of nails on a blackboard.

'No way in to the great Tom Shackleton. Don't look at me like that. Stop it. I did it for you . . . and now I'm being punished for it. Not you, no. You just go on. Tom . . .'

Her tone shifted suddenly, to pleading.

'Help me, please. Don't shut me out. Tom . . .'

To his horror she sank to her knees, crying, and wrapped her arms round his legs.

'I only did it for you. It wasn't meant to be like that. I didn't know he'd die. It was an accident. Tom. Talk to me, Tom. Tell me it's all right. Take it away. Please, Tom, please.'

She dissolved on to the floor. He stepped away from her, repulsed.

'Don't go. Please don't go. I can't stand being alone. Help me, I can't take any more . . .'

He walked to the door. To him she was being histrionic: her suffering was too operatic to be real.

'I'll call Jacinta, tell her to come over.'

Her reply was instant. 'No, don't.'

There was a pause then she sat up. The drama dropped away and she said quite simply and coldly, 'I slept with Robert MacIntyre.'

He stopped and turned to look at her.

Now she had his full attention, she was triumphant, back in control.

'To get you the Met, but do you know what? I was so good he made you Crime Tsar. Don't you turn your back on me! Tom Shackleton, Crime Tsar – made between his wife's legs. Watch my lips – Robert MacIntyre gave it to you because I let him fuck me. Couldn't have done it without me, could you? I put you where you are by letting him put his cock up my arse.'

She waited, sure of bitter victory.

When he spoke, it was quietly, with no emotion.

'Thank you. I hope it was worth it.'

He bowed his head briefly and left the room, closing the door behind him. Jenni stayed on the floor, unable to move, her eyes fixed on nothing.

Tom arrived at police headquarters to a barrage of press enquiries. Would he do the news on One, Two, ITV, Four, Sky, radio, broadsheets, tabloids? Instant stardom insulated him from thought and feeling. The day was cleared to make way for camera crews and interviews. The PM's spokesman was on the phone. The Home Secretary wanted him to return his call. The Home Secretary, the Gnome. Shackleton pushed the pictures of him with Jenni to the farthest, most stagnant unexamined backwater of his mind and joined the circus.

All day he spoke fluently, convincingly, modestly, of the need for a national database of criminal intelligence. The necessity in the twenty-first century of facing major international crime in a less parochial way. The importance of DNA and scientific advances. The world was a global village plagued with crime that respected no local boundaries. His responsibility was to coordinate the national response to national and international crime.

It was four-thirty in the afternoon before he had a moment alone. He instructed Janet to get the Home Secretary on the phone. He sat back and waited, his hands on the desk. Those expressive, capable hands. And on the third finger of his left hand a thin gold ring. Bought with money borrowed from his mother because Jenni had insisted they both wore rings.

'I want everyone to know you're married. I don't trust men who won't wear them. I always wonder why.'

She'd looked so beautiful as she concentrated on putting it on his finger. When he'd still been in awe of her. Grateful to her for rescuing him from ridicule and loneliness. He took hold of it in his right thumb and forefinger. He'd never taken it off since that Saturday morning, in his hired suit and squeaky shoes. He moved it up to his knuckle, resistance for a second, then it was free.

There was a knock on the door. Before he could say anything his secretary came in. She was sheet white and seemed to have tears streaming down her face.

'What's the matter, Janet?'

He stood up, aware that the woman lived with her elderly mother. It was going to be inconvenient organising all this media interest if she wanted time off to care for her or bury her. The old lady's timing had always been immaculate – she'd had a stroke the day Shackleton had needed Janet to work on a report he was preparing for the standing committee on prostitution. But he was all solicitude; Janet was too good to lose. He wondered, if the old lady had finally gone, if she'd consider coming to London with him.

'Your wife . . . Mr Shackleton . . . she's dead.'

*　　*　　*

Gary had been due to go to hospital to be assessed for cannabis pain-control trials at one o'clock, so Lucy had him ready in his wheelchair by a quarter to, ready for the ambulance. As it had had to collect two motor neurones and a Parkinson's it didn't arrive until two-fifteen, by which time Gary was tetchy and in pain, physical and mental. If he was accepted on to the trial he would have hope again but the thought of hope being refused him was agony. Lucy was kind and sweet but Gary wanted to lash out at her, to hurt someone as much as he was hurting. He told her he didn't want her with him, that he could manage, to stop treating him like a bloody cripple. He hadn't told her about the trial, though she'd nagged for months about getting on to it. He just told her he had to go in for a routine check-up. The thought of disappointing her again stopped him saying more, and he covered his fears with anger. If he was rejected by the cannabis trials she may finally, all hope lost, reject him too. He poured more anger on his doubt and shook her off.

As soon as he was bolted on to the ambulance floor by the smiling Sikh driver he felt sorry. He wanted to get off and apologise to Lucy, to wipe away the look of wounded incomprehension in her great animal eyes. But he couldn't get off, he couldn't do anything for himself, he was helpless, useless. He knew she'd understand but he didn't want that, he wanted righteous anger at his juvenile nastiness. But he wasn't well so she smothered him in patience, every gesture eloquent with martyred stoicism. There had been another subtle shift in their relationship. They couldn't even row any more.

Lucy went back into the house with tears in her eyes. Tears of guilt and confused love. She'd make it up to Gary tonight. Again she resolved like an addict she wouldn't see Shackleton again. They'd move away. She'd always wanted to try her hand at writing short stories – maybe this was the time to start. She got out the hoover and vacuumed every inch of carpet in the house, the noise of the machine deadening her thoughts.

Through it she heard the doorbell faintly. She went to answer it and got there just before the lanky youth drove off in his delivery van. Reluctantly he climbed out and brought her a polystyrene box.

'It says if no reply deliver it here. You'll have to sign for it.'

Lucy saw it was addressed to Mrs Shackleton and labelled 'Down-side Farm, Organic Meat and Poultry'. Lucy signed and the lad drove off.

Glad of something to do she took the box across the road. The burglar alarm wasn't on – she'd have to speak to Tom about that. Recently Jenni had taken to going out and forgetting to set it. Once in the kitchen she slit the tapes and unloaded the contents into the fridge. Then she left a note for Jenni telling her what she'd done. She got as far as the hall before the temptation to go upstairs to Shackleton's room overwhelmed her. She wanted to touch the pillows, to see if she could smell him on the sheets, to see if their little love was still in the bed.

Jenni was crouched, naked, at the door to her bedroom. Curled over like a beggar by a roadside. Lucy spoke her name but there was no response. As soon as Lucy touched her she knew she was dead. There was no similarity between live flesh and dead. Jenni felt the same as the slabs of meat Lucy had just been handling. She lifted her chin and was fascinated by the absence in Jenni's face. It looked like Jenni but wasn't her. The skin on the nose seemed to have been sucked in to the bone and cartilage and the lips were open in the way Lucy had seen dead rabbits' mouths gape in butchers' windows.

Time went out of step. She didn't know how long she knelt there, fascinated by the difference between life and death. She didn't want to leave Jenni there but knew she mustn't move her. Eventually she went to the airing cupboard and got out a clean white tablecloth. A beautiful expanse of embroidered cotton. It was warm. Lucy tucked it around the body. At first she had draped it over Jenni but thought the effect was too much like furniture covered by a dust sheet, so she rearranged it as if dressing an icon. Then she called Janet. She knew she couldn't tell Tom. He might hear the guilty hope in her voice. The gladness shining through the shock. After she'd spoken to Janet she sat down to wait.

She didn't want to leave Jenni alone. Jenni had always hated being alone.

Janet's self-control collapsed immediately after telling Shackleton the news. She simply stood in the middle of the room overwhelmed by the tragedy of the death of one so young, so good and so beautiful. Mrs Shackleton had always been so kind to her.

Tom didn't offer comfort. In this situation he didn't even know how to perform the platitudes. He just stood as well.

Finally, at a loss, he said, 'Janet, why don't you take a break. Till you feel better.'

She left the room grateful, though guilty she couldn't be more help.

Shackleton phoned his home. Lucy picked up after two rings.

'Lucy.'

Her voice was calm.

'Tom. I'm sorry. What do you want me to do?'

'Nothing. I'm on my way. Don't do anything.'

'Shouldn't I call the doctor?'

He hesitated. If he said no there would be questions as to why he'd delayed. He calculated how long it would take him to get there.

'Yes. Call her. The number's by the phone.'

He rang off. If it was a drug overdose . . . He knew Jenni well enough to know this might be her final gesture, calculated to damage him. He could see the headlines: 'New Crime Tsar's Dead Wife Junkie'. Bitch. But only hours ago he had been wishing for this. But then he hadn't thought of the implications. She shouldn't have died now. Not today. After. After she'd seen him crowned King. He didn't need this today.

He left the office leaving the still shaky Janet to deal with a news crew waiting outside. His instinct for self-protection stopped him thinking; he was grim and calm as he arrived home.

'Where is she?'

Lucy, acknowledging the distance between them, said, 'Upstairs. The doctor's here.'

Shackleton walked up the stairs. His control was extraordinary.

'Doctor. Hello. I came as soon as I could.'

They completed the niceties, then the doctor, a woman in her midfifties whose hair had started off in a bun at eight o'clock that morning but was now a halo of greying wisps, said, 'I'm so sorry, Mr Shackleton, rigor has started. It'll be distressing moving her. I've called the coroner's officer. Did you want a particular funeral director's to deal with it?'

He shook his head and composed himself to ask the next question.

'What did she die of? Can you tell?'

The long, worn face gave nothing away.

'I think it may have been her heart but of course there'll have to be an autopsy.'

'Of course.'

They looked in silence at the ruined remains of Jenni Shackleton. The doctor bent down and adjusted the tablecloth, for modesty. A modesty Jenni'd never known in life. Diplomatically the doctor left Tom alone with his grief and went downstairs.

He didn't give the body another glance but went quickly into his room and picked up his leather uniform gloves. Pulling them on he hurried into Jenni's room and cleared every pill and powder into an Armani bag he found in her dressing table. Wiping every surface capable of holding fingerprints as he did so. He wiped and carefully replaced the gloves then picked up the bag, holding a tissue round the handle.

As he passed Jenni's body on his way to the stairs, he stopped. Looking down at the draped corpse he saw again the beautiful adoring girl who'd bewitched him. But there was no art could find the mind's construction in the face and that beauty that had so ensnared him had masked a madness that infected them both. He wanted to ask her who the man was she'd been with that night in the car. And why. Why he couldn't be enough.

He turned away, unwilling to examine himself for any emotion, certain he was feeling nothing. Holding the bag tightly shut he walked downstairs and put it in the hall by the front door then joined Lucy and the doctor in the kitchen. He wiped his hands on a tissue and dropped it in the pedal bin.

The necessary paperwork had been completed and the older woman was anxious to go. Death was only a small part of her day's work.

Lucy saw her out then returned to the kitchen awkwardly. Shackleton had withdrawn into himself and she knew she couldn't find anything to say that would reach him. Yet again Jenni had spoiled everything.

'Lucy. I don't want to involve you in this but . . .'

He didn't remember ever saying before in his life: 'I need your help.'

She nodded, grateful to be included.

'The bag by the front door, would you . . . just keep it until this is over? Hide it. Can you do that? It's Jenni's – I just don't want . . . any unpleasantness. Do you understand? Lucy?'

Lucy went and fetched the bag. She resisted opening it. Shackleton knew if he flushed the drugs away in the house there was no guarantee forensic wouldn't find some trace if the autopsy proved the doctor wrong. It was too risky to keep them in the house and too risky to try to dispose of them himself. There must be no possibility of proving he had ever known they existed. He didn't want to involve Lucy, but . . . he couldn't delay calling his deputy any longer, the official wheels had to start rolling.

'Thank you, Lucy.'

He hesitated, he knew she wanted more, some sign that nothing had changed between them. He bent and kissed her on the cheek. It seemed to be enough. She squeezed his hand.

'I'll call you,' he said.

Mercifully she took her cue and left, taking the bag. There was nothing to link him with the drugs. Nothing but the fragment of his thumb print inside the yellow-pill container he'd knocked over in his haste. The gloves had been too bulky to allow him to pick it up and refill it with the spilled contents.

He breathed deeply and made the next phone call.

The coroner himself arrived in his battered old Daimler behind the discreet van from which his men emerged. The same men who'd cleared Geoffrey Carter away.

He was an extraordinary sight, small and dapper with a red carnation in his buttonhole. His hair was boot-polish black and its extravagant waves were controlled with Gentlemen's Pomade. There was something charmingly Dickensian about his scrubbed cherubic face and immaculate clothes.

'Tom. I'm so sorry.'

That word again.

'It was good of you to come yourself, St John.'

'Only proper, Tom, only proper.'

His Scottish accent was almost silenced by the voice of England's establishment.

'Did Jenni have any history of heart problems?'

Tom heard the unintended irony of the question.

'No. She was only forty-one. Forty-one in July.'

The coroner tutted his commiseration.

'We'll get the autopsy done as quickly as possible. Jackson's the pathologist – do you know him? Top man. Oh . . . and I know it's not the ideal moment but congratulations on the job. Best man for it in my opinion.'

The two men with him gently eased Jenni's rigid limbs to place her in the zip-up cover, so like a large suit carrier, and took her out to the van on a stretcher.

To the coroner Shackleton looked bewildered, lost in his sadness. They had been a famous love match. He couldn't know how fast the man's mind was racing, covering every possibility, calculating the damage Jenni could cause in death.

He had called his deputy while waiting for the coroner. Vernon was shocked, upset. Shackleton found himself fascinated by the reactions of each person who was touched by the widening ripples of Jenni's dramatic exit. Vernon alerted the area commander and they would arrive shortly. Jenni would have loved the attention.

Tom knew what he had to do next but wanted time before he did it. There was no time. He picked up the phone and called the Home Secretary. It took nearly ten minutes to be put through to MacIntyre.

'Yes, Tom. What can I do for you?'

Since last night the question begged a variety of unspoken replies.

'Jenni, my wife. She died suddenly this morning.'

There was total silence from the Gnome, then, 'I'm so sorry, Tom. What happened?'

'Probably her heart. There'll have to be an autopsy of course.'

'Of course.'

Another silence.

'It's unfortunate timing, Tom.'

'Yes.'

'Who's the coroner?'

'St John Clement.'

The Gnome seemed pleased.

'Good man. Very sound.'

Tom heard: Good, he's one of ours.

'I'll have a word with him. Obviously we want as little fuss as possible.'

'Obviously.'

'There wasn't anything else?' The question hung for a moment. 'No . . . circumstances?'

How much did he trust the Gnome?

'No. Nothing I know of.'

'Good. It would be unfortunate if anything tarnished your appointment. I know the PM would find it onerous to have another . . .

problem . . . it's very important to him the Anti-Crime Coordinator doesn't come under inappropriate press scrutiny.'

'Of course.'

'And, Tom, you have my total support. I was very keen you should have this job. I think we'll work well together.'

'I hope so.'

'You'll let me know when the funeral is, won't you. I was very fond of Jenni, you know.'

'Yes . . . she told me . . . It was one of the last things she said to me. How close you had been.'

The pause was just too long.

'Well, keep me informed. Anything you need . . .'

The doorbell rang and the house filled with his senior officers. Every one expressed their sorrow. Shortly after, two other officers arrived, unmistakable Special Branch. MacIntyre had been busy. Tom assured them all there was no cause for anything more than sympathy. They reassured themselves there was no question of suspicious circumstances and, by two o'clock, he was alone.

For the first time in his life he was alone· no mother, no wife, no family. Family. He realised with a shock that her children didn't know their mother was dead.

Another five minutes of freedom, then he'd call them.

The autopsy report was straightforward and produced within thirty-six hours of her body being found. Jackson was, after all, a top man. Jenni had died from a spontaneous rupture of the pulmonary artery caused by a structural weakness probably present since birth. Natural causes.

The funeral was arranged for the following week, the Wednesday morning. Burial, not cremation.

Tom continued to work and was admired for his strength and professionalism. His children re-inhabited his life and dealt with their grief and the daily influx of sympathy cards noisily and openly. Lucy offered help but was politely rebuffed. Tom's daughters were going to care for their father – they would clean his house and cook his meals; Lucy's lover was now speaking on television and radio as caring husband, father and grandfather. The bosom of his family stifled him and excluded her.

Desperate, she called his mobile. It was six o'clock, he should be on his way home. He answered quickly. That three-syllabled 'Hello'.

'Tom, I'm sorry to disturb you, but I wanted to know you were all right. Could I see you? It would be good to have a talk . . . about, well, what's going to happen . . . Tom? . . . Tom?'

She could hear voices in the background, a cocktail party or reception. She felt her face burning as she realised she'd interrupted him, she'd done the wrong thing. The public man had nothing to do with the one she was phoning. He didn't say anything. She could hear his breathing.

'Tom?'

Lucy panicked and rang off.

Shackleton wished everyone would go away, leave him to the empty house and his empty soul. He had felt nothing but was continually told by well-wishers that he would need time for mourning, when the funeral was over. When it really sank in. The loss. His great loss.

The press was sympathetic and soon the letters from lonely women, mostly written in green ink, began to appear in his office. Janet dealt with them, the ones who wanted to marry him, look after him, offer him comfort. Protected by her and his deputy he simply worked, unthinking and unfeeling, until the morning of his wife's interment.

St John Clement had seen the Home Secretary at his club on the evening of the autopsy. They met briefly on the imposing wooden staircase looked down on by past members of the great and the ostensibly good. Their conversation very quickly turned to Jenni Shackleton.

Clement's voice dropped to a low rumble.

'Yes. Natural causes . . . but . . .'

'But?'

The Gnome didn't want any buts.

'There was something else. The state of the organs. Wear and tear more than one would expect in a body of that age. Certain signs. My usual feeling would be to hold a second autopsy. Toxicology reports. Further investigation.'

'What's your suspicion, St John?'

The rubicund geniality gave way to an unexpected hardness.

'Drugs. Legal and illegal. Over quite a period. Maybe not years but . . . habitual, I'd say.'

MacIntyre thought for a moment. Then he said, 'Yes. Get Jackson to do another. But . . . let me have the result, eh? I don't think we need to let this go any further. We don't want to ruin Shackleton before he's had a chance to ruin himself, do we?'

Clement smiled his naughty-boy smile.

'No. Of course not. Wouldn't look good, would it? Adding to the burden of the grieving widower. And after that fiasco with Carter . . .'

The two men were thoughtful for a moment.

'Right ho, see you in the bar, Robbie.'

The coroner delivered the second autopsy report personally to the Gnome a couple of days later. No point in risking the discretion of a third party. He waited patiently while the Home Secretary read it.

'Tranquillisers taken shortly before death, traces of heroin and cocaine and alcohol . . . some evidence of Ecstasy . . . Good God, was there nothing this woman didn't get up to?'

'Very little, I'd say,' replied Clement. 'She also had a very neat case of syphilis. Not too advanced. Probably had no idea there was anything wrong. Not so usual in this country. Lots of it in the Eastern Bloc. Galloping. Breakdown of social fabric, of course.

'Oh, and there was evidence of severe damage to the rectum and anus. A small fistula, more a lesion really. Some infection. She must have been in quite a lot of pain. If Shackleton's responsible for both or either, I'd keep an eye on him. Whoever gave her those problems is a walking time bomb – someone definitely not to take home to your daughters.'

He missed the Gnome's expression as he produced a gold half-hunter and consulted it.

'I'm always surprised at what beauty hides. Anyway, I must be off. You going to *Traviata* on Thursday? Kitty's looking forward to seeing Lizie again, wants to talk to her about wisteria or something . . .'

When he'd gone the Gnome re-read the report. Of all the words in it the only one that had any meaning for him was syphilis. Dirty, degrading, degenerate, all words that had the power to excite him, but disease wasn't one of them. The long-conquered loathing for his physical self came back like a smell. A combination of unpleasant odours that made up the hated stench of his body, his feet, his groin, armpits, hair, stale skin and breath. And now decaying flesh.

He had no doubt Jenni had contracted it from him. An extra-ordinary female he'd met on an official visit to Macedonia came back to him. She'd been a hanger-on with some Russian delegation, ostensibly there to calm feelings in the wake of Milošević but actually to ensure the Trepeca Mine in Kosovo would be available to Serb protectors when the regime finally fell. A grubby girl, a memorable lay, but not worth what it was going to cost.

If he had impregnated Mrs Shackleton he had infected Lizie. Lizie, the only woman he'd never hurt.

What could he possibly say to her that would not destroy his marriage? With only words he was going to create that look of nauseous revulsion he strove to see on the faces of other women as he physically assaulted them. But not Lizie. Never Lizie. He had raised his wife above all other women, confident his depravity would never touch her. Now, as in some distorted Greek myth, she was his victim. The bitter irony was not lost on him.

There was a knock at the door. The secretary came in carrying a sealed box file.

'Are you all right, Mr MacIntyre?'

He nodded.

'Mr Hemsley sent this over, sir – it's the file on Dieter Gerhardt.'

'Sorry?' MacIntyre came back into focus. 'What were you saying, Susan?'

'The Austrian MP, sir, do you remember? Dieter Gerhardt, he's –'

'Coming for the conference, yes.'

MacIntyre snapped, annoyed at being spoken to like a backward child. Susan really didn't like him and she almost let it show.

'I was saying, Mr MacIntyre, Mr Hemsley was sent this file by the Austrian police along with information on all the other delegates to the conference. For security reasons, you understand.' It pleased her hugely to see how much her slowness irritated him. 'He seemed to think there might be something of interest to you in Herr Gerhardt's file.' She was still clutching it, warming to her subject. 'I used to enjoy his films enormously – I think he was a very good actor. Of course the fuss over his looks often obscured that fact. But maybe, when his career in politics is over, he'll return to what he does best. After all, you never know when they'll stop voting for you, do you?'

As Susan had been installed in Whitehall at about the same time as the Cenotaph she would be difficult to remove, but MacIntyre made a silent vow she'd be gone before the end of the year.

He sat for quite some time imagining Lizie's reaction when he told her. Perhaps, just perhaps, if he phrased it carefully, she would, might, eventually forgive him. Then again he had a very good relationship with a consultant at St Thomas's, over the bridge. He might, for a knighthood, give him something to slip in her food.

MacIntyre never lingered in despair for long.

Cheered by a chink of hope he opened the file.

Jenni Shackleton paying for a magazine was the top photograph. The cover was plainly recognisable. The next photograph: her hand holding a kiddie-porn video. He worked slowly through the rest of the file. The photographs that could have saved a life. In Vienna they had been no more important than blurred smudges from a speed-trap camera.

What if they'd come to light earlier? Messy, very messy. Carter would have not only been Crime Tsar but in an impregnable position. Shackleton would have been disgraced and possibly prosecuted with his wife. No, two deaths and a controllable anti-crime coordinator was a much neater result. Sad, regrettable but, in the final analysis, better. Poor Carter, at least it had been quick.

He opened his desk and took out an unmarked folder containing a great deal about Carter and Shackleton. MacIntyre tucked the photographs into the back flap. As he did so Carter's letter to Danny and another piece of paper dropped on to the floor. He bent to pick them up; the second letter caught his eye. He had deliberately put this one to the back of his mind, and the file. He re-read it.

Dear Mr MacIntyre,

My mother doesn't know I'm writing this letter and she would be very angry if she knew I'd sent it. But everyone is saying my father, Geoffrey Carter, has done things to boys. I know you are in charge of investigating him so I'm writing to tell you my dad has never done anything. He never hurt me or my brother. Please believe me, I don't tell lies and neither does my dad.

If you can tell everyone it's all right then I can go home and my sister can have the same name as me.

Thank you for helping,

Peter Carter.

*   *   *

MacIntyre looked at the childish writing. He would have liked to have helped, really he would, but to clear Carter's name now would be to undermine Shackleton's appointment. Yes. Wiser to save it. One day though, one day he'd give the boy back his dad. For the greater good, the little children would have to suffer just a little longer.

He put the letter in the file on top of a short report on Danny Marshall. A good man for the future and no friend of the new Crime Tsar. There was enough here to keep Tom Shackleton in order until he reached the end of his shelf life.

In the meantime he was perfect. Not as prone to brilliant inspiration as Carter, less likely to impress the public. Not such a good speaker or politician. And he was biddable, he wanted the trappings of success.

MacIntyre wondered why they had been so keen to have Carter in the first place. He would have become uncontrollable, inspiring loyalty in his men, respect in the media and the people. He wouldn't have been satisfied towing the Party line. Shackleton would be the government's man. Grateful. Always on message. Perfect.

The file was secure, back in the drawer. Good. Now to make an appointment with the clap doctor and buy Lizie something very, very expensive.

Jenni's funeral was gratifyingly well attended. Press and cameras were kept outside to record the arrival of celebrities, of which there were plenty. Jacinta and Tamsin in black suits flanked their sister Chloe, back from an orphanage on the Tibet border, wearing a version of Mother Teresa's blue-and-white sari enlivened with a large amount of silver jewellery. She looked like a heron in a parliament of crows.

Shackleton, followed by his daughters and grandchild, carried the coffin with Jason, Vernon his deputy, two undertakers, and Jenni's favourite editor. She could never bear those wheeled gurneys coffins were usually taken on, she thought they looked like dessert trolleys, and she hated the idea of strangers handing her into eternity. Everything was done according to the wishes her children imagined she'd had. Romanticised memories of her likes and dislikes.

Shackleton had kept out of it all, retreating to the dining room in the evenings, leaving them to bicker and plan in the living room. The church was filled with flowers, as if for a wedding. No chrysanthemums. Jenni hated chrysanthemums. Tom sat in his pew, knelt, stood, prayed with no thought of the contents of the coffin.

He saw Robert MacIntyre, head bowed with cares of state and subtle sadness. And Lucy, sitting with Gary at the back of the church. Lucy. She still had the drugs. Well, that wasn't a problem – there was nothing to link them with him. But he should talk to her. He should talk to all these strangers. Sometime. After. After today.

At the end of the service they shouldered their burden again. The coffin was heavy, ridiculously large for the seven-stone body inside it.

At the grave, in a light wind that caught the vicar's robe, more prayers were said then, in the Scottish tradition – the children said Jenni had thought it charming when she'd come back from a funeral in Perth – the pall bearers took up the cords, fine black ropes tied to the coffin handles, and lowered Jenni Shackleton into the deep shaft, room enough for three, which would be her final resting place. Her daughters dropped roses on to the pale wood then those who wanted to filed past throwing handfuls of earth into the grave.

Tom nodded to each, friends, neighbours, colleagues. Lucy held back. She had no right to give that final blessing, who'd wished for Jenni's death in abstract so many times. She reached for Gary's hand.

'Go on, Luce,' he said. 'Say goodbye.'

Numb, Lucy joined the queue, taking a pinch of dust from the priest. She and Tom stood on opposite sides of the grave, looking, unblinking, into each other's eyes as the earth trickled through Lucy's fingers on to the coffin so far below. She searched for recognition from Tom but saw none. She moved on. He didn't watch her but shifted his gaze to meet that of the next mourner.

It was such a shock to see those cowrie eyes, that black-scarred face, he almost fell. Almost toppled into the gaping grave at his feet. His son caught his arm. The three black women, their mourning dresses stirring like the feathers of ravens, faced him. As one they poured earth on the coffin. And then they started to sing. The sound was primitive and beautiful but bleak, without comfort, with no promise of eternal life and happy resurrection. It sounded like lonely wind in desolate places.

It was the sound of the death we all fear. Final, cold, pointless. As they stopped singing the heavens opened and rain fell in vicious, unforgiving needles. Everyone ran for cover. Within minutes the coffin was surrounded by water, the clay soil allowing no drainage. The earth liquefied to mud. The mourners slunk away to their cars and dispersed. The grave-diggers hastily threw a cover over the hole and went back to their card game.

Shackleton was deeply disturbed by the appearance of the three women. Fear and anger made him shake as he drove, alone and too fast, to the estate. He didn't know what he wanted to say to them but he had to see them again. What did they want? Who were they?

He didn't see Vernon and another officer following him. He just drove, determined to stop them ever coming near him again.

He screeched to a stop. Everything was exactly as it had been on his last visit, even the stained mattress outside the pub on which sat two drunks asleep with their cans of Special Brew. He jumped out of the car and ran over to the flat.

No, this couldn't be right. He looked at the rest of the block. Yes, he was sure this was it. But the garden had gone. In its place was a brown patch of weeds and rubbish. The doors and windows covered with aluminium shutters. Graffiti all over the walls.

There was an old black man coming out of the pub.

Shackleton called him over.

'The flats. Where are the people who live in the flats?'

The man looked at him with yellow eyes.

'No people there. No one been there since the fire, years back. I remember. Big fire, people die. Twas a bad business. They waitin' to pull the lot down. Too many rats and cockroaches. Too much bad stuff. No one lives there now.'

And he wandered off.

Vernon came up behind him.

'You all right, sir?'

Shackleton jumped.

Vernon had never seen his boss frightened. It was a surprise.

'I . . . I'm looking for someone. The people who live over there. In that flat. I need to speak to them.'

Vernon looked puzzled, like a dog trying to understand a command.

'No, sir. I don't think so. That block's been empty for ages. Like the old boy said, there was a fire. Three women died in it. Caused quite a stir. Before your time, sir. Three black women. Thought it was a race crime at first but forensic decided it was a candle or something. There was a rumour of magic, satanism, voodoo, but nobody believed it. It was just one of those things. Nobody's there now, sir.'

Shackleton ran to the boarded-up door, banging on it, shouting incoherently to be let in. He saw the metal sheet over the window was bent: he grabbed at it and put his face to the broken glass. Nothing moved in the darkness.

Vernon dared to put his hand on Shackleton's arm and lead him back to his car. He signalled to his colleague and sat Tom in the passenger seat. There was no resistance but Shackleton twisted to look back as they drove away. There was a man standing where the garden had been. A police officer. As the car turned the corner he recognised Geoffrey Carter.

Vernon had to restrain his chief as best he could. There was no way he was stopping before he'd delivered him to his house.

Shackleton kept talking about seeing Geoffrey Carter, then he was rambling about the black women being at the funeral, singing. Vernon had only said that morning he'd have to break down sometime, poor bastard, he'd lost his wife, for God's sake.

Shackleton disappeared for several weeks. Every day Lucy looked out for him but he didn't come home. The children had gone. Unwilling to stay in the place where their mother had died so tragically. Chloe scooped up her little brother and took Jason back to India to find consolation in the theology of reincarnation.

The house was empty. She'd stopped going over there: something about the place frightened her.

When she couldn't stand it any more she tried his mobile. Disconnected.

Controlling her panic, she phoned Janet.

'I just wanted to know if I should go in and clean. Water the plants.'

Janet was not forthcoming.

'I'm sure if Mr Shackleton wants you to go in he'll let me know.'

'Well, perhaps I should phone him. Do you have a number where he can be contacted?'

'I'm afraid not, but I'll tell him you called if he rings in.'

Lucy put the phone down, desperate now to speak to him. Aching to touch him. Obsessed as only denial can make us. He'd changed his mobile number. Why hadn't he told her? How could she find him? He needed her. He must need someone, and who else did he have?

Then one afternoon, unable to stop herself, she rang his office again and he answered. Lucy was thrown for a moment. Where was Janet? One o'clock. Lunch.

She was surprised at how normal her voice sounded.

'Oh, hello. I . . . er . . . I've been trying to get hold of you. I didn't expect you to answer.'

The self-deprecating laugh.

'I'm being a good boss, answering my secretary's phone. I must answer it more often.'

She felt a surge of hope. Maybe the intimacy was still there. She lowered her voice.

'Are you all right?'

His reply was formal. Polite.

'I'm fine, thanks, Lucy. How is Gary?'

She was burbling now.

'He's fine. Well, no, he's got to go into hospital for a couple of days . . . I mean . . . I've been worried about you.'

It was as though he hadn't heard her.

'I'm sorry, I have to go. I have a meeting.'

Lucy heard the desperation in her voice. Yet again he'd turned her into a supplicant.

'It would be nice to meet. If you want to talk. Well, um . . . you know, if Gary's going to be away, I'll be on my own till the weekend at least and well . . .' She trailed off hoping he'd come to her rescue.

But as if replying to a journalist he outlined his reasons for not being available: he had to draw up a national anti-crime strategy, he even detailed the government's policy towards recidivists.

When he drew breath Lucy said, 'So this is goodbye then.'

He was quick to reply.

'No, no. I don't want to say goodbye.'

Lucy was surprised at the strength in her voice.

'Well, I'm not going to phone up every six months to listen to the government's thoughts on repeat offenders.'

He was taken off guard by her turn. Defensive.

'But we were talking about –'

Lucy cut in. At last she was angry, indignant.

'Will I see you again?'

Pause.

'Probably not.'

Lucy knew she'd never been so coldly angry or so in control.

'Well, say goodbye then.'

Shackleton hated to give up anything that was his. When he spoke his voice was soft, reluctant.

'Goodbye.'

Lucy's voice was strong, loud.

'Goodbye.'

As she rang off she heard him say with a gentleness he only had with her, 'Take care.'

But it was too late. Lucy stared at the phone, the urge to call back not quite as strong as the desire to be free. But after a moment, regrets started to whisper, and she reached for the phone.

Then, through the window, she saw it pull up. A white flat bed truck. A nondescript man in jeans got out and heaved something off the back. He walked with it, like a suburban Christ carrying his cross, to Shackleton's gates. Then he tied the FOR SALE sign to the upright with metal ties. After checking it was secure, he returned to his van and drove off.

Lucy hadn't moved. She had barely breathed. She grabbed her bag and ran over to the house. Scrabbling for the keys she dropped the bag's contents on the front step. The key didn't work. It wouldn't turn. The locks had been changed. She leaned against the door and sobbed, sliding down it until she was sitting knees up and head down against it.

The same position Jenni had died in.

After speaking to Lucy, Shackleton had gone back to the work of putting his team together, meeting politicians, preparing his first statement of intent. It wasn't until after a rather fine dinner at the Athenaeum he thought about her again.

MacIntyre was also a guest and they found themselves sitting around the same low table in the bar drinking ancient brandy and savouring the burnt autumn smell of a large arrangement of lilies which dominated the otherwise soberly masculine room.

Their host, a desiccated wit whose life had been made comfortable by the Law, if not always justice, had the rare gift of making his guests relax into indiscretion and, occasionally, inebriation.

Neither Shackleton nor the Gnome was drunk but they were more relaxed with one another than they had been before. Jenni was no longer an uncomfortable presence.

The conversation roamed amiably and grazed on several subjects before MacIntyre said, 'How's that neighbour of yours? Lucy, wasn't it?'

Shackleton was so taken aback he didn't say anything but he could feel himself getting hot. His face and ears were burning. Red. For God's sake, he was blushing. He was confused – maybe he had had too much to drink. That must be it. He put his glass down.

The Gnome was watching him, amused. He'd never seen Tom Shackleton shaken before.

'I enjoyed meeting her. I thought she was a very . . .' He paused, swirling his brandy and summoning the right word. '. . . A very sweet person. Am I right, Tom? Is she sweet?'

He'd leaned in close to Shackleton now, close enough to see the fine hairs on the other man's cheekbones and the flushed skin underneath.

'I've no idea, I don't know her very well. She's a – she was a friend of Jenni's.'

The Gnome was smiling now. The alcohol was making him playful. He was in what Lizie called his 'kitten with a ball of string' mood.

'Really? I got the impression you' – a breath – 'were her special friend.'

Shackleton turned to MacIntyre and was surprised at the benign amusement on the dwarfish face. He struggled to maintain a tone of moderate outrage.

'For Christ's sake, what the hell gave you that idea?'

The Gnome shrugged and sat back, still watching Shackleton with a sort of elfish mischievousness.

'Oh, nothing really. Except she's in love with you.'

Shackleton clenched his hands together and suppressed a laugh.

It was a spectacularly inappropriate reaction and delighted the Gnome. He was always interested in unforeseen reactions to embarrassment. This was much more interesting than outrage or anger.

'Oh, while I think of it, we must have another meeting about budgets. That tight bugger at the Treasury's getting jumpy again. Another brandy?'

Having had his fun MacIntyre got up and went to the bar to join their host. There were waves of laughter from the men there. Shackleton knew they weren't laughing at him but it felt the same as when he was in the playground surrounded by laughter and didn't find out until his mother slapped him that his trousers were split, exposing his hand-me-down vest and pants. Group laughter had made him uneasy ever since.

He prepared to stand up but wasn't sure he could move. He must have drunk more than he realised.

Lucy. Bloody Lucy. Why couldn't she leave him alone? She'd made him say goodbye. That should have been it. The relief of a life without emotional clutter.

He got up. No, it wasn't too much drink, it was emotional poisoning. The residue of too much feeling in a hitherto emotional teetotaller.

Pleading pressure of work he said his goodbyes and didn't allow himself to think again until he was out of the building. He walked across the square to his car and looked back at the great gold Pallas Athene above the pillared entrance of the club. The goddess of wisdom.

He wondered who the goddess of rank stupidity was because that's who he needed tonight.

His driver opened the car door.

'No. No it's all right, thanks. You go. I want to walk for a while.'

The man looked sceptical but he just said goodnight and drove off.

It was cold. He put on his white raincoat, the one Jenni had derided as being far too Humphrey Bogart, and walked down the steps to the Mall. The buildings were luminous in the moonlight as he walked past the war memorial in the park, with the empty Horse-guards Parade on his left.

A car passed, illuminating the back of Downing Street. The pelicans he'd thought were swans on his first visit shone white on the rocky islands of the lake. The little gingerbread house opposite the Cabinet Office looked enchanted.

And he missed Lucy.

He sat on one of the low railings edging the grass, his back to Whitehall, his face to the quiet stirrings in the park, and allowed himself for the first time since the phone call to think about her.

Amidst all the guilt and confusion, the one thing he now realised, too late, was he missed her. He really missed her. It wasn't Jenni's absence he felt but that of cosy, loving Lucy.

'Oh Lucy. Lucy, Lucy, Lucy.'

A Canadian goose, disturbed by Shackleton's lovesick repetitions, honked.

At the same time a taxi, its old diesel engine shattering the romantic calm of the scene, clattered round the corner. Shackleton hailed it. If it had a third gear he might just make the eleven o'clock train.

The thought of Lucy alone in the house, and the residue of good wines and brandy, sustained Shackleton all the way to her front door.

Then the doubts set in. The sight of his house, the memories, the sheer idiocy of what he was doing. What was he doing? He wasn't sure. What had he come for? He didn't know. No. That wasn't true. He'd come to talk. Lucy was the only one he could talk to. She was a part of him. He sat on the step. If she was part of him she was the only good part. He saw how far he'd travelled when he realised he didn't want to lose that.

He remembered, in the warm, dark stillness of one of their nights together, he'd said, in reply to her probing for some sign of affection, 'If we were both free, our relationship would be very different.' As always, phrasing himself ambiguously. As always, open to interpretation. Well, now he wanted it to be different. All right, they weren't both free but they could talk, maybe make plans for the future, after Gary . . . when Gary . . . Shackleton stopped himself. Jenni had taught him the destructive power of allowing wishes to germinate. Leave it. Go back to London. The monster Hope had rarely visited his life – it wasn't the time to invite it to take up residence now.

But he couldn't stop himself. Lucy had become the one thing, the one person who could save him from the nothing that was threatening to envelop him. She had held him and told him he was alive. The black women had said only wood could defeat him. With Lucy and the scrupulous avoidance of splinters he'd make a life, a life like other people had, with happiness and tranquillity. He laughed out loud. That was it, Lucy was the key to life.

The front door opened behind him. He stood up like a guilty schoolboy.

'Can I help you?'

It was a woman in her forties with tightly curled rust-blonde hair, discreet reddish lipstick and blue eyeshadow unrelieved by either mascara or liner. Her dress was dark blue in the fashion of women who despised fashion. Her shoes sensible and suitable for anything required of a foot besides glamour. She was formidable and English, and born a century too late.

'My name's Shackleton, I'm sorry, I didn't realise the time, I was hoping to —'

She didn't allow him to finish, used as she was to a lifetime of completing the sentences of others.

'Pop in for a visit, yes. Now I see you in the light, you're that chap who's the new Crime Tsar. Used to live opposite. Lucy's mentioned you.'

'Is Lucy —?'

'Yes, come in. Oh how do you do, by the way, I'm Christine, Christine Stroud. We were just going to have hot chocolate.'

Shackleton followed her into the hall. His heart was beating fast. He hadn't felt like this for years. Or had he ever felt such excitement at the prospect of seeing a woman?

The house was smaller and shabbier than he remembered, but then he hadn't set foot in it for a long time.

Christine tapped on the door as she passed the front room.

'Visitor for you,' she called and went on to the kitchen indicating Shackleton should go in.

He was shaking and sweating. Out of breath. He'd been having breathless attacks since Jenni died. The doctors couldn't find any reason. Just stress, they said, reaction. Whatever the cause he was panting now, like a smoker after a flight of steep stairs.

The door handle was stiff and made too loud a noise as he turned it and went in. The heat of the room struck him immediately. It was stuffy with the blast of a very efficient radiator and heavily curtained windows.

Then he saw why.

Instead of Lucy there was Gary, lying in his bed with three pillows raising him to a half-seated position. Hanging by his side the urine bag hooked over the bed frame.

'I'm sorry, I thought –'

He wanted to run out of the house before Gary turned his head and saw him. But Gary didn't turn. He was asleep. His breathing steadier than Shackleton's and deeper.

Christine bustled in with a tray.

'Go on in. Sit down. I'll put Gary's under this little cover. I doubt he'll wake now he's had his medication. He doesn't usually go off this quick though.'

Shackleton didn't move.

'Well, why don't you stay a while – he might wake up. He'd be glad to see you.' She lowered her voice to a pitch that could summon foxhounds. 'I think he's lonely without Lucy here. Misses her dreadfully.'

Shackleton was lost for what to say.

'Are you a relation?'

He might as well have said, 'Do you support the disestablishment of the Church?'

'Good Lord, no. I'm a nurse, Mr Shackleton. Have been all my life. Lucy always asks for me when she's away. Not that she's away much, she's such a saint, no. She's gone off for a few days R and R. Apparently she lost someone close recently and has taken it rather hard. I'm sure you' – emphasis on the you and a rounding of the blue-lidded eyes – 'of all people will understand that.'

'Yes.'

'I'll leave you alone then. If you want anything I'll be in the kitchen.'

She'd put the tray down by the bed. Shackleton went across and looked down at Gary.

'You'd better drink it before it gets a skin.'

Gary spoke without opening his eyes, though the desire to see Shackleton's face was almost irresistible. He was rewarded by the sound of a cup being knocked over. He opened them then and turned to look at Shackleton.

'Don't worry, the Angel of Death will clear it up.'

Shackleton looked lost

'Nurse Stroud. I call her the Angel of Death. Every time she comes here she has yet another lurid tale of how one of her patients has "crossed over". Probably be me next. So . . . How have you been?'

'Fine . . . Fine. Good. I was just over at the house, checking everything's all right.'

'Oh Lucy could have done that for you. But of course . . . you changed the locks, didn't you?'

Shackleton avoided the challenge.

'I'm sorry it's so late – I hadn't realised the time. Why don't I come back another day?'

'When Lucy's here.'

'Well, yes, it would be nice to see her again. How is she?'

That tone of polite indifference really annoyed Gary.

'How is she? Well, Tom, what can I say? She's in love with another man who's just got a new job and moved away from the area. Suicidal might be a word I'd use only I don't think even Lucy could be so stupid as to kill herself for that piece of low life. And he's vicious low life, he's the sort of man who comes sniffing round when he thinks Lucy's husband is in hospital. Unfortunately for him there were no beds and Lucy's away visiting the rock pools and historic sites of Hastings.'

Shackleton looked like a stunned fish. Gary was gratified by the effect.

'I don't know what you mean.'

Gary exploded, and as the words poured out of him, he realised this was what he'd been missing in the politeness of disability. The opportunity of tearing into someone and feeling chunks of their flesh ripping under the onslaught. No, not someone, Tom Shackleton.

'Oh you nasty, cowardly piece of shit. Haven't you even got the balls to admit you've been sleeping with her? It wasn't even an affair for you, was it? She was just somewhere to put your frustrations, a soft repository for your ego. What have you come back for? Eh? To make sure she doesn't think too badly of you? Because you don't need her any more, do you? You've got rid of Jenni, you got rid of Carter and now it's Lucy's turn. But she doesn't have to die, Tom, does she? Not so anyone will notice, anyway. You found a much more subtle way to kill her, you just broke her heart. So, come on.

what have you come back for, you evil bastard? A last shag? Your bag of drugs?'

Shackleton, stunned by the attack, struggled to reply.

'Oh, it's all right, Tom, Lucy wouldn't let me do anything to hurt you, you're quite safe.' He paused, he was blazing like a consumptive and from somewhere found the strength to pull himself upright in the bed. 'Until I die, Shackleton. Until then. Don't ever forget a death-bed deposition is a statement. Admissible in court as evidence.'

Shackleton fought back.

'Evidence of what? There's nothing to link me with anything. Any accusation I would defend robustly.'

Gary was contemptuous.

'You can't defend yourself against a dead man, particularly if there are as many people as you've got out there just waiting for you to be brought low.' He was baiting Shackleton now. 'So come on, what did you come back for? And don't say to see me, try telling the truth, just for once, you might like it.'

When Shackleton spoke it was quietly but with a sort of defiance.

'I came back to see Lucy.'

Contempt took the anger out of Gary's words.

'Well, I know that. But why? Why do you want to see her?'

'To tell her I love her.'

Shackleton's admission, the first time he'd ever used the word love in the context of another human being, lay between them like a robin's egg. It was tiny, it was fragile, and it contained the possibility of new life.

Gary weighed it in silence then took great pleasure in booting it into touch.

'Enough to marry her? Enough to put her in the spotlight? Enough to take what they'll do to both of you when they find out you took her away from her disabled husband before your wife was cold in her grave? Can you imagine what the tabloids would do to her? And what would they do to you, the Teflon Chief Constable, now the Lord's anointed Crime Tsar?' Gary paused, but he hadn't finished. When he spoke again his voice was quiet, almost a whisper. 'How much do you love her really, Tom? I love her enough to die for her, if that's what she wants. I'm serious. If it's you she chooses, I won't stand in the way.' He laughed. It was an incongruous sound. Perfectly natural and genuinely amused. 'Stand? I should be so lucky to be able to. But I mean it, Tom. There's just one condition. You have to ask her. And tell her everything, I mean everything, all the stuff I can only guess at. Then let her choose.'

'I can't do that.'

'Why? Because you might lose? I don't think so.'

Gary was shocked to see Shackleton's eyes were bright with tears.

'No. No.'

Urban foxes, confident in the quiet street, shrieked as they played round the cars. An unlaid sewer pipe magnified their calls as they raced through it.

It was a moment of mutual rest in the fight between the two men but Gary wasn't going to relax. He knew he had Shackleton down but wasn't sure how or why.

When Shackleton looked up the tears hadn't fallen but he was able to speak.

'I don't want to hurt her.'

Gary let out a shout of derision.

'It's a bit bloody late for that. Have you any idea what you've put her through, you shit –'

'I know. I'm a bastard. I know.'

Gary was outraged now, and enjoying it.

'Oh no . . . you don't get off with a bit of self-pity and a mea culpa. All your life you've been doing that then carrying on just the same. You've got some idea that just saying you're a bastard absolves you of responsibility. Well, it doesn't. You've got to be sorry, Tom. Sorry enough to change. And I don't mean just reinventing yourself, which believe me I know is your usual trick. No, to change enough to make amends.'

He was sure Shackleton was beaten now. Gary hadn't tasted triumph in so long it hit him like neat whisky. He fell back on his pillows, dizzy and euphoric.

As he did, Shackleton stood up and leaned over him, dangerous, pressing his fists into the mattress.

'Finished, Gary? Right. Now I'll tell you what I think. Lucy is only staying with you because she feels guilty. Think about it, Gary, if you were well, if you and I were equal, which of us would she choose? Eh? If it was just a straight call, no emotional blackmail involved. She'd leave you, wouldn't she?'

Gary turned his head away.

Shackleton spoke in his most reasonable, most persuasive tone. 'If you really love her, then you must think about it. What have you got to offer her? Mmm?' He touched Gary lightly on his chest. 'This?' He lifted the urine bag so Gary could see it. 'This?' He reached across for the shaving mirror and held it in front of Gary's face. 'This?' He sat down. 'The difference between us, Gary, is I know I'm a bastard and you think you're a saint. But I'll tell you this. If you condemn Lucy to a lifetime of wiping drool off your chin and watching you rot you're a bigger bastard than I could ever aspire to be.'

He stood up and stepped away from the still body on the bed. The temptation to put his hands round that scrawny neck and squeeze was overpowering.

'More hot chocolate, gentlemen?'

Nurse Stroud spoke at the same time as knocking and entering the room. Completely oblivious to the poison air she sailed across, loaded the tray, tutted at the spill, mopped at it with a wad of tissues then turned and left with a cheerful wink at Shackleton.

'Open the door for me, will you, Mr Shackleton. Don't want to drop this little lot, do we?'

And she was gone in a cloud of Yardley Lavender soap and talcum powder.

Shackleton stood by the door. Not moving.

Gary couldn't see him.

'You still there? Tom?'

'I'm here.'

'Go over to the piano.'

Shackleton looked across at the bottles and boxes of pills, the tubes and sealed bags of equipment then walked slowly towards them. When he reached the piano he noticed without any recognition that it was a Steinway. All he knew about the name was that it was famous but for pianos or fridges he couldn't have said.

'You'll see a bottle on there, small green one – yes, that's it.'

Shackleton picked it up.

'No. Not yet.' Gary pulled himself more upright and did his best to pull his pyjama jacket closed. When he was satisfied he concentrated on Shackleton again. 'Tranquillisers. The bottle next to it, the tall plastic one . . .'

Shackleton picked it up.

'Yes, that one. Sleeping pills. And the packets of Coproximal, painkillers. You're ahead of me, you know where I'm going, don't you, Tom? I wouldn't like you to get bored. So here's my proposition. You give me those pills, all of them, and I'll take them.

'Now, I have to warn you, last time I tried to top myself it didn't work. But then even you, policeman though you are, will have grasped that one. I think this time though, between us, we could get it right. If you think Lucy would be better off without me, and believe me, I think you're right, I'll take them. I just don't imagine you'd make her happy. After all, Tom, you've never made anyone happy, have you?'

Shackleton knew that was deadly accurate. If anything, he'd gone out of his way to create a sort of unhappiness around him to stop intrusion. To prevent anyone seeing how little there was of him. But Lucy was different. She knew him. She understood him. She had promised never to hurt him. The hopeful child in him was facing the hopeless man across a chasm of experience.

'Give me the pills, Tom. Give Lucy what she really wants.' Gary held out his hand as best he could. His arm shook with the effort. 'Or are you afraid? Afraid to kill an old friend?'

Shackleton's reply was flat, unemotional.

'I've killed better men than you, Gary.'

'Come on then, Crime Tsar. Come on. You've got everything else you want. Take this too. It's easy . . .'

The devil looked at Shackleton with Gary's eyes. Yes. It would be easy. Why not? He might be prosecuted. No, he'd just say Gary asked for the pill bottles to be left by him. The caps? Unscrewed in case he wanted to help himself. Gary hadn't wanted to bother the Angel of Death.

Shackleton's mind worked fast, like a dog rounding up his flock of scattered thoughts.

He saw Lucy's face. Her fearful eyes looking up at him for protection and reassurance. He felt a surge of emotion towards her the like of which he'd never experienced. It was so strong he didn't know if it was pleasure or pain.

He gathered up the pills and took them to Gary.

Shackleton unscrewed the caps.

He put the containers on the tray table beside the bed.

It was all going to be so simple. Easy. Happy ever after.

Then he slowly pulled the table until it stood just out of Gary's reach.

Gary was trembling, his strength almost gone, but he seemed possessed as he looked up at Shackleton.

'Couldn't you do it, Tom? Couldn't you kill without Jenni there to hold your balls for you?'

Shackleton walked out of the house still hearing Gary's voice.

He almost ran back to the now dark and gated train station.

He sat down on a garden wall. Shaking. Sweating. Breathless.

Out of the station shadows a scruffy young man with a scruffier dog lying on a cardboard mat called, 'Spare some change, mate?'

Shackleton automatically felt in his pocket and produced two £1 coins. He walked across. His hand was shaking as he handed the money over. The young man was obviously high on something, his eyes dull and dilated, his speech just out of focus.

'Thanks, mate. Have a good night.'

Shackleton squatted down beside him.

'Could you spare me a cigarette? I don't normally smoke but tonight . . .'

The dog looked surprised – it wasn't often they were asked for favours. It laid its chin on the young man's knee while he rummaged under his blanket for a Marlboro packet that contained a selection of different brands and two rather suspicious-looking roll-ups. Shackleton selected a Benson and Hedges, the young man one of the thin roll-ups. They were lit with a blue throwaway lighter held in the young man's dirty hand. Shackleton noticed he bit his nails.

'Thanks.'

The smoke tasted dirty but it gave him an almost instant wave of pleasure as it infected his bloodstream.

'Thanks.'

'You all right, mate?'

Shackleton stroked the dog's ears. He took another deep lungful of the foul-tasting smoke.

'Yes. I think so. I didn't kill someone tonight.'

The young man was philosophical.

'That's always a good way to end the day.'

They smoked in silence.

'Why not?'

Shackleton flicked his ash before it was ready, enjoying the ritual and companionship.

'Tell me,' he said, staring across the road at nothing. 'If someone killed your dog so they could be with you, could you love them?'

'No fuckin' way.'

'What if you didn't know?'

'Fuck off, man. They'd have to be a murderer and a liar. I'd rather have me dog.'

The dog, knowing it was being talked about, looked from one man to the other, straining like a deaf mute to understand what was being said.

'Good choice,' said Shackleton. 'Only problem is, because I didn't kill him, I think he may have killed me.'

This appealed to the young man and he started laughing. Nothing had made him laugh for days and it felt good.

'Oh man, that's bad. What's his name? Me an' the dog'll go and get him.'

Shackleton laughed too. There was nothing funny but his muscles were contracting involuntarily, starting to ache.

'His name's Keith. Gary Keith.'

The young man's laughter now became uncontrollable at some picture in his head Shackleton couldn't see. He was gasping for breath when he explained.

'He's a fuckin' Woodentop. Like me, a fuckin' Woodentop . . .'

And with that he did an impression of a stiff marionette, dancing on its strings, and saying over and over again, '*Flob-a-Lob. Flob-a-Lob.*'

Both men found this hilarious. They couldn't speak. Shackleton was helpless, holding his stomach and wiping his eyes.

Finally he managed to say, 'Why? Why's he a Woodentop?'

The young man wanted to reply. This was knowledge.

'Because that's my nickname and he's got the same name as me, Keith,' he said, struggling to control himself. 'It's ancient Scots for Wood.'

Shackleton wasn't laughing any more.

*   *   *

On Monday it was raining. A dull day. Grey.

Lucy was playing Scrabble with Gary when the lunchtime television news came on. Neither was paying much attention when the announcer said, 'Today Tom Shackleton, the new United Kingdom Anti-Crime Coordinator, the so-called Crime Tsar, takes up his duties. It had been thought Mr Shackleton would stay in his post as Chief Constable of one of the largest police forces in the country but the Home Secretary, Robert MacIntyre, at a press conference said . . .'

Lucy didn't make sense of the rest of it. She saw the pictures of Tom and MacIntyre sitting behind a bank of microphones talking. Shackleton was smiling, answering questions carefully and quietly. Impossible. The man who had cried in her arms. The man who'd said . . . what? Nothing really. Nothing concrete, just the emotion of the moment. Not to be carried into the future. Not to be confused with reality. And then film of him going into his new office. Close to Whitehall, close to New Scotland Yard. Far away. Gone. Return to sender. Not wanted on voyage.

Gary didn't say anything. What was there to say? Lucy had come back from Hastings with a stick of rock and a determination not to think about Shackleton. Gary took the stick of rock, kissed her cheek and asked if she'd enjoyed herself. She said yes, the sea air had blown away the cobwebs, then she'd set about clearing out the kitchen cupboards. It was time for a good clear-out, she said. Gary said she was probably right.

She played her turn: 'Shit' with the H on a triple-letter score.

He added the E in his turn.

Lucy thought back to her childhood. Surplus to requirements. Tolerated. She thought of revenge, the papers. Kiss and tell, sex, drugs and the Crime Tsar. But where was the proof? The bag of drugs? Proof of what? Incriminating yes, but not of him.

She had taken a handful of water thinking it was an oasis. Better to have loved and lost? No. Never. Certainly never again.

Gary wanted to say something but couldn't think of anything that wouldn't sound triumphant.

'Gary?'

'Mmm?'

He tried to sound vague, unfocused.

'I want to tell you something.'

'Lucy, you don't need to.'

He looked at her, expecting to see that wounded vulnerability he'd got so used to, but it was gone.

'Gary, do I have WELCOME stamped across my forehead?'

She seemed to have gone from monochrome to colour. He judged his answer carefully.

'Not any more, no.'

'Maybe I should sell my story to the papers: "I was Tom Shackleton's Doormat". I could make a fortune. Oh Gary . . .' She covered her nose and mouth with her hand, looking over it as if at the scene of an accident. 'I can't believe how stupid I've been, how unbelievably cruel. I'm so sorry. I am so sorry.'

Gary nodded, afraid if he spoke his voice would crack. It was over, this time it was really over. But if there had been a bed in the hospital? If Lucy hadn't gone to Hastings? But there wasn't and she had. There was a God.

They played on.

'Luce? Put the radio on, will you? Radio Three. Let's live dangerously.'

Lucy dutifully got up and re-tuned the radio. The familiar and much missed sweetness of classical music filled the room.

'Oh I love this,' Lucy said as she sat down again, nodding to its lilting delicacy. 'What's it called? I can never remember.'

Gary wasn't sure he was going to be able to tell her. It was so perfect. Such a sign from the overcast heavens.

' "Sheep May Safely Graze." '

The beauty of the music blew through them as if the doors and windows of a shuttered house had been flung open to the fresh air of summer.

'I've been thinking, Luce.'

She looked up. Were her eyes as unnaturally bright as his?

'I think we should sell the house, get somewhere smaller that's cripple-friendly, and you should go back to work. We'll start again.'

Lucy wished she could start again, from the beginning, but this time she'd be elegant, beautiful and ruthless. She thought of Jenni slumped in death. Well, maybe not.

'Where you going, Luce?'

Gary, who'd never once shown how frightened he was of losing her, was suddenly panicked by her decisive getting up. She'd made a decision and he had no idea if it included him.

'To make a cup of tea. And I think I've got a Battenberg cake I put in the cupboard.' She let herself look at him honestly for the first time in years. 'Gary?'

He saw the seriousness in her face. No, he thought, I've done all I can, I've let my guard down. If you hit me now I'll never get up.

'Can I come home?'

'About bloody time too. God, it's been like living with a zombie.'

They both laughed. The relief at the abrupt end of a dark, fear-filled tunnel.

'I just cannot believe how stupid I've been.'

Gary was smiling as he said, 'Well, he's gone now. No harm done, eh?'

As if they'd woken to find the Bogey Man didn't really exist.

Lucy thought about the last stomach-churning months and her transformation into everything she despised. Gary's patience with her self-abasement, her worship of a false idol. Shackleton had been her Great Love. But Gary was her true love.

Yes, they'd move away and she'd go back to work. Use her talent and her mind again. Rejoin the human race. Self-respect would be a welcome change. And they would live happily ever after, each careful of the other's disability.

She shook her head.

'No, no harm done.'

'Oh, and Luce . . . I've been accepted on to the cannabis programme. I can start next week. And most important, maybe, the stem-cell research group –' He stopped, swallowing the excess of emotion. 'It may not work . . .'

Lucy interrupted him, overwhelmed with enthusiasm.

'But they can work miracles. And let's face it, anyone who doesn't believe in miracles isn't a realist.'

'I love you, Lucy.'

'Not half as much as I love you, Gary. Thank you. Thank you for putting up with me.'

They were laughing now, crying and laughing.

Lucy sat on the bed and they hugged each other, kissing clumsily and laughing all the more.

'Oh Lucy, it's all going to be all right.' He pushed her away slightly so he could look at her. He knew he shouldn't do it but he couldn't help it, like a murderer drawn back to the site of his crime. 'Luce, tell me honestly, and whatever you say, I won't love you any less. If you'd had to choose . . . who would it have been? Him or me?'

Lucy didn't hesitate.

'You.'

He saw her clear unblinking blazing honesty and had to look away. He had won. Finally, he had won.

Lucy made the tea and thought how much she'd changed. She would always love the man Shackleton had been but he'd made himself a stranger. He'd rejected her and the pattern was broken.

In some ways she was grateful to him for setting her free.

That night Tom Shackleton slept alone in his new London flat. He had everything, he was a success, he had planted his flag firmly at the summit. There were no ghosts to haunt him and no memories to tempt him.

But no friends travelled with him. His life was now no more than existence and sometimes he felt so cold he cried out for comfort.

By the bedside, on the bare table, under the lamp, lay the Russian wedding ring Lucy had given him, and when he woke from the nightmares that followed him he'd warm the three gold bands in his hands. Among all his trophies of success, the only one of love. Then holding it tightly, like a child, he'd hope for sleep.

The sleep of the dead.

Grateful thanks to Sue Clough,
Don Randall, Giles Smart, Crispian
Strachan, Rosemary Davidson, Mary Tomlinson,
Caroline Dawnay, Nigel Newton, and all
at Bloomsbury, David Parfitt and Saint Jude,
without whom . . .

A NOTE ON THE TYPE

The text of this book is set in Linotype Sabon, named after the
type founder, Jacques Sabon. It was designed by Jan Tschichold
and jointly developed by Linotype, Monotype and Stempel, in
response to a need for a typeface to be available in identical form
for mechanical hot metal composition and hand composition
using foundry type.

Tschichold based his design for Sabon roman on a fount
engraved by Garamond, and Sabon italic on a fount by
Granjon. It was first used in 1966 and has proved
an enduring modern classic.